White Buffalo

(New Beginnings)

Series

ISBN Paperback: 978-1-77354-382-6
ISBN e-Book: 978-1-77354-383-3

Published by Lauretta Beaver, Falher, Canada.

Publication assistance by

PAGEMASTER
PUBLISHING
PageMaster.ca

PASSIONATE ALLIANCE

WRITTEN BY: LAURETTA BEAVER

SERIES AND BOOKS WRITTEN BY LAURETTA BEAVER

Series #1: White Buffalo (New Beginnings)

Book #1: Passionate Alliance
Book #2: Raven & the Golden Eagle
Book #3: Revenge of the Silver Fox (Coming Soon)

Series #2: The Curse of the Celtic Dragon Medallion

Book #1: Dream Dancer & the Celtic Witch
Book #2: Twin Destinies
Book #3: The Seeker & the Shadow Hunter

I dedicate this book to Herman and Ruby Reum. Without their faith in me, I would never have finished writing this book. May they both rest in peace!

I would like to thank Shane Lambert for her good advice and criticism.

I also wish to thank Greg Macdaid for always being there when I needed him.

My heartfelt thanks go to Michel Pelletier for his help and friendship.

The Last White Buffalo Hide

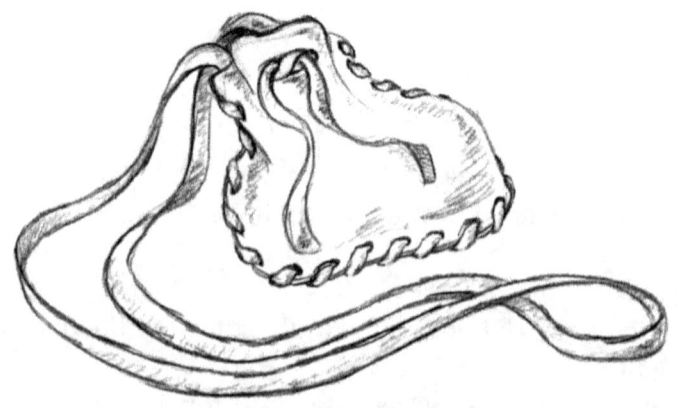

The Prophecy

When the majestic buffalo are almost driven into extinction
by the white man!
And the last white buffalo hide is given to the most
unlikely source!
The beginning, which will lead us all to the end... will be
upon us!

Montana

September 1805

A bright flash of lightning streaked towards the earth, when it was close it split into three separate bolts. A man walking out of the cabin stopped in astonishment. He stared in awe as the whole sky lit up unexpectedly in front of him; it was so bright he had to squint in order to see. However, even the wonder he felt at nature's fury didn't lessen the tears streaming down his face.

Before counting to two, the building behind him shook as a booming clap of thunder resounded deafeningly through the cabin; making him duck down instinctively to protect himself. It was an automatic reaction, even though death right now would be welcomed. It was so loud the ground beneath him also quivered in reaction.

He looked up infuriated at the black and purple clouds hovering above him. He grimaced in anger as the rain began to fall. Several drops fell on the bundle he carried... he sighed resignedly. Doing his best to ignore the miserable weather, he marched purposely to the grave he dug earlier. He clutched his burden protectively, trying to shield it from the rain. He mumbled to himself irritably. "What a lousy day for a burial!"

Any day was a bad day, especially this sort. He knelt; gently the man set the white bundle down beside the deep pit to look one last time. His hand trembled in reaction as he eased the cloth away from the faces of a woman and child. He raised his head to glare up at the heavens... though he couldn't see much in the pouring rain. He screamed out in rage. The frustration and agony in his voice were plain to hear when he managed to gasp out past his constricted throat. "WHY?"

He looked again at the woman in remorse before reaching out tenderly. Gently, he stroked her ice-cold cheek regretfully. He shook his head in bewildered disbelief... how could they do something so unspeakable?

How anyone could hurt a woman, especially one so obviously with child; it was completely beyond his understanding how a person can be so cruel!

His gaze turned to the young boy; his breath hesitated on

another sob. His hand dropped from the woman's cheek to his son's coal-black hair. He brushed it back sadly. His son had just turned ten this past summer... now he would never reach manhood.

He dropped the hand into his lap before lowering his head and wept bitterly. He couldn't help remembering that Daniel was alive when he found them. Unfortunately, there was no way to save him; he did try desperately, though.

The boy was still lucid when he first arrived from his trap line. It appeared to the man his son had kept himself alive by sheer will alone. Long enough to tell his father what happened, so he could die in peace...

"I tried to help Mom, but there were three of them. After they stabbed me, they thought we were all dead so started talking about Dakota; wanting revenge against some woman who had killed their brothers. Then they laughed about how Mom put up such a good fight. 'Unfortunately, not as good as the Indian squaw's they found two years ago'... they said."

The boy lived long enough to give a vague description of the three men to his father before he died; fortunately, he heard them call one another by their first names. His son's fascination with horses meant he remembered what they looked like also...

"There was a man with blonde hair who rode a black gelding, they called him Marty. The second man had hair that was black; he was riding a big grey mare, his name's Sam. There was a third one, his hair was brown; he was even taller than you are Dad. His horse was a red stallion, a mean brute... I heard them call this man Jimmy. The only thing the same about all three was their dark blue eyes."

With his dying breath, the boy described what the men did to his mother. The man pushed the thought away; it was just too painful to remember.

Gazing at his family one last time in anguished disbelief, he gently wrapped them back in the sheet. Once done, he jumped into the hole then pulled it towards him. Carefully, he lifted the lifeless bundle before putting them into the deep pit. He jumped out with a repulsive shiver as he picked up the waiting shovel. Slowly, he began filling in the grave... his heart hardening with each scoop of wet soil. Tossing the dirt over the shell of his dead wife and sons, would he feel anything but hate or anger again.

When he finished, he dropped the shovel in distaste. Quickly, he piled the large rocks he collected earlier on top of the mound to mark it. It would also help to keep scavengers from digging them up. He placed a makeshift cross at the head of the fresh mound of dirt that he painstakingly carved with his own two hands; 'My beloved family'... it read.

Although, he didn't remember most of the **Our Father** prayer; he mumbled a few words of the verses that he could recall. Tears of grief continued to fall unchecked, while he pleaded desperately for forgiveness for having left the two of them on their own for so long.

Rage took over suddenly as the tears vanished. His face turned bitter with hatred before he looked up towards the heavens then made a solemn oath to his family. As he made his vow, he lifted his fist to the sky in fury; he shook it threateningly, his voice now lethal in promise. "I will not rest until I have found and punished those bastards. No matter how long it takes... even if I have to pursue them into hell itself!"

Before he could drop his hand, lightning lit up all around him... giving him a sinister eerie glow; a crack of thunder shook the earth seeming to seal his vow as if God himself approved.

*****

A dark-skinned man watching the burial from the safety of the woods stepped out... revealing himself. He didn't understand the words the white man was saying, but he guessed at their meaning. As he remembered his own pain that was still with him even after two long years.

The white man tensed at a whisper of sound behind him, spinning away from the grave... he turned; at the same time, his hand was moving in a blur of motion. Drawing his gun, he pointed it at the stranger staring at him impassively.

The Indian gazed at the revolver pointed at him without flinching. Looking at the tall black-haired man with no fear... he spoke calmly; his voice was low pitched, giving his native language a majestic ring. "You are the one that the Blackfoot named, 'Grey Wolf'?"

Grey Wolf gave the big man a searching look. He didn't recall ever seeing this particular Indian before. By the war paint on his face, he was obviously a Cheyenne. The white man had him measured in moments; he lowered his gun feeling no threat from the Indian, so he put it away. He answered in the Cheyenne language guessing the native didn't speak much English... few could or would. He nodded in confirmation, as well as curiosity. "Yes, I am. What do you want with me?"

For a moment, the Indian was silent as he took in the white man's size... wondering again if this was a good idea. Most white eyes were untrustworthy, but he heard good things about Grey Wolf. Like how he always spoke truthfully to both whites and natives. He also remembered hearing that this man was quick to anger; although, he never drew his gun unless given no choice. There were great tales of how he helped both the whites and Indians when trouble brewed between the two nations. He was usually successful in quelling any disputes.

The Indian didn't miss the speed with which Grey Wolf moved either. He knew instinctively, everything he heard about this man was true. He smiled in satisfaction, knowing he found the white man he was searching for all this time. Finally, the native broke his long silence; he motioned in sympathy at the mound of rocks marking the grave. "I am sorry about your family."

Looking deep into the Indian's eyes for a long moment, Grey Wolf relaxed his stance slightly at what he saw in them before nodding... accepting the condolences. He repeated his question, more persistently. "What do you want from me?"

The Indian frowned in disapproval at the abrupt tone the white man used, he wasn't very patient. He finally pointed at himself in introduction. "I am called, Chief Giant Bear."

That was a good description of the Indian. He was huge for a Cheyenne, about six-feet and so husky he looked like a bear; especially, with the bearskin wrapped around his shoulders. Most natives were skinny and slight, being that they were mostly undernourished... neither were they usually as tall as this one.

Grey Wolf smiled, guessing at how Giant Bear got part of his name. He knew that the Cheyenne Indian's named their sons on merit. He wondered how the Indian earned the rest of the name... 'bear', in particular. Maybe it was just because he looked like a bear. The polite curiosity was plain in Grey Wolf's tone. "How did you get such an unusual name?"

Chief Giant Bear kept his face impassive; proud of the unique name he earned, but not wanting to seem boastful... he spoke without a trace of arrogance. "I saved a small boy from a grizzly bear when I was eleven summers. I killed it with only an eating knife, so earned the name, 'Giant Bear'."

Grey Wolf nodded impressed; a bear as large as the skin hanging from the Indian's shoulders would be almost impossible to kill with just a knife. He guessed correctly, when he figured that was the hide Giant Bear was wearing now. The big Indian must have jumped the animal from behind then went for its eyes in order to get a kill... its throat could be vulnerable too. A bear's thick fur, plus its tough hide would stop a knife anywhere else.

Not speaking again, Grey Wolf knew that Giant Bear saw the approval on his face; he knew it's all that would be required. The white man waited for the Indian to tell him why he was here and what he wanted, getting more curious by the moment.

Giant Bear waved towards the grave behind Grey Wolf. Not looking away from the white man; he tried to convey how serious he was as he made his offer. "I would like to help with your search for your family's killers."

Staring in surprise, Grey Wolf was taken off guard by Giant Bear's offer... not having expected it; he hid his surprise well before inquiring curiously. "Why would you want to do that?"

Gazing at the horizon briefly; Giant Bear kept his face void of emotions, remembering his pain from two summers ago at the death of his wife... then his sister. Finally, he looked at Grey Wolf before letting his emotions blaze to the surface for a second.

Seeing the agony in Giant Bear's eyes, Grey Wolf watched the pain turn into hate and vengeance before the Indian's face became impassive again. The white man recognized the sorrow instantly; he was surprised the chief would show it to him at all.

Balling up his fist in fury, Giant Bear shook it. This was all the emotion he now showed. "Two years ago, the same men that killed your family; raped then murdered my wife. They did the same to my sister before leaving her and my daughter to die, but they made a mistake... she survived. Three days later, naaxaa'eheme told me what they did to her then took her own life because she couldn't live with her dishonour. I vowed to my family and the Great Spirit to hunt them down. Unfortunately, I've been unsuccessful so far since they're always disappearing."

After an infuriating pause, Giant Bear continued. He motioned sharply in frustration... clearly enraged. "It's difficult for a lone Indian to hunt in white man's territory. I tracked them here, but I was too late to help your family; I arrived after you."

Grey Wolf turned; gazing sadly one last time at his family's grave. Wishing, Giant Bear had arrived in time. He didn't blame the Indian though he blamed himself. He put his family in danger by ignoring his father's warning not to bring them here... why didn't he listen!

Bringing his attention back to the native, Grey Wolf's face turned pensive trying to decide whether he should bring an Indian Chief into the white men's territory. He sighed resignedly, knowing if he were Giant Bear, he too would find a way... regardless of the consequences. The white man finally conceded his mind made up. "I would be honoured to have you by my side; I cannot do anything more here, let's head out."

Giant Bear inclined his head slightly, relaxing noticeably at the good news. He watched the white man turn then walk towards the cabin before disappearing inside.

The Great Spirit was right after all; Giant Bear mused to himself. After meditating in the sweat lodge for several days before leaving his people, he saw a vision telling him how to find his wife's killers. He didn't understand at the time why he was to go northeast to search for this cabin, now he knew why. It was necessary because he just found the man the Great Spirit promised would not only become his friend, but would help him find the killers. Without Grey Wolf to teach him about white people, he would fail then die... his soul afterwards would wander restlessly for eternity.

Smiling unemotionally in satisfaction, Giant Bear turned away to go get his horse. As he walked, he couldn't help but wonder who the sacred white hide was meant for. He had received another vision the night he left his people; it told him to bring the last white buffalo hide with him on this journey. The chief figured it would be given to the person who helped him, but Grey Wolf already had an Indian name... now he was mystified.

A few minutes later Grey Wolf rode up to Giant Bear with a packhorse following obediently. The white man nodded in approval at the chief's sturdy-looking Indian pony. "Let's go!"

Motioning to Grey Wolf that he was ready, Giant Bear shrugged off his confusion about the hide. He knew that it would be revealed to him when the time came; there was no doubt about that, whatsoever. He stayed close to his new friend, the closer the better the Great Spirit told him... he definitely agreed.

CHAPTER ONE

North Dakota 1814

Melissa Ray stopped her high-strung stallion; she looked around suspiciously, instantly knowing something was amiss. A quiver of foreboding rippled down her spine before she felt the hairs on the back of her neck standing erect. Glancing around again, she touched the butt of her revolver on her right side in reassurance. Just to be on the safe side, she unhooked the strap holding it in place. Looking around nervously once more... what was making her so jumpy? At first, nothing seemed out of the ordinary.

Once again, a shiver of forewarning rippled down Melissa's spine; it was all the warning she needed. Desperately, she kicked her horse hard into an urgent gallop. "Ayah!"

Lightning squealed in surprise before surging forward at his mistress's frantic command. In less than a heartbeat, he was at a full gallop. A shot rang out behind them; the bullet was a second too late though, it hit the dirt where the horse had been only a moment ago.

Glancing over her shoulder, Melissa searched. She wondered if she should turn back to find out who had taken that shot at her. Grinning knowingly when she saw three men charging out of the trees, she kept going recognizing one of the horses.

The men gave up, turning they returned to wherever they came from.

Slowing her horse to a lope, Melissa figured the danger was past... she laughed in exhilaration. She won again; she patted Lightning in apology for the rough handling.

If anyone was watching Melissa from a distance, they would never believe she was a woman. She wore a man's checkered flannel shirt, a tan coloured vest... with dark blue pants. A black hat pulled low over her forehead effectively hid her hair; she also carried not one, but two colt revolvers at her hips.

The people in town were used to seeing Melissa in this strange attire; most strangers laughed at the guns in disbelief though, until they saw how well she could handle them.

Melissa kept her horse at a lope going north. The thick

forest on her left continued to keep her heading straight. She looked to her right, smiling in satisfaction at the newly planted seedlings. They wouldn't become saplings until at least four feet. Her men did an excellent job at replanting; she would make sure she mentioned it to them tonight.

Skirting the seedlings, it wasn't long before huge towering trees enclosed her once again. Melissa turned west, following a small game trail that was almost invisible unless you knew it was there. She continued on the trail as it twisted then turned back on itself for about a quarter of a mile... until she reached an open valley. A creek meandered through this little meadow. The trees surrounding it effectively hid her hideaway from prying eyes. Here the grass was lush with new growth; wildflowers of every description were just starting to bud.

This was Melissa's favourite spot; her eyes sparkled in pleasure at finding it just as lovely and peaceful as she remembered. She dropped the reins then slid off her horse prepared to enjoy the peace and quiet of her haven... having been gone far too long.

Melissa was tall for a female; at five-feet-eleven and a half inch, she topped most men. However, she was every bit of a woman. This was evident when she removed her hat, as she did now. When she stood with her dark blonde hair flowing around her... she was quite striking. Clouds of curly hair framed her delicate features of which the most memorable, were her eyes. Looking into the depths of those turquoise beauties would make a person think she could read their soul. It made many people nervous, particularly the men.

At this moment, Melissa's eyes sparkled in satisfaction at the thrill of the chase; she wondered if her men had given up yet. They tried several times a month to surprise her, but still had not caught her off guard.

If anyone asked Melissa why she was unmarried at the unheard-of age of twenty-seven; she would snort then answer in amusement. "I have yet to find a man who can out-shoot or out-ride me!"

That her life became very lonely at times, she would admit to no one... not even to herself.

Walking to the creek, Melissa sat down on a small rise beside the water's edge to gaze into the crystal-clear water.

She didn't have to worry about her horse straying, for the bond between them was unbreakable. Turning she admired Lightning as he nibbled at the tender sprouts of green grass growing along the edge of the forest. Her thoughts went back to the first time she saw him as a frightened colt...

Scrambling up a steep ridge, Melissa heard a horse screaming in terror. She urged Pepper to pick up more speed as the desperate sound continued. When she crested the knoll in front of her, she saw a man using a whip on a small silver-grey horse; quickly, she made her way down.

Instantly infuriated... Melissa jumped off her mare quickly; she rushed forward to prevent the man from hitting the frightened yearling again. Grabbing the whip from the man's hand in rage, she threw it as far as possible into the thick brush behind him.

Whirling around angrily, the man raised his fist in fury at whoever dared to interfere. Being so intently focused on his colt, Brian had not heard anyone approaching. Quickly, he dropped his arm in surprise when confronted with a deadly revolver pointed straight at him. He lifted his head in apprehension before gazing into icy turquoise eyes. Immediately, recognizing who was facing him... he swore silently to himself in frustration.

Melissa stared at the sandy brown-haired man in disbelief; he had dark blue eyes with a brown handlebar moustache, which he always kept neatly trimmed. He was slim, almost too thin, plus shorter by three inches at five-feet-eight. Her face-hardened when she recognized the only man other than her father, she respected... until now! The admiration disappeared from her eyes in a heartbeat!

Brian Jenkins winced before swearing silently to himself; he watched the esteem he so carefully nurtured instantly fade from Melissa's eyes... he knew he just made a grave error.

Disillusioned, Melissa put her revolver away; spinning away from Brian in loathing, she looked at the frightened colt... it was love at first sight.

Recognizing the look when Melissa turned back towards him; Brian immediately knew what he would have to do. He turned, gazing at the white thoroughbred for a moment in regret. He couldn't help thinking of all the trouble, plus the expense the stud had caused him so far. In the past, before he cared what she thought he would have trained his horses at his ranch. However, Mell was so against people beating horses... he needed to hide his true nature.

Sighing in frustration at losing such a valuable animal, Brian knew he didn't have a choice. He needed to take the look of disgust off Melissa's face. It had taken him too long to get where he was with her; he wouldn't lose everything because of a stupid horse, no matter how much it cost him. He shrugged in resignation before turning back then handed the halter rope to her. "Here, I give him to you as a gift... with my apologies. I can't do anything with him anyway."

Melissa stared at Brian in disappointment... a scowl of disbelief still on her face. "I cannot believe that you of all people would harm an animal; you know how I feel about any kind of abuse!"

Brian lowered his head in apparent shame, giving himself time to come up with a good excuse. He shrugged as he looked up at Melissa pleading for understanding. "I didn't really want to hit him; I bought him from a rancher in South Dakota as a welcome home gift for Mary. I have been working with him here for over a month now in secret so she doesn't find out about him. Unfortunately, I just can't seem to do anything with him. Every time I get close, he kicks and rears up completely out of control. I got so frustrated this time I lost my temper so took out my whip... that's when he came after me like a mad dog. I needed to use it to protect myself! When you got rid of the whip, he calmed down."

Watching Melissa's expressive face, Brian continued his charade when he realized he was fooling her. "I just realized that the sound of your voice is what stopped him from attacking me further. Perhaps, it was a man who abused him that's why he has a violent reaction when I get near him. He is way too volatile for Mary; I thought of making him a gelding, but he's too beautiful as a stallion. Here you are he's all yours. I just hope you have more success with him then I did."

****

Since that time, a close bond formed between Melissa and her horse; it took her a long time, with a lot of patience to get Lightning to trust her... it was definitely worth it in the end.

Melissa's thoughts returned to the present. Wanting to

wade into the inviting looking water, she turned to face the creek before removing her boots; her socks followed. Her face was pensive as she reflected on the excuse Brian gave her for his cruel treatment towards the colt. It made sense at the time, until she met Mary that is. Reflecting now on their conversation, she realized his account was lame... even absurd.

Why would Brian purchase such a valuable animal for his sister, when it appeared to Melissa, he didn't even like her? Was she a thorn in his side, could it be possible he even hated her? She didn't press the issue afterwards, since she had no way of knowing what he actually planned for the stud. After all, she couldn't call him a liar without proof... could she!

Not long after this incident, Brian changed for the worse. Melissa started avoiding him as much as possible; especially, after he asked for her hand in marriage and she refused him. The fury on his face took her by surprise, leaving her feeling... uneasy.

"NEIGH!" Lightning trumpeted a warning call... just as Melissa heard the menacing growl of an animal. She looked up in shock as a large black wolf came out of nowhere then sprang towards her unexpectedly. She heard hoof beats clattering on the ground behind her as her horse sped towards the scene.

Melissa instinctively put her left arm up to protect her face. She grabbed desperately for her right revolver, which she thankfully hadn't tied down yet. She screamed at Lightning in order to keep him from getting in harm's way; she needed to be able to shoot the animal without having to worry about her horse getting shot by mistake. "Stand Lightning, stand!"

The revolver came loose just as the big wolf surprisingly jumped right past Melissa; shocked... she almost fell backwards in astonishment. She watched in amazement, as he grabbed a large rattlesnake not more than a foot away from her back.

Lightning came to an abrupt halt at Melissa's sharp command; he quivered in fear at being so close to a wolf. The stallion stood his ground though, refusing to leave his mistress.

Melissa sat there bewildered and dazed with her revolver hanging limply in her hand. She watched the wolf kill the deadly rattlesnake. It was then she noticed her horse was headed in the direction of the snake... not towards her as she first thought.

A sharp whistle sounded to Melissa's left. Watching in stunned amazement, she saw the animal drop the rattlesnake. Afterwards, he ran to sit docilely beside a white man dressed in buckskin pants. He also wore moccasins, plus a fringe doeskin shirt. The man stood at least six-feet-five or six-inches tall with large hands; they appeared surprisingly gentle as he stroked the wolf's head tenderly. His murmur was husky and quite deep. With an English accent that was only, slightly noticeable... he praised the animal for killing the snake.

Melissa felt a cold nose poke at her shoulder as Lightning nudged her checking to see if his mistress was all right... she ignored him. Hastily, she put her gun away but didn't tie it down just in case she needed it. Mell quickly pulled her socks back on before jamming her feet back into her boots. She jumped up instantly when another man emerged from the trees, further left of the first man. Her hand automatically reached for her right revolver; she didn't draw it though since they just saved her from a rattlesnake. Cautiously, she kept her hand on her gun.

Taking small hesitant steps towards the two men for a better look; Melissa got close enough to notice that the second man was native, or maybe just part Indian. He was the largest one she had ever seen in this area. Approaching cautiously, she examined them more closely.

The white man's face was rugged and masculine; his nose came straight down with only a slight flare around the tip, fitting him perfectly... not too big or long. His lips were full, almost too large. With a chin, that jutted out giving him an appearance of arrogance. Long coal-black hair hung down to his shoulders. Studying his eyes, she was startled by their misty light blue colour. Gazing back at her, he seemed to see right through her. His expression seemed sober until he grinned in reassurance. Tiny laugh lines appeared at the corner of both eyes with a small dimple appearing on the right side, near his lip. The smile softened his face significantly. When he smiled, it was devastating!

Shivering slightly, Melissa felt the effects right down to her toes. She could tell a lot about people by studying their faces. It was part of her job to assess a person quickly... she was one of the best at it. What she saw in the white man's features relaxed her considerably; she removed her hand from the butt of her gun.

Melissa turned her head to study the second man intently. She revised her thinking when she got a better look. He was definitely a full-blooded Indian... Cheyenne, she figured. There were a couple of scattered bands over the border in Montana, but most had moved and settled further west. She could tell he was a leader or a chief just by the way he carried himself. His clothes gave him away too. Mell happened to know all the chiefs in this area; she didn't recognize this one, so he must be from western Montana. What was he doing this far from home? In addition, why was he travelling with a white man?

Grey Wolf studied the tall dark blonde woman approaching them; she intrigued him... what was she doing way out here all by herself. He frowned in annoyance at himself as he gazed into her deep turquoise eyes, feeling the first stirrings of desire since his family died years ago. He gave a small sigh of relief when she turned away from him to study Giant Bear.

When the white woman got closer, Giant Bear stepped into the background not wanting to cause trouble for his friend; he allowed a bit of a smirk to cross his face, impressed by what he saw in the woman's eyes. She didn't hesitate to approach them, nor did she show any fear as she studied them intently.

Melissa stopped suddenly, looking from one man to the other curiously; her firm no-nonsense voice demanded an answer... immediately! "Who are you?"

The white man stepped forward quickly. Wanting to put the woman at ease, he answered for both of them. He motioned towards himself, making sure to give her his white name first before adding his native name afterwards since the chief would be using that name; pointing at Giant Bear next, he introduced him too. "My names Jed Brown, I'm from Boston... my Cheyenne friends call me Grey Wolf; my traveling companion is Chief Giant Bear."

Jed pointed to the wolf before looking down to make introductions. He grinned fondly at the comical looking animal, who was sitting there scratching an irritating itch behind his ear. "This is Three Toes; we gave him this name because he ended up losing one, thanks to the trap we rescued him from as a pup."

Looking back at the woman in amusement, Jed noticed her strange clothing. The smile disappeared as he eyed her in displeasure. Studying her more closely, he frowned in disdain. Grey Wolf could hardly believe his eyes; she was dressed in men's clothing and carried two lethal colt revolvers on her hips. From the worn looks of the two guns, they were definitely well used. Were they hers... or did she take them from her brother or father? In spite of the odd attire she was a beautiful woman, he grimaced in aggravation at himself as he felt a slight stirring in his loins.

Shaking his head in exasperation at himself, Jed tried to clear his thoughts. He waved towards the woman invitingly, wanting to put her at ease; he smiled encouragement. Grey Wolf was hoping to distract himself from this unexpected attraction. "And who are you, if I'm not being too bold to ask? I am sorry if we frightened you, but I didn't have time to warn you about the danger you were in."

Giant Bear watched the two with silent interest for a moment. Turning, he melted soundlessly into the trees before heading to their nearby camp to get their horses. He knew instantly, they wouldn't be spending another night here.

Melissa didn't notice Giant Bear leaving at first, since she was too preoccupied with Jed. She tensed suddenly in mistrust when she glanced to the left and realized he was absent; quickly, she looked back at Jed threateningly... her hand automatically dropping to her gun. "Where did your friend go?"

Jed saw her quick reaction towards the gun on her right hip. He couldn't help noticing immediately the speed of her hand. He felt a touch of respect... she might even be faster than he was. Grey Wolf wondered silently why she wore two guns when she only reached for one. Perhaps, she only used the one on her left as a backup or if there was more opponents. It left him to speculate why she would feel the need for such protection; unless, there was trouble with outlaws in the area which was always possible. So, judging by her quick response the guns must be hers. Her movements were too smooth and practised for them to be someone else's.

Grinning disarmingly, Jed put his hands up soothingly... showing he wasn't a threat to her. "Giant Bear went back to camp to gather our belongings; we are looking for work in this area, but so far we have had no luck."

"I could use a couple men on my ranch." Melissa scowled furiously at herself; she immediately lamented her thoughtless outburst. Unfortunately, it was too late to take back the offer when she saw Jed nod in acceptance... not even hesitating.

Jed turned away instantly; having noticed Melissa's grimace of regret, he didn't want to give the woman a chance to change her mind. Hastily, he spoke over his shoulder before heading in the direction his friend went. "I will go get Giant Bear and we will follow you to your ranch."

With that comment, Jed disappeared into the trees quickly before Melissa could run off without them. His curiosity was definitely aroused by her offer, as well as by the woman herself. Not only did she carry two revolvers, but she also owned a ranch; she said 'my ranch', not our ranch... was she a widow? Whatever the reason, his interest was piqued. Grey Wolf knew there would be no leaving now until he found out all the answers to this mysterious woman.

Giant Bear met him halfway then they both returned immediately to the creek.

*****

Melissa led Lightning to the water for a drink. She rested against him waiting for the two strangers. Her thoughts were on the man she wanted to know about... still, she couldn't help regretting her offer. Instantly thinking about him brought a mental picture of Jed to her mind, she felt that strange tingle once again. Shrugging in frustration not sure if what she was feeling was a warning or premonition, but she desperately needed to find out what was causing it. Mell learned long ago to listen to that warning shiver; it had saved her life more than once in her lifetime.

When the two men appeared, Melissa sprang up on her horse to lead the way.

Melissa took the opportunity to study both men closely as they rode along and liked what she saw. You could tell a lot about a man by the horse he rode, as well as by the gun or guns he used. Jed was riding a bay gelding larger than Lightning; he looked well treated with no spur marks on his side or a chaffed bleeding mouth from a cruel bit. She had noticed immediately when they first met that his six-gun lay low on his hip, it would take only a flip of his hand to grasp it... telling her he had experience using it.

Giant Bear rode a smaller paint mare. His saddle was a worn brown blanket; his halter plus the reins was made of homemade rope with no bit in the horse's mouth. The Cheyenne Chief wore no spurs or guns, but he had a rifle in a homemade beaded pouch hanging from the saddle blanket... from what Melissa could see, it looked okay.

Catching Melissa staring curiously at them, Jed smirked inquiringly, but didn't make a comment.

Flushing in embarrassment, Melissa averted her head.

The grin Jed flashed towards the woman turned into a mischievous smile as Melissa looked away. He allowed his own gaze to roam over her figure assessingly. When he first glanced into her expressive eyes, he saw honesty with a stubborn resolve... as well as a great deal of determination. It made him think she was a widow bound and determined to keep her ranch. However, the girlish flush at being caught staring baffled him. It changed his mind slightly; it brought to mind a young girl mortified when caught looking at a man. Grey Wolf frowned confused. She was definitely a beautiful woman, not young either perhaps in her late twenties. She must have been married at one time. He shrugged slightly to himself, but his interest was piqued he needed to understand what she meant by, 'my ranch'.

Jed lowered his gaze to Melissa's stallion in appreciation; he approved of the way she handled her horse, not once did the stud look towards Giant Bear's mare and she was in heat. He wondered how she managed to keep him under control... she almost seemed a part of him.

Melissa at that moment was wondering what Jed would think when she told him how she acquired the ranch or what her profession was. She grimaced slightly in anxiety, what would he say? Mell was sure he wouldn't understand... most outsiders didn't. Many of the townspeople hadn't understood it at first either. Of course, they didn't know she was a woman when she first started working there. Over the years, she had proven herself to them countless times; they knew she was just as capable of doing the job as any man.

After riding south for most of the day, they turned southeast for several hours before cresting a hill just as the sun was sinking. Melissa heard Jed draw in a deep breath of amazement; it brought out a smile of satisfaction from her.

The view before them was spectacular. Nestled in a valley was a long two-story ranch house, painted white with red trim surrounded by trees on three sides. There were two large corrals to the left neatly constructed. They were both painted white; one with two-dozen mares and their foals. In the other corral was six horses, some for breeding... others for gelding. The barn situated between the two corrals was painted red, with white trim. Further left Jed could see two bunkhouses side by side both black with white trim. Further, back he saw a couple other small buildings probably for chickens, pigs, as well as a milk cow or two.

Amazingly, there were no logs not even at the corrals, everything was built with lumber; this was an unusual sight in Dakota. Another large building could be seen about two miles north... deeper into the trees.

Hearing a warning shout from the ranch yard, Melissa saw half a dozen of her men galloping towards them. She slowed her horse frowning in disapproval, knowing now why she didn't see Joe at his post; he must have seen them coming so rushed ahead to forewarn the other men that strangers were with her. Mell stopped to wait for them with a scowl of annoyance. The others in her party reined their horses in waiting with her.

The wolf growled a warning.

Instantly, Jed snapped his fingers sharply in command not wanting him shot by mistake. "Three Toes come over here, you better lie down now."

Three Toes obediently moved closer to Jed. He dropped down to his belly dutifully, observing the newcomers closely with no more show of hostility; his job of alerting his master now done.

Jed watched the man in front closely, guessing correctly that he was the bailiff of the ranch. He had dark brown hair and was clean-shaven. Grey Wolf estimated his age to be early forties with hair slightly greying. The closer the man got the more he could see; his skin was leathery looking from obviously spending a lot of time outdoors. When the foreman was close enough, he saw straightforwardness with a great deal of honesty in the man's brown eyes. The Englishman grunted in approval at Melissa's choice of stewards before chastising himself, most times he still couldn't help thinking in British terms... even after all these years.

The men came to a halt a few yards in front of Melissa. The foreman eyed the strangers suspiciously. Speaking for all his crew waiting anxiously behind him, he looked at Mell before nodding towards the two men; with a slight hint of command in his tone... he inquired. "Do you have a problem here?"

Sighing in vexation, Melissa shook her head in disbelief at her foreman; she waved slightly in furious reprimand at her men. "Of course not, you all know that I can take care of myself."

Melissa's men looked abashed smiling sheepishly at one another, but it was the foreman who spoke for all of them... he smirked without any guilt on his face. Wade shrugged in explanation at his angry boss. "We can't help it Mell, we worry about you; I guess you will just have to put up with us!"

Nodding resignedly, Melissa was well aware her men would never change. She chuckled slightly in humour at the look of amazement on her men's faces now that they could look the strangers over more carefully.

After introducing everyone, Melissa motioned to her foreman as she pointed at the chief. "Wade, I want Giant Bear to work at the ranch... Jed will help me in town."

Jed frowned in surprise wondering what Melissa could be working at in a town that he would be any help with. He shrugged; Grey Wolf knew he would find out tomorrow.

Turning to Jed in forewarning, Melissa gestured to the south. "Be ready to ride before the sun is up; Wade will show you where to bunk down for the night."

Melissa glanced down at Three Toes before looking back at Jed; she cocked an eyebrow in inquiry.

Jed shrugged in apology; he smiled at Melissa's question concerning the wolf. "Three Toes chooses his own path."

Looking at the wolf, Melissa nodded in acceptance; her expression softened considerably. "He can go where he wants on my land; it's the least I can do since he saved my life."

Wade gave Melissa a quizzical look when she looked back at him, but he didn't comment. He knew she would explain things to him at their customary meeting later tonight. The foreman beckoned Jed to follow him; the new hand obediently turned his horse towards the ranch.

Figuring Jed's friend would be more comfortable with Daniel, who happened to be half Cheyenne; Melissa waved for him to take the Indian Chief to the bunkhouse. "Dan you can take Giant Bear with you... help him settle in."

Giant Bear had eyed the Cheyenne in curiosity as Melissa and her foreman were speaking. Dan was in his early thirties with the typical light dusky skin of a half-breed; his eyes were dark brown, with black shoulder length hair. He also wore a headband that showed he once lived with his Cheyenne family. His gaze was direct... without shame for having chosen to live with the white man rather than his native family.

Inclining his head, Giant Bear nodded in thanks towards Melissa at her choice when he passed her but didn't comment.

Nudging Lightning into a trot, Melissa headed for the ranch house after waving to the rest of her men to go about their business; Mell was glad to be home in familiar surroundings where she could get her bewildered thoughts together.

Melissa entering the ranch yard headed for the barn. Her horse slowed in order to step upwards. A sharp hollow sound came from his hooves before they reached firm ground again. After two strides, Lightning stepped off the planks that were laid along the ground as a sidewalk going from the house to a door on the left-hand side of the horse barn. More planks went from the door then turned left towards the paddocks. It went to a small gate that Mell's father could open to go through; a ramp was on the other side allowing him to coast in his wheelchair to firm ground. The sidewalk had been constructed to help him get to the barn as well as the corrals without assistance... when he needed to.

Looking down, Melissa was surprised to see Three Toes following her; laughing down at him in permission, she nodded in amusement. "Okay, you can come too if you want."

Melissa dismounted not far from the barn doors.

Immediately, young Tommy appeared from the stables to

care for Melissa's horse. When he saw the wolf, he stopped short; standing there petrified, he trembled in shock.

Smiling in encouragement at the young boy, Melissa held out her reins invitingly. "He won't hurt you, Tommy... I promise; he saved my life!"

The young Tommy was taking no chances; he grabbed the horse's reins then ran back into the stable without comment.

Laughing at the retreating Tommy, Melissa shook her head in humour; he was only ten, with brown hair, dusk skin, and blue sorrowful eyes... the high cheekbones pointed to his half-breed Indian status. He hadn't left the ranch since his mother brought him here at the age of six for Mell to look after.

Shaking off her reflective mood, Melissa turned away from the stables. She raced across the yard to the veranda before taking the four steps two at a time then walked towards the front door. Further to the right was a gently sloping ramp for her father's wheelchair; he used it to get to the sidewalk, which allowed him to move about more freely.

Three Toes slipped by Melissa when she opened the door before trotting inside uninvited. Having completely forgotten about the wolf following her, she made a grab for him but missed. "Oh no, you don't!"

However, it was too late; the wolf looked back at Melissa with what she could only describe as a wolfish grin. She chuckled in surrender letting him have his way. "Okay, I said you could go anywhere you wanted to so you can stay."

Glancing around in pleasure as she began removing her outer clothing, Melissa was quite proud of her home; it was bigger than most others in the area were. Inside, it was more open since Mell had all the doors to the rooms removed, except for the kitchen, den, and Alec's rooms. There was even a second floor, only one other ranch could boast about having a second story... it belonged to Brian.

There was a huge front entrance with two large windows, one on each side of the main door... giving lots of sunlight since Melissa had the wooden shutters removed. Once inside, a wide hallway going the full length of the house greeted you. To her left a stairway went up to the second floor. The banister was made of oak intricately carved at the top and bottom with a wolf's head. Upstairs, there were five bedrooms. The one on the left was hers. It was the master bedroom, which boasted its own sitting room. On the right, there were two guest rooms tastefully decorated. Mell's maid Gloria and her fostered son Tommy occupied the remaining two bedrooms. All the bedrooms had small fireplaces in them for cold winter nights.

Frowning, Melissa's thoughts returned to Tommy. She just couldn't help herself. Her foster son was such a sad boy for his age... quite intelligent, but too mature for one so young. He is Mary's son, who happens to be Brian's sister. The boy was half Cheyenne because of that fact his uncle hated him. Brian threatened to harm her son so Mary brought Tommy to Mell in the hopes she would foster him... he's been with her ever since. She tried again to shake off her thoughts of the troubled boy as she continued disrobing.

Melissa's contemplation once again returned to her home; on the right side of the main entrance, there was a formal drawing room with a western decor. It boasted a piano, a huge fireplace along the far wall, with a large portrait of her mother hanging above the mantel. This room was rarely used now that she lived here, only twice could she recall having guests in it.

The next room was the dining room. Beyond that one was the kitchen; she had added swinging doors... mostly because of smoke when cooking, plus it made it easier for her father to get in and out on his own.

On the opposite side of the kitchen counter there was another door; it would take you to the back entrance. The back entryway wasn't big. It did have two more doors though when you walked in from the kitchen. The one along the far wall would take you into the cellar, the one to the right led outside.

Across the hallway from the kitchen were Alec's living quarters. Once inside, a doorway on the left gave him direct access to the den from his room. The den was large enough to hold two Victorian chairs and a small two-person sofa... along with a large fireplace. A desk with several armchairs surrounding it was against the far wall. Here, her father did the daily ranch business; the den's main entryway though, was almost directly across the hallway from the dining room.

Once through the door of the den from her father's room, the library archway was straight ahead. When entering this room there was a large sofa and one armchair with two tables for putting books, another cozy fireplace greeted you. The library was across the hall from the formal drawing room. Of course, both the main entrance to the library and living room had no doors. Since Melissa's father came to live with her, she redesigned the downstairs of her home to accommodate him. Mell got rid of all the excess furniture so he would have more room to manoeuvre his chair around. The bookshelves in this room lined each wall, which held books of every description. Some belonged to the previous owner and her father added all his to the collection... filling them to overflowing.

Hanging up her outside clothes, Melissa also added her gun holster to pegs along the wall before putting on her inside moccasins; she turned then headed down the hallway calling out expectantly. "Dad, where are you?"

Hearing the squeak of wheels coming from the den; Melissa hurried past the stairway and library before turning left then pushed the door open, since it was ajar. When she entered... she stopped short in surprise; there was Three Toes sitting on his haunches regarding her father fixedly with his head cocked to the left. Alec was staring just as intently at the wolf in awe wondering if it was okay to move, they were at eye level Mell couldn't help noticing.

Taking the opportunity, Melissa studied Alec while he was occupied with Three Toes; her smile was full of love with a touch of sadness apparent as well. She inherited his curly dark blonde hair, but his eyes were crystal blue, hers were turquoise like her mothers. Before the accident put him in a wheelchair, he stood at six-feet-eight inches which accounted for Mell's height. Her mother died in the same accident that put her father in the chair. Pain, with plenty of worry lines filled his craggy face... which at one time only held love and laughter. She pushed thoughts of her mom away it was still painful for her, even after all these years.

Melissa eyed Alec's chair in pride; Mell, with the help of her men custom-made it for him plus his outside chair. The wheelchair allowed him to keep his pride making it possible for him to be independent.

Several years ago, Melissa read about a new type of chair the Boston hospital was using... called a wheelchair. It was made especially for crippled people. In excitement, she rushed there to investigate this newfound invention. When she saw the huge ungainly high-backed chairs they used, she knew there was no way Alec could maneuver the cumbersome thing around by himself. After Mell returned from Boston, she gave her men a sketch that the attendant in the hospital gave her so they could see it for themselves. She couldn't help expressing to them her deep disappointment, it would be too difficult for her father to go anywhere in one of those chairs; the men decided to try to build him a better one.

They took a sturdy wooden chair then cut off the legs. One of Melissa's hands made two wheels similar to a wagon wheel, but smaller. They were not too tall, only a foot above the arms of the chair so he could push them both making them roll forward. A long round wooden bar was riveted to them holding the wooden seat up with two even smaller wheels in the front. It took them quite a while to figure out how to get all four wheels to roll freely when any weight was put on the seat. The two wheels on either side of his chair were twice as thick as wagon wheels... making it sturdier. A wooden platform in front held Alec's legs up, so they were not dragging on the ground; this put the small wheels directly under his feet.

It was only made of wood, so was not sturdy enough for outside. However, while Melissa was in Boston, she bought two of those new bicycles; of course, one of her men just had to come up with the idea of using them for an outside chair. It didn't take them long to figure out how to put it together... it work even better than the wooden chair. Mell lost her bicycles, but it was well worth the loss to see the look of relief then contentment on her father's face.

Shrugging off her thoughts, Melissa laughed at the sight of the two staring at each other so intently. She shook her head in amusement as she walked over to Alec's chair; bending, she kissed him on the cheek. "Hi Dad, how was your day?"

Alec Ray looked away from the wolf for a moment as he accepted Melissa's kiss then glanced up at her in loving pride. "Mine was the same as usual, how was yours?"

Grinning down at Alec, Melissa patted his shoulder in reassurance; she motioned towards the wolf making introductions. "Just great; Dad, this is Three Toes."

Melissa looked over at the large wolf before snapping her fingers sharply in invitation. "Come boy, and meet my father."

Three Toes instantly dropped to his belly whining eagerly then crawled forward. He approached the chair ever so slowly. When he reached it, the wolf raised his head until Alec's hand was touching him; still non-threatening he lifted his head to sniff at the hand Melissa's father turned over for him.

Alec beamed in delight as he leaned forward to touch Three Toes fully when the animal licked his hand in greeting... introductions complete. He looked at Melissa inquiringly as he continued to stroke the wolf's silky fur in enjoyment. "He's a fine-looking animal where did you find him?"

Smiling down in appreciation at the wolf's antics, Melissa looked back at her father before gesturing casually. "I hired a couple of new hands today; Three Toes was with them. He decided he liked me better so followed me into the house. He saved my life so I couldn't refuse to let him in."

Bringing his gaze back to the wolf quickly to hide his expression, Alec frowned slightly in surprise but didn't ask any questions. He knew Melissa would resent his concern... she was way too independent for even his peace of mind. His face under control once again he looked up then waved towards the kitchen. "Gloria came in a few moments ago to call us for supper, but I decided to wait for you. How about giving your old man a helping hand?"

Melissa chuckled in humour when her dad referred to himself as, 'old man'... really, he wasn't that old. She walked around her father's chair before taking hold of the handles; gladly Mell pushed him into the kitchen where supper was waiting.

CHAPTER TWO

After supper, Melissa and Alec went out on the veranda to watch the sun go down; they did this every night to discuss the day's events before their ride. Now that the days were getting noticeably longer, soon they would be able to take further evening rides which her father thoroughly enjoyed.

Alec, unable to keep silent any longer cleared his throat loudly... his curiosity was getting the best of him. He wanted to know more about the two men Melissa hired. Her father was mystified at her decision to hire them without first discussing it with him, as was her custom. Even though technically, the ranch was hers. Still, he now had a share in it. "How about telling me about your new hands and the wolf saving your life?"

After thinking about it seriously, Melissa decided not to tell Alec about the three men who chased her earlier... not wanting him to get upset. She knew they couldn't have been her own men; despite the resemblance of one of the horses, because Wade would have mentioned it to her when she arrived back at the ranch. Instead, Mell told her father about the rattlesnake then the rescue by her new companions.

Looking away to hide his hopeful expression; Alec turned back once his face was under control again before continuing hastily when Melissa finished her tale. "I want to meet them!"

Melissa sighed in resignation already knowing what he was up to; he would check Jed out to decide whether he was marriage material. Afterwards, he would try to play matchmaker... again. It happened every time new hands were hired. She shook her head in irritation, but could not refuse her father anything. Even after all these years, Mell still felt her actions that long ago day contributed to her mother's death. Pushing that painful thought away, she motioned persuasively hoping to distract him. "Do you want to ride tonight, Dad?"

Beaming over at Melissa in pleasure, Alec tried his best to give her an innocent look. "That would be absolutely wonderful!"

Sighing resignedly, Melissa wasn't fooled at all by her father's expressionless face. She went to the barn to ask

Tommy or Dan to saddle up Lightning and Lady for their evening ride, while Alec left to change.

Melissa saw her foreman standing by the corral as she was leaving the barn; she beckoned him over. "Wade, please bring Jed and Giant Bear over to meet my father."

Wade snickered knowingly; guessing it was Alec who asked for the introduction. He shook his head teasingly at Mell. "Are you sure you want me to do that?"

Grimacing in embarrassment, Melissa flushed slightly; at one time, Alec tried to match her up with Wade. It was a standing joke in the men's bunkhouse as to whether her father would ever succeed in finding Mell a husband.

Turning, Wade sauntered slowly towards the bunkhouse; he made sure his boss heard him as he mischievously whistled a loud wedding tune.

Melissa frowned in annoyance as she waited for Alec, thinking they would be laughing about it in the bunkhouse for the next six months. Oh well, she thought shrugging there was nothing she could do; her dad would never change.

Alec wheeled his outside chair down the ramp before going over to Melissa; he smiled up at his daughter... still trying to look innocent. "Well, where are the men you were talking about?"

Just then, Wade came around the corner with Jed and Giant Bear.

Whistling in appreciation, Alec was amazed at the size of the two men... especially the Cheyenne. "Boy, you sure weren't exaggerating about their size; it's not often I find anyone even remotely near my height, the white man looks pretty close though."

Jed walking towards Melissa was surprised to see an older gentleman with her. It didn't take him long to realize the man was probably her father, he had the same thick curly blonde hair as she did. He would also be just as tall as Grey Wolf was... maybe taller, if it were not for the chair he was in; that would account for her height, but Mell's dad had crystal blue eyes. Therefore, she must have inherited her mothers.

While waiting for introductions, Jed eyed the funny looking chair with wheels that the older man was in... what kind of contraption was that? Shaking off his curiosity, Grey Wolf shook Alec's hand firmly.

Alec could see the interest in Jed's eyes as they shook hands. He liked the young man's firm, but not crushing grip; the honest integrity was plain to see in his eyes. Melissa's father could also see a pain... a deep-rooted agony that went beyond the physical. Only someone who experienced the same loss would be able to recognize it. It brought his personal torment rushing to the surface instantly. He let go of the younger man's hand then turned away hiding his expression for a moment.

Once Alec's face was back under control, he turned his attention to Giant Bear. He eyed the large Indian in surprise, there didn't seem to be an ounce of fat on him. The native reminded Melissa's father of someone, he frowned perplexed when he couldn't remember who the person was. Familiar with his language, he began to talk to the chief in his own tongue; trying to make him feel more welcome.

Jed was surprised at Alec's fluency in the Cheyenne language, few white men could converse so easily in the native dialects; he turned to Melissa inquisitively... or Mell, as her ranch hands affectionately called her.

Melissa looked over at Jed knowingly before smiling broadly at the surprise on his face, she gestured towards her father. "We can both speak in three native languages."

That surprised Jed even more, his admiration for Melissa went up a notch; even he could not speak three Indian languages... only two. Grey Wolf gazed around the homestead in admiration it was a beautiful place.

Dan walked towards them leading two horses.

Jed wondered who was riding the other horse.

Wade moved Alec's wheelchair over to the mare.

Alec clucked his tongue at his horse in command.

Instantly, the mare dropped to her haunches waiting patiently... familiar with this routine.

Wade helped Dan lift Alec; they took him to the sitting mare before placing him in the saddle.

Reaching out, Alec grabbed a hold of the extra-large saddle horn; he made sure his grip was as tight as possible. It was custom made so he could use his arms instead of his legs to keep himself in the saddle. It also had a way higher back which helped him stay firmly in the seat. The muscles in his arms bulged... straining them; Mell's father kept his body in place, allowing Wade and Dan to let go of him.

Once sure Alec wouldn't fall off, the two men quickly turned to put his feet in the custom-made stirrups that enclosed the front of his boots. Now Mell's father was straddling the mare properly. Afterwards, Wade and Dan, both positioned themselves so they could hold tightly to his thighs and back; making sure he would not slip out of his saddle when the horse stood back up.

If there was an emergency and Alec needed to get up on his horse by himself... he used a different whistle. She would lie completely down so he could crawl on her before getting up slowly; with Wade and Dan there though, she didn't have to be as careful with him. When he was settled, Mell's father whistled another one of his special signals. She stood up quickly then waited quietly for the two men to strap his legs down.

Wade had taught the mare these tricks to make it easier for them to help Alec mount; it was just too difficult lifting him that high. The foreman also trained her to stay lying down so Melissa's father could mount on his own... if he needed to. He started slowly by sleeping with her when she was a foal. At some point during the night, he would make sure to lie on her somewhere. Until, she got used to staying down when something heavy was crawling on her.

Things just progressed from there. By the time the mare was three years old, Alec was able to pull himself over to her then crawl on her by himself. Once in position, he would wrap both arms around her neck. When he was ready, he would give a different whistle; telling her to rise cautiously, until she was standing then he could sit up on her. Once or twice a year, they did this little stunt just to make sure she wouldn't forget.

Lucky for them there had never been an occasion where Alec needed to do it on his own, but it was better to be prepared.

Jed stared in amazement... never having seen such a sight before; he continued watching in interest as Wade took a rawhide rope and threaded it through the girth. The foreman strapped Alec's stirrup with his leg against the horse's side, to hold him in place for when the horse went faster than a walk.

Grey Wolf admired the way the older man sat on his horse,

even with his useless legs. Obviously, Mell's father was not always in a chair. He was impressed that he didn't let his handicap stop him from riding.

Melissa turned to Jed and nodded goodbye with a slight insistent note in her voice. "I will see you at the barn by five o'clock sharp; I want to be out of here no later than five-thirty!"

Looking towards Giant Bear, Melissa didn't give Jed a chance to comment; she nodded farewell to him as well. "I hope you will like working here."

Giant Bear grunted in acknowledgement as he watched Melissa expertly mount her horse; he couldn't help mumbling to himself in a low tone. "I think it might be... interesting."

Jed watched them ride away; he noticed Three Toes loping along beside Alec's horse. Grey Wolf looked at Giant Bear before laughing good-naturedly not in the least put out. "It looks like my wolf adopted Melissa and her father."

Giant Bear smiled at his friend, but made no comment. He left soundlessly, walking towards the bunkhouse since he hadn't eaten yet; he left Jed standing there staring after Melissa.

Standing for a while longer, Jed reflected pensively on the pain he had seen in Alec's face; just like the older man, Grey Wolf had recognized it in his face almost immediately. He shook off thoughts of Melissa's father then thought of the afternoon he spent with Wade. The foreman talked a lot, but really hadn't told him much about Mell. All he learned so far was she lived in the saloon when she first moved out here, since there was no hotel in the town at the time. He also learned she worked in town for about ten years before she moved to this ranch about six years ago. How she acquired the ranch... nobody would tell him.

That was all the information Jed could get out of Wade. He asked about Melissa's job in town of course, but the foreman just smirked in humour refusing to answer... much to his disappointment. Shrugging his shoulders resignedly, he reminded himself patience was definitely a virtue; Grey Wolf would learn more in the days to come, he was sure. Now though his curiosity about Alec was piqued as well, he wanted to know about the pain he saw reflected in the older man's eyes.

Finally, Jed went into the bunkhouse for some dinner; he was just too busy settling in earlier to eat. The only men still at the table were Giant Bear and the man from the stables... Dan looked more Indian than white. With any luck, he could find out some information from him about the woman he was looking for. He dished up some stew the cook left on the back of the wood stove to keep warm. Afterwards, he went over to sit beside his friend. He put out his hand to shake Dan's in introduction. "I'm Jed Brown to the whites and Grey Wolf to the Indians."

Dan shook Jed's hand firmly in return before inclining his head slightly in greeting. "I am Dan here or Red Eagle when I'm with my Cheyenne family."

Grinning in acknowledgement, Jed dug into his stew ravenously. After eating in silence, he pushed the bowl aside before turning to Dan inquiringly. "How long have you lived in North Dakota?"

Dan eyed the inquisitive Jed thoughtfully wondering where this was going, but didn't see any harm in the questions so answered honestly. "I've lived on this ranch for twelve years now. I was born and raised in town; although, I did go stay with my Cheyenne family for a while."

Jed sighed in relief, hopefully now he could get some answers. "Good, maybe you can help me then; I'm looking for a white woman."

Chuckling knowingly, Dan waved towards town. "I can introduce you to a few at Chelsie's Bar. Although, she usually doesn't like her girls getting close to the men; she does look the other way occasionally. Or Pam's Ladies at the local fancy house, I don't get any time off until next week though."

Hooting in amusement, Jed shook his head negatively at the misunderstanding. "No, I am not looking for that kind of woman. I'm searching for a particular one. I can't tell you much about her because I have no idea who she is. All we know is she should be in her late forties or early fifties... we think. Somewhere around fourteen or so years ago she killed two men then turned three others over to the sheriff; the three men later escaped. I don't know why she turned them in either, my guess is that they tried to kill her or were rustling her cattle."

Gesturing with a decisive motion, Jed continued after a brief pause of thought. "Probably both... would be my guess!"

Sitting back, Dan rubbed his chin thoughtfully for a few minutes. He stared into the distance thinking back before finally shaking his head negatively. He looked at Jed regretfully. "No, I've never heard anything like that happening around here; I most definitely would have since North Dakota has only recently been civilized. Fourteen years ago, the town was just beginning so there was only a couple of white women around... none outside town. Another point to consider is we have the only law in the north. If something happened anywhere nearby, our sheriff would have taken the outlaws into custody before bringing them to town to stand trial."

Dan watched the disappointment flicker over Jed's face; he motioned intrigued as he leaned forward enthusiastically sensing a good story. "Why are you searching for this woman... if you don't mind me asking?"

Jed exhaled noisily in aggravation; he thought for a moment there his search was over, but yet again he was disappointed. He shrugged gravely at Dan before answering honestly. "We are looking for the three men that got away. We think they're around here somewhere, searching for the woman. If we locate her, we should be able to find the men."

Sitting forward, Dan tapped his lower lip with his index finger reflectively for another few minutes; trying one more time to remember something that might be helpful. He knew Jed was not going to tell him anymore, but he wanted to help... suddenly, he motioned towards Grey Wolf inquisitively. "Are you sure she lives in North Dakota?"

Jed shook his head negatively. "No, why do you ask?"

Dan smiled confidently figuring he had the answer... he waved towards the south dramatically. "Could she be from South Dakota, I only ask because it was civilized a lot longer?"

Grumbling reluctantly, Jed shrugged not really having any clue. "We don't know for sure, all we have is the name Dakota."

Heaving a sigh of disappointment, Dan gestured in regret. "Not much to go on; you can talk to the old timers tonight, it might help. I'm betting the woman you are looking for though is living in South Dakota... or did at one time. Around nine we usually have a poker game going on in the bunkhouse, come join us."

Scowling dejectedly, Jed turned to Giant Bear resignedly before motioning in frustration. "I guess we will just have to keep looking. We will stay here until the end of the month or until those men resurface again... whichever comes first."

Pushing back his chair, Dan got up to leave. "I'm sorry I couldn't be more help to you."

Turning to look at Giant Bear inquisitively, Dan tried once more to get him to change his mind. "You sure you want to sleep in the barn?"

Giant Bear nodded his head that he did, but didn't answer.

Frowning in disappointment, Dan really wanted to spend more time with Giant Bear; he missed his people at times. Oh well, tomorrow would do he supposed. He turned back to Jed before nodding expectantly at him. "I will see you later tonight at the poker game then?"

Dan turned with a final wave; once Jed inclined his head slightly in confirmation that he was going to play poker with them. The young man left for the barn to finish his chores while he waited for Melissa and her father to get back.

*****

Melissa led Alec towards Devil's Rock; they were not going that far though, since it was a five-day trip... if you weren't in a hurry that is. She always tried finding different routes to travel so her dad wouldn't get too bored.

As Melissa rode along, her thoughts kept returning to the three men who shot at her earlier. Who were they... why were they on her land? She was definitely going to have to find out tomorrow when she went back to work; there was just no way, she would allow anyone to trespass on her place shooting at people without trying to put a stop to it. If Mell had known it was not her men in the beginning, she would have turned back then followed them to see what they were up to. Unfortunately, she didn't know and to go back now would be futile they would be miles away.

They were about an hour away from the ranch when Alec rode up beside Melissa. He cleared his throat noisily to catch her attention as he motioned curiously in concern. "What's the matter, Mell? You have been too quiet tonight; it's not like you to be this preoccupied... something must be troubling you?"

Melissa turned to look at Alec then grimaced in apology. "I'm really sorry, Dad; do you mind if we cut this short. I have a few things to figure out and I'm just not in the mood for riding tonight?"

Alec inclined his head in understanding; not even hesitating he turned his horse... heading towards home. "Did something happen at work I should know about, or does it have something to do with the two new men? I have never seen either one of them before, and it's not like you to hire complete strangers without talking to me first."

Looking over at Alec in reassurance, Melissa smiled before shaking her head negatively. "No, Dad nothing happened at work, everything was quiet. As for the new hands, I don't really know why I hired them since we don't need anyone right now. It was just a spur of the moment decision made because of curiosity. I've never seen an Indian Chief travelling around willingly with a white man, especially in our territory. Hopefully, I will find out the answer tomorrow when I take Jed to work with me. I'm also hoping he is more open-minded than most men are, if I get the typical reaction from him that I get from others... I'll be very disappointed."

Nodding in understanding, Alec remembered how disillusioned Melissa was in the town men when they first found out she was a woman. He thought of the tall, good-looking dark-haired stranger with the tormented blue eyes and grinned. "You like Jed... don't you?"

Glaring at Alec in dismay, Melissa frowned in forewarning as she gestured sharply in rebuke. "I do not even know the man, and don't you start your matchmaking with him! For all we know, he might be a killer or a hired gun; until I know more about them, you just stay away from both men!"

Alec smirked shrewdly at Melissa. "I think you protest too much!"

Holding up his hands in surrender, Alec hooted in amusement when he saw Melissa gearing up to give him another blast. "Okay, Mell... I'm sorry; I will stay out of it until we know more about this Jed fellow."

Heaving a sigh, Melissa was relieved when they came in sight of the stables not wanting to continue the conversation.

Dan and Dwayne came out to help Alec into his chair before

tending to the horses.

Melissa thanked them both then pushed her father to the house.

Three Toes followed them inside; without even hesitating, he trotted into the library since the den door was closed. Alec smirked knowingly, figuring the wolf was headed into his favourite room... without even waiting for them.

Beaming up at Melissa in pleasure, Alec motioned after the retreating wolf. "It looks like Three Toes has adopted us; he even knows which room I spend most of my time in already."

Smirking in agreement down at her father, Melissa made no comment; she pushed him into the library, through the archway into the den before taking him to the table where he kept his pipe, tobacco, and his current book.

The wolf was already underneath the table sleeping contentedly.

Gloria, Melissa's maid, popped her head through the door to make sure it was her boss making the noise. "You are back early; do you want your tea now, or should I wait a bit?"

Eyeing the slightly plump middle-aged maid, Alec couldn't help but grin. Gloria, at four-feet-nine inches with light hazel laughing eyes always seemed to get a smile from him... even on his worst days. However, don't let her sparkling eyes fool you; she had a strong will and would take no back talk from anyone. Plus, she was fiercely loyal to them. His grin widened as he thought of the first meeting between her and the wolf.

Looking at Three Toes sternly, Gloria shook a chiding finger at him before growling in warning. "You better behave yourself; I don't tolerate nonsense or begging in this house... no messes either."

The wolf didn't faze the maid one bit, even though sitting Three Toes was just shy of being at eye level with her.

Looking at Gloria with his head cocked to the right, Three Toes turned it to the left inquisitively... staring at her quite intently; suddenly, he whined pleadingly and raised his right paw as if he wanted her to shake on the deal.

Alec watched in utter amazement as Gloria tentatively reached out then shook the wolf's massive paw; her expression was deadly serious. Mell's father's guts were killing him as he held in his laughter trying not to let the maid see his amusement. When she left, he doubled up holding his side in torture... laughing in glee, unable to help himself.

Motioning plaintively over at Melissa in explanation, Alec didn't look away from Gloria as he chuckled quietly to himself remembering earlier; he still had a hard time keeping a straight face around her, wanting to laugh every time he thought about the wolf incident. "Mell didn't feel like riding anymore so we came back early, you can bring the tea anytime... there's no rush."

Nodding agreeable, Gloria ducked back out of the door.

Turning to Melissa after she settled on the couch; Alec's expression sobered in thought as he brought the subject back to their two new hands. "So, you think these men are up to something?"

Shrugging indifferently, Melissa wasn't really sure what was causing her apprehension. Not wanting Alec to read anything special in all this... she kept her tone casual. "I don't know for sure; I'm hoping Jed will confide in me tomorrow."

Scowling thoughtfully not fooled by Melissa's tone; Alec eyed her speculatively, not wanting to give up talking about the men yet... he continued. "Do you think there is anything at the sheriff's office on them, maybe you should look through the wanted posters tomorrow, too?"

Sighing in exasperation, Melissa really wanted to get off the subject of her unease. She gestured in appeasement. "I don't know Dad, but I will look into it tomorrow when I go into town... I promise."

Gloria entered with a tray; she put it down on the table before pouring tea for Alec and Melissa. Wade came in, so she poured a cup for him then another for herself... afterwards, they all found seats. This was an evening ritual, since Wade was foreman and Gloria was the only housekeeper; they wanted reports from them first before the others arrived to give their versions of daily events.

Wade helped himself to a cake from the tray, and turned to Melissa as he motioned in aggravation. "That new man of yours, Jed; he keeps asking about three men and a woman in her forties or fifties. When he couldn't find anything out about them, he began fishing for information about you two."

Shrugging, Melissa was unperturbed that the new men were asking questions about them. "It's only natural for him to want more information about us, since now he will be working here; I will be taking Jed with me tomorrow so I'll find out what he is up to then... I hope."

Wade nodded in satisfaction and thankfully changed the subject. "Mell, you only have about a week or two before you have to start riding your gelding instead of Lightning... it's that time of year again!"

Exhaling noisily in displeasure, Melissa nodded; she hated leaving him behind, but they had several mares he needed to breed. Everyone in the room could hear the disgruntlement in Mell's voice when she concurred. "Let me know when you need him, I'll switch horses."

Chuckling at Melissa's tone, Wade didn't say anything more; he didn't really have anything all that interesting to report tonight, so the four sat quietly drinking their tea.

Melissa looked at the mantel where her clock sat; right on time, she heard the hum of voices as the hands entered the library then the den. They mingled, talking quietly among themselves for a bit before everyone quieted respectfully when Mell rose from her chair. She cleared her throat to get everyone's attention. "Does anyone have anything interesting to report tonight?"

Watching them all shake their heads in denial, Melissa frowned pensively; well, obviously nobody else saw the three strangers she had seen earlier. It relieved Mell's mind slightly, they were probably just passing through... fortunately.

Smirking mischievously when she looked over at Jed, Melissa decided to tell her men about her run in with the wolf; she beckoned the two new men to step forward. "As you are all aware by now, we have two new hands... Jed Brown and Giant Bear of the Montana Cheyenne."

Both men nodded acknowledging the introductions.

Looking underneath the table, Melissa smiled fondly at the sleeping wolf before waving down at him. "This is their wolf... Three Toes; even though he seems to have adopted us for the moment. Let me tell you how he saved my life!"

The ranch hands all listened eagerly as Melissa told her story.

Jed grinned in humour; he listened to Melissa as she embellish the story, until all the men were jumping in reaction at all the right places. They gasped in surprise when

Mell snarled like a wolf then jumped towards her men... as if attacking them.

Even Three Toes looked up at that; seeing no other animal around, he laid his head back down and went back to sleep in disinterest.

Leaning towards Giant Bear; Jed made sure to whisper quietly, so the others wouldn't hear him. "Mell's quite good at that... isn't she?"

Giant Bear grunted before nodding in agreement. "She would make a good story teller."

Melissa finished with a smirk of satisfaction at her excited men, as they talked among themselves appreciating her dramatics. One by one, the men went to Mell to wish her goodnight before each one stopped then shook Jed and Giant Bear's hand; they introduced themselves then left.

Jed followed closely by Giant Bear was the last ones to wish Melissa a goodnight before leaving.

A hush descended, as the four remaining finished their tea in silence.

Wade got up then looked down at Alec. "I will see you in the morning to go over the supplies list, instead of tonight; I think I'll retire early."

Turning to Melissa once Alec nodded agreement; Wade tipped his hat respectfully before leaving.

Gloria stood up hastily, as soon as Wade was gone; she turned towards Alec, and bobbed her head goodnight before she looked over at Melissa eagerly... motioning hopefully. "I can bring you the list of supplies I need tomorrow, as well. So, if there's nothing else, I'll take the tray to the kitchen then call it a night also."

Beaming up at her maid, Melissa wondered what all the rush was tonight before waving for her to go impatiently. "It's okay Gloria you can leave now; I will put the tray on the counter on my way to bed."

Mumbling thanks hurriedly, Gloria scurried out of the room as if her skirts were on fire.

Smiling at Alec, Melissa got up then walked over to his chair for a goodnight kiss. "I am going up to my room, Dad; I think I'm tuckered out since there was a lot of excitement today. Is there anything you need, another book? Or would you like more tea before I take the tray away?"

Shaking his head, Alec accepted his daughter's kiss. "No, I don't need anything; I will probably stay up late, so my chair can sit by my bed."

Melissa leaned down further after kissing Alec... she gave Three Toes a good night pat before picking up the serving tray. Mell walked out the door; immediately, she turned left then went to the kitchen. Pushing open the swinging doors, she deposited the tray beside the kitchen sink then turning back, she hurried out. Going back down the hallway, she passed the den and the library heading towards the front door. Suddenly, she turned right as she hurried up to her room.

*****

Out in the bunkhouse, Jed sat down at the poker game. Once again, he was introduced to everyone. There was Dan the half-breed that he had met earlier; he was dark like the Indian's, and husky almost fat... like some white men.

There was Cookie, who was the bunkhouse cook. He looked like a typical cook, too; with his chubby cheeks, double chin... plus he was just about as round as he was tall.

Jerry was next with his cowboy look; he was one of the horse breeders. He was painfully thin... wiry, with honest hazel eyes, and light brown hair; he had a habit of slouching so was taller than he looked.

Dwayne sat next to Jerry, he had black hair and green eyes with a medium build, he was only average in height. Being a gambler down on his luck, he helped with the horse breeding reluctantly; he nodded arrogantly at Jed not bothering with any greeting.

There were two others at the table both older than the rest, but he didn't catch their names. Jed was not interested in them anyway... except maybe for information; he could tell just by looking at them they were just ordinary cowpokes. Wade wasn't among the players. A couple were lying on their bunks sleeping.

Dan smiled over at Jed then explained the rules. "We don't play for big stakes here... Melissa doesn't allow it; we open the game with a penny and you can't go any higher than a dollar."

Jed threw a penny on the pile while the cards were dealt out; he tried to bring the conversation around to what he wanted to talk about. He assumed a talkative tone, pretending he wasn't interested in the answers. "There seems to be a lot of men working here?"

Cookie frowned over at Jed pensively, unsure if he should tell the new hand anything or not. Finally, he decided just to give him vague answers. If he wanted to know more, he would have to ask Melissa. "Well, most of us worked here for years... Bradley Henderson was the first owner, back then there were a lot of cattle here. When the town took it over, they sold all the cattle, but left us on anyway to look after the place. When Mell and then her father took over, they let us stay on; even though they don't really need all of us. Most of the time they seem to find something for us to do."

Nodding distractedly, Jed didn't care why there were so many men here; he just wanted to keep the cook talking. He threw another penny into the pot for two more cards before inquiring. "What happened to Alec, how did he lose the use of his legs?"

Shrugging, Cookie wasn't sure of the answer for that question. "All we know is he was in some kind of carriage accident which also killed his wife; the doctor said he would never walk again."

Jed scowled in disappointment, but it did explain the anguish he saw reflected in Alec's eyes. He decided to try another question, he looked at his cards in interest; he had a full house... kings and threes, so threw a quarter into the pot. Assuming a casual tone, not wanting the others to know how interested he was. "What job does Mell do in town?"

All the men exchanged looks then grins, not fooled by Jed's tone at all; however, it was Cookie who answered for them. He grinned mischievously at the new hand and couldn't help a teasing note from creeping into his voice. "You will have to ask Mell that question."

Nodding in dissatisfaction, Jed dropped his cards on the table face up. "A full house kings high!"

The men groaned before throwing their cards into the center as Jed raked in his winnings.

Cookie gathered up the cards before shuffling them again.

Jed sighed in exasperation, still unable to get any answers about Melissa. He thought it best to turn to a different subject of discussion; he would try again later to find out more about her. "How long ago was the town built?"

Now the official spokesperson, Cookie continued to answer Jed's inquiries as he dealt out the cards. "They started building our town about fourteen years ago... there weren't many people at the time; it wasn't until four years after it was built that we had enough people to call it a town, but it was lawless then. The sheriff was old, we did have a few women around, but they were ladies you don't want to marry."

Grimacing, Jed exhaled noisily in frustration already knowing the answer but asked Cookie the same question he asked Dan earlier anyway... just to be sure.

Looking at the two older cowboys for confirmation, Cookie saw them shake their heads negatively; he turned back to Jed before shaking his own head in denial as well. "Never heard of anything like that happening around here, sorry."

Jed scowled in disappointment at the answer; he picked up his cards and began playing again, without asking more questions.

CHAPTER THREE

Melissa woke while it was still dark outside as she usually did, wondering why she felt peculiar this morning. Perhaps, it was just nerves because she was taking Jed with her. Again, she hoped she wouldn't get the customary reaction from him she received from other men. Mell shrugged, there was only one-way to find out. She got up and lit a candle before getting dressed; it was time to go to work!

*****

In the bunkhouse; Jed finished dressing. He had a few minutes to spare, so sat back down on his bunk to think about last night's poker game. He quizzed everyone about the three men he was tracking, but nobody seemed to know anything about them. Grey Wolf was also frustrated because he couldn't get any information about Melissa, or about what kind of work he was going to be doing. Everyone just snickered... it was really making him nervous. The worst of it was, he didn't know why he felt it was so important to find out what she did for a living. Maybe, it was because he did not want her to be a madam of a whorehouse or a saloon owner with women of questionable means.

Jed shook his head irritably before telling himself to quit thinking about Mell... she is what she is; it wasn't up to him to criticize. He needed to keep his concentration on finding those men and the mysterious woman, not on his new boss.

They tracked the three men slowly across Montana then into the Dakota Territory; afterwards, they disappeared... again. It seemed every time he got even remotely close to catching up to them, unexpectedly they would vanish without a trace! There was no wanted poster out on them because they never left anyone alive to identify them. Unfortunately, Jed only had a vague description from his dying son. The sheriff he talked to in Montana said it was not enough to go by.

In Montana, they were referred to as... the Shadow Killers. They seemed to kill for no reason, but only hit the elderly or women with children who were left alone. That is why he was looking for the woman his son mentioned. Unfortunately, he had no description of her either. Every time he heard of them killing again, he would rush there; of course, they were already gone by the time he arrived. Well, he would just have to keep his ears open. Eventually, they would kill again they couldn't seem to help it then he would be able to continue the chase. Right now, it was time to get moving. He strapped on his gun and walked towards the door.

Cookie intercepted Jed before he could escape. The cook was holding a bowl of porridge; he handed it to the new hand with a merry twinkle in his eye. The big man used a firm no nonsense tone, as he shook a beefy finger at Grey Wolf in warning. "Eat before you leave, I cannot in all good consciousness let you go until then."

Jed nodded in thanks and took the bowl obediently. Eating quickly, he gave it back before leaving... it was almost five o'clock. Hurriedly he rushed into the barn, but slowed when he heard voices. Grey Wolf was just in time to see Melissa slap Wade on the back, with a laugh of pleasure at something her foreman said. Stopping abruptly, he scowled at the pair; he had to restrain himself all of a sudden from marching over there, and stepping in between them.

Melissa caught sight of Jed suddenly then halted what she was going to say to Wade; she smirked at her new hand in humour instead. "What took you so long?"

Giving Mell a strained smile, Jed fought against the jealousy he couldn't help feeling. "I'll be with you in a moment."

Oblivious to the battle Jed was having with himself, Melissa turned to Wade inquisitively. "You have your instructions; do you or any of the other guys need anything from town?"

Wade smirked perceptively after Jed; unlike Melissa, he caught the furious green-eyed look on the man's face. He turned to Mell before putting his arm around her. He just couldn't help himself... the look he saw on the new ranch hands face made him do it. "Yeah, Mark wants a plug of chewing tobacco and Dwayne wants a pack of his favourite cigars."

Instantly moving away from Wade; Melissa was taken by surprise, but not before she elbowed him in the ribs in rebuke... she continued mystified. "Okay, I will see you tonight if nothing unusual comes up."

A groan of agreement was all Melissa got from Wade... as he massaged his sore ribs. The foreman smirked devilishly at Jed as he walked past; trying hard to hide the fact that Mell had jabbed him hard in reproach.

Taking a hold of her horse's reins, Melissa shook her head in puzzlement at how strange Wade was acting all of a sudden. She led her horse out of the barn with her packhorse tied to her saddle, so he followed her too. She mounted as soon as she was clear of the door.

If Melissa could have seen Jed's furious face as he led his own horse out, she would have been even more bewildered.

Jed struggled to conceal his feelings of jealousy; unfortunately, he was unsuccessful as he heard Wade laugh teasingly behind him. Finally, succeeding in controlling his look of fury... he swung into his saddle before turning to Melissa. She had her hair tied back today instead of hidden under her hat. He couldn't help noticing that the ends brushed against her horses back. Grey Wolf's eyes turned to look at her packhorse next in surprise. He speculated again about her work, but knew better then to ask.

About half way to Smyth's Crossing, Jed's curiosity got the best of him; he looked towards Melissa and motioned at the horse following Lightning. "Mell, what is the packhorse for?"

Melissa grinned naughtily over at Jed before giving him a vague answer, not wanting him to know yet. "I started taking a packhorse with me because sometimes I have to be on the trail for days... mostly without notice."

Opening his mouth to ask Melissa again what her job was, Jed quickly snapped it shut audibly. Grey Wolf swore silently to himself; he wouldn't ask again even if it killed him. He sighed in frustration... it just might!

Nudging her horse into a canter once he was warmed up; Melissa effectively forestalled any more questions. She was running a bit late as it was, since it took a good two hours of hard riding to reach Smyth's Crossing from here. If Mell kept them at a leisurely pace, it would take them half of a day to get to town... that was unacceptable!

They rode into town just after eight o'clock in the morning.

Jed looked around speculatively, it was bigger than he figured it would be. On the left was the smithy with a barn attached; he could just hear the whoosh of the forge as it was brought to life. A few horses milled around in a small paddock pawing at the ground impatiently. They snorted in anticipation when a short black-haired kid ran out with water and hay... he was running late for the morning feed.

On the right was the general store with three wagons unloading supplies; there was groaning and complaining from the five youngsters struggling with sacks of flour, sugar, coffee... plus several other staples that were needed in town.

Chuckling in sympathy, Jed turned to his left; he was just in time to see the saloon sign which read 'Chelsie's'. It was two stories so either had rooms to rent or fancy women. He shook his head to himself; Dan said Chelsie frowned on that sort of conduct so it was probably rooms for rent... it could possibly be for dancing women too.

It was quiet at the saloon this time of the morning, with a drunk sleeping it off on a porch swing. Jed spotted movement in the alley where a man had fallen asleep against the building. He nodded in approval to himself when he saw the barn and the two-story saloon close together... it was a good idea; this way horses were brought there, instead of left out in the street.

Next to the saloon was a three-story hotel. Jed could smell fresh bread cooking; he sniffed appreciatively it was definitely coming from the hotel. The sight of people moving around in front of the windows caught his eye. The hotel patrons probably smelt the bread too. It was making his mouth water... even way out here. Grey Wolf had no doubt it would be drawing them down for breakfast.

Jed turned to the right again; there was a dentist office, as well as a doctor's office all in one. He chuckled; probably the same man did both jobs.

Next to it was a barbershop; a short, older man was sweeping the porch getting ready for the day.

A sign on the next building read; 'Barrister Timothy Rowling at Law'; under that was... 'All your lawyer's needs'.

When Jed turned his head to the left again, there were a few houses; he smiled a greeting at a young woman as they passed by. She stopped hanging clothes in order to wave hello, he tipped his hat respectfully... returning the greeting.

A courthouse was the last building, unless you looked further down; Jed could see a three-story house a little way out of town. The building was dark, as well as totally isolated. Grey Wolf figured it had to be the brothel Dan told him about last night.

The people out at this hour called out good wishes to Melissa. "Morning, Mell; have a great day!"

One informed her everything had been quiet since she left.

Shaking his head, Jed was completely bewildered now. Obviously, Melissa wasn't a madam. He continued looking around in interest... he turned to his right. The sheriff's office was next, he chuckled knowingly; he was sure the lawyer had his office next door, so he could get extra business.

Jed could see beyond it was the stagecoach office with a stage just getting ready to leave. He heard a loud 'crack' of a whip, followed closely by the snap of the reins before a thunderous bellow from the burly driver rent the air... "Giddy up!"

Melissa halted outside the lawman's office; interrupting Jed's contemplation... he looked around grimly. Although no posters were out on him that he was aware of, he had no use for sheriffs. Grey Wolf found most of them to be obnoxious bullies. Mell dismounted before tying her horse to the hitching rail, but left the packhorse tied to her stallion.

Jed sighed in relief; they must not be staying long. He dismounted too then followed her dutifully, when she beckoned him to come with her.

Walking into the building, Melissa stopped to wait for Jed to enter. After removing her hat, she hung it up then walked around the desk and sat down. Taking out a sheriff's badge, she pinned it on before reaching again into the drawer; Mell pulled out a deputy's badge and placed it in front of her new hand... right on the corner of her desk.

Standing there gaping in astonishment for a moment; Jed's mouth opened then closed several times as if to say something... nothing came out. He visibly pulled himself together as he sat down hard in a chair. He shook his head in disbelief before motioning in bewilderment. "How did you get to be a sheriff, when most women can't get any job outside the home without jeopardizing her reputation? What about your father or the men in this town, did they actually agree to this?"

Shrugging self-consciously, Melissa gestured for Jed to take a seat. "It's a long story so you better sit back, while I try to explain everything."

Settling in the chair, Jed was still having a hard time

believing Melissa was a sheriff; he watched as she got up and poured them both a cup of coffee that someone must have made for her earlier... probably a deputy.

Melissa handed him a cup then sat back in her own chair; her face turned pensive as she thought back to the time before her mother's death...

"I was born and raised in South Dakota in a town called Windy Creek. My father was the foreman of the Triple Horse Ranch just a few miles out of town. Except for me, all the children out there were boys so naturally I learned everything they did. I was riding before I could walk; I learned how to shoot a rifle at five years old. At the age of seven, I was learning how to use a revolver then how to track people and game. When I was ten, I could out draw, out shoot... plus out track most of the boys I grew up with. By the time I was thirteen, I was out wrestling and out boxing most of the men. I was taught to speak three Indian languages, mostly from the half-breeds working there. How to speak French by one of the cowboys, whose family was from France."

Hesitating, Mell couldn't help smiling lovingly thinking of her mom before continuing...

"My mother taught me reading, writing, then arithmetic; she also tried her best to teach me the ways of a lady; although, she despaired of me ever using the knowledge. I also learned how to survive off the land, winter or summer for weeks or months at a time if necessary. After I proved myself, I was officially allowed to help with roundups and was a great help when problems arose. Most often, the ranch hands forgot I was a girl; I was late in blooming so I resembled a young boy until I was older. My mom couldn't do anything about it I was a real tomboy. I wonder though if things would have been different if my parents could have had another child... preferably a boy."

Melissa halted then got up to pour more coffee, there was only half of a cup left for each of them so she added some whiskey to their cup. She didn't usually drink, but she knew she was going to need it to finish her story; Mell sat back down and tried to collect her thoughts before she continued.

Jed sat quietly waiting; he wanted Melissa to continue in her own time. He was beginning to understand what made Mell the strong independent woman she was today; he was totally engrossed in her remarkable story.

Taking a fortifying sip of her whiskey-laden coffee, Melissa continued. Her brow creased in pain, remembering the day her world was shattered then changed forever...

"Everything was going great until I was fifteen. I was out tracking some rustlers with a few of the hands. Luckily, we found them quickly at a fork in the trail that leads to town; it was not far from the ranch. There were five rustlers all together and four of us. After the smoke settled, we managed to kill two of them then took the other three to the sheriff in town. You should have seen their faces when I took my hat off to wipe the sweat off my forehead, and they realized I was a girl. They started shouting insults, as well as loud lewd comments that I didn't understand at the time before they talked about getting revenge."

Melissa sighed resignedly; she sat forward, and rubbed her forehead then took a big gulp of her fiery coffee for courage... to continue on. Settling back once more, she took a deep breath then continued.

"My parents had gone into town earlier in the day, so after we dropped off the rustlers... I went looking for them. I asked around town, but they already left. Which, I figured was strange because we should have met them somewhere along the way. After we headed out of town, I started looking for their wagon tracks. They were easy for me to find, because one of the back wheels had a deep groove in it from a rock that left its mark years ago. When I found them, I followed. I just had this gut feeling something was terribly wrong. It didn't take us long to get back to the bend in the road, we used earlier to capture the outlaws. I noticed some odd marks; it looked like horses pulling a carriage reared then bolted. We followed the tracks going east. I knew for sure then something was definitely wrong because the trail we were on led to a dead end with a ravine at the bottom. When we got to the top, I could hear a horse screaming fearfully in pain. We climbed down quickly, the first thing I saw was one of our horse's half-sitting attempting to stand up. He was full of blood, we knew by the look of him he wouldn't make it, the other one was dead."

Stopping quickly, when an unwilling sob caught in her

throat; Melissa took several deep breaths before she could continue...

"I looked in dread to the left then saw my mom lying there; I almost passed out right there when I realized she was dead. Her head, arms, and left leg were at unnatural angles obviously broken. Only the sound of a groan coming from underneath the carriage kept me from going crazy. When we lifted it, Dad was laying there breathing heavily but still alive. We wrapped my mother up in a blanket and put her on my horse. We built a stretcher for my father out of the broken wagon so we could take them both to town. The doctor couldn't find anything wrong with him, except for a large lump on the back of his head. However, when they turned him over, we noticed a lot of swelling at the base of his spine. The doctor figured his back was broken... he said Dad would never walk again. I hoped he was wrong at first. Especially, since he was only a vet doctor so didn't know much about doctoring humans. What he did know, was from helping others a few times with no real doctor around. Unfortunately, he was right."

Lifting both her hands, Melissa rubbed her moist eyes angrily; she hated letting her emotions get the best of her. Dropping her hands back to the desk once she was back in control, Mell continued...

"We buried Mom the next day knowing it would be impossible to figure out when my father would regain consciousness. It was six months before he came out of the coma. The first word spoken was my mother's name. When I broke the news to him, he was devastated. The only thing he said, was he should have been the one who died. Six months after the incident, he finally told me all the details of the accident. They came around the bend just before the fork, one of the bullets flying around hit the dirt in front of the horses. It made them rear up in fright; they jerked the reins from my dad's hands before bolting. All he can remember was going over the lip of the ravine. It took my father a year to recover, except for the use of his legs... although, he rarely smiled after that. My dad's partner was a real help to us at first, but then he began to notice I was starting to develop into a woman."

Blushing at this point, Melissa turned her head before

gazing out of the window as she continued in embarrassment...

"He started trying to touch me or would corner me at different times of the day. Usually, I was too fast for him and managed to escape; unfortunately, there were those times when I needed to use wrestling tricks to keep him at bay. It was about a year after the accident before I felt my father was recovered enough to enable me to pack up my gear then leave the ranch. I decided to leave South Dakota entirely because I knew I would never get another job on a farm out there, since everyone knew I was a girl. So, I left and headed to North Dakota where nobody would know me. I travelled from one town to another picking up odd jobs never staying long... searching for something. I didn't know what, though. Finally, I hit this town just after my seventeenth birthday."

A nostalgic smile caused Melissa to stop for a moment; she really missed her old mentor. She took another sip of her coffee before continuing...

"They were having lots of trouble with a group of outlaws terrorizing the area. The lawman at the time tried to organize a posse of men to try to stop the desperadoes. Regrettably, nobody wanted to help him; they were all too afraid, so I offered my assistance... that is how I became a deputy sheriff. When we left to track the gang, there was only the old sheriff, his original deputy, two volunteers, as well as myself. We tracked them for about three days then cornered the leader and three others. It was a bitter fight. Thankfully, we managed to kill the leader then captured the other three. The original deputy with the two volunteers took the men back to town to stand trial. The lawman and I took off after the final outlaws by ourselves. It was another two days before we track them down, finally we captured the last four. When we arrived back, we were welcomed as heroes. They convinced me to stay on as their new deputy. The sheriff taught me everything he knew about the law, anything he didn't know I learned on my own. It took a full year of acting as his deputy before the lawman discovered I was a girl. At first, he was going to fire me but then the other deputy got shot. I managed to talk him into keeping me on for another year. He agreed, as long as I didn't let anyone else know I was a woman. While I was away, the old bugger got himself shot by an outlaw he was chasing. I was visiting my father at the time; when I got back, the townspeople already elected me, sheriff. Everything was relatively quiet for about a year except for a few drunks plus a couple of hot heads wanting to test me occasionally. I was found out by the rest of the town because of a boy I didn't know."

'**Thwack!**' Melissa slapped the desk unexpectedly; making Jed jump slightly in surprise, she chuckled in humour remembering the black-haired boy's reaction then continued with her story...

"I went to a pond I figured nobody knew about. It was quite a way back in a thick wooden glade completely isolated, or so I thought. I found it by accident, when I was out tracking an outlaw the year before. Taking my hat off, I began removing my clothes. Suddenly, I heard an in-drawn breath of shock. Spinning around quickly with gun in hand, I spotted this black-haired boy resting beneath a tree. He obviously skipped school to sit by the water to fish. I did not know the boy, so I didn't think he knew me. When I yelled at him to get on home, he took off like a scared rabbit. It was funny watching him peek over his shoulder to see if I was in pursuit. It never occurred to me to worry. I was so confident of my disguise, that I leisurely finished my bath then headed back to town. As I rode down the street towards the office, I noticed everyone staring at me funny. I checked my sombrero, which I bought from one of the Mexicans working at Windy Creek because it effectively hid my face, since it had a wide low brim. I couldn't feel any hair on my neck, so it shouldn't be showing and the hat was on my head properly. Finally, I shrugged. Everything seemed to be in order so I continued on my way. The townsmen followed me; when I got close to the hitching post by my office, I could see quite a crowd gathered... maybe even the whole town. After I slid off my horse, the judge who also happened to be our mayor approached me then asked me to remove my hat. It wasn't till then I saw the young boy from earlier standing there gawking at me. I knew I was caught red handed, so I gave a resigned sigh and took it off reluctantly. You should have seen their faces when my blonde hair tumbled down my back. I had made a promise long ago to never cut my hair. Especially after my mother died, my fondest memory was of her combing my long hair at night before bed."

Melissa grinned in humour then smirked; remembering the townspeople's reaction to her long hair, she leaned back and continued once more...

"The women gave outraged cries while the men gave wolf whistles, some stood there gaping in astonishment not sure what to do or say. The judge told me that because I'm a lady, it wouldn't be proper to allow me to continue as sheriff. I tried everything to make him change his mind. I pointed out all the ways I made this town a safer place to live in. I even used some feminine wiles then pleaded prettily, but he was unyielding and insisted on paying my salary immediately. He even paid me extra to keep me quiet about being a woman so he could save face. I packed up my gear then left town; although, I didn't go far because I knew the young kid they planned to hire would not last two months. Besides, I had come to think of this place as home. I decided to look for a ranch since I had saved my wages for a year, I figured that I should have enough to buy a small place. Finally, I found a ranch that I wanted a month later. Unfortunately, the price was a bit too high. I learned Smyth's Crossing owned it because the previous owner died leaving no heirs. Soon after this, my prediction proved true as the new sheriff picked a fight with the wrong person and died... I went after his killer then brought him in. With the reward, I still didn't have enough money to buy my ranch so I just kept on hanging around waiting for an opportunity to make more money. I picked up odd jobs here and there for the next few months."

Affectionately, Mell paused in contemplation. Unable to help remembering the day that she assisted a couple, who would ultimately become her best friends; she finished with a flourish...

"One day while travelling along the trail to town, I came upon three men holding up a coach. I managed to take them by surprise, because they were in the process of dragging a woman out of the carriage when I appeared... so they didn't notice me. The man who accompanied her was tied up so couldn't help her. It wasn't until I got closer that I recognized our judge and his pregnant wife. I quickly untied him, immediately he hurried over to comfort his sobbing wife. He described how their town turned lawless after my dismissal then went on to ask if I would take my job back. It would be my reward for saving his wife and unborn child. I told him that much as I would like my old job back, they didn't pay enough money. I explained I was saving up to buy the old Henderson place. The judge's wife quit crying then was quiet until that point, but she winked at me suddenly before whispering something in her husband's ear. He visibly brightened, and said he would throw in the property with the job offer. After thinking it over carefully, I accepted the proposal; on the condition, the ranch would still be mine if sometime in the future I quit my job to get married. The judge stuck out his hand to finalize the deal. I went back to my office the next day then I proceeded to clean up my town. I moved out to my ranch as soon as I could and got everything organized so I could send for my father, we have been here ever since."

Jed sat quietly for a while mulling over what Melissa said, as well as what she hadn't said. It was obvious to him she was deeply affected by her mother's death, even though she tried hard to hide it. He also started wondering if this was the woman that he had been searching for all this time. If so, it was no wonder he could never find her; when Grey Wolf asked his questions they were always about an older woman. It never occurred to him she could be so young... the time frame matched. He sat forward eagerly as he motioned inquisitively. "Mell, what happened to the three rustlers you first captured?"

Melissa eyed Jed in surprise for a moment at his inquiry; she couldn't help wondering what was so important about that incident... why would he want to know more about it? She sighed in irritation, seeing no harm in the question she shrugged unknowingly. "They got away shortly after we handed them over to the sheriff. At first, I was uneasy checking over my shoulder constantly thinking they would come looking for me. Thankfully, they disappeared after escaping from jail."

Leaning forward fervently; Jed was so close to Melissa's desk, he needed to put his hand out to keep himself upright. The urgency was plain in his voice. "Can you describe them to me?"

Melissa frowned at Jed in speculation. Of all the things he

could have asked about her profession, she couldn't figure out why he was so interested in the rustlers. However, since he seemed so intense about it, she decided to continue telling him... more out of curiosity now, though. At least he didn't put her down as most men did when they found out she was a sheriff. Mell gazed into the distance thoughtfully trying to recall that long ago day then looked at Grey Wolf as the image of the three men formed in her mind. "From what I saw and heard they were either brothers or related in some way. Their eyes were all the same blue, but with different hair colours. One had black hair, there was one with dark brown hair, and the last one's hair was a blonde, I think. Their names are even etched in my memory. Although, I'm not sure which one is which; Marty, Jimmy, and then Sam."

After Melissa told Jed the names, she could plainly see the visible fury in his face.

"**BANG!**" Melissa jumped in shock when Jed drove his fist into her desk before getting up unexpectedly.

Jed stood there glaring angrily for a long moment. Unexpectedly, he started pounding on his leg with a balled up impotent fist as he began pacing... muttering to himself in agitation. "You should have killed them all!"

Melissa scowled grimly as she watched her new hand pace frantically. Clearly, he knew who these men were. She stiffened in surprise at what she heard him saying; she leaned forward in cautious concern getting just a little upset at his words. "What's the problem, Jed?"

Spinning around, Jed looked at Melissa in shock; as if just remembering her presence in the room. He gave a weary sigh before sitting down. Sadly, he described the massacre of his family plus Giant Bear's. After he finished, Grey Wolf frowned in apprehension. "They are known as the Shadow Killers. We have slowly tracked them across Montana then finally here into North Dakota. We were also looking for you, but we didn't know who you were. You see... before my son died, he told me he could remember them saying something about going to Dakota to find a woman who killed their brothers. They did not describe you at all, so we didn't have any idea who we were searching for or what you looked like."

Melissa sat for a moment contemplating her new hands story. Being that she was a sheriff, she had heard a lot of stories concerning the Shadow Killers. With no description of them, she never linked them with the outlaws of her past. Suddenly, Mell sat up straighter in her chair in excitement... remembering yesterday. "Jed, three men chased me just before I met you. I thought they were my men because once or twice a month some of my hands try to sneak up on me; they do this to keep me on my guard, it has saved my life more than once."

Picking up the deputy's badge, Melissa handed it to Jed.

Jed pinned the badge on without any hesitation; he got up in excitement before turning for the door. Quickly, he threw over his shoulder not even waiting for Melissa. "Let's go boss!"

Hurriedly, Melissa grabbed something out of her desk drawer before jumping up; she was taken completely by surprise at Jed's rush, and dashed around the desk after him. Mell grabbed her hat off the rack quickly.

However, before either of them could reach the door, Melissa's regular deputy walked in; Greg smiled in greeting. "Hi, Sheriff..."

Greg stopped what he was going to say, as soon as his gaze fell on the stranger. The deputy watched the man jump behind Melissa instantly to avoid being hit by the office door. Another time he probably would have laughed at the mad scramble; now, he was staring in shock at the deputy's badge pinned to the man's shirt. It wiped the smile off his face in a heartbeat.

Nodding pleasantly at her deputy in greeting; Melissa was completely unaware of his feelings, as she motioned in apology. "Good morning, Greg... thanks for making me coffee this morning. I have to ask you a big favour, I hate to since I just got back but I need you to make the rounds for me today."

Melissa's brows drew together in a troubled frown when her deputy didn't answer, but just kept staring at something over her shoulder. She turned to see what he was looking at before finally remembering her manners. Mell moved to the side so the two men were facing each other and belatedly introduced them. "Greg, meet Jed Brown... he will be working with us from now on. Jed, this is Greg Warren; he acts as my deputy in the evenings and when I need him. Usually when I am on the trail, he keeps everything here nice and quiet for me."

Jed stared hard at Greg assessing him; he had dirty blonde hair with dark blue eyes. He had a large forehead with thick brows that only had a minimum break in the middle, giving his eyes a bit of a sunken look. He stood just under six-feet, so was a bit taller than Melissa. The deputy was hefty, but not fat. Grey Wolf frowned thoughtfully in surprise when he saw something flickered in the man's eyes. It was only there for a moment; could it be panic perhaps? It disturbed him for the second it was visible... suddenly, it was gone.

The two men shook hands as they both mumbled greetings; you could tell right from the start they didn't like each other.

Scowling in bewilderment at the two men, Melissa ignored her disgruntled deputies; she turned to Jed without commenting on the dislike on both men's faces. "I have to make a stop at the general store and another at the ranch before we hit the trail."

Turning back to Greg, Melissa sighed apologetically at having to leave him again. "I don't know how long we will be gone; sorry, but you might have to look after things for a day or two."

Greg frowned perplexed; he motioned in confusion. "What's up, Sheriff. Where are you headed now, you just got back the other day."

Melissa told Greg about the three men who shot at her yesterday, explaining that they were outlaws wanted for robbery and murder. She never mentioned that they could be the Shadow Killers; they were not a hundred percent sure yet anyway. Mell was in too much of a hurry, so she didn't tell him about Jed's involvement in the case or her own either... not wanting to take the time. She waved for her deputy to move out of their way.

Standing for a moment more blocking the doorway, Greg sighed in surrender as he moved reluctantly; silently he followed them outside. Standing on the porch, the deputy frowned anxiously as he watched the two leave.

That new deputy was going to cause them grief; Greg just knew it. He shrugged resignedly, nothing he could do about it. He turned and went back inside mumbling irritably to himself, wondering if he should make a trip out to the ranch to give a warning. He finally decided against it. His cousin would find out on his own... eventually.

*****

Jed followed Melissa out to where their horses waited. They mounted then rode down the main street headed out of town.

Making a quick stop at the store, Melissa picked up cigars and chewing tobacco for her men... as promised. She also added extra supplies for the trail in case she needed them; seeing a hunting knife she liked; Mell bought it then tucked into the back of her shirt as an afterthought.

Jed purchased some bullets, tobacco, and rolling papers.

Melissa had the clerk add Jed's bullets to the town's tab, as well as her own; she also included the hunting knife. They finished then left for the ranch to go speak with her father.

As they rode along Melissa turned towards Jed... she pulled out the extra deputy's badge to show him. "I brought along another badge for Giant Bear because he's just as involved in this as we are; I thought he might like to join in our search."

Turning, Jed looked at Melissa in amazement as she held out a badge for him to see. "You would deputize an Indian?"

Stiffening instantly, Melissa wondered if Jed was criticizing her. However, the thought quickly vanished when she realized he probably thought most sheriffs were prejudiced; of course, he wouldn't know she wasn't one of them. Mell smirked over at him before putting the badge back in her pocket as she nodded decisively. "Yes, I would deputize an Indian... actually he won't be the first one I have had as a deputy."

Looking up at the cloudless sky in relief, Melissa sighed thankfully; as long as it didn't rain the outlaws trail would be easy to follow. If the three men who chased her yesterday were the same three Jed was looking for... she hoped to find them quickly before they found her or killed again.

Melissa turned to watch Jed, he was obviously thinking about his dead wife and child. His jaw was rigid as if he was in severe pain; he also had a hard resolute expression on his face. She cleared her throat loudly to get his attention so she could distract him. "See the line of trees over there?"

Pointing to a hill ahead of them, Melissa waited for Jed's nod. She smiled over at Grey Wolf when he turned to her enquiringly... she continued. "That's the beginning of the border to my place; it extends east for at least two and a half days ride then west for another two days. If you wanted to ride the outskirt of my land, you will turn east here for a couple days.

Thinking quickly, Mell shrugged indecisively. "It could even be another half a day or so depending on where you end up. You would then turn north again before following the trees all the way; until you arrive at the bottom of those mountains in the distance. It marks the end of my ranch. We call those mountains Devil's Rock. They are about a five and half day's ride from here. You need to turn west from there and follow the edge of the mountains. It would take you another five days to reach the turn off then you would have to turn south, which would bring you back towards town. On your way south, you would pass the spot where we met. It is a four-day journey south before you would turn east for two more days in order to reach this point. Of course, those lines are not straight. We only use a small portion of the land now. I have thought of selling some, but I might decide to use more later on so I haven't. Right now, I only raise horses and harvest lumber, but later when I retire... I might get into raising cattle. It was lucky for us the town grew northward so now they are only two hours of hard riding away from the border of my land. Once you get here, I am only another hour away so if they have need of me for any reason, I can get there pretty quick."

Jed nodded as he looked around speculatively; he turned to Melissa then gestured around him. "From what I have seen so far you have pretty good land for cattle, if I owned this place, it's one option I would look at."

Congratulating herself on distracting her deputy, Melissa nudged her horse into a canter; they rode the rest of the way in silence, content in each other's company.

CHAPTER FOUR

Melissa and Jed slowed their horses when they got closer to the ranch yard, to let them cool down a bit; both horses were sweaty, but not foaming or blowing hard.

When they reached the bunkhouse, they could see that the door was slightly ajar. Melissa called out loudly hoping her foreman or the Cheyenne Chief was inside. "Wade and Giant Bear; come out I need to talk to you both."

Wade appeared in the doorway instantly; he jumped off the veranda to follow them to the barn. He looked up at Melissa in concern. "What are you guys doing back so early, it's not even noon!"

Melissa slid out of her saddle; she walked around her packhorse before rummaging around in the saddlebags for the cigars and chewing tobacco. Turning she handed them to Wade. "Where is Giant Bear, I need to see him too. When I was out riding yesterday, three men rode out of the trees shooting at me... I managed to out-ride them, but we are going after them now."

Scowling irritably at Melissa, Wade waved in bewilderment. "Why didn't you mention this before; it wasn't any of us this time!"

Grinning confidently, Melissa motioned soothingly. "I know that already, Wade; if it had been any of you, it would have been mentioned last night at the meeting."

Appearing around the corner, Giant Bear stopped short in surprise when he saw Melissa and Jed.

Handing her horse's reins to Wade, Melissa turned to leave for the ranch house; she threw a quick explanation over her shoulder at the Indian Chief. "Jed will explain everything to you... I need to go up to the house to talk to my father."

Giant Bear nodded after Melissa in uncertainty, even though she didn't see him; he looked at Jed inquisitively.

Running to the house, Melissa entered in haste; she didn't even bother removing her outer clothes this time or her guns... she called out immediately. "Dad, where are you?"

Not even taking the time to remove her boots; Melissa walked down the hallway quickly at her father's distant call. "I'm in the den, Mell."

Melissa stepped inside, the first thing she saw was the wolf stretched out watching Alec; she giggled in amusement as she motioned towards the animal in humour. "I guess Three Toes has become your guardian for the time being."

Alec gazed down at the large wolf with affection before looking back at Melissa. "Yes, he has hardly left my side all day. He follows me when I go outside; he even sleeps beside my bed. You are home early, Mell... what's up?"

Sitting down in a chair, Melissa explained everything she learned today to Alec. After she finished, apprehensively Mell waited for her father's reaction.

Frowning anxiously, Alec leaned forward intently before gesturing fearfully. "Mell, I know you have been a deputy since you were seventeen then sheriff for the last six years, but are you sure you can handle this?"

Noticing a frown of painful disbelief on Melissa's face, Alec added quickly before reaching out to take her hand. "Mell, I'm not trying to say you are incompetent or anything... think about it carefully. Whenever you needed to go after anyone it is always someone or circumstances that do not concern you personally. This time you are directly involved, these men are out to kill you; not because you're the sheriff, but because you hurt them by killing two of their brothers. Can you keep your emotions out of it or would it be better to let someone else handle it? I have already lost your mother to these killers. I couldn't handle losing you too."

Carefully, Melissa considered all that her father said as she analyzed her feelings cautiously. She stared at him pensively, needing to find the right words; finally, she squeezed his hand in reassurance before gesturing resolutely with her free hand. She spoke calmly, but decisively. "I know that this hit's closer to home than any other job I have ever done. Dad, I'm also very much aware of just how deeply my emotions are involved in this. You of all people know though that if I don't do everything in my power to stop these men from hurting anyone else... I would have to give up my badge right now. I would never be able to forgive myself, because indirectly it's my fault the men have murdered all those women and innocent children. If I had killed them or at least made sure that they hanged when this all started, all those people would still be alive. So, please understand. I have to do this for myself, as well as for every woman or child they have put into an early grave."

Alec's chest puffed up in pride as he gazed at his only child. He couldn't believe sometimes how well Melissa had turned out, even though she hardly ever acted like a woman! He also understood nothing he could say now would dissuade her, but he had to try once more. "You were only fifteen at the time so how can you blame yourself for not killing them... I didn't raise my daughter to be a murderer!"

Melissa motioned pleadingly with her free hand hoping for Alec's understanding. She heaved a sigh forlornly as she shook her head remorsefully. "I know that, Dad; I still can't help feeling responsible."

Smiling in sympathy, Alec conceded as he let go of Melissa's hand. "I understand how you feel, Mell; you must do what you think is best. Are you taking Jed with you?"

Grinning in relief, Melissa got up to leave. "Yes; I'm also taking Giant Bear."

Alec visibly relaxed as he received that information, at least she wouldn't be alone.

Leaving Alec in the den; Melissa ran upstairs, to gather a few things from her room before she said a final goodbye to her father.

Sitting in his chair with an apprehensive look on his face, Alec cursed the fact his legs were useless. He pounded on them in a powerless fit of temper. A shiver rippled down his spine as a premonition hit him that nothing would ever be the same after Melissa returned; he also felt strongly that someone would die before this was all over... who, was anyone's guess.

Three Toes sensing his new friends panic went over to his chair, and put his head on Alec's lap... he whined in concern.

Absently, Alec stroked the wolf's head; thankfully, it calmed him down a lot. By the time Melissa came in to say goodbye, he managed a calmer expression and his daughter didn't see just how distressed he really was.

Dropping a light kiss on Alec's forehead, Melissa looked down at the big wolf in command. "You take good care of Dad, Three Toes... I'm counting on you!"

The wolf whined at Melissa as if he understood what was going on. He settled back down beside Alec's chair and continued to watch his charges every move.

Chuckling in amusement at the wolf, Melissa turned to Alec... she patted his shoulder in farewell. "I will see you when I get back, Dad; you are in good hands with Three Toes on guard."

Leaving the den, Melissa headed for the door; she paused then turned back when she heard her father call out to her.

Having pushed himself into the hallway, Alec gestured solemnly towards his daughter. "No matter what happens out there, Mell... remember that I will always love you!"

Melissa blew a kiss lovingly towards Alec; she waved a final goodbye before turning to leave without commenting. Mell didn't hear her father's whispered prayer to his dead wife to keep their daughter safe.

Rushing over to the barn where Jed and Giant Bear were waiting impatiently; Melissa dug in her pocket taking out the extra deputy's badge that she grabbed on her way out of the office... Mell handed it to the chief.

Giant Bear accepted it without hesitation then immediately pinned it to his buckskin shirt.

Looking at the two men gravely, Melissa with an unyielding profound tone recited the deputy's oath that she at one time had also taken. "I want you both to raise your right hand then repeat these words after me. 'I', state your full name, 'solemnly pledge my oath to uphold the laws and protect the innocent even unto death... as long as I shall live.'"

Jed and Giant Bear both repeated the vow gravely; their identical expressions were deadly serious. Both aware of what significance taking such an oath meant. Once it was done, they turned to ready their horses.

Melissa went over to Wade before gathering her reins from him; she frowned in edginess. "Who's on watch tonight?"

Wade smiled soothingly; he backed away so Melissa could mount. "Joe has first watch until twelve fifty... Dwayne will take over before one o'clock."

Nodding, Melissa was relieved; Joe was one of the older hands, he was quite capable. She mounted quickly then looked down at Wade intently. "Please ask them to keep a particularly vigilant watch tonight just in case, there's something in the air... it's disturbing me!"

Frowning nervously, Wade watched Melissa leave with her

two new deputies following her. Usually, when his boss gets one of her feelings... it doesn't bode well for any of them. He shrugged no use fretting about it; all they could do was take a few extra precautions and hope for the best. He turned towards the bunkhouse to go inform Joe of Mell's warning.

*****

After several hours of hard riding; Melissa found the spot where she saw the three men going into the thick woods. She turned to Jed before pointing at the trees headed west. "They came out of there, fired one shot at me then went back. I didn't get a good look at them... I'm not even sure they are the ones you are after."

Giant Bear threw an inquiring look over at Melissa but didn't speak.

Nodding in consent, Melissa knew exactly what Giant Bear wanted; he took the lead in the direction she indicated. Mell followed then Jed brought up the rear with the packhorse.

It took them the rest of the day to find the outlaws abandoned camp; when they did find it, they decided to stay there as well since plenty of firewood was left over from the last occupants... dusk was falling fast. In less than an hour, they wouldn't be able to see anything because of the thick trees.

Frowning in apprehension, Melissa squatted beside the small crackling fire that Jed had quickly started. She looked at the two men for confirmation of her opinion. "It looks like they are headed for town."

Jed nodded, but didn't look up as he continued to feed the small fire to get a good blaze going.

Melissa's scowl deepened; she held her hands out to the warmth of the snapping fire as it greedily consumed the kindling being fed to it. It was still cool out in the early spring evenings, especially in the trees. Out in the open where the sun reached the ground it was a lot warmer. However, the small blaze was not big enough yet to cook their food or to warm her up much. Her thoughts were in turmoil as her mind turned back to the outlaws and she began to fret more... Mell rubbed her hands together. She finally turned to Giant Bear inquisitively. "What do you think?"

Waving towards the other side of their camp where all the tracks he had studied earlier were, Giant Bear nodded decisively. "I agree... I'm sure they camped here again after they chased you yesterday then they headed to town; they have not returned."

Standing up, Giant Bear beckoned them to follow him. The two obediently got up, eager to see the signs he discovered. "This was where they picketed their horses."

Giant Bear squatted down; his hand followed the trail so Melissa could see what he saw. "This is the way they left later in the afternoon and their trail definitely leads southeast towards town, but they could have come out somewhere further down... we can track them better in the morning."

Looking around at all the signs, Melissa tried to figure out what the outlaws were up to; unless they were just looking for information. If that was the case, why did they disappear? They couldn't have gone into town or Greg would have mentioned strangers around before they left. They wouldn't need to go to town in any case to find her since everyone around here knew where she lived. Unless, they already figured out she was now a sheriff which might have scared them off. She shook her head to herself... bah. Highly unlikely they would scare off that easily, so where did they go?

Giant Bear decided to do a little hunting to get fresh meat for their supper instead of using their supplies; he stood up then motioned towards Melissa before pointing to his left. "I am going hunting if you have no objections? I also noticed a creek over there if you are interested, Mell."

Melissa grinned in relish at the thought of a bath; it would be cold, but... oh well. "No, I don't mind if you go hunting and I would love to have a bath, if the creek is deep enough that is."

Going to her packhorse, Melissa grabbed her soap; plus, a towel she always liked to carry for just such an occasion. Quickly, she turned back towards the promised creek in anticipation before disappearing through the break in the trees that Giant Bear had indicated.

The creek Melissa was heading towards, was the same one running through her favourite spot; she could see quite some ways down the path that the water took, it most definitely headed straight towards her haven. This part was a little deeper by the looks of it... she should have no trouble bathing in it. Lucky for Mell it was warmer once she left the trees then strolled out into the open, but she knew it would still be a cold bath.

Leisurely, Melissa walked towards it with a pensive frown... a million questions plagued her. How did those men happen to be in this area? Did they know she was nearby, or was it a coincidence that brought them here at the same time she was passing by? Had they known it was her when they took the shot? If so, why did they not pursue her further? She shook off her feelings of agitation as she dropped the soap and her towel on the ground so she could undress. Mell took her hat off next letting her dark blonde hair flow down her back in a waterfall of silky curls. She reached for the buttons on her shirt.

*****

Jed watched Melissa depart with a preoccupied frown and didn't even notice Giant Bear leaving to go hunting. He finally wandered towards the fire pit on his own; he swore irritably when he noticed his fire was almost out. Squatted down, Grey Wolf stirred up the ashes before adding more wood. Once the fire was crackling again, he sat down on a large rock to think.

What was there about Melissa that caused him to have thoughts of settling down again? Every time he was near her, he couldn't help speculating; wondering what she was hiding underneath the strange assortment of clothing she wore. Just thinking about the first glimpse he had of her, with a riot of dark golden curls fanning about her shoulders... caused his manhood instantly to harden in desire. Before he could stop to reconsider his actions, he rose then strode purposely towards the creek where Mell went to bathe.

When Jed arrived... Melissa was removing her shirt, beneath which she wore a white binding coiled about her in layers; she used this to flatten her chest so no one would guess at the abundant flesh it hid.

*****

Melissa's thoughts turned to Jed, wondering why she felt warm and shivery every time she was near him... was there something wrong with her? She unwound the tight binding from around her chest then took a deep breath of air. Mell instantly felt a surge of relief as her large full breasts sprang free. She gently touched one and felt a peculiar sensation as her nipple hardened. She frowned perplexed. Usually, her nipples only got hard when it was chilly out; she was not that cold yet.

Unexpectedly, Melissa heard an in-drawn breath; immediately, she spun around in disbelief then saw Grey Wolf watching her from a distance. Suddenly she became entranced, with a sense of anticipation as that strange tingling sensation came over her again. Not thinking about what she was doing or the consequences involved, almost as if she was dreaming. Mell kept her eyes locked on Jed's... she reached for the buttons on her trousers.

Jed tensed in desire; he watched Melissa in fascination as her long-tanned fingers started undoing the top button on her pants. Slowly, she lowered her trousers until they pooled around her feet... she stepped out of them. Finally, she stood there naked. Grey Wolf moved towards her cautiously, afraid she would bolt before he could get to her, but she didn't move an inch. Not wanting to frighten her away, he continued walking slowly getting more confident of himself the closer he got. He whispered caressingly as he reached out for Mell. "You are even more beautiful than I imagined."

Hauling Melissa to him roughly, Jed slowly lowered his head; it was almost as if he was giving her a chance to pull away, but she remained... he moaned in pleasure as their lips met for the first time.

Melissa immediately melted against Jed in surrender as he deepened the kiss; unsure what was happening to her, but knowing she needed more of something.

Jed groaned in desire... he slid his hands down Melissa's arms then paused in anticipation. Tentatively, he let the back of his left-hand brush against the curve of her breast. When Mell didn't protest, he took his right hand away from her arm before trailing a finger across her chest; until he touched one of her tender swollen nipples.

Crying out in pleasure, Melissa shuddered uncertainly but didn't move away.

Taking this as a sign Melissa wanted more; Jed's caresses became more persistent. Suddenly, his ears caught the sound of someone walking through the trees some distance away... making an awful lot of noise. Grey Wolf stiffened immediately, groaning in reluctance he pulled away unwillingly; guessing who wanted to be heard. He tenderly stroked Mell's face as he stared down at her in regret with a look of thwarted need plain on his face. "Giant Bear is back, I better leave before he comes this way looking for me."

Nodding incoherently, Melissa watched him walk away in frustration. She turned and waded into the creek to cool off her overheated skin; shivering, the icy cold-water hit her full force causing her to come back to herself with a jolt of shock. Shaking her head grimly... feeling mortified. She couldn't understand what came over her. Mell was ashamed of the way she practically threw herself at Jed. Never had she felt such strange feelings towards any man.

At the same time, Melissa wondered how far they would have gone if Giant Bear hadn't returned; she finished her bath in record time before getting dressed quickly. She headed back towards camp, her emotions now under control... or so she thought.

*****

Frowning in concentration trying to ignore his need, Jed skinned the three rabbits the chief got for their meal; his friend fashioned a spit to cook them on, while he was busy with that. Grey Wolf skewered the rabbits as soon as Giant Bear handed him the spit, he put them over the fire before turning to look intently at his companion. "What do you think of Melissa, Giant Bear?"

Looking towards his blood-brother and long-time companion steadily; Giant Bear could see Jed was falling in love with Melissa. He had made sure to make plenty of noise on his way back to camp guessing that Grey Wolf went to the creek after he left. "She is very beautiful plus highly spirited, but my friend you do realize you will never be able to change her... do you not?"

Frowning at Giant Bear in surprise, Jed motioned in confusion. "What do you mean by... change her?"

Choosing his words with care, Giant Bear didn't want to offend Jed or have his meaning mistaken in any way. "Melissa is a strong determined woman. She knows what she wants and is willing to do anything to accomplish her goals. She will never give up her job as sheriff nor will she leave her ranch to go roaming around the countryside with you. She is also extremely honourable for a woman... I can see it plainly in her eyes. If you think you can love her then leave her, you will hurt her badly. She is more the marrying kind; you need to remember this if you plan to get involved with her."

Staring at Giant Bear in amazement, Jed frowned musingly; that was the longest speech his Indian friend had ever given in all their years together. Sometimes, it was easy to forget he could speak so well now. His English improved immensely compared to when Grey Wolf first met him, but usually all he did was grunt... nod his head or he didn't say anything at all. It made his words even more worth taking heed of; he knew the Cheyenne Chief was speaking from his many years of wisdom. He also knew his friend was right, Mell was the marrying kind.

Walking into the clearing at that moment, Melissa's eyes were drawn unwillingly to Jed's. She couldn't help turning scarlet with embarrassment... as well as suppressed desire. They stared at each other intently for several seconds, until Giant Bear cleared his throat noisily to remind them of his presence.

Melissa turned away from Jed quickly; her face became an even darker red, but this time from mortification as her gaze met Giant Bears.

The Cheyenne Chief heaved a resigned sigh; he could tell by Melissa's expression she was already in love with Jed. Hopefully for her sake Grey Wolf would get over his dead wife then settle down. Giant Bear knew his two friends could find a great love together... if they let it happen gradually. If they did become one, he knew their relationship would be anything but smooth. It would be a constant struggle between two strong willed forceful people.

Finally wrenching her gaze away from Giant Bear's, Melissa walked over to the fire; she sat down with her eyes lowered thinking.

Eating was a quiet affair, and only Giant Bear seemed to be able to eat anything; not letting the atmosphere between his two friends get to him.

After they finished eating, Jed rolled three cigarettes; he lit them then handed one to Melissa and one to Giant Bear then sat with his back to a tree, puffing on his own pensively. He was still thinking about Mell and his blood-brother's words of warning.

Melissa inhaled deeply on her cigarette then heaved a sigh

before she broke the silence. She looked towards the two men gravely. "I will take the first watch... it is about nine o'clock now. I'll wake you up at midnight, Jed; you can wake Giant Bear for the last watch at three o'clock."

Both men nodded; they threw their cigarettes into the fire before getting up obediently, and heading over to the sleeping area.

Going to her saddle, Melissa unhooked her whip before moving into the shadows of the trees for a good view of the camp. She was hidden enough that anyone approaching wouldn't see her; this way she could surprise them... if need be. She had decided to take the first watch knowing she would not sleep, anyway. She needed to sort out her thoughts then decide what to do about Jed and her confused feelings about him.

Spending the next three hours trying to figure things out, Melissa eventually gave up... it was no use. She just couldn't resolve anything; she decided that she was just going to have to ignore this unwanted attraction until the outlaws were apprehended. For now, she would just pretend he was just one of her men. With that resolution in mind, Mell went to wake Jed for his watch.

Stretching, Jed watched Melissa leave then yawned tiredly before walking over to take her place; he hadn't really slept since his mind refused to shut down. When he looked directly at his new boss, he had seen a grim resolve in her eyes. He knew instinctively Mell decided to ignore her feelings, and he silently agreed with her; neither of them could afford to get distracted right now or someone could die... just the thought made him flinch in fear.

Jed knew what Giant Bear said earlier was right. If he wanted Melissa, he would have to marry her then settle down here. However, after the trauma of losing his family, did he really want to go through the pain of loving someone and possibly losing them again? Mell's work was very dangerous; there was always a chance that one of them or even both of them could get killed. His friend was correct though in saying she wouldn't give up her job as sheriff... could he live with that. Could he love someone so opposite to his dead wife?

Victoria had been not only a beauty; she was also a debutante. She was too soft and sweet for the likes of him.

His social butterfly had been quite demanding at times, until he brought her to Montana that is. Once out of her element she ended up being timid, afraid of her own shadow. Not once did she ever dare argue with him when he insisted on something, always she would give into his judgment... right or wrong. Jed couldn't help thinking, it would have been nice if she stood up for herself more. It was too late now to regret making them come out here with him, but there was no way of knowing what would happen. If she absolutely refused to come with him to Montana maybe Victoria, as well as his son would be alive today.

Jed chided himself for his thoughts; there was no use continuing to punish himself after all this time. Especially over something he could never hope to undo, he had done enough of that in the beginning. If it wasn't for Giant Bear taking the bottle of whiskey away from him, he would still be drunk in the first town they stopped at. Then there was his promise to his dead wife... he must not think of a future love until he avenged his wife, unborn child, and son.

Love! That thought slammed through Jed's brain like a hammer. Unlike the confused Melissa, he knew what love was like. He sighed in frustrated anger, it all depended on finding the killers of his family; until then his life was on hold. He was certainly getting tired of chasing those men with never any success in getting remotely close to them in all this time. It has definitely been a long nine years, but finally the end was getting near. Those men are so close now, Grey Wolf could feel them. Now that Melissa was in the picture, he was even more eager to put the past to rest... needing to get on with his life.

Standing, Jed stretched tiredly; he decided to walk around their camp before waking Giant Bear. He made a full circle and found himself standing over Melissa watching her sleep. He hadn't planned on going anywhere near her, but here he stood unwillingly. Grey Wolf turned away then strolled over to sit in the same place so he could continue watching the camp. He tried hard to ignore the need to go over to continue watching Mell sleep. The urge got so bad he finally got up to march over there once again... unable to help himself.

Turning at a noise behind him, Jed sighed relieved to see Giant Bear coming towards him to take over guard duty. Grey

Wolf tried to smile, but it was more of a grimace before mumbling hastily. "Goodnight!"

Jed rushed quickly to his bedroll without saying another word and fell on top of his bed staring upwards sleeplessly.

Watching his blood-brother walk away without comment, Giant Bear shook his head in disapproval. He had watched Jed earlier and decided he better take over the watch; his friend was in no condition for guard duty tonight. He probably wouldn't even notice how early it was.

Sighing resignedly, Giant Bear sat down in the shadows of the big tree. He listened with half an ear to the chirping of the crickets; smiling in contentment, he heard the deep croaking of the frogs... the night deepened. The Cheyenne Chief shifted as his eyes grew heavy, but suddenly everything went deathly quiet.

Instantly wide-awake, Giant Bear stiffened looking around cautiously. He heard the hoot of an owl right above him. He looked up in surprise at a pure white owl staring down at him intently. For a full two minutes, the great horned owl gazed at him without moving an inch; unexpectedly, he opened his huge wings before launching himself into the air... he flew up above the treetops.

Giant Bear watched him circle above them; since they were in a slight clearing, the bird was clearly silhouetted against the large brilliant full moon for a moment then the owl disappeared from view. He frowned troubled; usually the sight of an owl during the day was a forewarning... not generally at night, though.

The strange behaviour of the horned owl made him nervous; Giant Bear got up and hurried over to his saddle blanket before taking out his rifle... just in case. Making himself comfortable, he settled back to watch over his two confused friends. It was going to be a long evening. The chief felt better once the crickets and frogs continued their nightly songs, but the apprehension continued throughout the night.

CHAPTER FIVE

Back at the ranch, the quiet was shattered suddenly as two men galloped in with guns firing wildly.

The men sleeping in the bunkhouse staggered outside in confusion; disoriented, they were more asleep than awake. Most of them died before they even realized what was going on or even where all the bullets were coming from.

There was a third man shooting also, but nobody could see him since he was hiding strategically up in the barn... facing the bunkhouse. He was shooting at anyone who stumbled outside.

Three Toes' warning growl woke Mell's father, instantly. He caulked his head listening wondering what had upset the wolf. Suddenly, Alec sat up in bed with a stunned jolt when the sound of gunfire exploded outside. He reached for a loaded pistol that was kept in his bedside drawer; he didn't quite make it before a strange man burst into his room.

Snarling savagely, Three Toes jumped towards the intruder swiftly; the wolf was a second too late though, as the man fired a shot at him... he fell to the floor twitching.

The distraction the wolf caused gave Alec time to grab a knife hidden under his pillow; he shoved it into his long underwear... hastily he removed his hand before the black-haired outlaw could see what he was doing.

"Hold it right there!"

Immediately, Alec put his hands up at the man's ominous shout; he grimaced in rage impotently. "Who are you and what do you want?"

The man grinned wickedly over at Alec; without a hint of remorse, he viciously kicked the wolf as hard as he could in the head in pleasure on his way around the bed. "You are coming with me!"

Three Toes stilled immediately.

The stranger turned to the closet without hesitating; he pulled out the wheelchair stored in there.

Alec stared in astonishment when he saw the strange man retrieve his chair then wheel it to his bed.

The stranger went back to the closet and threw Alec a pair of pants plus a shirt. Impatiently the outlaw waited as the cripple struggled to get dressed as fast as he could. Grunting in satisfaction the man turned back towards the closet when Melissa's father finished. He pulled out the spare boots that were always kept in there; still without saying a word, he checked for hidden knives as he walked over to the bed then helped the old man put them on hurriedly. He pointed at the wheelchair in command expecting no disobedience. "Get in... NOW!"

Not daring to argue, Alec was well aware of his inadequacies in defending himself with useless legs. He eased himself off his bed into his wheelchair. The stranger wheeled him around, Melissa's father caught sight of the wolf lying on the floor dead.

Shaking uncontrollably, Alec had to forcibly control his emotions. He shook his head in bewilderment; furious, he muttered to himself quietly so the killer couldn't hear him. Someone must have betrayed them but who would do such a thing? There had to have been somebody because this man knew exactly where his chair was stored, few people had access to his private living quarters.

Alec knew it couldn't have been anyone living on the ranch; the outlaw didn't know about Three Toes, the astonishment on the man's face just before he shot the wolf attested to that.

So deep in thought, Alec didn't even realize they reached the barnyard area; when he did his face paled in shock when his gaze fell on the dead bodies of his hired men... littering the ground. The only one still alive was Wade. He was holding his left arm close to his side obviously wounded.

Wade and Alec gazed at each other intently for a moment... a silent message passed between them; they both knew who these men were, but they were unsure why they left the foreman alive.

The black-haired outlaw pushing Alec walked around the wheelchair then up to Wade before handing him a letter remorselessly. He pointed in the direction Melissa went yesterday afternoon. "Take this to the woman; tell her she has five days to produce herself or her father will die!"

Taking the letter unwillingly from the obvious older brother and leader of the three outlaws, Wade inclined his head unpleasantly... he didn't say anything. His thoughts were churning as he contemplated angrily who had betrayed them, there had to have been someone; how else would they know to hit the ranch at ten minutes to one. Just before shift change? The foreman was unaware Alec also figured it was an inside job.

A blonde, skinny, gawky looking cowboy brought two horses from the barn. He was not as tall as his brothers were... not having reached six feet; he handed the reins of Wade's horse to him before bringing Alec's mare over to Melissa's father without any hesitation.

Alec and Wade quickly shared another glance both now aware the other knew it was an inside job.

Mounting his horse slowly in obvious agony, Wade almost blacked out from the pain shooting up his arm; he shut his eyes then leaned against the pommel of his saddle to steady himself before the foreman was finally able to ride away.

The largest outlaw among the three stomped over to the wheelchair. He had greasy brown hair with black rotten teeth. He grinned evilly down at Alec.

The outlaw was close to his own height Melissa's father figured at six feet eight, but the large man was huge and beefy unlike his own slender frame. There was a blank cruel look on his face; it made the older man shudder in revulsion figuring the big man must be simple. He was obviously younger than his other two brothers were. He was extraordinarily strong too. Easily he hoisted Alec into his saddle by himself without any help from his brothers or needing to have the mare sit down first... before strapping his legs in.

Alec remained silent even though he was having a hard time keeping quiet, wanting to find out what was going on... he didn't want to antagonize the outlaws either; he heard the blonde skinny man mutter to his older black-haired brother.

"Smart man, he knows when to keep his mouth shut; you better put that blindfold on him. He doesn't want the old man to know who he is just in case something goes wrong."

Sitting quietly when they tied a bandana around his eyes, Alec wondered who the person they referred to as... 'he' was. As they rode out, he realized his earlier premonition that someone would die had proven true. He prayed to God no one else would die before this was all over. Melissa's father felt the knife he hid in his underwear earlier and was comforted a little; at least he wasn't completely defenceless. What he would do with a pitiful knife against all these killers he didn't know, but it helped him to stay calm which was the most vital thing right now.

Alec heard another horse racing to catch up to them; there was a mumbled discussion then the horse was racing away again. The exchange of words was too low for him to hear, but he was sure whoever it was had betrayed them all. Melissa's father didn't have time to see if anyone from the ranch was missing. He was still positive it wasn't one of their own men who was the betrayer... he hoped; still he couldn't be absolutely sure either, he just prayed Mell would be able to get to him in time.

*****

Wade rode hard for several hours as he followed Melissa's tracks; good thing there was a full moon to see by and she didn't feel the need to hide her trail. Even with the glow from the moon, he still managed to ride right past where they had turned off. It took him a good half hour to decide he lost the tracks... he turned back then picked up the trail before turning into the forest going west.

When Wade entered the trees, all the moonlight vanished instantly. He had to close his eyes to adjust to the darkness. When he opened them, again; he became conscious of the fact that there was no way he could track any further. It was just too damn dark. He decided to ride west in the hopes he would stumble into Melissa's camp. He tried to go as straight as he possibly could, but ended up going more northwest.

As Wade weaved through the trees... his thoughts were busy. The foreman was trying to figure out who betrayed them and why? Only a handful of people knew the routine of the ranch. Only four people other than the hands knew that the watch changed at ten minutes to one. It was too coincidental that the outlaws hit them at twelve forty-five; just when the first sentry was getting drowsy and before the new sentry who would be fully alert, arrived. They also knew where the watch was located because he passed Joe's dead body.

Stumbling across Melissa's camp just after six in the morning, Wade let them know it was him approaching; he called out Mell's name as loud as he could, so he wouldn't get himself shot... again.

Melissa rushed anxiously towards Wade; just as he finally wavered then fell weakly to the ground, having lost too much blood. Mell gasped in disbelief when she saw the blood trickling down her foreman's arm and knelt beside him in fear, her voice trembled in panic. "Oh my God... what happened? Why did you leave the ranch untended?"

Hurrying over, Jed dropped down beside Melissa in concern; giving her a gentle nudge... he moved her over a bit. "Mell let me patch him up while he answers your questions, or he is liable to die from loss of blood before he can tell us anything!"

Jed looked for Giant Bear, but the chief was already heading to his pack to get his medicine bag; Grey Wolf nodded in relief, next he sent Melissa for the kettle they just started heating for coffee... he ripped open Wade's shirt to examine the wound.

Jed nodded thanks distractedly when Melissa knelt beside him once again; she brought not only the pot of warm water, but also a bottle of whiskey. She always carried one for emergencies. Grey Wolf ripped a strip of cloth from Wade's shirt and wet it to clean the bullet hole in the foreman's shoulder. It was the best he could do out here, when it was clean he poured a generous amount of the whiskey directly on the injury.

Bellowing in agony as the whiskey hit his opened wound; Greg did manage to tell them about the terrible events that took place at the ranch... once he got his breath back.

Wade handed the note to Melissa; as soon as she read it, her face became bloodless... she swayed slightly on her knees. For a moment Jed thought for sure Mell was going to faint, but she visibly pulled herself together.

Giant Bear brought Jed the medicine bag; lucky for Wade the bullet went clean through his arm so it didn't need to be dug out. Grey Wolf searched through the bag then found the roots he was looking for before turning back to the foreman to dress the wound.

Finally, Melissa spoke, but her voice cracked in strain as she fought for control of her emotions. "They are taking my father to Devil's Rock; there is a trail leading up to the old miners shack... that's where they want me to meet them. I have five days or Dad is dead it says. They also warn me not to bring anyone with me or they will kill him instantly!"

Interrupting Melissa, Wade grimaced painfully as Jed packed his wound with herbs. The foreman gritted his teeth trying to talk through the agony. "Me and your father think it's an inside job."

Melissa looked at Wade in astonishment. "When did they let you talk to my dad?"

Shaking his head negatively at the misunderstanding, Wade explained. "They didn't let us talk, but we could see each other; it was obvious to both of us when they knew which horses we rode. I knew we were right when I passed Joe dead at his post. Only four men know when each shift changes, or even where the sentry is posted... Greg, Brian, Victor, as well as the judge. They are the only ones who would have that information except the hands, but I'm pretty sure they are all dead."

Jed scowled angrily, thinking sadly of all those men he just came to know then gestured anxiously at the thought of his wolf. "Is there anyone else alive at the ranch? What about Melissa's housekeeper, the boy Tommy... or Three Toes?"

Shaking his head sadly, Wade's thoughts turned to Tommy then Gloria. It was an excruciating decision for him to leave without checking on them. He had wanted desperately to return to the ranch. After seeing Joe dead, he even turned his horse right around to do so. He changed his mind though knowing he would never make it to Melissa's camp if he did, so he gritted his teeth enraged then reluctantly turned away. "I don't know they made me leave right away. It was too risky for me to go back; I wasn't even sure I would be able to get this far. I figured Mell would want to stop at the ranch first anyway to check for survivors before burying the dead, so I never went back."

Nodding decisively, Melissa wiped her tears away before grimacing grimly at the idea of having to bury her men. "Yes, you did the right thing coming to find me. We will go to the ranch first then we can find out which trail they took to Devil's Rock. Nobody's aware that I used to go up there by myself when I had time off to explore. I know the area like the back of my hand; that's the only advantage we have right now."

Melissa and Giant Bear quickly broke camp while Jed finished tending to Wade.

Helping Wade to stand after bandaging the wound, Jed guided the still wobbly foreman over to Melissa's horse... Grey Wolf assisted him in mounting behind her. He jumped up onto his own horse afterwards; they left the camp with Giant Bear in the lead.

Their progress was painstakingly slow, not wanting to jostle Wade's wound too much. The bullet had nicked a vein, so they didn't want it to start bleeding again before they could get him to the ranch to tend to it properly. They were all really quiet; trying hard to prepare themselves for what awaited them at Melissa's ranch.

*****

Several hours later, the four riders approached the bunkhouse solemnly sure they were prepared for what was to come; they were not!

Melissa gazed around in horror all her men were dead lying exactly where they had fallen; several scavengers were already hanging around hoping for an easy meal. Squawking in disappointment they flew or slunk off... back to where they came from.

In silent shock; the two deputies dismounted before helping Wade off Melissa's horse then they walked around checking all the bodies for possible survivors or for anyone missing.

As soon as Wade dismounted; Melissa raced to the ranch house as fast as her horse could go. She jumped off him in a panic before he could even stop fully. Taking the stairs two at a time, Mell ran into the house to look for anyone still alive in there. Entering quickly, she didn't even bother to close the door. Racing down the hallway urgently, she searched calling out in anguish... fearing the worst. "Gloria, Tommy, where are you?"

Melissa received no answer; she ran back to the entryway and turned right going to the stairs leading up to the bedrooms. She took them two at a time then paused at the top in dread. Mell inhaled a deep steadying breath to quiet her nerves before hurrying to Tommy's room first.

The walk down the hallway seemed to take forever; Melissa wasn't sure if she would ever reach the end, but finally she paused in front of Tommy's door... she really didn't want to go in there. She looked up at the ceiling imploringly, praying to God for all she was worth before closing her eyes trying not to fall apart yet. Mell managed to open them and put her hand over the doorknob. She twisted it slowly, fearing to push the wooden door open as she continued praying. "Please God no! I don't think I could bear it!"

Holding her breath, Melissa pushed open the door all the way; stepping inside, she looked around frantically... no one was there. Instantly, she clutched at her stomach before dropping to one knee then put her free hand out to keep herself from falling; she weakly let out the breath she had been holding for way too long. Mell steadied herself then got up in relief, her hopes lifted slightly.

Leaving Tommy's room, Melissa walked slowly almost dragging her feet to her maid's room next. Again, that short little hallway seemed to take forever to negotiate. Mell wondered if her foster son ran to Gloria for protection and that is where she would find them.

Again, Melissa looked up imploringly praying for all she was worth. Her heart was in her throat as she held her breath once more. Slowly, she turned the knob and pushed opened the squeaky wooden door. It creaked slowly open... she shivered fearing the worst. Mell cried out in disbelief before slumping against the door this time. She clutched at her stomach; the fear and uncertainty made her feel physically sick, but she managed to keep herself upright.

*****

Jed turned over the last one, but sighed in disappointment at the eyes staring up blindly; he looked at Giant Bear before shaking his head sadly. "Help me take him over to the others, please!"

Giant Bear nodded grimly; he gently lifted Cookie's shoulders before walking over to the trees where they put all the other bodies... in preparation for the burial. They put him down then the chief looked over at Jed solemnly. "Such a sad day this is my friend!"

Jed nodded in agreement unhappily, not even one person survived the massacre; Grey Wolf frowned resignedly before looking towards the house, hoping Melissa was having better luck.

*****

Melissa unable to move for a long moment stared at the empty room in elation. Her thoughts were chaotic, jumping from one scenario to another. Did the outlaws take them too? Shaking her head decisively, she highly doubted that... if not where could they be? Finally, turning ecstatically with another hopeful expression, she raced back downstairs. Half way down she vaulted over the railing and landed in the hallway in a crouch, getting up she ran towards the kitchen. It was the only way to get into the back entryway where the cellar door was located. Mell tried the handle frantically when she reached the door; she pulled hard, but it wouldn't budge. It had to be barred from the inside. She exhaled noisily relieved then banged on the wooden door repeatedly and kept calling Gloria's name desperately, until finally the hard wood door creaked open slightly.

Gloria opened the cellar door a smidgen; too afraid to open it all the way, just in case it was a trick... she peeked out cautiously. When she saw Melissa, she allowed it to swing open fully but she was still unable to move any further. She stood in the doorway quivering in fear as tears streamed down her chubby cheeks. The maid's voice was barely coherent as she whispered almost too low for her boss to hear. "We were absolutely terrified when we heard the shooting. I got to Tommy's room quickly. Afterwards, we crept down the upstairs hallway before slipping down the stairs. We were planning on getting your father and barricading the three of us in the root cellar. Just as we reached the bottom of the steps, we heard a shot coming from your dad's room. Grabbing Tommy, we ran to the kitchen and into the back entry so I could lock us in the cellar. I'm so very sorry Mell, I think Alec is dead! Really, I didn't know what to do I had no way of protecting us!"

Bursting into fresh tears, Gloria finally able to move threw herself bodily at Melissa crying hysterically.

Holding her for a moment, Melissa murmured soothingly slightly shocked to see Gloria break down so completely... usually nothing fazed the formidable housekeeper. She tried pushing her at arm's length to explain that her father wasn't dead, but her maid clung to Mell desperately; refusing to release her as she sobbed feverishly.

Continuing to babble hysterically, Gloria refused to listen to anything Melissa had to say. "Oh, Mell... it was terrible; we were so very frightened, I didn't know what to do!"

Melissa's patience gone, tried again to break loose from the clinging inconsolable housekeeper. She had to resort finally to shaking her slightly to get her to listen... Mell just hoped she wouldn't have to slap her too. "Gloria enough, please go make us something to eat there are still four of us alive; Jed, Giant Bear, Wade, and me. My father isn't dead either they took him prisoner, which is why they raided the ranch."

Gloria quit crying instantly; she stepped back and stared at Melissa hopefully. "Are you sure Alec and Wade are both alive?"

Nodding mutely, Melissa watched in confusion as Gloria's frantic crying stopped suddenly. "Yes, they sent me a ransom note so Dad is alive for now. Wade caught a bullet in his arm that went clean through; he did lose a lot of blood before he found us... otherwise he is unhurt."

Quickly, Gloria wiped her tear-stained face with the back of her hand; she reached down calmly smoothing her dress before turning slightly. She gestured impatiently behind her, towards Melissa's foster son who was still inside the cellar unable to get out with the housekeeper blocking the doorway. "Tommy, what are you still doing in there? Come out this instant... I'll need help with lunch."

Rolling his eyes resignedly; the young Tommy knew better then to remind the plump housekeeper that it had been her doing, keeping him stuck in the cellar doorway.

Melissa stared after the two retreating figures completely bewildered. She watched as Gloria walked away very much in control now as if a few minutes ago she wasn't totally hysterical. She shook her head perplexed... she would never understand women; even though Mell was a woman herself, she was never prone to such mood swings so didn't have a clue how to deal with someone who did have them.

Shrugging baffled, Melissa closed the cellar door; she turned, following the two into the kitchen but went straight through it into the hallway before crossing to her father's room looking for Three Toes. She walked into the bedroom then found the wolf lying on the floor beside her dad's bed still as death. Turning away to go give the sad news to Jed; she saw one of the wolfs legs twitch, unexpectedly. Mell had to strain hard to hear a painful low whine coming from deep in his throat. She instantly ran back to the doorway to yell across the hall at her maid. "Gloria, send Tommy to go get Jed! His wolf is still alive in here, but hurt!"

Rushing back into the room, Melissa knelt beside Three Toes before whispering soothingly to him... trying to keep him calm and still. She stroked his head in encouragement, waiting impatiently for Jed. Hearing footsteps behind her, Mell turned to Grey Wolf with tears in her eyes. "Please tell me he is going to be all right!"

Jed knelt on the other side of Three Toes before examining him for injuries. He looked over at Melissa and smiled thankfully as he sat back, grinning relieved; Grey Wolf nodded in reassurance. "Yes, it looks like his head was just grazed by a bullet leaving him more stunned than anything. Good thing he has so much fur it slowed the bullet enough it didn't cause too much damage, only knocked him unconscious. He should come around soon since he has been out for a while, I cannot find any other bullet wounds... thank God!"

Three Toes opened his eyes a few minutes later... he licked Melissa's hand as she stroked his nose gently. The wolf managed to stagger to his feet on his own then wobbled over to Jed. Unknown to them, was it was a kick to the head the big wolf received keeping him in a daze for so long. He licked Grey Wolf's face in greeting; he whined slightly in pain before turning away after getting a reassuring pat.

Going over to the bed next, Three Toes smelt it before sniffing around on the floor searchingly. When he found the scent that he was looking for... he turned. The wolf followed the smell out of the room, down the hallway, and out the still open front door; without pausing, he went down the ramp into the yard.

Jed followed by Melissa trailed Three Toes; once outside they watched him intrigued as he sniffed around the yard.

Wade and Giant Bear came over to stand beside them as they too surveyed the big wolf, wondering where he was going.

Three Toes staggered, but continued doggedly on as he followed the tracks out of the ranch yard. He trotted faster when he came to the trail leading to the north approach to

Devil's Rock; unexpectedly, he stopped. The black wolf turned expectantly as he looked back at Jed... asking permission.

Nodding in consent, Jed cupped his lips with his hands then called out loudly to the massive wolf. "Okay, Three Toes... go find Alec!"

Lifting his head into the air, Three Toes howled forlornly at the loss of his friend before turning back towards the mountains; he started loping drunkenly towards Devil's Rock. The determined wolf was still very unsteady from the head wound, but that didn't stop him as he put his nose to the ground... he never looked back again.

Melissa frowned in apprehension as she turned looking at Jed in concern. "Will he be, okay?"

Jed smiled in reassurance; his face softened at Melissa's worried expression. "Yes, he will find your father then watch out for him until we catch up to him."

After watching the wolf disappear, the four of them returned to the house to decide on a plan.

As they gathered around the table, Gloria entered and started setting out lunch.

Melissa noticed a look of adoration in Gloria's glance as it rested on Wade; she couldn't help but smile in pleasant surprise when her foreman returned the look.

Gloria turned away with a gratified look on her face; she saw Melissa watching her. Blushing deeply, she hurried out as Mell's grin widened.

Now Gloria's hysterical actions earlier made more sense.

When lunch was finished, Melissa turned to the three men resolutely already having a plan in mind. She waited until Gloria was back in the room before she began. "There are three entrances to Devil's Rock; two are hidden, unless you are familiar with the area you wouldn't know about them. I will take Giant Bear to the one leading up to the cabin where they are holding my father. Jed can go to the other one leading to the cliffs... he will be watching from above."

Taking a fortifying breath, Melissa's face became hard and expressionless knowing the men wouldn't like her plan. However, that didn't matter her father's life was at stake; she'd do just about anything she had to in order to save him, even give up her own life if need be. "If we ride hard, we should be able to get to Devil's Rock in three days... four at the most. Once I show you where the hidden trails are, I need to ride up to the bend just before the main pass then make camp there. That will give you both a chance to find a good location before first light of the fifth day so we can all see clearly. On that morning, I will ride up the trail to take attention away from your goal, which is a miner's shack where they are holding my dad."

Melissa turned to her foreman next; she waved towards the southeast where their nearest neighbour lived. "Wade, I want you to stay here. Later on, you can send Tommy to the Johnson's place to get someone to help dig graves for the men who died... scavengers would be a problem otherwise. We will have a service when we return. Gloria, make sure you have everything you will need on hand in case anyone is hurt badly enough we cannot fix it on the trail."

Wade nodded agreement relieved, but just as Melissa figured Jed and Giant Bear didn't like it.

Frowning angrily, Jed gestured sharply as he argued vehemently. "Mell, you can't sacrifice yourself; your father wouldn't want that!"

Melissa sighed in aggravation as Jed questioned her authority as sheriff; she had known he would have eventually. Now was a good time for him to do so, this way he would see she did know what she was doing... even if it didn't seem like it. She smiled reassuringly over at the disgruntled Grey Wolf as she motioned consolingly. Mell explained her motives, even though she didn't think she should have to. "Jed, think about it. They waited until I was gone from home before they grabbed my father. If they wanted to kill me outright, they could have come in the other night and ambushed us. Obviously, they already knew where I lived. I think that is why they chased me the other day without really trying to shoot me. The killers must have known I would go searching for them, once I found out it wasn't my men shooting at me. That would get me away from the ranch because they want me to suffer before killing me. They aren't going to just shoot me on sight if that is what you are worried about. This will give you plenty of time to rescue my dad then help me afterwards."

Giant Bear frowned thoughtfully as he nodded towards

Melissa. "I think you are right about them wanting you to suffer; what if you are wrong though and they have your father with them when they go to meet you... what would we do then?"

Shrugging in unconcern, Melissa waved towards both of them not worried in the least. "I guess my two deputies will have to rescue both of us. It is the only way I can see to keep you two hidden... at least until it is too late for the outlaws to retaliate."

Jed growled angrily; **'bang'**... he smashed the table with his fist to emphasize his point. "I don't think we should take that kind of risk!"

Melissa's face became expressionless; she leaned forward irritably not wanting to argue anymore. She pointed a finger towards Jed in warning, deadly serious. "It's a good plan, if for some reason it doesn't go as I anticipate. I trust you both to help my dad first! I can look after myself but he can't... is that understood?"

Jed opened his mouth to refuse; he snapped it shut sullenly when Giant Bear poked him in the ribs under the table to get his attention. The chief knew Grey Wolf was about to say something he would regret later, because he feared Melissa would do something foolish to save her father. They didn't need her to disappear on them either... besides, the Cheyenne Chief figured she was right.

Wade motioned for Tommy to come help him in the barn, needing to get the horses ready. Unfortunately, he couldn't handle it himself yet; the foreman still felt a bit weak. Although, Gloria's tender touch earlier and the food helped immensely.

Throwing his hands up in surrender, Jed gave up; obviously, he wasn't allowed to talk Melissa out of sacrificing herself. They left the table and went to change before preparing to ride out again.

*****

Melissa took them in a different direction from the one Three Toes had taken. It would mean a few hours longer, but she wanted to make sure the outlaws wouldn't spot them; Mell was positive they would have someone watching for her.

Looking around him in pleasure as they rode along, Jed turned to Melissa in approval. "This is all yours?"

Nodding over at Jed, Melissa smiled in pride at his obvious pleasure in her ranch. "Yes, I not only look after this town but once a month I ride to all the smaller settlements. When I rescued the judge and his wife, they gave me the ranch on two conditions; number one, I would not draw any more wages. Two, I would have to administer the law to all the places that are remote enough they don't have a sheriff. The town pays my deputies plus all my expenses for travelling around."

Jed stared at Melissa in astonishment. "How do you find the time?"

Beaming in pleasure at Jed's interest in her, Melissa waved in reassurance. "Well, it's not hard really. I have one deputy in each small settlement, when there's a problem, they send someone for me. My own town is quiet now except for a few drunks getting out of hand occasionally. I'm not there very often; usually Greg looks after things for me. Actually, I just got back a couple of days before I met you. I finished my rounds for the month so I don't have to go again for another three weeks or so."

Jed thought about it for a moment before motioning in understanding; he turned back to Melissa. "Okay, I see how it might work, but what do you do for money when you get no wages?"

Melissa shrugged in unconcern. The money never really mattered to her. Jed wouldn't know that, of course. "Well, when I'm on the trail all my expenses are paid for. The supplies such as the ones I acquired from the store yesterday... even yours; are billed directly to the town. Did you notice a building in the trees about two miles from my ranch?"

Nodding attentively, Jed thought of his first view of the ranch. "Well yes; I figured it was somebody else's or abandoned."

Smiling teasingly, Melissa shook her head negatively. "No, it's not; you did notice that the ranch house, barns, corrals, and both bunkhouses are made of lumber not logs... didn't you?"

Frowning thoughtfully, Jed remembered yesterday. She actually mentioned it on their way from town, but he had been too upset and distracted. He hadn't really been paying attention to what she was saying. Grey Wolf grinned back at Mell perceptively. "Oh, I see; you have a sawmill that is why I saw such small trees when we first met."

Chuckling, Melissa winked playfully. "Why do you think our town is so large; they don't have to wait for lumber, the town's mayor just puts in an order. We will haul it anywhere, mostly into Montana right now it's our biggest market. I have about a dozen wagons out selling now. When they get back, I will start cutting again. We don't cut wood continuously because we don't want to deplete our supply. We also make sure to plant more trees as we cut them down. I do okay selling, breeding, and breaking horses too. Most people who see my stud fall in love with him so want their mares bred to him."

Jed shook his head in amazement. "Haven't you ever thought about settling down with a man... getting married; you know, maybe raise a couple of kids?"

Shrugging self-consciously, Melissa nodded wistfully. "A few times, but I have never met anyone who could accept me the way I am; I'm not the stay-at-home look after the kid's kind of woman. I love my job and everything that goes along with it... few men would accept that."

Sighing in understanding, Jed recalled Giant Bear's words on the same subject. Grey Wolf lapsed into silence once they urged their horses into a full gallop, since they were now warmed up enough... they raced towards the mountains urgently.

It would be a gruelling three days with little sleep.

****

Alec held tightly to his saddle horn so he wouldn't be tempted to lift the blindfold; he knew if he tried it, the outlaws wouldn't hesitate to kill him... no matter what the consequences. It was late the evening of the fourth day and he was half-asleep when they started climbing a steep hill. Melissa's father woke instantly knowing where they were at, he knew his daughter's lands very well. According to the time that passed as well as a change in terrain, they must be going up Devil's Rock.

Hearing a horse galloping towards them unexpectedly, Alec tensed as his ears picked up another sound; he frowned pensively or maybe there were two horses... he couldn't tell for sure. His optimism rose hoping it was Melissa and Jed coming to rescue him; he waited eagerly ready to urge his horse into a run immediately. His hopes plummeted since the call to run never materialized.

There was a hurried conference, which dashed Alec's thoughts of a quick rescue. Hearing a lot of arguing, he concentrated... trying hard to hear what they were saying; unfortunately, he couldn't before the horse was galloping away again. He was sure this time there was only one horse. They started riding again and after a couple of hours of riding up some steep terrain, they finally reached their destination.

The big outlaw lifted Alec off his horse. He was carried into a building before being put down roughly on a bed... or cot by the hard lumpy feel of it. His hands were put behind his back before they were tied; the blindfold was removed after almost four long days of wearing it.

Cursing silently in disappointment when they tied his hands, Alec frowned. Now he wouldn't be able to get to his knife. His one hope was to retrieve it and if the worst happened, to take at least one outlaw to the grave with him. He looked around inquisitively; Melissa's father saw the three outlaws that hit the ranch lounging around. It took him several minutes to notice another man... he was standing in the shadows.

Alec's eyes widened in shocked surprise and recognition; he exhaled in incredibility... stunned for a long moment! He knew now he was a dead man as the outlaws let him see the traitor!

****

The three rescuers were quite exhausted and so were all the animals by the time they reached the bottom of Devil's Rock. They had stopped only a couple times, when their horses were just too weary to go any further. They would sleep for a few hours before racing on again; tonight, they all knew they would be able have a good night's sleep. It took them just over three gruelling days to arrive here. It was late almost midnight when they halted the horses.

Melissa was silently thanking God for the quick uneventful trip here; thankfully, they should only be a day behind the outlaws. Unknown to them was that they almost caught up to the kidnappers. If they would have stayed on the trail instead of going around, they would have caught the killers in the pass.

Devil's Rock was not a huge mountain; it was more like a mountain range with cliffs protruding everywhere. A main pathway ran upwards almost in the center up to an old miner's cabin. At the west end was a thick forest that hid a back entrance going up the steep cliffs. Melissa found it years ago when exploring, on one of her rare occasions off.

The old miner who lived up there would come to town mumbling about devils stealing his things, so it became known as Devil's Rock.

Once you reached the cabin there was a small valley with lots of trees behind it, which is where Melissa found the first hidden pass. There was a spring with the sweetest tasting water behind the deck. She tried to find the source of it, but after searching for a week she gave up; it did help her find the second hidden entrance though. When she had more than one day off in a row, which was rarely... this was where she would come to hideout.

Melissa guided Giant Bear to the trail he would take alone; it would bring him directly behind the cabin her father was held captive in. Just before leaving the Cheyenne Chief, Mell gave him some additional instructions. "Find a place to sleep tonight then go first thing tomorrow morning. It will take you a full day to navigate the cliffs when you get past this forest of trees. Once you find a good place up there, you can rest again until daylight of the next day. I will ride up the path at that time. You will be closest to the miner's shack so in the best position to rescue my father. I want you to go in and get him out while I distract the outlaws... Jed will watch your back. He will also have a clear view of what goes on when I ride up. This way if anything goes wrong, both of us have back up."

Giant Bear nodded without hesitation before horse with its rider melted into the trees without a sound.

Turning her horse away, Melissa urged him into a canter going east... the other entrance was close to the main pass she would be taking. The two remaining rescuers continued riding for three more hours before they left the forest behind; finally, scraggly brush took the place of the trees.

Behind the bushes, Jed could see huge rocks with boulders protruding everywhere; how he was supposed to get up them he had no idea, but Melissa seemed so sure... he would just have to trust her.

Melissa took Jed around a sharp turn; she halted her horses before dismounting in silence.

Following Melissa's lead, Jed looked where she was pointing. He inclined his head in acknowledgement when he saw an opening behind the bush before dropping his horse's reins. Grey Wolf walked towards Mell purposefully; he stopped in front of her... motioning in demand, his voice held a desperate sound of urgency. "Are you sure your plan will work!"

Before Melissa could even answer, Jed clasped her by the upper arms before pulling her towards him... he pleaded urgently. "Don't do anything rash Mell; I don't think I could bear to lose you! I want to finish what we started at the creek."

Once again, Melissa tried to speak but her words were stifled as Jed's lips covered hers relentlessly in a searing kiss full of unleashed passion... as well as promise.

Pushing her away suddenly without speaking or even giving her a chance to speak; Jed quickly grabbed his horse's reins and disappeared into the thick brush.

The path Jed followed wound up the cliff before coming to a small cave he could sleep in. He didn't have as far to go as the other two, so he explored his little niche closely after bedding his horse down for the night. Grey Wolf followed the path upwards. He came to a shelf which gave the best view of the cabin, and main trail leading up to the miner's shack. From here, he would be able to see everything happening. Satisfied, he climbed back down as the first rays of dawn lightened the horizon. Thankfully, he had the whole day plus an evening to rest up; he knew he was going to need it then grabbed his bedroll. Rolling himself into it, he was fast asleep almost immediately... too exhausted even to think about the kiss he shared several hours ago with Melissa.

*****

Staring after Jed in amazement, Melissa softly touched her bruised lips; shaking her head in bewilderment, she turned away and remounted her horse before riding further east.

It took Melissa several hours to reach the main trail leading up to Devil's Rock. Unfortunately, the sun was already peeking over the mountains... causing her to frown fretfully. She needed to get to her nook before daylight arrived, so she could sleep. Mell hid behind a wall of rocks, waiting patiently for the dark cloud that she could see in the distance to cover the rising sun. Hopefully, it would give her a bit more cover; just in case they had someone this far watching for her.

This was the first part of the pass. It was wider here, so Melissa figured the outlaws would wait farther up closer to the cabin where it was narrower. There was a place just ahead, which was her goal. It branched off into a deep nook... almost a cave. It was not big, but Mell could sleep comfortably in it. She could even put her horse behind her; it would mean a cold meal until later when she could safely have a fire.

A raindrop fell on Melissa; she looked up at the darkening clouds in the distance as they covered the sun then the rain began to fall. Darn it, she wanted the clouds... not the rain.

Melissa turned to her saddlebags before rummaging inside. She pulled out four sheets of cloth with rawhide threaded through going all the way around. Sound carried here for miles and she was not taking any chances. Mell put three on the ground then clucked softly. Obediently, Lightning lifted his front foot... familiar with this indignity. He snorted in rebuke; she chuckled quietly as she slipped the cloth over his hoof then tied it to keep it in place. Patting her horse in silent apology, she went to his other hoof until all four hooves were covered.

Leading her horse quietly up the trail, Melissa whispered a prayer for everyone's safety as she hurried along... suddenly, she disappeared.

****

Alec stared in absolute shock at the man standing in the shadows; of all the men, he thought of then discarded as the traitor. Melissa's trusted deputy from town wasn't one of them.

Greg stepped into the light; he sneered viciously and cackled in satisfaction at Alec's shocked stare. "Surprised to see me?"

Nodding in furious disbelief, Alec eyed Greg wearily. "Now I know how they knew so much about the routine of the ranch; I'm a bit confused... how did you know where I keep my chair?"

Shrugging in unconcern, Greg waved negligently. "Not hard to find out if you ask the right questions."

Sam the black-haired oldest brother, plus their leader walked over then turned his back to Alec to block his view of Greg. He spoke harshly to the deputy; unfortunately, it was too low for Melissa's father to hear what he was saying.

Greg stiffly nodded his head in frustration at Sam, without saying a word. He glared down at Alec when Sam moved aside to let the deputy pass; obviously blaming Melissa's father for the reprimand before stalking out... in obvious rage.

Sam and Jimmy followed him, so only Marty the blonde gawky cowboy remained on guard duty.

Alec laid down as best he could with his hands bound behind his back, thinking furiously... he frowned perplexed. If Greg was here, who left on horseback? Was there someone else involved, or did Greg ride ahead of them? He finally dozed too exhausted to stay awake any longer.

At one point, Alec jerked awake thinking he heard a different voice in the background. However, when he turned around only Marty was there. He was standing in front of the door staring fixedly at it... no one else seemed to be about.

Managing to go back to sleep, Alec still wondered if his imagination was playing tricks on him.

*****

It was just breaking dawn when Alec woke again. He cocked his head listening, trying to discover what roused him this time. Looking around guardedly, he saw Marty sleeping in a chair. He was snoring softly but it wasn't loud enough to wake him up. He could hear the rain drumming on the roof, but that shouldn't have woken him either. Suddenly, he heard scratching against the wall outside and a low pleading whine. He smiled widely in joy; Three Toes hadn't died after all, he whispered as quietly as possible. "I'm okay, boy... go find Jed!"

Three Toes whined plaintively at not being able to reach Alec; he caught up to them the second day of the kidnapping. Unfortunately, the wolf couldn't get close enough. He stayed in the background watching his friend closely. As long as nobody tried to hurt Melissa's father, he followed from a distance... knowing his master was coming!

Scratching at the dirt under the cabin for a bit longer, Three Toes finally gave up and Alec didn't hear the wolf again.

Alec looked towards Marty, but the man hadn't moved. Melissa's father sighed relieved then wiggled around trying to get more comfortable, now able to sleep better... knowing help was on the way.

CHAPTER SIX

Melissa arrived at a narrow opening farther up the trail, with huge rocks rising high on both sides; this was the entrance to Devil's Rock, which is why the old miner added rock to the name instead of mountain... she guessed long ago.

It was around eight o'clock in the morning; with the days getting longer, it was full daylight already. Thankfully, it stopped raining early last night. Melissa camped in her hiding place around ten o'clock yesterday morning further down the trail. Exhausted, she slept the day away. Luckily, she was able to have a fire later in the evening before it quit raining... to cook supper. Mell's breakfast this morning consisted of last night's leftovers, of course.

Riding through the opening, Melissa saw three men coming towards her. She lifted her arms non-threateningly to show she wasn't holding any guns. At first, she didn't recognize any of them. As they got closer Mell drew in an outraged intake of breath when she finally identified the traitor, Greg... her deputy at Smyth's Crossing.

Furious by the time the three men got close enough to hear her, Melissa's voice trembled in fury... fighting with herself, she tried to control her rage. Mell managed to get the words out past her clenched teeth. "Bugger your soul to hell, Greg... how could you betray me so blatantly!"

Sneering maliciously, Greg waved to his companions in introduction. "Let me introduce you to my cousins."

Greg chortled in mockery at the stunned look on Melissa's face. "That's right Sheriff you killed two of my cousins, so you will pay for it with your life; get down off your horse... **NOW**!"

Turning to the huge man on his right, Greg motioned in caution. "Jimmy, the sheriff carries a knife in each boot top; she also carries two revolvers. Don't overlook the whip behind her saddle either... she can be lethal with it!"

Melissa as well as a man called Jimmy both dismounted. She stood stiffly while he stripped her of her weapons. Mell looked up into his face hoping to see some sign of compassion; instead, she stepped back hurriedly in revulsion at the cruel... hateful look.

Thankfully, Greg didn't know about the knife Melissa had

purchased when she left town with Jed; it was hiding under the sheriff's shirt, with a small pistol she always kept out of sight unknown to anyone... even her father.

Greg pointed to Melissa's horse remorselessly. "Mount up Sheriff and behave yourself or your father is dead!"

Glaring up at her deputy intently; Melissa's voice became whisper soft in lethal promise as she gestured unflinchingly, before mounting. "Did you hurt him, Greg... if you did, you are a dead man!"

Melissa's tone was ominous; she saw Greg's hand shake slightly in reaction.

Lifting his hat to wipe the sweat of his brow, Greg hid his momentary panic from his cousins. He snickered at Melissa's warning before sneering in derision as he jammed his hat back on. "That's a mighty big threat from someone who is going to die soon!"

Not fooled for a moment, Melissa could tell Greg knew it; she turned then mounted silently with no further comment... her dire warning already given.

Jimmy giggled with his cousins, unaware of the deputy's apprehension before riding ahead with his older brother; letting Greg and Melissa ride together.

****

Meanwhile, Giant Bear cautiously approached the cabin looking for a sentry; the three outlaws confident in Melissa's compliance only left one man inside alone. The Cheyenne Chief peered into a side window of the miner's shack to see who was left inside. The first person he noticed was Alec sitting quietly on a cot in the corner... his hands were behind him; he was staring furiously at someone who was standing not far from the front door.

Giant Bear's glance flew in that direction; he froze immediately when the rage instantly sprang to the surface. He looked at the man his sister had called Marty. She had described him perfectly. She even explained to her brother in detail how he got his broken nose. The chief's wife had hit him in the face with a rock during the struggle as he was raping and strangling her. They went on to rape his sister repeatedly, which is why she took her own life but not until after she told him what happened. The dishonour was too much for her to bear, now there he stood with his back to the

Cheyenne Chief... taunting Alec.

Creeping towards the door, Giant Bear slowly pushed it open hoping it wouldn't creak. His silent prayer was answered as the old wooden door opened soundlessly. He took the step hurriedly that separated them before grabbing Marty from behind then spun him around quickly... the chief locked the unfortunate outlaw in a bear hug.

Marty was taken completely by surprise; he didn't even have a chance to call out as he looked in horror at the huge Indian in shocked alarm.

Giant Bear's eyes narrowed remorselessly. He stared at the dumbfounded Marty straight in the eye. Not once did he look away and there was no hint of repentance for what he was about to do. His voice echoed through the cabin savagely, void of all feeling except for satisfaction. "You raped then killed my wife before raping my sister and left her to die. As I slowly crush the life out of you, your death will be filled with agony; while you stare into my eyes you will remember they both were avenged. They will haunt your afterlife forever as you see them reflected in my eyes."

Groaning agonizingly, Marty strained against the arms holding him fast, but he was caught like an animal in a trap; he couldn't break free or even look away from the enraged Cheyenne Chief... even though he tried desperately to.

Shuddering in excruciating torture, Marty felt his ribs break slowly one by one. As each one snapped... the sound echoed eerily in the quiet of the cabin. The jagged pieces started piercing his lungs, an inch at a time. He could feel them as they entered the soft lining, and penetrated completely. The outlaw let out a stifled scream when blood gushed into his mouth, choking then gagging him slowly. The blood finally overflowed his lips; it dribbled down his chin faster and faster.

Keeping his merciless gaze locked on Marty's face, Giant Bear relished every moment of agony the outlaw suffered. He knew the moment death found its mark then he dropped the limp body to the floor without any show of emotion. Taking out his hunting knife; the chief bent down before grabbing hold of the man's hair and scalped him. He stood up slowly then raised the scalp towards the ceiling, as if to show his sister and wife he had avenged them. He let out a bloodcurdling shriek of satisfaction!

Muttering under his breath as if saying a prayer, Giant Bear dropped his arm and tucked his grisly trophy in his belt; before going over to a bucket of water to wash his hands clean... plus his knife. The Cheyenne Chief turned finally then went over to Alec to release him.

Alec sat silently shuddering as he witnessed Giant Bear's revenge. He had cringed each time he heard the outlaw's ribs break as it echoed eerily throughout the cabin; he said nothing though, respecting his friend's Indian ways... not judging him.

Giant Bear sliced the ropes binding Alec's hands in one quick motion.

Sighing in relief, Alec finally felt a tingle of circulation slowly work its way through his hands. He beamed up at Giant Bear in gratitude before bringing his hands out in front of him; he massaged his wrists hoping to return more feeling to them. "Thank you."

Casting an apprehensive look at the door searchingly, Alec didn't see Melissa. He looked up at the Indian Chief anxiously. "Is Mell nearby?"

Eyeing Alec respectfully, Giant Bear was impressed; Melissa's father didn't shy away from him, even after witnessing the death of the white man; although, he probably would have done it differently. He only sighed in relief when the chief washed his hands before releasing him.

Giant Bear nodded in admiration down at this crippled white man he was proud to call his friend. His voice clearly reflected his approval. The chief waved towards the door of the cabin. "Yes, she is with the other outlaws; hold onto me tight while I take you to your horse. I must leave you in a safe place so I can go help the others."

Alec complied; he put his arms around Giant Bear's neck trustingly... without any qualms. The huge Indian bent down to scoop him up.

Tenderly enfolded Alec in his huge beefy arms, Giant Bear stood up before carrying him from the cabin; he had to step over the body of the outlaw, but neither man spared the dead man a glance.

Looking down at Melissa's father when they got outside; Giant Bear motioned with his head towards the cliffs on their right. "Alec, wave your hand so Jed will know you are all right."

Obediently, Alec did what Giant Bear asked even though he couldn't see Jed way up there.

****

Up on a ledge overlooking the cabin... Jed watched Giant Bear disappear inside then emerge later with Alec in his arms.

Giant Bear's head lowered and he appeared to be saying something to Alec.

A moment later, Mell's dad waved his hand in Jed's direction to let him know he was okay.

Jed sighed in relief glad Alec wasn't hurt. He didn't wave back in acknowledgement afraid the outlaws would see him. He turned away then climbed down the ledge cautiously so he was kneeling over the lip. Now Grey Wolf was ready to ambush the killers. Unfortunately, this spot was not to his liking... backing away from the edge he turned.

Hearing a rustling in the bush, Jed turned then immediately went for his gun. Grey Wolf dropped his hand with a sigh of relief when Three Toes appeared beside him; stroking the wolf's head tenderly he whispered, so only his wolf would hear. "Good boy... follow me now."

The pair followed the edge of the cliff until Melissa and the remaining outlaws came into better view on the trail below; he crept into position. He silently directed the wolf to take down the simple Jimmy.

Looking down at the black-haired Sam, Jed felt the rage he kept bottled up for so long seep back to the surface in a heartbeat... remembering that horrible day long ago. His dying son had kept himself alive to tell his father who killed his pregnant wife once everyone raped her. The outlaw then plunged his dagger into her belly viciously; turning he plunged the same knife, still dripping with her blood and the blood of his unborn child into his ten-year-old son leaving him to die too.

Jed waited patiently then gave the large wolf the signal to attack before jumping down himself, knocking Sam out of his saddle; they both fell hard to the ground as Sam's horse spooked by the smell of the wolf bolted up the trail... the outlaw swore savagely as he fell.

Three Toes jumped off the cliff knocking a shocked, bewildered Jimmy out of the saddle. The large outlaw landed hard on the rocky ground; with a loud gasp of disbelief the air was driven out of his lungs forcefully. His horse screamed in fear before racing up the pathway.

The wolf landed lightly on his paws and turned quickly... he grabbed the disoriented Jimmy by the arm, unable to get close to the huge man's beefy throat.

Getting to his feet quickly, Jed drew his knife out of its sheath. Not even bothering with his gun, wanting Sam to die the same way his Victoria had; he prepared himself for a fight to the death.

Sam growled in furious disbelief... glaring up in astonishment at the stranger towering over him. "And who the blazes are you?"

Jed opened his mouth to answer, but snapped it shut again in fear at the sound of a horse screaming in pain behind him... making him jerk around in panic. He glanced quickly in that direction to make sure it was not Melissa's horse who was hurt. Grey Wolf realized Mell was attacking the fourth outlaw, so brought his attention back to Sam quickly. He cursed at himself for his lost opportunity; the leader of the Shadow Killers was now standing in front of him holding his own knife.

Taking the opportunity of Jed's distraction to get to his feet, Sam drew his knife; he didn't want to attack though. Usually, he would have if someone was stupid enough to give him his back, but he wanted to know who the stranger was first.

Jed smirked threateningly as he pointed at himself in introduction answering Sam's earlier question. "My name is Jed Brown; I have been tracking you and your brothers across Montana. My search started in Western Montana where you raped then killed my pregnant wife before stabbing my ten-year-old son and left him to die. Now at long last I will destroy you for it... avenging their deaths."

Inclining his head thoughtfully, Sam remembered that day then he beamed in satisfaction evilly... before teasing Jed playfully. "Oh, yes the beautiful brunette. The greatest whore I ever had as I felt the blood of her child gushing out of her body, enveloping me with blood!"

Attacking in a furious frenzy; Jed lifted his arm to plunge

the knife into the man's throat, unable to hear him give further description of the terrible massacre of his wife and son. However, he didn't make it there. He stumbled backwards in grief instead, when he heard a gunshot followed by the howl of an animal in pain. Out of the corner of his eye not daring to look away from Sam completely, he saw the huge wolf fall to the ground... he groaned in regret.

Giant Bear emerged from the hills moments too late to save Three Toes; he tackled Jimmy furiously, livid at losing one of his friends... especially since he helped raise him from a pup.

Sam also turned in surprise at the gunshot. His mouth dropped open in disbelief when a Cheyenne emerged from behind Jimmy; the outlaw could hardly believe his eyes, that was the biggest Indian he ever seen!

Eyes bulging out of their sockets in shock, Sam felt a sting in his lower chest... not even realizing Jed had struck at first; he clawed at the knife in panic trying to stop it from penetrating deeper, as he groaned in agony.

Holding his knife in place firmly unrelenting; Jed kept his gaze locked on Sam's face, enjoying the moment. He drove it still further in, until it was buried almost to the hilt... he smiled in pleasure. "I would have done this more slowly, but I have friends to help out."

With that, Jed savagely twisted the hunting knife as deep as he could into Sam's chest before ripping it upwards... through the outlaw's black heart; he felt grim satisfaction as he watched the life drain out of Sam's eyes. He dropped the lifeless body in contempt, remorselessly.

Jed looked in Giant Bear's direction just in time to see him scalp his victim. His friend didn't need his help, so he walked over before kneeling down beside the dead wolf sadly; he took a brief moment to gently pat the stiffening body in farewell then got up to find Mell.

****

Melissa was listening grimly to the conversation ahead of her... the men riding in front were describing in detail how they were going to kill her; it would be a long slow process according to them.

Suddenly the voices in front of Melissa stopped in astonishment. She watched in satisfaction as their horses unexpectedly reared screaming in fright. Both riders were unseated from their saddles as Three Toes then Jed leaped from the cliffs above. This was what Mell was waiting for; not wasting any time, she shouted a command to her horse. Obediently he reared and twisted towards the horse Greg was riding.

Greg barely had time to register his surprise at the turn of events when the stallion beside him rose upwards. Lightning's hooves landed on the back of his horse's neck, forcing him to the ground. The deputy would have been crushed under his horse, but Melissa jumped at him; causing them both to fall out of their saddles. He landed hard on his back with a grunt of shocked pain.

Curling herself into a ball, Melissa rolled before springing up cat-like as she crouched there with her left hand pressed to the ground. She reached behind her back with her right hand, jerking the knife from its hiding place. Mell stood up slowly then with deadly assurance plain in her voice, she stared down at her deputy threateningly. "You will die now, Greg! I promise you are going to pay for your betrayal!"

Pulling a knife from his boot top, the former deputy got up as well.

They circled each other looking for an opportunity or weakness.

Hearing a shot and a howl, Melissa kept her concentration focused on her prey. She saw a flicker of movement when Giant Bear showed up to help, so heaved a sigh of relief. That second of distraction almost cost her... her life; as Greg took the opportunity to attack without warning. She managed to sidestep him neatly before aiming a swift kick, which connected solidly in his stomach. She smirked in satisfaction, glad now for all the wrestling and the boxing she did as a kid at the ranch her father looked after. Her mother had been horrified when she caught Mell fighting with the boys behind the barn.

Greg doubled over in pain holding his abdomen in disbelief not having expected that at all.

Melissa ridiculed her deputy. "What's the matter Greg, getting old?"

Roaring in frustrated rage, Greg stood up then charged Mell again.

This time Melissa slipped under his left arm before coming

up behind him; for a moment they were standing back-to-back. The agile Mell turned quickly before Greg even figured out what she was up to or where she went. The sheriff stabbed him in the right shoulder just below his collarbone... she taunted. "This is for killing my friend Joe!"

Greg groaned in agony when he realized Melissa planned to cut him to ribbons before she finished him off; he became desperate. Spinning around to face the sheriff... he lunged for her again.

This time Melissa took a quick step to the right so Greg would end up charging right passed her; when he went by, she spun around quickly once she had enough room. Bringing her knife up, she plunged it into his back in the left shoulder, again just below his collarbone. "That is for Dan my stableman."

Catching a flicker of movement out of the corner of her eye, Melissa knew immediately that Jed and Giant Bear arrived to watch the knife fight. She couldn't chance acknowledging them or she risked losing her concentration. However, just that second of hesitation gave Greg time to leap at her again. Unexpectedly turning around swiftly, the deputy managed to get under her guard. Mell faltered slightly as she felt his knife pierce her left shoulder.

*****

Jed couldn't help admiring Melissa's surprising unconventional handling of a knife, but when Greg wounded her... he couldn't stand by any longer; he stepped forward to help her.

Putting a restraining hand on Jed's shoulder, Giant Bear pulled him back to stand beside him. The chief shook his head at his friend compassionately when he glared at him infuriated. "I'm sorry Grey Wolf, but this is her fight... you must let the sheriff deal with her deputy."

Giant Bear watched Jed's face patiently waiting for him to agree; there were actually two reasons why the Cheyenne Chief refused to let him go. One was because he wanted his friend to watch Melissa in action in order to understand her better. It would build his trust in her for when Grey Wolf needed her in the future. The second reason was because Jed's first wife had been a wealthy debutante in Boston. When he described her to the chief after they met, he always used words like fragile and delicate. He needed to see that Mell was completely opposite to his deceased wife. The sheriff could take care of herself without help or he would forever be racing to save her when she didn't need it... sooner or later, she would resent him for it.

Jed's angry frown eased as he nodded in reluctant agreement before turning back to the fight in time to see Melissa rally back. He could hardly believe what he was seeing; she was cutting Greg to ribbons. Every time she cut him. She named someone else from the ranch that died. He could see the deputy tiring from the many wounds he had sustained already as he desperately tried to get under the sheriff's guard, but was outwitted at every turn. Grey Wolf watched Mell in stunned fascination... her moves were cleverly executed. She didn't rush in then stab, but used her feet and body in perfect symmetry like a dancer. Her deputy outweighed her by a lot, but she was quicker with longer legs, which she used to her advantage.

Greg was becoming more frantic. He charged wildly for Melissa. Again, she evaded him then kicked out catching him square in the jaw; it snapped his head back painfully. His eyes bulged in surprise and astonishment when the deputy felt a sting in his chest, even before he realized she struck.

Going in for the kill, Melissa buried her knife blade to the hilt into Greg's chest before twisted it viciously; ripping it upwards, she made sure her deputy was dead as she painfully gasped out in exhaustion. "This is for my father!"

Melissa thought she whispered her words to Greg, but it was more of a shout; both the men watching heard Mell's last words to her deputy. The fatally wounded man fell dead at her feet.

Breathing heavily, Melissa stood for a moment gazing down at the dead man in disbelief; what had she done! She swayed in weakness when the loss of blood caught up to her. Sinking to her knees, Mell dropped to the ground. She felt someone put their arms around her; thankfully, pulling her away from Greg so she wouldn't fall on him. She trembled exhausted, Jed drew her closer tenderly.

Giant Bear left without a sound to get Alec and the horses as soon as he was sure Melissa was okay.

Glancing around dazed, Melissa knew she had just crossed

the line... what would happen to her? She saw Giant Bear returning leading five horses; one was carrying someone; she sighed reassured as she recognized her father apparently safe and unhurt. At this point, Mell's eyes closed wearily then everything went black. She crumbled in Jed's arms without uttering a sound.

Jed was frantic, he called Melissa's name desperately; shaking her in panic. "Mell, wake up... don't you dare die on me now!"

Melissa slowly opened her eyes before staring up at Jed pleadingly as she whispered weakly. "You can quit shaking me now, I'm not dying; I'm just very tired, is everyone all right?"

Grinning thankfully, Jed gazed down at her in reassurance before nodding. "Yes, except for Three Toes. He was shot before Giant Bear got close to the outlaw he was struggling with."

Relieved that they had only lost one, Melissa closed her eyes weakly as she whispered softly. "Jed, I think I love you!"

Faintly Melissa heard his soft reply as she once again lapsed into unconsciousness.

"I love you too, Mell!"

****

The man watching from the cliffs above moved back slowly and as quietly as he could; not wanting to be discovered. The anguished wrath on his face gave him a menacing evil appearance. When he was far enough back that he was sure they couldn't see him, he turned to leave. He only went a few steps before turning back suddenly then raised a furious fist as he spoke under his breath so nobody below could hear him. "I will get all of you for this... I swear on my life!"

****

Camp was set up for the night at the same place Melissa used last night. It was crowded, but big enough without the horses inside for injuries to be treated. Mell's wound wasn't serious; she lost quite a bit of blood though, making her exhausted both physically and emotionally.

Giant Bear had knife wounds in his right leg plus his left shoulder from his struggle with Jimmy.

Cleaning their wounds, Jed packed them with a poultice of dried raspberry and oak leaves he found in the Giant Bear's medicine bag... it would draw out any poisons; he boiled the rest for tea then made them drink it, which would help stop infections inside the body.

Alec decided it was best for Melissa to rest another day; she would need to get some of her strength back before undertaking the long trek back to her ranch. He needed to watch his daughter closely anyway right now. Knowing her the way he did, he knew the sheriff would be beating herself up for killing a man. She wouldn't care how deserving it was, the fact that she crossed a line she had always prided herself on maintaining would be eating her up inside he knew.

CHAPTER SEVEN

Melissa's party arrived at the ranch around noon of the ninth day. It was a weary sober group that dismounted from their horses; still, they made good time it only took them four days to return.

Jed insisted they bring back the body of the wolf... he felt strongly that Three Toes deserved a burial with the rest of the deceased men at Melissa's ranch.

Giant Bear and Jed lift Alec of his horse then carried him up onto the porch and gently put him in his outside wheelchair.

Refusing all offers of help with Three Toes, Jed knew he needed to do this on his own. Once everyone went inside, he returned to his horse then led his gelding over to the burial site. Tenderly, he pulled the dead animal of his horse; Grey Wolf winced at the loud... '**Thwack**', the stiffening body made as it fell to the ground. Grey Wolf knelt beside his companion remembering with fondness the tiny pup he rescued. He stayed there for several minutes gently stroking the soft fur while the tears ran down his cheeks, dripping onto the animal's thick black coat; not only was he saying goodbye to his animal friend, but he was also putting away the ghosts of his first wife and son.

Standing up, Jed grabbed the shovel lying on the ground then started digging a grave; as he was digging flashes of the past with his wife, son, and Three Toes came then went. Once they faded, he tucked them into a part of his heart to be stored away but not forever. In the future Grey Wolf would be able to revive them now without all the festering rage and bitterness... in order to share with new loved ones.

When Jed was finished remembering, he was only half done with digging the grave. He spent the balance of the time exorcising the feelings of hate, and despair... plus the grief he carried around for so long. When he decided the grave was deep enough, he pushed Three Toes in then knelt down before arranging him inside tenderly. Grey Wolf paused and put his hand onto the wolf's soft fur one last time before sitting back. He stared down sadly then murmured quietly. "Goodbye my friend, take good care of my wife and son for me; someday, I will join you!"

Getting up again, Jed rapidly shovelled the dirt back into the gaping hole until it was completely full. He dropped the shovel before standing up straighter; he looked up towards the heavens, smiling in pleasure completely free for the first time in nine long years.

At that moment, the sun came out from behind a fluffy cloud; its rays surrounded Jed completely all the way from the top, down to his toes. His smile widened as he lifted his head further so the sunshine was directly on his face. Grey Wolf felt immense pleasure in the golden rays encompassing him through the trees. He tilted his chin listening to the beautiful songs of the birds all around him, they seemed to sing a melody just for him... as if God approved.

Jed felt like a new man; he laughed out loud, raising both arms in delight to the sky he thanked God for allowing him to live again... instead of existing only for revenge. He opened his heart wide open; it allowed him to feel plus see the beauty surrounding him which he had missed for the last nine years. Dropping his arms, Grey Wolf turned before hurrying to the ranch house to join the others.

*****

Gloria and Wade met the returning party in the hallway relieved to see everyone alive.

Tommy stationed outside for the last two days as a lookout, ran inside to tell them as soon as he saw Melissa coming.

Immediately, Gloria ushered Melissa and Giant Bear into the den to examine their wounds. She worked on Giant Bear first; after taking off the bandages, she nodded in approval at Jed's expertise in treating injuries. She left it off; satisfied both his wounds were healing okay.

Melissa told both of them the gory details as the housekeeper turned to her next.

Listening to Melissa absently, Gloria cleaned the wound in relief at the healthy pink skin around the scab that had already formed. It would leave a nasty scar, but Mell wouldn't care about that. Her boss had several now, one more wouldn't hurt her. Again, the maid threw the bandage in a corner, still listening absently.

Just as Melissa finished her account of events, Jed entered the room and told his story.

Later a quiet group sat around the table trying to force food into their mouths; finally, they gave up then pushed their plates aside. As if of one mind, they all rose together before heading for the door.

Jed stopped to help Alec into his outside chair.

As they walked along Wade looked over at Melissa explaining what he did after she left. "I sent Tommy to the neighbours like you said; he returned with Franklin and Joseph. They helped us dig the ten graves. I didn't say anything in the way of a memorial, cause I knew you would want to be here for that. Oh yeah... Tommy helped us too."

Nodding soberly, Melissa sighed. "Good work both of you; thank you!"

They gathered around the graves solemnly then Melissa began by singing a hymn. The others all joined in; at the closing of the song, Mell asked her father to say a few words in prayer.

When Alec finished, there was not a dry eye in the group as they headed back to the ranch house.

Melissa was hit the hardest by the senseless massacre; those men had been with her since the day she moved to this ranch. They were not just her ranch hands they were her friends too, most of her grief she kept bottled up inside for now needing to be strong for the others.

Once inside they headed to the den for a meeting; after sitting, Melissa turned to her father first inquisitively. "Dad, can you tell us what happened to you after you were taken from the ranch?"

Reflectively thinking back, Alec was still mystified by a few things. He motioned in bewilderment as he scowled confused. "Two things puzzled me. First off... after Wade left, they put me on my horse then blindfolded me. One of those men, Marty, I think it was; the skinny blonde one said, 'he did not want me to know who he was'. I figured he meant the traitor, but when we got to the cabin, they took the blindfold off and there was Greg standing in the shadows watching me. Why would they do that? I knew as soon as they let me see your deputy they were going to kill me in the end. The second most confusing part of it all was when I woke up during the night; I thought I heard someone else. The voice sounded vaguely familiar, unfortunately I couldn't place it. I'm not a hundred percent sure about that though."

Frowning pensively for a few moments, Melissa looked at Jed and Giant Bear to see if they saw anyone else; they both shook their heads in disagreement... the chief spoke for both of them. "Nobody else was there, when I went to get your father, I studied the tracks carefully I only found five different horse shoe indents!"

Nodding at the two men, Melissa agreed with them before turning to her father... she gestured in reassurance. "I have to concur with Jed and Giant Bear. It would have been easy for Greg to find out about your horse since he has been at the ranch several times unsupervised. I never kept it a secret from him where you sleep or where you keep your chair either; it's doubtful that anyone else is involved, I'm pretty sure we got them all."

Alec sighed comforted, but he shifted slightly still uneasy; he finally deferred to their judgment "Like I said before I'm not sure, if you think we have them all... I won't worry about it anymore."

Melissa eyed her father's troubled expression pensively before shrugging off his apprehension. "Well, I guess that is about it. I want everyone to get a good night's sleep; tomorrow I will take Jed with me to town, we will need to give a report to John."

Turning to Jed, Melissa explained to him who John was since he wouldn't know who she was talking about. "John Elton is the mayor and also happens to be our judge, which is the reason I have to inform him of what occurred. He will want to know where the outlaws' bodies are located to send someone to bury them. I will also go to the ranch hand's families to let them know what happened here. We will send them everything we have here that was theirs plus all the wages owing to the men. I also need help to recruit more men; it's not wise to leave the ranch untended for any longer than we have to. We still have men out selling lumber, but who knows when they will be back."

Turning to Wade, Melissa waved towards her foster son. "I want you to take Tommy home to his Uncle Brian's; he can spend a few days with his mother."

Tommy gave an angry snort of denial. "No Aunt Mell, please!"

Looking sadly over at Tommy, Melissa knew he wasn't going

to like this at all. "I'm sorry, but I need you to go stay with your mother; just until things settle down here."

Frowning fearfully, Tommy interrupted her heatedly. "Aunt Mell, Uncle Brian doesn't want me there... he hates me!"

Walking over to Tommy, Melissa put her arm around him consolingly. "I know, just try to stay away from him. I'm sorry, but it's the only thing I can think to do for now. Your mother hasn't been able to come here for a while and once she hears about this, she will be frantic; she will want to see for herself that you are not hurt... I promise it will only be for a few days!"

Stomping off furiously to pack his clothes, Tommy muttered under his breath as he left.

Sighing sadly, Melissa shook her head regretfully.

Jed exchanged concerned glances with Giant Bear; mystified at the obvious hostility on Tommy's part towards his uncle. With silent understanding, the Cheyenne Chief got up to follow the boy.

Opening the door to go out, Giant Bear suddenly getting a hunch changed his mind. The Indian Chief closed it again before stepping into the shadows to listen.

Going over to talk to Melissa, Jed was anxious about Tommy's safety if his uncle really hated him as the young boy said. "Mell, what is this about Tommy's uncle?"

Frowning unsure if it was her place to tell the story; Melissa finally sighed before deciding to reveal Mary's past to Jed not seeing any harm in it. "Tommy's mother got married to a Montana rancher just over ten years ago before I moved out here. They were on their way back to his ranch when a Cheyenne war party attacked them, her new husband died along with the two ranch hands with them. She ended up being a captive or so she thought at first. After they took her to the Indian village, she was told the chief was on a rampage looking for three white men who murdered his wife. After a time, she fell in love with the Cheyenne Chief so they were married. They were only married a short time when he left her to hunt for the white killers again, leaving her with his young daughter from his first wife behind. Soon after he left, she found out she was pregnant. When her husband still did return after four months, she decided to leave to go home to have her baby there. When she reached her brothers place, she realized she made a mistake. Brian had changed over time for the worst. As soon as he figured out that she married a Cheyenne Indian, he was furious. He was constantly calling her names. Thankfully, he only dared hit her once... that's when I stepped in. After Tommy was born, Brian began calling him nasty names. The older the boy became the more her brother mentally abused him. It got so bad Mary asked me to take the little one in. She is still pining for her lost husband, which makes her brother even angrier."

Listening carefully to Melissa's story, Jed waited for her to pause not wanting to interrupted her; he frowned pensively. "You know, Mell. That Indian Chief sounds like."

"Me!" Giant Bear stepped out of the shadows unexpectedly.

Everyone turned to look at him in amazement; nobody had seen him come back into the room.

Giant Bear couldn't keep a mental picture of his beautiful blonde wife from emerging; who he thought was still in his Indian village before sharply motioning infuriated. "So, my Golden Dove is here. All this time I thought she remained safe with my tribe, which is all that has kept me going for so long. You say I have a son I didn't know about, I must go to her then take her home... my son as well!"

Frantically, Melissa rushed after the chief when he turned to leave. Grabbing a hold of his arm desperately, she held on to him before he could escape out the door. "No wait, Giant Bear, please. You cannot go over to Brian's ranch! You will be shot on site without them blinking an eye... no questions asked! Already one Indian has been killed, which is the cause of the rift between us. He's been after me to marry him for years. It would be a good match since our land borders each other. I keep turning him down because I could never marry anyone that has such hatred for people, just because they are different. If you wait for a moment, I think I have a plan that will work."

Turning to Gloria hastily; Melissa didn't dare release the chief afraid he would leave, anyway. "Go tell Tommy we talked it over and decided to keep him here. You can tell him we need the extra help because Wade doesn't think he can handle things... he's still hurt. Just don't let on Giant Bear is his father, his mother should be the one to reveal that important news."

Gloria nodded relieved; she didn't like Brian at all! She left the room quickly with the good news. Glad Tommy's uncle wouldn't be given another opportunity to hurt him again.

Melissa turned her attention to her foreman next. "Wade, I need you to go to the creek at ten o'clock tomorrow morning; Mary usually goes there for her daily rides. Bring her here, but only tell her what you have to get her to come. Don't mention anything about what is going on, I want to be the one to let her know about her husband being here!"

Looking back at Giant Bear, Melissa squeezed his arm gently in support. "I need you to stay out of sight until I have a chance to talk to Mary; I don't want her to pass out from shock."

Melissa glanced around; it seemed that everyone agreed except for Giant Bear. He stood undecided for a moment before slowly nodding his head reluctantly in consent. Mell sighed thankfully and let out a breath she hadn't even realized she was holding.

*****

Later that night, Melissa lay in bed exhausted after allowing her emotions to come to the surface then cried into her pillow for two hours non-stop... until no tears were left. Now she couldn't sleep; her mind kept running over the events of the past two weeks. Could she have done anything differently, did she inadvertently cross a line by killing Greg the way she did? Maybe she should have taken the outlaws into custody to be hanged, no she did that once and she regretted not killing them at the start. They escaped then massacred those innocent women and children. She was right to end it as she did, second guessing herself now did no good. She knew though that until she spoke to the judge her badge was on the line, only he could absolve her of any wrongdoing. The sheriff sighed grimly then tried to put the memories of the killers away before bringing her thoughts to what happened afterwards.

Recalling how she passing out in Jed's arms after killing Greg, Melissa remembered whispering to Jed that she loved him; did she really tell him that or was it just a dream? No, she was sure she said it aloud. She was also positive his reply was... 'He loved her too'. However, if it was true why did he ignore her afterwards? All the way to the ranch for four days

Grey Wolf didn't even glance at her. Maybe, she wanted him to say it so badly she imagined it. Mell sighed in aggravation before turning over again then tried to go to sleep.

Just as Melissa started to doze off a faint knock on her door sounded; she grinned figuring it must be her father. She smiled remembering all the times in the past when he always got two of the ranch hands to carry him and his chair upstairs to visit her. Every time she was hurt or had a narrow escape. He would come to sit by her bed then hold her hand until she fell asleep. He said it was because she needed comforting, but she knew deep down he did it to reassure himself she was okay. She sat up before calling out softly in anticipation... forgetting for a moment all of her men were dead. "Come in!"

Melissa's smile died immediately when Jed entered her room; instantly, her first thought was concern for her father. "Is something wrong?"

Jed shook his head negatively in reassurance. "No, I wanted to talk to you for a minute; privately, if that's okay?"

Walking over, Jed sat on the side of Melissa's bed without giving her a chance to protest or think about it; afraid she wouldn't let him in otherwise. Noticing her tear ravished face, Grey Wolf gently reached over before brushing a tear away. "Is your shoulder hurting you, Mell?"

Shaking her head negatively, Melissa smiled slightly in surprise at Jed's gentle touch. "No, not as much now it's more of a dull throb."

Nodding in relief, Jed explained why he was there. He took Melissa's hand, holding it in both of his tenderly. "I didn't come up here earlier because I knew you needed some time to grieve. Admittedly, I also needed time; mostly for putting away old ghosts, so I could come to you whole... in mind, body, and spirit. I couldn't wait any longer though to confess how much I love you. Will you marry me tomorrow or whenever you want!"

Comforted, Melissa sighed relieved; now she knew she didn't imagine Jed saying he loved her. "I also have a lot of love for you, but.... "

Grinning encouraged, Jed gently covering Melissa's lips with his fingertip to keep her from saying anything more; he needed to finish what he wanted to say. "Hush, don't speak yet let me say what I have to first then it will be your turn... I promise."

Removing his finger, Jed was confident Melissa would let him continue. "I know you have some concerns like your work."

Melissa tried to interrupt. Jed held up his hand to silence her. She closed her mouth sullenly with an audible snap that Grey Wolf heard quite plainly; she sat with a stubborn look on her face fearing the worst. Mell expected him to ask her to quit her job. If that was the case... he could forget about marriage!

Jed just smirked indulgently when Melissa sat there in a huff because he could guess at her thoughts, but she was wrong. "Now about your job I doubt very much you want to give it up. However, I do require some stipulations. First, I wish to remain as your deputy. Secondly, when we decide to start a family... you will have to put them first. Your job must wait until each child finishes nursing at least. I will act as sheriff until you can resume your duties at the appropriate time. As to the ranch, I think you manage it beautifully. I'm not much of a rancher myself so I'll leave you and your father to handle it. However, I might decide to buy up some more land later then maybe bring in some cattle if the two of you agree. So, Mell what do you say; can I go to Alec tomorrow and ask for your hand in marriage?"

Watching Jed closely, Melissa feared asking this question but needed to know. She studied his face closely to see his reaction. "Are you sure you can handle having your wife as your boss, it'll require taking constant orders from me; do you think it would work? It might be a bit hard to handle... even for you!"

Holding her breath, Melissa waited tensely... dreading Jed's reply.

Frowning thoughtfully, Jed stared intently at Mell then tried to be as honest as he possibly could. "Well, I have thought about it long and hard. I'm not saying I'll always agree with your methods or decisions. We might even get into a few fights about it, but I will never dispute you in front of others! I do expect you to listen to me though when I give my opinion; all I ask, is you give me a fair hearing. In the end, it will be your decision. I don't say these things because you are a woman or my wife. If I worked for a man, I would expect the same consideration... boss or no boss."

Satisfied with Jed's answer, Melissa smiled widely in approval showing her pleasure. She nodded her permission to his all-important question with no more hesitations. "Yes, Jed... I will marry you! You can talk to my father tomorrow if you wish."

Whooping in joy, Jed enfolded Melissa in his arms; she continued speaking not wanting any misunderstanding between them as she went on to explain a few things. "I must confess that although I make some decisions about the ranch, I leave them mostly up to my dad so you need to discuss buying cattle with him. He takes care of the buying, selling, and breeding. He has never allowed me anywhere near the mares during their season. Even my stud is off limits to me at that time, I have to use a gelding for a month."

Jed was bewildered by Melissa's father's old-fashioned views; considering how open-minded Alec was about letting his daughter do a man's job without any protest. However, he had other things on his mind now so changing the subject. "Mell, I have waited for you for so long! I need you badly, please let me love you tonight... I don't think I can wait another moment."

Melissa couldn't help hearing the love in Jed's voice; a deep passion was also quite evident when she moved back to look up at him. She whispered softly as she reached up then stroked Grey Wolf's cheek in permission. "Yes, oh yes!"

Lowering his mouth to hers, Jed nibbled tasting Melissa's lips. He didn't want to scare her because he knew she was innocent. Grey Wolf knew it that day at the creek when he first kissed and touched her. Her untutored responses were blazingly apparent. He wanted her first time to be one of joy... not pain; he planned to take it slowly even if it killed him. He continued kissing Mell as his hands drifted to the hem of her nightgown then lifted it upwards before removing it altogether. At this point, he sat up straighter to get a better view and murmured caressingly. "Let me look at you - you are so beautiful!"

Reaching for Melissa's hand, Jed laid it in his lap so her palm was flat against the bulge in his pants. "Here feel how much I need you."

Hesitantly Melissa touched Jed's manhood through his

trousers and felt it quiver in reaction. When he moaned in pleasure... Mell jerked back in fright thinking she hurt him.

Jed chuckled at Melissa's hesitant response then smiled encouragement. "It doesn't really hurt, Mell... it just feels good; I want you to explore so you can get to know my body that way it won't frighten you."

Melissa frowned puzzled by Jed's remark... her afraid, bah; never in her entire life had she feared any man, what could happen to make her scared of him?

Unaware of Melissa's thoughts, Jed would have groaned at how naïve and innocent she was. Grey Wolf opened the buttons on his trousers so his manhood was free; wanting Mell to explore him more fully.

Gingerly, Melissa felt Jed's bare flesh before becoming bolder; she applied more pressure than put her hand totally around it. She was surprised it felt so velvety soft, but at the same time strong and hard... this time she didn't flinch at the twitching reaction.

Moaning in pleasant torture, Jed encouraged Melissa to continue her exploration. While she was busy with that, he began stroking, investigating her sexy body which she hid quite effectively in her oversized men's clothes. Grey Wolf paused at her breasts; he used his fingers to tease her nipple before bending his head to suckle first one then moved on to the other one gently.

Groaning and shuddered, Melissa arched her body upwards to give Jed better access.

Taking Melissa's hand away unexpectedly, Jed got up; she groaned in denial thinking he was leaving her. Grey Wolf just smiled reassuringly and removed his clothing.

Gazing at Jed in awe, Melissa couldn't help noticing that he was massive. His chest was bulging with muscles; plus, it was covered in a light dusting of dark curly hair. She caught sight of his arm muscles causing her to shudder. It had a touch of panic to it though... surprisingly a flicker of pleasure intruded. She couldn't help thinking Grey Wolf could probably break her in two with one tight squeeze. The two emotions warred within her for a long moment. Fighting, she tried to get over a touch of fear. She felt tiny and delicate for the first time in her life, which caused her to shiver slightly in uncertainty. Mell wasn't sure if she liked the feeling at all.

Lowering her eyes to Jed's hands, Melissa continued. They were also large and roughly callused, but had been so gentle when he touched her breasts. Travelling still farther downward, she encountered his slim belly with thick black hair tapering down to the juncture of his thighs. Her eyes became huge at the sight of his large fully erect manhood with the sac below. The fear took over instantly; she couldn't seem to stop it... even though she tried. Her cheeks flushed heatedly as she looked up at Grey Wolf for a few moments. She wasn't sure if she should continue before taking a deep breath of courage.

Needing to finish her exploration, Melissa's gaze went lower. Jed's thighs were well muscled and his long legs were covered with hair. Grey Wolf was so beautiful to look at, but also alarming... she never seen a man unclothed before! Mell wrenched her vivid turquoise eyes up to his; her look a mixture of terror with equal parts of desire. Both were intense and warring against each other trying to overcome the other!

Jed realized this was going to be more difficult than he thought; obviously, no one ever explained to Melissa what took place between a man and a woman after they were married. The first thing he needed to do was take the look of distress out of her eyes; he wanted this marriage to be different from his first one. There was no way Grey Wolf would hide himself this time, do his duty then turn away unsatisfied. He tried making his marriage better but every time he attempted to rid his wife of the blanket that she held in a death grip... she screamed until he relented. After a year of this, lovemaking became an unpleasant task with a blanket always between them.

Deciding to try something different this time, Jed hoped to make this marriage more satisfying. He turned, snuffing out the light. He sat on the side of the bed then felt Melissa scoot to the other side quickly. Grey Wolf laid down facing her before pulling the blanket over both of them making sure his lower body was covered. He had made a mistake showing her his whole body so soon. She was such a strong woman in so many ways... even being stabbed hardly fazed her much; he hadn't realized she was so innocent, though. He sighed in frustration when his lady sheriff curled up in a ball keeping away from him as far as she could, without falling off the bed. Reaching out he took her hand before holding onto it gently. "Mell, do you trust me?"

Thankfully, with the moonlight shinning through the window Jed was able to see Melissa nod her head that she did. "Okay, I'm going to make you a promise. We will plan to marry a week from tomorrow; there will be no consummating our relationship until our wedding night."

Visibly, Melissa relaxed as she listened to his promise.

Jed smiled in triumph as the tension noticeably eased on Melissa's face; he continued even more confident now his plan might work. "But we will sleep together every night. I will touch every part of your body as well as taste you and I want you to do the same to me. I'm doing this to allow you to become more comfortable with me... hopefully by our wedding night you will be ready to become my wife in every way."

Melissa felt relief then confusion; her body wanted Jed so bad but he scared her, which bewildered her even more. She couldn't figure out why he made her feel so small and delicate, Mell was completely out of her element. She needed time to get used to Grey Wolf's naked body plus the idea of an intimate relationship without any undue stress. "Thank you, but are you sure you can wait that long... you look like you're ready to explode or something!"

Chuckling at Melissa's naïve question, Jed shook his head in amazement. "Do I ever have a lot to teach you; your first lesson for today is that both of us will burst tonight and every night. There are many ways of making love without consummating our relationship. Come here so we can cuddle for a while... I'll show you."

Obediently, Melissa scooted closer to Jed; trustingly she rolled over onto her back before waiting tensely for whatever was going to happen next.

Leaning over Melissa, Jed gave a pleasurable snort. "Okay, I will go first, but everything I do to you; you will have to do to me... is it a deal?"

Nodding hesitantly, Melissa waited anxiously as Jed slowly bent his head making her wait in anticipation. He touched his lips to hers almost in a butterfly kiss it was so light and subtle she hardly felt a thing... her lips quivered in response wanting more.

Flicking his tongue out; Jed daintily ever so gently, traced first her top lip before moving down to her lower lip.

Moaning, Melissa lifted her head for a deeper kiss.

Snorting in satisfaction, Jed backed away slightly. He kissed Melissa's cheek with the same velvety touch he gave her lips; he moved to her ear before flicking her earlobe with a light stroke of his tongue. Grey Wolf trailed it delicately ever so slowly down her neck. Every few minutes he would lightly nibble as he went farther down... still as gently as he possibly could so Mell would only feel it faintly.

Melissa felt intense tremors running up her spine as Jed suckled... unexpectedly he gently bit at her neck. He then proceeded to soothe the bite by licking it before blowing on the wet spot. She shuddered in shocked pleasure as the cold air of his breath hit the warm saliva on her hot skin. Mell shivered again in delighted surprise as Grey Wolf's hands lightly skimmed down to her breasts; tracing her nipples teasingly with his fingertips.

Bringing his right hand up, Jed put his first two fingers into Melissa's mouth to moisten them before returning his fingers to her nipple. Deep moans of ecstasy came from Mell's throat when her nipples hardened even more into erect buds of desire; they were so hard now... they almost hurt.

Lifting his head, Jed watched the expression on Melissa's face expectantly as she responded to his caresses. He brought it back down satisfied she was feeling everything he wanted her to experience. Grey Wolf flicked Mell's hardened nipple with his tongue; afterwards he blew on it lightly.

Melissa gasped for air in amazement as the goose bumps intensified all over her body before arching up in excitement and torture. It was pure torment... every nerve was screaming; she felt moisture seeping from her secret place. Mell clamped her legs together in alarm hoping to stop the excretion, but it was no use.

Feeling Melissa's responsive shivers, Jed knew it was time to advance further; he slowly slid his hand down her belly... Grey Wolf's touch was so light it tickled.

Gasping in pleasure, Melissa giggled in surprise; she just couldn't help herself.

Jed felt Melissa's muscles bunch and tighten against his

fingertips. He smiled knowingly to himself, she was ready. He reached his goal and played with her triangle of curls teasingly at the apex of her thighs; trying to entice her, hoping she would open for him but they were tightly clamped together. Grey Wolf brought his mouth back up to her lips before whispering softly against them pleadingly. "Mell, open your legs for me... let me touch you there."

Hearing the entreaty in Jed's voice, Melissa instantly responded to it... she did what he told her to do without knowing why. Grey Wolf parted Mell's petals to reach her inner core before she could change her mind then he began lightly stroking her silky bud.

Melissa felt pressure below, it was building up in her loins and she fought the feeling at first unsure what was happening to her; as Jed's strokes increased in pace, the pressure became stronger. She felt a weird sensation it was almost painful. It was also intensely pleasurable at the same time. Mell continued to fight the phenomena but couldn't hold out for long... she groaned in denial.

Jed could feel Melissa fighting the passion. He brought his mouth back to her lips and whispered desperately. "Mell, let yourself go... don't hold back sweetheart; I promise, it will be the greatest pleasure you have ever felt."

Continuing to stroke Melissa enticingly, Jed pressed slightly harder against her bud.

Groaning in surrender, Melissa felt the pressure building to a peek; she erupted against her will unable to fight it any longer... bright lights, with pulsating stars seemed to explode in her brain. Mell opened her mouth to scream out in pleasure and shock.

Quickly, Jed fused their mouths in a searing kiss... effectively cutting off Melissa's cries of gratification. He waited until he felt her relax before lifting away then laid back; he pulled Mell up against him tenderly. Grey Wolf just held her as she slowly came back to earth.

Curling herself around Jed contentedly, Melissa was hardly able to move or speak. Finally, she couldn't help asking him drowsily. "Is it going to be that intense all the time or is it only the first time?"

Snickering mysteriously, Jed teased. "It just gets better, Mell; you have only just tasted part of the pleasure."

Sitting up instantly, Melissa grimaced in simulated apprehension. "Darn... if it gets better then tonight; I might not live through it!"

Jed's eyebrow rose in surprise when Melissa used a curse word, but he didn't comment on it. Grey Wolf chuckled again at her expression as he teased. "Oh, it does get better Mell and I promise you... you will survive it; now it's time for you to explore me like I did you."

Turning slightly, Melissa eyed Jed shyly. "What do I do?"

Smiling with great anticipation at what was to come; Jed tweaked Melissa's nose playfully. "Whatever your heart desires, but to get you started... you can kiss me first."

Melissa leaned down to reach Jed's mouth and tentatively touched her lips to his; he opened his mouth a little to entice her. Getting brave, she pushed her tongue inside then began moving it around experimentally. Satisfied, she stopped before covering him in little kisses all over his face around his eyes and down to his arrogant chin. Next, she began nibbling on his neck before blowing on the wet spot she left. She smiled in delight when she tried his stunt and it worked on him too. It caused her quite a thrill when he moaned then tremble at the contact of the cold air against his hot skin. Mell shifted, now she was kneeling slightly... it helped to free up her hands. She brought both up to his chest before running her fingers through his springy black curls. They tickled her palms. She giggled slightly at the erotic feeling. Her hands slipped lower then touched Grey Wolf's nipples hoping they were as sensitive as hers were.

Jed moaned in pleasure when Melissa became bolder and moved down to his nipple; she started sucking on one as he had done to her. He squirmed groaning in delight when he felt her copy his method of wetting the nipple then blowing on it. Grey Wolf didn't know how much longer he could control himself as the pressure continued to build in his loins. He gritted his teeth and fought the sensation trying to give her more time to explore. As Mell's hands moved slowly downwards, he had to grind them together harder... she tentatively touched his engorged manhood. He prayed he could hold on until she finished but he doubted he could, it's been over two years since he was with a woman.

Melissa ran her curious fingers up then down Jed's manhood

before going a little further and picking up his sac. She could feel two hard round balls inside; Mell made a mental note to ask him later what they were for.

If Jed could have heard Melissa's thoughts at that moment, he would have laughed hysterically in disbelief at her naïve curiosity; instead, Grey Wolf was emitting gasps of pleasure mixed with pain... still fighting to hold on as Mell reached again for his manhood.

Touching the head with the tip of her finger curiously, Melissa frowned in surprise when she felt a sticky substance before jerking back quickly... thinking something was wrong.

Grabbing Melissa's hand tenderly, Jed put it back demandingly... he managed to gasp out passed his constricted throat. "It's all right Mell; the same thing happened to you before you reached your peak; the moisture is a natural lubrication that happens before making love."

Looking at Jed anxiously, Melissa grimaced. "I don't know what to do!"

Beaming in encouragement, Jed held onto her hand for a moment more. "Just keep stroking and squeeze gently, every once in a while, pump your hand up then down... it will make me explode like you did."

Doing as Jed asked, Melissa held on tightly to him... once he let her hand go. Using both hands, she knelt above him since one hand didn't seem to be enough. Grey Wolf pushed upwards against Mell; until he finally felt his control disappear then he found his own release.

Melissa caught her breath in amazement when her hand became sticky with a white gooey substance; Jed's manhood continued jerking in her hand emptying itself. After a few minutes, she could feel it beginning to shrink. Startled, Mell dropped it in shock then sat back incredulously unsure what to do now. Watching in fascination, she saw it shrivel up to about a quarter of its previous size.

At the perturbed look on Melissa's face, Jed couldn't help bursting into uncontrollable laughter. He tried to stop, but that look just made him laugh even harder.

Scowling down at Jed in mock anger at his amusement, Melissa planted her balled up fists against her waist waiting for him to finish. She couldn't help wondering what was causing him such hilarity. Grey Wolf was laughing so hard the tears were leaking from his eyes. Her curiosity got the better of her though, ignoring his laughter she demanded indignantly. "Why did it shrink, what's that white stuff and why doesn't it stay the same size?"

Jed finally got himself under control enough to answer Melissa's questions. He reached out then pulled her down beside him. They cuddle while he tried to describe it to her as best he could. "No, the size you see now is its natural shape; it only grows larger when I get excited or first thing in the morning when I have to go to the outhouse. The white stuff is my seed... it's what makes babies."

Nodding pensively in understanding, Melissa bit her lower lip not sure if she should ask but only for a second; as she thought of another question which made her frown... the concern was obvious in her voice. "Oh, that makes sense, doesn't it hurt when it grows bigger though?"

Smiling indulgently at Melissa's curiosity, Jed tried to answer as best he could; it was a little difficult trying to explain how it felt to a woman. "No, after it reaches full erection there is pressure but it doesn't really hurt."

Melissa's expression became skeptical when she thought of Jed's earlier remark about lovemaking getting more intense; she didn't know how that could be possible. "Are you sure lovemaking gets better?"

Grinning mischievously, Jed nodding emphatically as Melissa looked at him curiously. "Yes, it does, and tomorrow night I'll use my mouth down there... instead of my hand."

Getting up, Jed went to the washbasin then put water in a bowl and washed himself; he brought a cloth to Melissa so she could wipe her hands clean.

While Jed was busy, Melissa mulled over his comment in surprise before shaking her head in shocked denial when he came back; after she was finished cleaning both hands... she looked up at him in objection. "I don't think I'll like that at all!"

Laughing in delight at Melissa's horrified expression; Jed threw the cloth in a corner then crawled back into bed before winking teasingly... with the utmost confidence he snickered. "Trust me, you'll like it. Now lie down and go to sleep we have a big day ahead of us tomorrow."

Melissa yawned too tired to argue with Jed one-way or the

other then laid her head on his chest in contentment. Mell
stretched into a more comfortable position. "Oh, I forgot to
tell you tomorrow we have to stop at Brian's and let him know
Mary's husband is here; when we do, get ready for an
explosion... he will be furious."

Jed nodded already guessing from what he heard about
Brian so far, he was going to be quite upset over this. He
yawned worn out... Grey Wolf turned to Melissa for a
goodnight kiss before falling asleep contentedly.

For the first time in years Jed slept through the night with
no nightmares about his wife and son's brutal murder. Now
his dreams were full of a long life with Mell, as well as the
children yet to come.

CHAPTER EIGHT

Melissa woke first; she could feel Jed's hot breath against her neck then felt a shiver of desire, with quite a bit of embarrassment... recalling their actions of the night before. Was this how married people acted? She didn't know for sure, but knew she would have to ask her father if she wanted an answer to her question. Mell remembered Grey Wolf saying he was going to use his mouth, 'down there'. She felt her face burning at the thought, maybe asking her dad wasn't such a good idea after all.

Jed woke with the strong feelings of an over abundance of love, hope, and contentment. He felt Melissa curled up against him... he smiled in pleasure. It was the first time in years he didn't feel any hate, rage, or despair when he first woke in the morning; it felt so good. He hoped Mell didn't have any feelings of regret about what happened last night. Grey Wolf knew by her breathing that she was awake, so he brought his hand up to her breast then began fondling her nipple playfully.

Rolling away quickly, Melissa took the top bed cover with her as she frantically searched the floor for her nightgown... Jed had stripped it off her last night; of course, she just had to forget to put it back on before she fell asleep.

Grimacing anxiously when Jed saw the acute embarrassment on Melissa's face; he knew he would have to act quickly before she had time to think. Going after her, he grabbed her around the waist and threw her on the bed before jumping on top of her. He pinned Mell beneath him, Grey Wolf made sure though to keep his weight on her left side because of her injured right shoulder.

Taken completely by surprise, Melissa lost the blanket as her arms flailed around; shocked, she found herself flat on her back underneath a grinning Jed.

Once Jed figured Melissa was subdued; he smiled down teasingly at her before lowering his head and gave her a quick, thorough kiss. He lifted himself up so he could see her expression as his manhood instantly hardened in desire. He couldn't help panting slightly when he also became excited. Grey Wolf watched in satisfaction as passion returned to her expressive face. "Mell... a wife-to-be, gives her husband-to-be at least a good morning kiss before she jumps out of bed!"

Melissa looked up at Jed's smug face before smiling slyly up at him. Her grin turned devilish suddenly; it's all the forewarning she gave him. "Oh, she does... does she?"

With no other warning, Jed found himself lying flat on his back with Melissa lying on top of him holding him down with a smirk of vindication; she then proceeded to kiss him thoroughly in return. When she ended the kiss, she pushed herself up to gaze down at Grey Wolf's flushed cheeks and passion filled eyes in satisfaction. Mell had to clear her throat in order to tease him roguishly in return. "Good morning... husband-to-be!"

Quickly, Melissa jumped off Jed before scampering away; unfortunately, she didn't escape totally unscathed.

Leaping up, Grey Wolf managed to smack Mell's bare bottom for her impertinence before she could get away fully.

Squealing in playful shock, Melissa couldn't help smirking in satisfaction when she managed to get across the room relatively unhindered. She happened to glance out the window as she was passing by... Mell's face lost all playfulness as she swore in surprise. "Oh drat, it must be eight or nine o'clock. I have never slept this late in my life!"

Hurriedly, Melissa scurried into her clothes.

Winking over at Mell suggestively as Jed was putting on his pants; he couldn't help teasing her a bit. "We could shock everyone even more by not going down until ten o'clock. I can think of a few things to keep us busy for another hour or so!"

Feeling something soft hit him full in the face before Jed could get the last word out... he sputtered in indignation. Melissa burst out laughing as her nightshirt fell to the floor in a heap at his feet. She turned instantly then ran for the door as Grey Wolf started running after her; Mell yanked it open and disappeared down the hallway.

Stopping quickly, Jed turned back into the room when he realized he wasn't finished dressing. Grey Wolf grabbed his shirt before following her... he smiled in relief and pleasure at her teasing then congratulated himself on getting Mell to forget her embarrassment; he followed her down more slowly.

*****

Everyone was already sitting around the kitchen table when Melissa and Jed came into the room.

Alec glanced intently at Melissa in concern at her flushed face, he wondered if she was getting a fever as she took the seat beside him. Searching his daughter's face grimly, he couldn't help wondering how she was coping with killing her deputy. He knew how she felt about taking another's life and was fully aware she would hide her fear about the repercussions to follow... even from him. She didn't know he watched the fight from behind the rocks; not wanting to distract her, he stayed hidden. He knew she crossed the line somewhat and was aware she wouldn't hide that fact from the judge. "How is your shoulder doing, Mell?"

Melissa shrugged unconcerned then tried to hide her face. "It's fine, just a twinge here and there."

Gloria brought the coffee first; afterwards, she served breakfast since they all decided to wait for the latecomers. At the end of the meal while everyone was relaxing with a cup of coffee, it became quite apparent Wade was uncomfortable. The foreman was squirming around in his seat as if he had gotten the bullet in the backside... instead of his shoulder.

Just as Alec was about to ask Wade if there was a problem; Melissa's foreman stood up before clearing his throat in embarrassment. "I want to make an official announcement, Gloria and I have decided to get married... as soon as possible."

With that statement finally out, Wade sat down quickly; he took out his handkerchief then wiped his face in relief at getting his speech done with.

Instantly, Melissa jumped up in surprised pleasure before rushing over... she hugged her maid ecstatically. "That's great news, Gloria; I'm so happy for you both. We can have your wedding a week from tomorrow, it will give you time to become used to Wade."

Giving Melissa a strange disgruntled look after Gloria stepped back... she waved in bewilderment. "What do you mean by that; I think I'm already use to him!"

Frowning in puzzlement, Melissa's face flushed this time in discomfort. "Oh, I thought all brides and grooms needed to get to know each other before they wed."

Blushing deeper, Melissa saw everyone staring at her in

bewilderment. She heard Jed start to chuckle behind her; she spun around then planted her balled up fists against her hips demandingly as she glared at him heatedly... glad to have someone to direct her ire at. "What do you find so funny?"

Holding up his hand's palms outward in a placating gesture, Jed wisely ignored Melissa's question. Still, Grey Wolf couldn't help another snicker from escaping as he turned to congratulate Wade.

Jed turned to Alec when he was finished with the foreman... his expression became serious. He had planned to ask Melissa's father later for permission, but since they were on the subject of marriage; he decided to leap in with both feet, so to speak. "Sir, while we are talking about marriage, Mell has consented to marry me. I would like to have your blessings."

Alec looked up at Melissa's flushed face in surprise then looked over at Jed before beaming in satisfaction; he raised his hand to shake Grey Wolf's in glee. "I couldn't be happier... of course, you have my approval. It looks like we will be having a double wedding!"

Turning when an idea suddenly blossomed, Alec looked at the Cheyenne Chief intently. He knew an Indian ceremony was not considered a legal marriage to the white's; he smiled enticingly over at Jed's friend. "Unless you and your wife want to renew your vows as well Giant Bear then we could have a great celebration... a triple wedding! What do you say?"

Giant Bear's stoic expression softened somewhat when he thought of his Mary... he nodded in agreement. "I think my Golden Dove would like to get married in the white man's way then no one can take her away from me again."

Gloria started clearing off the table before grinning as a plan tickled her imagination... she looked over at Alec for consent. "How about a small engagement supper tonight so we can all celebrate?"

Everyone nodded in excitement then Gloria left the room humming happily to herself; she was already planning what she could make for such a grand occasion. She went out to the back entrance to head down to the cellar for a look at their supplies.

Wade instantly got up and followed his fiancé to say

goodbye to Gloria privately.

Turning nervously from the cellar door at a noise behind her; Gloria wilted in relief before rushing over to Wade for a passionate kiss... the supper completely forgotten for the moment.

Lifting his head after several minutes of passion, Wade looked at Gloria's flushed cheeks in pleasure. The foreman chuckled at her eager expression before kissing her again for good measure; stepping back reluctantly... he tweaked her nose playfully. "I will see you in a few hours try to behave while I'm gone!"

Gloria's look turned sober and her expressive face showed a momentary fear. "Be careful, there Wade; I thought you were dead once. I don't want to ever have that feeling of hopelessness again."

Nodding in sorrow, Wade thought about the tragedy they had all endured the last couple of weeks. "I'll be careful, I promise."

Wade turned away from Gloria then slipped out the side door before walking around the house. Tommy was already trotting out of the barn with his horse. When the foreman got to him, the young boy handed him his reins. "Well thank you, Tommy; do you have Mell and Jed's horses ready too?"

Tommy's face lit up with a huge smile as he beamed at Wade proudly. "Almost, Giant Bear came out a few minutes ago... he is helping me. I was watching at the barn door so came out when I saw you coming this way. When I see Aunt Mell and Uncle Jed all I have to do is bring their horses then they will be on their way."

Chuckling at the boy's enthusiasm, Wade swung up onto his horse; he looked down at Tommy curiously. "You're calling Jed, uncle already?"

Smiling shyly up at Wade, Tommy nodded matter of factually. "Of course, I knew right from the start Aunt Mell would marry Jed so when Giant Bear told me a few moments ago... I wasn't surprised at all!"

Looking at Mary's son in dumbfounded surprise, Wade shook his head in wonder; it really surprised him how perceptive Melissa's foster son was... that uncle of his was sure stupid to give up a fine boy like Tommy, just because he was part native.

Waving goodbye without another word, Tommy raced back to the barn to finish getting ready for Melissa and Jed's arrival.

Kicking his horse into a trot to warm him up, Wade finally urged him into a run... heading for the creek where Mary always went. It took him several hours to get there. He slowed his gelding in appreciation before patting his neck in gratitude for the speed. "Sorry about that, old boy; we can slow down now, we made good time."

Wade's horse whiffed at him as he blew hard at the demanding ride; pleased by the pat of gratitude as if he understood what his master was saying. The foreman chuckled at his horse's attentiveness.

Getting to the creek just in time, Wade saw Mary mounting her horse to leave; he sighed thankful, he hadn't missed her.

Mary tensed in surprise, instantly suspicious when she heard an unfamiliar horse coming. Nobody ever came here except her; she readied herself just in case she needed to urge her horse into a run for a quick getaway. Golden Dove didn't relax again until she recognized Melissa's foreman. She waited until he was beside her before warmly beaming up at him then nodded pleasantly in greeting. "Good morning, Wade, what are you doing here at this time of the day?"

Tipping his hat cordially before his expression sobered, Wade told Mary all about the tragedy at Melissa's ranch.

Shuddering in horror by the time Wade finished, Mary shook her head in disbelief. "I can hardly believe Greg could do such a terrible thing; Melissa has always been such a good judge of character. Are you sure my son is unhurt?"

Nodding sadly, Wade frowned none of them had suspected Greg... even Melissa didn't think him capable of such treachery. The foreman smiled reassuringly then reached over and patted Mary's hand soothingly that was sitting on the pommel of her saddle. "Your son isn't hurt physically, but Mell thinks you should still come to the ranch who knows how this could affect him later. We figured you'd want to stay for a couple of days just to make sure Tommy is okay; plus, the ladies will need some extra help until more hands can be found."

Mary nodded, instantly concerned for her son. She turned her horse towards Melissa's place; not questioning why she was needed when the sheriff should have a better understanding of how to handle this kind of tragedy.

****

Melissa and Jed walked out of the house heading towards the barn; they were about halfway when Tommy came trotting out with both their horses, plus the customary packhorse... even though they wouldn't need him today. Still, it was better to be prepared then sorry later, she learned a long time ago to always expect the unexpected. She grinned knowingly at Jed. He nodded pleased that Mary's son was thinking ahead of them. They both stopped to wait for the boy to get to them. Mell smiled in approval and thanks at the youngster before taking her reins from him. "Why thank you, did you saddle the horses by yourself?"

Shaking his head negatively, Tommy beamed at Melissa in pleasure. "No, Giant Bear helped me then I waited until I saw you coming."

Grinning in appreciation, Jed took the reins from Tommy. "Thanks to the both of you, I appreciate it!"

Grinning, Tommy was ecstatic at their approval wanting to be as useful as he possibly could. Not wanting his aunt Melissa, who he adored... to talk about sending him away ever again.

Squatting down, Melissa's tone became serious; she looked her foster son straight in the eye so her words would carry their critical nature to the young Tommy. "I have a big favour I want to ask you... this is really important to me. You will not understand right now, but I promise to explain it to you later."

Tommy nodded attentively well aware that when his aunt Melissa talked to him like this, it meant change of some kind in his life. "Aunt Mell, I love you... you can ask me anything. You don't need to tell me anything either, if you don't want to; I will still do whatever you want me to without asking why."

Looking at her foster son sadly for a moment, Melissa knew she would lose him soon then gathered him into her arms impulsively; trying to hide her tears as she whispered brokenly. "I love you too, Tommy... I promise, I'd never ask you to do anything that would hurt you or anyone else."

Smiling shyly at Melissa when she finally let him go, Tommy put his hand over his heart. "I know, Aunty Mell; I trust you with all my heart."

Melissa sighed as she hid her heartache then managed a crooked grin for Tommy. She was so proud of the young boy she helped raise; he had turned out so well despite his uncle. She cleared her throat noisily so she could speak past the lump of emotion choking her up. "Wade is bringing your mother here today. I don't want her to go to the barn so you will have to come get her horse before she goes there. I also do not want you to talk about Giant Bear or Jed in front of her; do not even mention their names when she is around. I'm going to tell her when I get back about what happened, as well as about my upcoming marriage. Okay, can you remember this... it's very important to me?"

Grinning happily at such an easy request, Tommy beamed in delight at having a secret his mother wasn't to know yet. He looked at Melissa seriously before making a solemn vow... he put his finger over his heart again, but this time he made the sign of the cross over it. "That's easy; I promise not to say anything to her, cross my heart."

Chuckling at the dramatics, Melissa gave Tommy another hug in praise before she pushed him away so she could tell him her last request, but held onto his shoulders. "Thank you, I do have one more favour to ask of you though; the bunkhouse needs to be cleaned out, can you ask Giant Bear to start then let Wade know about it so he can help him when he gets back?"

Tommy nodded then stood back so Melissa could get up off her knees; he watched his aunt mount her horse before voicing his own request as he looked up at her earnestly. "Aunty Mell... do you mind if I help them?"

Grinning down at Tommy, Melissa nodded her consent. "Sure, you can, but don't forget your lessons with grandpa. There are several burlap sacks in the tack room of the barn give them to Giant Bear; ask him to put all the articles of the ranch hands in them... I'll send it to their families later."

Without further comment, Tommy turned then ran back to the barn to give Giant Bear the message before he forgot anything.

Melissa and Jed rode in silence for a few moments then he turned to her before smiling in admiration as he thought of Tommy. "That boy loves you very much... I was impressed;

you and Mary did a good job raising him, Giant Bear will be quite pleased."

Sighing sadly, Melissa gestured grimly. "I didn't realize how much Tommy had grown until today; with no other children around, I suppose he couldn't help but grow up faster. I'll be sorry to lose him when he goes to Montana with his parents... he's like my own son. I always pictured him staying with me then taking over my ranch if I never have any kids. You do realize I'm almost thirty. I might be too old to have children."

Jed laughed in delight and shook his head negatively in reassurance. "Believe me, you are not too old; my mother was pregnant with me when she was about thirty... I wasn't her last child either."

Smiling in relief, Melissa motioned eagerly. "Good; I was worried about that, I'm hoping to have at least two children."

Chuckling teasingly before his voice became serious, Jed waved for emphases. "As many as you would like, I miss my son very much. I hope we have one boy at least... a girl would be nice too; I want you to know if it never happens though, it's okay as long as we are together it is all I need to make me happy."

After a few minutes of silence, Jed looked back at Melissa then changed the subject. "What are we going to do first when we hit town?"

Melissa sighed in aggravation not wanting to have the moment spoiled at first. She shook off her happy thoughts of a life with Jed resignedly before she turned to him and the matter at hand. "I want you to go to Chelsie's Saloon then Pam's Place; it's the fancy house just outside town. Let everybody know we are looking to recruit six men to work plus live at the ranch. After you choose the six men you want, take each of them aside to let them know what happened here that way they can decide whether to take the job... or not. They could change their minds since it is dangerous to work for me, if they do you will know right away so can pick someone else in his place. I'll go see the families who live around here and tell them about the deaths of their loved ones then give them the money I owed the men. Afterwards, I will meet you in front of the courthouse so we can go in together."

Jed nodded thoughtfully before looking over at Melissa. "It's a good plan; I would like to give you some advice though."

Melissa laughed at Jed teasingly before waving incredulously at him as she joked. "Disagreeing with me already, are you?"

Smirking good-naturedly, Jed shrugged negatively. "No, but since we don't know how long the other person is going to be we should meet in the hotel instead for lunch. I will bring the men I choose with me and you can meet them; this way if you do not like some of my choices, I can look for others."

Nodding Melissa smiled over at Jed in approval, but waved away his offer in dismissal. "Going for lunch is a good idea. As for meeting these men, I don't need to; I have complete trust in your judgment."

Beaming in pleasure at Melissa's confidence in him, Jed gestured in appeasement. "I'm glad you have faith in me; although, I wasn't thinking in terms of trust. My thoughts were more along the lines that you know these people better than I do. Besides, we are all going to have to get along and just because I like a person... doesn't mean you will."

Sighing pensively pleased that Jed made such logical points, Melissa inclined her head slightly. "True enough; okay, we will do it your way."

Snickering in devilish delight, Jed grabbed his chest as if in total shock. "Oh, my first victory; I should probably mark this occasion down, I have this feeling you will not be this easy to convince in the future."

Melissa smirked in amusement at Jed's antics and leaned over her horse for a quick kiss. Grey Wolf nudged his horse over then tried to meet her halfway; leaning precariously, Mell almost fell out of her saddle... quickly she straightened with a fiery blush at her boldness.

Jed laughed uproariously at Melissa's surprised expression and inflamed face. When he got himself under control, he tried for a more serious appearance but wrecked it by chuckling again. Grey Wolf's tone finally turned all business once more. "Now these men you want me to hire... should we get all single men or family men?"

Sighing in disappointment at having the moment spoiled by business. This was only the second time Melissa heard Jed's unrestrained laughter, it was deep, as well as very masculine; she definitely enjoyed hearing it. Hopefully, Grey Wolf would continue to do it more often in the future. Shrugging thoughtfully Mell sighed sadly at the thought of what had happened to her ranch hands again. "I think single men would be better... especially with what happened."

Frowning wistfully, Jed remembered the love he shared with his son Daniel. "I would like to hire at least one family if you don't mind. It wouldn't take long to build them a cabin; this way when you and Gloria are ready to have children there will be another woman around to help out."

Melissa exhaled noisily aware suddenly of Jed's sadness then tried to lighten the mood. "Good idea, I never thought of that; come to think of it... Wade and Gloria will probably want their own cabin, as well."

Shaking off his sad thoughts, Jed winked teasingly over at Melissa; he couldn't help giving an exaggerated wave of his hand. "I am sure they would love to have their own private place. Mind you I just met them, which makes it hard for me to judge. I'm pretty positive though, they wouldn't appreciate having to stay in the bunkhouse with the other men."

Chuckling at that thought, Melissa nodded contemplating. "We have plenty of lumber on hand for two cabins; it will only deplete our reserves a little. Once we have more men, we can cut some more if need be."

Sighing irritably as they rode into town, Jed wanted to continue the conversation. He shrugged resignedly to himself. Oh well, there was always later. Grey Wolf waved goodbye to Melissa before turning towards Chelsie's Saloon without further comment. Mell headed to her office first to make out the report she was dreading having to make.

Jed dismounted at the hitching rail of the saloon then tied his horse loosely. He checked wanting to be sure his badge was in plain sight before entering, wanting everyone to know who he was. Grey Wolf sauntered into Chelsie's and looked around curiously never having been to this place before. He walked up to the cedar bar. Thankfully, the scent of cedar overpowered the stench of whiskey, cigar smoke, and the unpleasant odour of vomit one could always associate a saloon with. He smiled in greeting at the hefty, five-foot-five red headed woman standing behind the bar. "You must be Chelsie; my name is Jed Brown... I'm the new deputy in town."

Sticking out her rough calloused hand in greeting, Chelsie

grinned in pleasure as she eyed the rugged... tall, dark, and handsome stranger standing in front of her. Her smile became slightly enticing before her Irish drawl thickened in invitation; normally, she didn't allow for such going on's, occasionally though she made an exception. "Hi, I heard the sheriff hired a new deputy."

Shaking Chelsie's hand firmly, Jed ignored her obvious attempts at enticement; he leaned over the counter to whisper in conspiracy so there would be no more advancements. "I'm also her fiancé... do you know where I might pick up a wedding ring?"

Jed looked for his wife's ring, but it was gone when he found them. It had upset him at first because it was originally his grandmother's wedding ring. It wouldn't matter; he preferred to give Melissa a new one, anyway.

Chelsie's expression instantly lost the flirting look in surprise... she eyed Jed in disappointment. Until she thought about what the new deputy said then her smile lit up her whole face in congratulations as she slapped the bar before chortling loudly in delight. "Drinks are on the house; the sheriff is finally going to get herself hitched!"

Everyone there cheered at the news of free drinks, and came over to Jed one by one then shook his hand before introducing themselves as they offered best wishes.

Beckoning one of her girls over to tend bar, Chelsie turned and motioned for Jed to follow her. "Come with me, I might have what you are looking for."

Nodding perplexed, Jed obediently trailed after the heavy set but beautiful redhead. He guessed she was Irish by her red hair, the thick burr when she was excited also pointed to an Irish background. She seemed opened and friendly, but he could well imagine the temper this one would display when miffed. Chelsie reminded him of his dead wife; heftier though, plus more outgoing than his wife had been. He followed the saloon owner to her office in the back. Grey Wolf watched her curiously, as she opened a safe hidden behind a cabinet before taking out a large jewelled box.

Chelsie brought it over proudly and set it on her desk carefully, she looked up at Jed. "Not too many people buy jewellery from me yet, so I have a good selection on hand... I make my own, of course. I get my gold mostly from the gold miners wanting a few drinks. I also hunt the creek bed just outside town for special rocks, or crystals if I can get them, they work the best. My father was a goldsmith in Ireland. He even made jewellery for the king when he would come to visit his estates. My dad never had a boy which is why he passed it on to me instead. He remarried when my mother died; she was not a nice person. I had to leave, that is how I came to the new world. I hoped things would be different out here for a woman. Most of the stuff I have is just plain gold bands, which I sell from one to three dollars. I do have a few unusual ones I only show to special customers though."

Opening the box lovingly, Chelsie turned it so Jed could see the treasures inside.

Jed caught his breath in wonder... completely taken by surprise as he stared at the beautiful jewellery displayed inside before looking up at Chelsie in speculation. "Why do you own a saloon when you do such exquisite work with gold?"

Smiling in pride at the praise Chelsie shrugging sadly. "The saloon is just a sideline there isn't enough business in this small town for an actual goldsmith shop yet... I do everything here. I hope to open a shop one day, until then this place puts food on the table; most of the work I do now is done on commission or special orders. If you are going to Melissa's place later, I would appreciate your help in getting a package to Alec for me without his daughter finding out?"

Nodding, Jed watched as Chelsie walked towards the safe to get Alec's parcel.

Chelsie came back then handed it to Jed.

Putting the package in his shirt pocket under his vest, Jed didn't want to lose it. He went back to studying the rings, necklaces, pocket watches, and other jewellery artfully displayed inside the box; Grey Wolf picked up a ring that just seemed to jump out at him suddenly.

Chuckling in delight when she saw which one Jed was holding, Chelsie nodded in approval. "That one would be perfect for Melissa... luckily I just finished it two days ago. Actually, the inspiration for that ring came from Alec's commission; it would go perfectly with the bracelet and earrings I made for Mell at her father's request. He had the stones shipped to me so I could make them for him. There was a sliver of the gem left so I made the ring. If you didn't pick it yourself, I would have showed it to you then recommended it."

Smiling in thanks for the advice, Jed looked back down. He pushed a few rings around, but didn't find what he was looking for; Grey Wolf looked back up at Chelsie inquiringly. "Is there another ring to go with it?"

Shaking her head slightly in disappointment, Chelsie hadn't gotten around to one yet. "No, I didn't have time to make one but that's okay because you wouldn't want to spoil the looks of that ring, anyway. I think one is sufficient for most women... especially Melissa, she's not into fancy jewellery."

Jed nodded well aware that Melissa was a plain simple woman not prone to elaborate things; he totally agreed with Chelsie's character description of his fiancé. "Okay, I can run across to the bank while you wrap it up for me. Oh, I suppose I should ask you what you want for the ring."

Chelsie laughed in delight at his flustered question before taking it from Jed. "I want thirty dollars for the ring because of the unique stone it contains."

Grimacing then smiling in embarrassment as Chelsie laughed at him, Jed looked back down at the rings to hide his momentary discomfiture. His grin widened when he thought of the perfect wedding gift for Giant Bear and Mary. "Fair enough, but before I go to the bank, I will need two more rings; just plain wedding bands for my friend who is getting married with us... it would be a perfect gift for him and his wife. Afterwards, I have business to discuss with the men in your saloon. Actually, maybe you can help me. I need to hire six men for Melissa's place preferably single and one family to come live at the ranch also."

Frowning in concern, Chelsie went back to her safe and brought out a plain box; the saloon owner set it on her desk before looking down. She rummaged inside for two plain matching bands for his friends. "What happened to all the men already out there, have they been fired for some reason?"

Sadly, Jed shook his head when Chelsie looked up then held out two rings for his inspection; he took the bands in approval before telling her everything that happened the last two weeks.

When Jed finished; Chelsie sighed sadly and wiped tears away. She had known them all of course. The saloon owner had even been bed partners with one of them. Shuddering in sympathy, she wondered how Melissa was handling it. "Oh, how terrible the sheriff must be devastated!"

Nodding Jed frowned in worry as he wondered how Melissa was holding up right now. "Yes, she is; while I'm recruiting more men, she went to tell the families what happened."

Sighing forlornly, Chelsie wiped more tears away. She eyed Jed's worried frown then fidgeted with her box concerned. "That will be extremely hard on the sheriff; now I see why you want single men, but why do you need one family out there... if you don't mind my asking?"

Jed's expression lightened considerably; he beamed hopefully. "Well with us getting married, plus Gloria and Wade want to get married too; we hope to have children running around soon, so the women will need extra help around the ranch."

Grinning mischievously, Chelsie asked slyly. "Will Melissa be quitting her job now or are you man enough to handle having a sheriff for a wife?"

Laughing in delight at Chelsie when she challenged his manhood, Jed shrugged in dismissal before becoming serious... he shook his head resignedly. "Do you really think I could get away with telling Melissa she has to quit her job? No way would she consider marrying me if I even asked, she loves her work too much; no, she will remain the sheriff until we decide to have children then I will take over her duties until she is ready to come back."

Chelsie sighed in relief at Jed's wise decision; Melissa was so lucky to find a man who accepted her as she was. She hoped someday to be so fortunate. "Good! Come on, I'll help you pick out the men you need. I also have the perfect family that would love to go work for the sheriff."

Pocketing the three rings once Chelsie wrapped them; Jed followed her into the saloon after she put her jewellery box back in the safe. Discussing the price of the other two rings Grey Wolf wanted they went back to the barroom.

****

Melissa walked out of the bank with eight banknotes filled out to each family of the deceased; the manager almost had heart failure when she told him each one needed to be one thousand dollars. She frowned thoughtfully, looking up and down Main Street undecided who to see first; finally, she decided to go to Cookie's sisters. Walking towards the hitching post, Mell mounted her horse. Turning south, she rode out of town.

Leaving her packhorse tied to the hitching rail in front of her office, Melissa knew she wouldn't need him now. The farm she was riding to wasn't very far away; dismounting, she dropped the reins on the ground so Lightning could wander around to eat but would stay close by if she needed him. Mell went to the porch slowly dragging her feet not looking forward to this at all. She walked up the steps before approaching the wooden door and couldn't put it off any longer... she raised her hand then knocked on it hesitantly.

A petite brunette opened the door instantly having seen Melissa coming... she smiled in pleasure at the unexpected visit. "Well, hello there, Sheriff; this is a pleasant surprise? Come on in, I will make us some tea."

Going in, Melissa removed her hat respectfully; she had tied her hair back with a ribbon knowing she would be removing her hat a lot today. She walked over to the kitchen table then sat watching Ruby fuss over arranging cake on a plate. It gave Mell the time she needed to muster up the courage to tell her friend that Cookie was dead, and it was her fault. She sighed sadly, watching the tiny mousy brown-haired woman thoughtfully. Ruby was quite a bit slimmer than her brother had been... shorter too, but she did have the same hazel eyes. She waited until the older woman sat down once the tea and cake were set on the table before the sheriff looked Cookie's sister straight in the eyes searchingly.

Ruby stared at Melissa in concern, finally taking notice of her friends upset expression then eyed the sheriff's badge; she frowned knowingly as she sat forward anxiously. "This isn't a social call, is it?"

Shaking her head sadly, Melissa reached out for Ruby's hand in support. "No, I'm terribly sorry; Cookie was gunned down over two weeks ago at the ranch with all the other men... except for Wade and my father."

Melissa told the whole story first then held Ruby consolingly while she cried on Mell's shoulder.

Getting herself under control, Ruby sat back. She wiped her tear-stained face on her apron then looked up at Melissa in gratitude. "Thank you, Sheriff, for coming to tell me personally. I also want you to know I appreciate your thoughtfulness in burying him at your place; Cookie loved you and the ranch."

Sighing in relief, Melissa hadn't realized she was worried about it until now. In her subconscious mind, she wondered if she was doing the right thing in burying the men at her place... instead of in town at the church graveyard. She frowned sadly before reaching out then patted Ruby's hand in sympathy. "It was the least I could do. I have something for you."

Taking out the bank note with Ruby's name on it; Melissa pushed it across the table towards her.

Ruby stared at it then gasped as she looked up in shocked surprise at Melissa, but didn't touch the note. She had never seen that kind of money in her life. "Mell, you don't have to do this; Cookie knew when he decided to stay working for you it was dangerous. We talked about it many times, he was always aware that because you were the sheriff you would have enemies that might come after you at any time."

Taking Ruby's hand again, Melissa squeezed it gently in reassurance and support. "I know I don't need to do this, but all the men earned this money just for sticking with me all these years. Even though I couldn't pay them much in the beginning, I now have more than enough money to look after their families since they cannot; as you can see the note is only in your name, this is your inheritance from your brother. Put some money in the bank for each of your children, take the rest... spend it on yourself. A horse and buggy would be a great investment so you can come to the ranch as often as you wish. I will also send you all his belongings which are still at the ranch once we have them all sorted out, okay?"

Standing up, Ruby reached over before hugging Melissa in gratitude. "Thank you so very much for your thoughtfulness; I'll take your good advice."

Returning the hug enthusiastically, Melissa smiled in pleasure as she sat back down. She waited for Ruby to sit before continuing. "Good... now to change the subject, I do have another reason for being here. I would like to invite you to the ranch next week for my wedding; I will bring you a proper invitation later. It will be a good opportunity for you to see where we buried your brother."

Ruby's eyes enlarged in shocked surprise at the news of Melissa's marriage; she grinned in delight and congratulations at this turn of events. Her smile of wonder turned mischievous as she smirked teasingly then guessed correctly. "I'm absolutely amazed and ecstatic for you... let me guess, you are marrying the new deputy you hired not too long ago."

It was Melissa's turn to be shocked; her eyebrows rose in baffled inquiry "How do you know I hired another deputy?"

Laughing pleased with herself for guessing correctly, Ruby hesitated; unsure if she should tell Melissa but she gave in quickly unable to keep a secret for long... she shrugged good-naturedly. "Greg went to Chelsie's the day you brought the deputy to town. He was complaining to everybody who would listen about him. My James happened to be at the saloon at the time so he ran home to tell me."

Smiling in humour, Melissa couldn't picture the black haired, short, chubby James's rushing home; because Ruby's husband never ran... ever! He was too fat to hurry anywhere, but she nodded in understanding then stood up to leave. "You're right I'm marrying my new deputy. I also want you to know before I go that you can come out to the ranch anytime you like to visit Cookie's grave."

Ruby inclined her head in thanks as she got up and gave Melissa a farewell hug before she left.

Going out the door, Melissa whistled to her horse; mounting she turned back towards town then headed for Dan's mothers.

CHAPTER NINE

Melissa rode up to the hotel and climbed wearily down from her horse then tethered him loosely to the hitching post. Exhausted both mentally and physically, the strain showed plainly on her expressive face; Mell climbed the stairs before entering the main lobby slowly.

The clerk looked up instantly then smiled in pleasure at the sight of her; he waved down the hallway towards his private rooms. "Afternoon Sheriff your new deputy took a private dining room... if you follow me, I will take you to him."

Nodding, Melissa didn't comment as she followed the tall skinny clerk. She always joked that the man was so thin and sombre looking he should be an undertaker. He had a long thin face with a beak nose he liked to look down when talking to someone... with hair plus eyes midnight black; it just added to the effect of a mortician, which they liked to be called now.

The clerk ushered Mell into a room silently then bowed his way out.

Jed waited until the hotel clerk was gone before walking over to gather Melissa into his arms in sympathy; no words were needed, her expression said it all. He released her after a few minutes then led her to the table... he sat her down in a chair. Grey Wolf picked up a glass waiting then handed her a generous shot of whiskey, he watched her swallow it in one gulp. He chuckled as she sat there shuddering for a few minutes in reaction before taking a deep breath. Finally, she was able to relax back in her chair gratefully. Kneeling beside Mell, he took her hands in support then frowned in concern. "Are you okay now?"

Nodding in thanks, Melissa beamed down at Jed as she squeezed his hands in reassurance. "I'm fine, when did you get here?"

Getting up now that he was satisfied, she was all right, Jed sat across the table from her before answering; he waved towards the saloon. "Chelsie suggested I take a private dining room just in case you needed time alone."

There was a discreet knock on the door suddenly.

Frowning in irritation at the interruption, Jed sighed resignedly before looking towards the door then called out loudly. "Come in."

A pretty plump blonde woman came in with a tray, she served them lunch and coffee before leaving without saying a word or even looking directly at them; she had been told to be discreet... she took her job very seriously.

Jed continued the discussion after the serving woman left. "I got here twenty minutes ago. Chelsie was a big help, if it were not for her, I would probably still be looking. The six men I hired will be here in less than an hour to introduce, themselves; I also hired Brad Anderson to move out to the ranch."

Smiling in pleasure, Melissa thought of her friend Jane. "Good; you did an excellent job, Brad and his wife will be perfect... thank you."

They finished the rest of their meal in silence before pushing their plates away; sitting back, they enjoyed their coffee.

Standing up to leave, Melissa was getting impatient now to get the rest of the day done. "Why don't we go talk to the judge now? I will leave a message with the hotel clerk for the new hands to head out to the ranch instead... I can meet the men there later. If we don't leave soon the trip to Brian's will take forever and we probably won't get back to the ranch until well after midnight; we would end up missing our engagement supper."

Nodding Jed smirked saucily at Melissa before bowing obediently. "As you wish... I serve and obey!"

Laughing in delight at Jed's impertinent answer, Melissa slapped him playfully for his insolence before leaving the room. They walked into the lobby where the clerk was waiting; he was all too happy to give the men the information.

Taking Jed to her office first, Jed gathered up the report she filled in earlier for the judge before they headed back across the street then turned right. They walked a block to the courthouse and entered the building. Mell went up to the desk to talk to the secretary first.

Following behind Melissa, Jed was unsure where to go.

Melissa smiled cheekily at the steel grey-haired formidable secretary that had been with John Elton since he took office. John was both the judge and mayor of their small town. Lucy was almost as tall as Mell, but she was brawnier not fat at all just husky; she was also exceptionally strong from helping her father on the farm. If Lucy didn't want to let you into the judge's office she would stand in your way physically. Once planted, it was impossible to move her. "Hi Lucy, is Judge Elton in today, I need to speak to him... it's important."

Lucy looked up then nodded before grinning at Melissa as she motioned towards the judge's office invitingly. "As a matter of fact, he is; you just caught him before he left for lunch, so you can go right in... Sheriff."

Snickering down at Lucy teasingly, Melissa gestured impatiently before planting her fists on her hips in demand. "How many times do I have to tell you to call me Mell?"

Shrugging dismissively, Lucy smiled in pleasure before bantering back playfully. "Sorry, Sheriff, when you are on duty and I'm on duty formalities must be observed."

Melissa threw her hands up dramatically in anger. "I give up you will never change, Lucy."

Beaming in guiltless gratification, Lucy waved them towards the judge's office.

Jed chuckled in delight at Melissa's theatrics as they walked down the hallway; he looked over at her curiously before lowering his voice... not wanting the secretary to hear him. "Does it bother you that much?"

Shaking her head negatively, Melissa smirked in amusement as she pointed behind her at Lucy. "No, but it has become a routine with her; only once did I forget to ask her to call me Mell... she wouldn't speak to me for two days afterwards."

Snorting in understanding, Jed didn't comment further.

Knocking Melissa pushed open the door to the judge's office before entering; she walked up to his desk and waited patiently for John to look up.

John lifted his head, quite annoyed at being interrupted. Until he saw who it was; a big smile lit up his robust face in surprised pleasure and greeting. "Well, hello, Sheriff! I haven't seen you in over two weeks... where have you been. It's not like you to stay away for so long unless you are on the trail."

Nodding in greeting, Melissa's expression sobered instantly; she put her report down on the desk in front of John before gesturing seriously to emphasize how important the report was. "I have two good things to tell you... one really bad thing and an invitation as well."

Laughing knowingly, John propped his elbows on his desk and put his chin in his hands in attentiveness. "Well, what else is new; it's always a mixture of good news and bad with you... you can definitely start with the good first."

Melissa nodded gravely before beckoning Jed forward then pointed to him in introduction. "Judge John Elton, I would like you to meet Jed Brown; he is my new deputy."

John sat up straight all business now before standing up.

Jed leaned across the desk offering his hand.

The two men sized each other up silently, neither letting go until they were satisfied with what they saw.

Assessing the rotund judge with his rosy plump cheeks and his almost complete baldhead; Jed saw mirth, honesty... plus compassion in his expressive hazelnut brown eyes. When he had stood up Jed noticed that Judge Elton was only half an inch shorter than Melissa. Grey Wolf liked John's handshake it was firm but not crushingly so for such a big man. After staring intently at each other for a few minutes, both men smiled an approving smile; just like that, they were friends.

Letting go of John's hand, Jed stepped back out of Melissa's way.

Melissa shook her head in dumbfounded amazement at the both of them before continuing... she didn't comment on their quick friendship. "I deputized Jed in the field so you will have to deputize him properly since he will now be my full time, deputy; I also deputized a Cheyenne Chief, by the name of Giant Bear."

John nodded in confusion... wondering what happened to Greg. He took out his bible without hesitation knowing Melissa would explain after he was done; within minutes, Jed was officially a deputy.

Frowning thoughtfully to herself, Melissa listened to John's words. Yep, she had known she didn't get the deputies' oath right. Oh well... it wouldn't hurt either man to think themselves responsible for the innocent, 'as long as they lived'; instead of, 'as long as they wore a badge'.

Rummaging in his desk, John pulled out a contract that Jed needed to fill out then sign. Judge Elton handed it to the new deputy before looking at him intently to explain what it was for. "This is a required form; in case anything happens to you we will know who to get a hold of in your family. Melissa and I decided we needed this kind of information when a former deputy of hers died in the line of duty. We couldn't find out where he was from or who to contact; afterwards, we made this up to help in future cases of emergency."

Nodding Jed took the paper to a chair; he sat down to read the contract before filling in the document.

John motioned towards Melissa, curiously. "Do you want to take a deputy's contract to your chief; I would suggest that we just add his name to our list of part time ones... if you don't need him all the time."

Melissa inclined her head in agreement. "Just add him to the list, please."

Smiling down smugly at John after he sat back down; Melissa motioned casually. "I will also need you to come out to the ranch in eight days to be a witness at my marriage."

Staring up in stunned disbelief for a moment; like Melissa's father, John had almost given up on the possibility of Mell ever finding a husband. Judge Elton whooped in joy as he jumped back up then leaned across his desk to hug her ecstatically. "When did this happen... who are you marrying?"

Melissa pointed behind her at Jed when John released her so he would see her gesture. "There is your culprit right over there, I was officially asked last night. This also brings me to the invitation... we are having a supper tonight; I would like you and your wife to come. Oh, I guess I should tell you that Wade is marrying Gloria so they will be married with us. Chief Giant Bear wants to remarry his wife, Mary, in the white man's way. So, they will renew their vows before he takes them home to Montana. You and your wife will be the only guests tonight then a week from tomorrow we will be having our wedding."

Dropping into his chair in astonishment at all the marriages happening at once; John held up his hands in confusion to stop Melissa's excited explanation... it wasn't making any sense to the judge anyway. "I think you better start from the beginning and take it slowly."

Nodding Melissa sat down, she told the story knowing her job was on the line; even knowing that she told the whole truth without leaving anything out.

John listened to the whole sordid story from beginning to

end without asking even one question; if Melissa forgot something Jed would remind her. Judge Elton watched the sheriff closely. He had known her way too long to be fooled by her calm guarded expression. She crossed a line she had put in place herself... and they both knew it. The new deputy would be unaware of this he knew, since Grey Wolf didn't know Mell well yet.

Voice trailing off in uncertainty, Melissa waited tensely for what was to come. The silence dragged on until she wanted to scream. John's fingers began drumming loudly on his desk as he stared off into space. She knew he was deciding her fate; her body tensed even more... fearing the worst. Just when Mell figured she couldn't take any more, Judge Elton's fingers stilled.

Sitting forward resignedly, John propped his elbows on the desk then put his head into his hands, rubbing his face tiredly. Judge Elton lowered his hands onto the desk; folding them, he looked towards Jed grimly, ignoring Melissa. "Shadow Killers, I always thought they were a myth made up to scare people away from Montana. Now you are telling me they are real... plus, it just happens to be our sheriff who started them on their killing rampage against women!"

Jed nodded sadly. "Yes, it looks that way."

John turned to Melissa. He stared at her intently until she began squirming in her chair uneasily. Knowing her the way he did, the mayor knew he had to come up with some kind of punishment to appease her. Sighing, Judge Elton sat forward then pointed at her grimly. "You crossed a line you yourself put in place. On the other hand, it is nice to see you are human and make mistakes like the rest of us... sometimes I wondered if you were. You will go to church then confess your sin to Father Renolds. Afterwards, the slate will be wiped clean; this discussion never took place and nobody except us or the ones involved will know about it. Is that clear to the both of you?"

Opening her mouth to argue, Melissa snapped it shut when John held up his hand to forestall her. "I will hear no arguing on this matter; one mistake can't undo all the years of good you have done for this town... now go!"

Jed looked from one to the other in confusion, unsure what that was all about."

*****

Melissa and Jed finally walked out of the judge's office... she turned to Jed with a weary sigh. "Well, I am glad that is over. We finished everything now except for seeing Brian. All the new hands should be on their way to the ranch by now. All the relatives of the dead were informed except for one; I have to send a letter by stagecoach for that one. Let's hurry to Brian's so we can get home at a half decent time it's been an exhausting day already."

Nodding thoughtfully, Jed followed Melissa across the street to collect the packhorse before strolling back to the hotel for their horses. He couldn't help thinking as he mounted that the next few hours could be the most difficult of the day. Brian wasn't going to be too happy with all the things Melissa must tell him. Number one, he needed to be told about his friend's death... plus Greg's betrayal. They would also inform him that his sister's husband wasn't dead, which he believed all these years; then they would be letting him know Giant Bear was taking Mary and their son Tommy away with him.

Brian would also be informed that Melissa was going to marry Jed. He wasn't sure which piece of news the man was going to take the hardest; Grey Wolf would bet money though, that losing Mell would hit him harder than the loss of his sister or even the death of his friend.

*****

It was a long ride from town going more northeast whereas Melissa's place was straight north from the town. It took them three hours of hard riding; thankfully, there weren't a lot of trees so it was easier going making it good land for cattle. They rode mostly in silence... not looking forward to what was to come.

At Brian's ranch, they both dismounted in front of the hitching rail. They draped the reins of their horses over the railing; neither tied them, just in case they needed to leave in a hurry.

Jed looked around curiously. The ranch house was the only other two-story house out here besides Melissa's. It was a plain house with no paint... unkempt looking. There were old harnesses, broken wagon wheels, with lots of other junk lying around. Grey Wolf was not impressed even a little; especially, after being at Mell's place hers was so neat compared to this. They walked up the stairs then across the veranda slowly, both still dreading the confrontation to come.

Lifting her hand to knock, Melissa jumped back instead when the door swung open violently; she almost fell inside.

Brian sneered in anger as he stared at the two trespassers belligerently. "What do you want?"

Both of them could hear the fury plain in Brian's voice; although, it was Jed who smelt the liquor first. He took a small protective step towards Melissa... he just couldn't help it. Grey Wolf eyed the man assessing him intently. He didn't like what he saw at all. He was shorter than Mell by a good three inches. He was not fat, but husky with a quick temper by the look of him. Mary's brother had mousy brown hair with a thick handlebar moustache that he was obviously proud of and squinty blue eyes. He looked older by about ten years, which would make him around forty-five. There was quite a bit of grey around his temples with the start of a receding hairline. He would probably be bald in another five years or so. He was not handsome or ugly, more in-between the two, making him unremarkable in a crowd.

Melissa smiled coaxingly at Brian before motioning calmly. "Hello Brian, can we come in; I would like to talk to you for a few minutes if you don't mind?"

Brian moved back obediently before moderating his tone a little; both visitors could still clearly hear the anger in his voice. "Come in then if you must!"

Leading the way into the den, Brian turned to look at his visitors in inquiry; he continued to keep a hostile chill in his voice, though. "Do either of you want a drink... brandy or whiskey maybe?"

They both shook their heads negatively.

Melissa scowled in disapproval at Brian's back when he turned away then picked up a glass. "No Brian, you know I hardly ever drink; especially while on duty."

This afternoon had been an exception of course but he didn't need to know about that.

Snorting in derision, Brian walked over to his chair before dropping into it disrespectfully as he looked up. He didn't invite the two unwanted visitors to sit. "Yeah, I know... so, I will ask you again; what, do you want?"

Jed and Melissa sat down on the divan facing the chair that Brian slumped into, even though they hadn't been invited to. She eyed the brandy glass he put down beside his chair in surprise, looking around she saw several empty decanters littering the place. Mell decided to ignore it. She cleared her throat then gentled her tone not wanting to hurt him too much, at one time they were quite good friends. "Just over two weeks ago my ranch was invaded by a group of outlaws... almost everyone was killed; the only ones to survive it were Gloria, Wade, Tommy, and my father. We unfortunately were away looking for these outlaws when they hit the ranch."

Interrupting heatedly, Brian sat forward in his chair; he waved his hand around in fury. "What has that got to do with me?"

Melissa couldn't help being taken aback by the resentful challenging tone of Brian's question; she motioned placating in reassurance. "Well, nothing directly."

Pausing only for a moment in surprise, Melissa watched as Brian relaxed back in his chair as if in relief... before she continued as if she hadn't been interrupted. However, her puzzled frown remained at Brian's strange behaviour. "I wanted to be the one to tell you because Tommy is your nephew. It is important that you hear it from me, because it was Greg who betrayed the ranch then ended up dead; everyone knows how close the two of you were..."

Scowling deeply perplexed, Melissa quit talking in mid-sentence at the rage on her former friend's face.

Brian interrupted Melissa enraged; he sat forward intently before gesturing in furious denial as he shouted at Mell in an angry frenzy. "Tommy is... 'NOT' my nephew, I don't want you to ever call him that again!"

Melissa stood up instantly in agitation totally frustrated; she started pacing back and forth just as irate now as Brian was. She couldn't believe how stubbornly bull-headed he was when it came to his nephew. Mell suddenly stopped pacing then stared down at him in livid incomprehension before motioning imploringly. "He is so your nephew whether you want to admit it or not. The other reason we stopped here is to let you know that Tommy and his mother won't be coming here again. Mary's husband will be taking them to his people, contrary to what you believe the Indian you killed that day wasn't her husband."

Jumping out of his chair in a heartbeat, Brian stood toe to toe with Melissa; he balled his fists ready to swing forgetting for a moment that she was a sheriff. "NEVER... I will kill them both first!"

Stepping back hurriedly, totally taken by surprise; Melissa didn't expect that reaction from Brian at all. Instinctively her hands automatically dropped to her guns in reaction. Instantly, she was ready to draw if she needed to.

Jed had been watching silently up to this point. When Brian jumped out of his chair in a temper to confront Melissa; Grey Wolf also sprang up off the settee before putting his hand over his gun... in warning.

Brian saw movement behind Melissa when she stepped back; it wasn't till then he noticed Jed's movement towards his gun. He threw his hands up in surrender before falling back into his chair dejectedly. He hadn't seen Mell's quick reaction either, not until he looked at her and saw her hand hovering over her gun.

Walking over to the mantle, Jed turned to face the two of them; now he had a better view of what was taking place. He stood quietly letting Melissa handle this but making sure the man knew he was there. Grey Wolf kept his hand on his gun in warning so Brian wouldn't get any more wild ideas.

Sighing in relief, Melissa dropped her hand from the butt of her gun... she backed up and settled back on the divan. Mell gestured consolingly at her former friend as she continued the conversation. "Brian, I know this is difficult for you but your sister loves Giant Bear. I will leave you now to think about coming to grips with your hatred of Indians; I hope you can come to terms with your feelings by next week. If you do, you can come to the wedding."

Brian sat forward apprehensively as he stared at Melissa then demanded indignantly. "Who's wedding? According to Mary... she's already married to that damned Indian!"

Nodding before exhaling noisily in resignation, Melissa tensed for an explosion that she knew was imminent. "Wade and Gloria are getting married next week."

At this good news, Brian began to relax back into his chair in disinterest.

Ignoring his reaction not finished yet, Melissa continued to speak calmly. "Your sister and Giant Bear will also be renewing their vows; plus, I will be getting married too."

Instantly surging to his feet again in shocked rage, Brian motioned in disbelief. "Who the hell are you getting married to?"

Melissa frowned in relief, at least he had forgotten about Mary for the moment. She looked up at Brian but didn't rise herself as she spoke softly in an apologetic voice. Mell was aware he had wanted to marry her all these years; she pointed towards the mantle where Jed was standing. "I'm marrying my new deputy."

Standing for a moment in a state of indignation, Brian pointed over at Jed incredulously. "You are marrying him?"

Brian sputtered, so infuriated he was unable to say anything or move for a few minutes... too stunned at first. He pulled himself together before bringing his hand back in front of him and gestured sharply in demand. "Why, you don't even know him? He comes out of nowhere, a drifter then you decide to make him a deputy before marrying him; he is probably after you for your ranch and money!"

Taking a menacing step forward in anger, Jed paused when Melissa lifted her hand towards him to stop his advancement. Grey Wolf backed up to the mantle once more to listen; interested in how she was going to handle this.

Melissa's tone turned frosty with warning before she stood up heatedly. She watched Brian's expression closely as she demanded in a deadly soft voice. "First off, Jed knows the ranch goes with my job so he couldn't get it even if he wanted it; as for money, nobody knows anything about that... where did you get your information?"

Unprepared, Brian was completely caught off guard by Melissa's question; he stood there sputtering... not sure what to say at first, then apprehensively cleared his throat uneasily. "Your father told me."

Narrowing her eyes skeptically, Melissa highly doubted her dad told him anything. She decided to let it go for now, Mell would check with Alec later. She didn't want to accuse Mary's brother of anything until she knew for sure. She sighed in exasperation. "Brian, my deputy doesn't know about any money. Technically, I don't have any... it's my father's, not mine. Jed isn't a drifter either; he was searching for the men who murdered his family. Now that they are all dead, his family can rest in peace so he is ready to settle down. As for just meeting him, well that one did rather take me by surprise. You have heard of love at first sight though, haven't you?"

Brian inclined his head mutely in reply not sure what to say.

Melissa nodded thoughtfully remembering their first meeting and the tingling feeling that had confused her at first. "I fell in love with Jed almost the first moment I laid eyes on him... I make no excuses for that. Now, if you can overcome your feelings of hatred; I'm sure your sister would love for you to come to her wedding."

Glaring at Melissa in disbelief, Brian turned towards Jed then glowered at him with intense animosity; he turned back to Mell, spitting out in anger with balled up impotent fists... he shouted. "NEVER..."

Shrugging her shoulders in resignation at Brian's stubbornness, Melissa turned to leave. Mell threw one more statement over her shoulder in parting. "So be it, but that is a real shame. Plus, your loss! Come on Jed; let's get out of here!"

It took them just over an hour but to Jed it seemed more like several; thankfully, they were finally riding away from the ranch. He took a moment to ponder all he heard during their encounter with Mary's brother. He had known it was going to be difficult coming here from everything he heard about the man they just left. Grey Wolf learned a few unexpected things about Brian... about himself as well.

The first thing Jed noticed were the empty brandy decanters sitting on the mantle. It was as if Brian was in deep mourning; it didn't make any sense, how could he know about Greg before they told him. Nobody else knew until today, unless somebody rode out from town to tell him while they were with the judge. Or, maybe the neighbour who helped Wade to bury the men at the ranch told him. That couldn't be it either, nobody knew at that time about Melissa's deputy.

In addition, why was Brian so jumpy when Melissa mentioned the massacre at the ranch? Despite the drinking, the two men couldn't have been that close of friends. He didn't mention or commented on Greg's death; not even once after he was told, as if not surprised by their news. So, someone must have gotten there first, it's the only thing that makes logical sense.

Jed was right in surmising that Brian would be more upset to learn of Melissa's upcoming wedding then about the news of his sister's leaving. He also wondered how the man learned about this money belonging to Mell... like his fiancée, he doubted Mary's brother found out from Alec. Whenever she mentioned her neighbours name, her father would frown apprehensively and tense up; it was obvious to Grey Wolf that he didn't like him much.

Then there was what Jed learned about himself. Although, he promised Melissa last night when he asked her to marry him that he would let her handle things as sheriff. He did have self-doubts that he would be able to hold back if she were actually threatened. He now knew he could... up to a point. Grey Wolf looked over at Mell before frowning curiously; he motioned inquisitively. "What is all this about money, what was Brian talking about if you don't mind my asking?"

Melissa looked over at Jed and shook her head negatively, she didn't mind his questions at all. She was actually relieved he asked her about it. Mell didn't want anything to come between them now. "Before my dad met my mom, he liked gambling a lot. One night he went to a high stakes poker game that he knew was being held. He won a lot of money plus a deed to a house. When he went to look at it, he was extremely shocked to find out he was now the owner of a fancy house and gambling den. There was no way that he was going to run such a business, so he sold it right away for a substantial profit. When he married my mother, he bought a half interest in the ranch that he worked on as foreman. The owner was in financial trouble at the time. After the accident that killed my mom, dad sold his share of the ranch for a profit back to the original owner then came to live with me. About ten years ago, he bought into a dry gold mine that a friend of his said was not dry. My father gave his friend five thousand dollars to buy the land and equipment needed and wouldn't you know it; the man was right. They struck a new vein of gold three years ago, now my dad is well off. The lumber business is also quite lucrative. We have tried to keep it quiet because he didn't want anybody to know, so how

Brian found out is beyond me. I'm sure my father didn't tell him... that money is his, it has nothing to do with me whatsoever."

Jed nodded his head thoughtfully; he was somewhat in the same boat himself. He came from a wealthy family back east but because he didn't make the money himself, he felt he had no right to it. The estates he has back home he let his friend manage for him so the money just keeps building up. Grey Wolf sighed knowingly then motioned in sympathy. "I know how you feel my family moved from England when I was a baby to Boston. They went into shipping, which was a good choice since they have done quite well. My father had a title in England. Thankfully, he left it behind when we moved. Since I never had anything to do with the business, I never felt I had any right to the money or the titles. My whole family was angry with me for going to Montana. When I talked my wife into coming with me, my dad almost had a fit. Especially since, I was the only one in my family to have a boy at the time. Everyone else had girls so he would have been the next heir to father's shipping company. As it turned out my dad was right but there is nothing, I can do about it now."

Melissa frowned sadly when Jed mentioned his dead son; she couldn't help wondering what his family would think of her... she waved unhappily at Grey Wolf. "I suppose your family will not like me because I'm a sheriff."

Shaking his head negatively, Jed laughed in delight as he imagined his father's reaction to his new wife. He gestured towards Melissa in reassurance. "Now there you are wrong, my dad especially will like you; I even know what he will say after he finishes yelling at me for taking my family into the wildness with me and not looking after them properly. He will look you over carefully then say... 'Well, I must say, at least you found someone as strong as you are this time. I will expect strapping grandsons from such a fine figure of a woman, tall ones too'!"

Laughing at Jed's imitation of his father's British accent, Melissa shook her head at him in disbelief. "You're just making that up; he will not say any such thing."

Smiling knowingly, Jed put his hand over his heart significantly. "Cross my heart; I'm not lying that is exactly what he will say."

In amusement, Melissa shook head in incredulity before grinning at Jed's theatrics. "How many brothers and sisters do you have?"

Sighing in resignation, Jed grimaced in false horror as he waved in aggravation playfully trying to be melodramatic. "Too many... I have two older brothers, one older sister, and two younger sisters."

Laughing at Jed's expression of suffering, Melissa's face turned wishful. "Was it really that bad?"

Nodding vigorously Jed scowled dramatically again. "You have no idea! We all fought constantly; my mother would be so fed up with the lot of us she would chase us all out of the house with a broom. My mom never believed in having nursemaids, she wanted to raise us herself. She told me once that when she lived in England, she never saw her parents ever. Just her nurse was around and she didn't want that for her kids. We did have a huge black housekeeper who helped her a lot. When that woman bellowed at you... you better run for your life."

Melissa chuckled in amusement; she pictured an older feminine Jed screaming at the top of her lungs then chasing her kids outside with a broom. Once she got control of her laughter. Mell sighed wistfully again... she looked back at Grey Wolf. "I always wanted a brother or sister but after my mother died, I stopped wishing."

Jed smirked in invitation. "If I could do so I would give you a few of my siblings; it's not all that fun you know."

Smiling over at Jed in sympathy; although, Melissa didn't really feel all that sorry for him. "Maybe, but if you were an only child; you would want a few siblings, as well."

Laughing in agreement, Jed sighed after a bit. "Yeah, you're probably right; at least we all loved one another and helped each other out when we could."

Heaving a sigh in anticipation, Melissa waved eagerly. "I can't wait to meet them all."

Chortling in forewarning, Jed shook his head in horror at the thought of Melissa with his brothers and sisters. "You might change your mind later."

Shaking her head negatively, Melissa answered him seriously. "No, I don't think so."

Jed just smiled knowingly, but didn't comment further.

Smirking back confidently, Melissa didn't continue the conversation either. She nudged her horse into a canter wanting to get home. They rode the rest of the way in silence, immersed in their own thoughts; neither paid any attention to the beautiful sunset as they rode west towards Mell's ranch.

CHAPTER TEN

Melissa and Jed rode into the yard thankful to be home; they both saw Tommy running towards them at the same time so they halted immediately... dismounting they waited for him to get to them. Mell smiled at her foster son in greeting, as well as thanks when he took the reins from her. "Well hello sweetheart, how's everything going so far?"

Tommy grinned in pride at getting everything done Melissa wanted him to do, plus a few things extra. "We cleaned the bunkhouse like you asked; good think Uncle Wade showed up to help, we just got finished when the new hands got here. He suggested cleaning the barn next... we finished that about an hour ago. Giant Bear wanted to have a bath afterwards, so I took him to the creek. I offered to fill a tub for him but he wouldn't go for that. He is all dressed up in a fancy buckskin outfit pacing, he seems upset about something. Uncle Wade came to the barn just before we went to the creek then talked to the chief. It seemed to help for a while."

Nodding in approval, Melissa's her expression became serious. "And your mother is here?"

Vigorously, Tommy shook his head yes before his chest puffed up in satisfaction as he boasted. "Yes, she is; I did what you asked, not once did I let Mom anywhere near the barn. I didn't tell her anything about Jed or Giant Bear either."

Grinning in relief, Melissa ruffled Tommy's hair in affection. "Good boy... you did an excellent job today. You can take the horses to the barn and ask Giant Bear to unsaddle them for me; it will keep him occupied for a bit. Afterwards, go up to the house and help there for the rest of the night. Since you look like you already had a bath you won't need one, but I do. You can start heating water for me please."

Beaming up in delight at having another job to do, Tommy nodded eagerly. "Yes, ma'am when I went to the creek with Giant Bear, I decided to have a bath there too. It was really cold; I wouldn't want to do that in the winter... I would freeze to death."

Turning without waiting to hear Melissa's reply, Tommy ran to the barn with the three horses following him obediently.

Looking over at Jed, Melissa pointed to her left; not far from the west side of the house but not too close. "That is where I want to put Wade and Gloria's cabin."

Turning more, Melissa gestured to her left again, it was closer to the barn but further back... she waved. "That is where I want to put Brad and Jane; the screen of trees between the two cabins will give them a little privacy from each other."

Nodding, Jed looked in the directions she indicated then he turned back to Melissa... he motioned in appreciation. "Those are really good spots, there are a lot of trees behind where the cabins are going to be giving them more privacy; it will also make a good windbreak for warmth in the winter."

Grinning in pleasure at his praise, Melissa turned towards the bunkhouse expectantly. "Let's go meet the new ranch hands you picked out."

Melissa led the way but let Jed go into the bunkhouse first to make sure everybody was dressed and ready for an inspection; Grey Wolf beckoned the all clear to her... Mell walked onto the porch then through the door.

The new hands were standing in a row waiting to be inspected.

Smiling in pleasure, Melissa recognized the youngest and went up to him first. "Hi, Dusty; I saw your mother today. I didn't know you wanted to work for me or I would have asked you before."

Beaming shyly at Melissa, Dusty fidgeted slightly in embarrassment when she went to him first. He shrugged off his shyness enough to answer her truthfully. "I would have asked sooner but Pa still needed me; now that my brother is old enough... he said I could go."

Nodding before shaking Dusty's hand warmly, Melissa tried to put him more at ease. "Good to have you aboard."

Dusty was Lucy's son... she was the judge's secretary. Her son was one of the hardest workers Melissa had ever seen. He was good looking and the same height as her right now. He had midnight black hair with deep brown expressive eyes. The girls just loved him, but he was so bashful he would stammer in their presence then run away before any of them could even say hi. He was only seventeen years old and a bit awkward with his big feet. Unless he had a job to do; instantly, he would forget about his feet and shyness long enough to get things done efficiently. Mell definitely approved of Dusty being chosen.

Melissa turned to the next man. He was the exact opposite of Dusty. His looks were only medium with no shyness in him at all. If she remembered rightly, he was quite bold and extremely outspoken. It had gotten him into trouble a few times, nothing serious though that she could recall. He did have a bit of a gambling problem. She didn't allow high stakes here anyway so it shouldn't be an issue. The man had brown hair with laughing hazel eyes. He was painfully slim, plus wiry, not afraid of work either. She shook his hand in greeting; Mell liked the firm, but not crushing grip he used. She also liked the fact that he looked her in the eye with a straightforward gaze... she nodded pensively. "Kenneth, right?"

Grinning pleased that Melissa remembered him, Kenneth smirking in delight... remembering the last time they met. "That's right Sheriff, but you can call me Ken; you helped me get out of a few scrapes the last few years."

Melissa smirked recalling the last time he got in a brawl at the saloon; she intervened to save his hide, but she didn't hold that against him. "Welcome aboard."

Turning to the next man in line, Melissa looked at him intently as she frowned in reflection. "I don't think I know you."

The man beamed good-naturedly at Melissa; he reached out to shake her hand enthusiastically in introduction. "No, you don't... I'm Darrel. I used to work in the next town, but they could only keep me on until after round up. When your man happened to come into the saloon offering a yearly job I jumped at the chance; Chelsie vouched for me, so did one of the hands I worked with."

Darrel was attractive but not as handsome as Dusty. He was the oldest man there with more salt than pepper in his hair, it brought out the pale blue colour of his eyes. The man was husky, not anywhere near fat though. He smiled or squinted a lot by the looks of the wrinkles around his eyes and mouth. The new hand was taller than Melissa, she also liked his handshake... it was firm and he had an honest face; she smiled at him in welcome before nodding approval. "Welcome aboard."

Paul was next... Melissa shook his hand in greeting. He was the only black man there, he had tight curly black hair with dark brown sorrowful eyes; he was not quite the shortest one there, although close to it. Mell had always liked him, ever since he moved to town about a year ago. Not once did she see him in the saloon or going into Pam's house! He was quiet, very shy with never much to say but he was always polite. "Hello Paul, nice to see you here; I'm glad you could come to work for me."

Shaking her hand with a grin, Paul enthused. "Yous Deputy came to me house; I could no pass up the chance to works for yah."

Grinning pleased, Melissa nodded in approval. "Good!"

Melissa turned before frowning in surprise at the two men she didn't expect to see here. "I know both of you, Mark and Tomas I believe."

They both nodded then shook her hand one at a time as Melissa eyed both men closely; curious to hear their explanations. "I thought both of you worked for Victor Gray... so, why are you here?"

Shrugging with a confused expression plain on his face, Mark seemed unsure himself what was going on... he spoke first. "They fired me this morning with no warning or reason; just told me to collect me pay then skedaddle."

Mark was quite good looking with sandy blonde hair; he had a scar that ran down his right cheek... it gave him a rakish look. He had green eyes and was a head taller than Melissa. She remembered having only one problem with him when he drank too much and got rowdy. Other than that, he seemed a pleasant enough fellow. Mell accepted him as well. "Welcome aboard."

Looking intently up at Tomas for a long moment, Melissa frowned. He was a big burly man almost fat and just about as tall as Jed was... although not quite. He was sinfully ugly, with greasy dark brown hair. Plus, small blue squinty eyes which didn't quite match his big forehead and deep brow line; giving him an awkward look.

When Tomas first moved to town five years ago, Melissa looked through her wanted posters... she couldn't find anything on him, though. It wasn't because of his grotesque look that she checked; he just seemed familiar. As if Mell seen him somewhere before, unfortunately she could never remember where it was at. Even today, she felt that she knew him. The hairs stood up on the back of her neck in suspicion, but the sheriff never really had anything to cause her unease. In the last five years, not once was he in any trouble with the law!

Tomas shrugged dismissively not in the least concerned. "He fired me too for no reason at all."

Nodding hesitantly in welcome but not in approval, Melissa wished she had met the new hands at the hotel. She wouldn't have accepted Tomas. She wasn't sure she would have accepted Mark either; unfortunately, it was too late now. "Welcome."

Turning to the last man in relief at getting that interview completed, Melissa smiled in delight. "Brad how are you doing; did you bring Jane with you?"

Grinning back in pleasure, Brad shook his head negatively. "Nah, Jane didn't come today, cause your man wasn't sure what you were going to do with us; she will be coming tomorrow with Mrs. Elton though."

Sighing in disappointment, Melissa inclined her head in satisfaction at being able to see her friend tomorrow. "Good."

Brad was a short, plump, good-natured man... bald with grey green eyes. His wife fit him perfectly; she was slightly shorter, even chubbier than her husband. The two of them were both jolly, always laughing at each other. They were painfully honest, too much so at times.

Backing up so she could look at all seven men at the same time, Melissa motioned in caution. "Jed explained the dangers of working for me I hope?"

All seven men nodded in agreement.

Waiting for all their nods, Melissa continued. "Okay, please follow me; I'll give you a tour then let you know what will be expected of you tonight. I'm not sure what all your strengths are yet so over the next few days, Wade... my foreman, will talk to each of you separately. He will decide where to place you, as well as what job suits you best."

They all walked out of the bunkhouse and kept close to Melissa so they could hear her as she explained some of the rules.

Melissa spoke as loud as she could so none of them would

miss anything. "The first rule is that my name is Mell, not Sheriff while you work for me. The second rule is no drinking allowed while on duty... ever. When you are off duty, you can drink if you want; I will not say you can't, but remember just because you work for me doesn't mean there will be any special privileges if you get out of hand."

Smiling over her shoulder to take the sting out of that comment before turning around... Melissa continued walking and talking. "You can play poker after work, but I only allow small pots; you can only go up to a dollar per game. I started this rule because one of my hands got beat up by the others because he won all their pay for two months, now I make sure it will never happen again."

They reached the corrals then stopped.

Turning to face the men; Melissa allowed a touch of menace to enter her voice... needing them to heed her warning. "There is absolutely no beating, using whips, or cruel spurs on my horses."

Melissa looked at each man intently in turn to get her point across.

The men nodded their understanding when Melissa's gaze fell on them.

Moderating her tone once Melissa was sure they understood her. "As you are probably aware, we raise horses on the side. I have a few people that bring their mares here for us to breed Lightning to or to get broke. As you can see, I have two large corrals; one of the projects for you gentleman is to fence off a larger pasture, we want to pick up more breeding stock sometime this year."

Turning, Melissa walked towards the barn. The men followed dutifully as she continued. "Everybody also takes a turn on guard duty, Wade will organize you guys on that job. My Father takes care of the breeding, foaling, as well as the wages; you will all need to go up to the house one at a time to meet him. Wade as you know is the foreman, I will send him out to meet you all later, any specific questions you have will be directed to him... or my dad."

Opening the barn doors Melissa entered; she looked around, but didn't see Giant Bear anywhere. She looked questioningly at Jed. He shrugged then pointed up at the hayloft in silent answer to Mell's question... Grey Wolf figured correctly that his friend was hiding up there.

Melissa nodded agreeing with Jed before she turned back to the men. "We have twelve stalls in here; the horses that are used every day are kept here... as well as both stallions. There is a tack room to your left it has everything you will need. Whatever isn't in here can be found in the second bunkhouse which we use as a storage facility in the summer. In the fall, we use it for the loggers when we start harvesting trees. If you need a horse, we will supply one. If you want to buy a horse, talk to my father and he will take small payments out of your pay each month. Another plan for this year is expanding the barn or maybe even building a second one. We haven't decided yet which way we want to go."

Walking out of the barn without waiting for questions, Melissa led them towards the area she picked out for the two cabins. "The first order of business for you gentlemen... is building two cabins. Wade will take some of you down to our saw mill; it's about two miles from here, in order to bring up some lumber to get started."

When they reached the spot for Brad's cabin, Melissa turned to him inquisitively. "You have three children; one boy and two girls... am I correct?"

Brad nodded then smiled in delight as he thought of his rambunctious children. "Yes, the girls are seven and eight; my son is about to turn ten."

Melissa inclined her head already aware of that... she just wanted to make sure. "Okay, starting tomorrow you gentlemen will start building a cabin here for the Anderson family."

Looking back at Brad, Melissa gestured inquisitively. "Would you like to help me draw up a plan, Brad?"

Brad shook his head negatively. "I would be obliged if you could do that, I'm not good with plans."

Nodding, Melissa took the lead again as she moved towards the spot she picked for Wade and Gloria's cabin; she turned back to the men then continued. "After Brad's cabin is done, I want another built here. This one will be for my foreman and his intended... who will be getting married next week. I would also like all you bachelor's to know if you ever decide to marry, a cabin here will also be offered."

Waiting for the men to nod that they understood, Melissa

finished up. "Now a few other things you need to be aware of is that my father, Alec, is in a wheelchair; it's the reason we have a wood sidewalk going from the house, to the barn, corrals... as well as the bunkhouse. If you want to work with the horses or at the mill you will have to talk to my dad. If you need something that cannot wait until payday, you have to discuss that with him too. Any other concerns should be brought directly to Wade, Jed, or to me. Jed is my Deputy, but occasionally I need extra ones. If you are interested, let me know later. He is also my fiancé we will be getting married next week so any orders coming from him are to be obeyed. You can start cleaning around the spots for the cabins. If there are any other duties needed tonight, Wade will let you know. If you don't have any questions, you are free to go. Except for Dusty and Brad, I have other tasks for you tonight."

The two men singled out stayed; the other men left to start cleaning up the ground of dead brush, as well as debris. Melissa smiled at both men then waved towards the ranch house. "I am having a small dinner party tonight so I would like you two to work at the main house. The ladies could use a couple of strong men to haul water and such... if you have no objections to working inside that is."

Both men inclined their heads in agreement then waited for further instructions.

Pointing in the direction of the side door, Melissa continued. "Go to the back entrance since it is closer and tell Gloria I sent you to help out tonight; she will put the two of you to work."

They turned then left obediently without comment.

Melissa and Jed followed, but slower; she looked over before grinning at Grey Wolf earnestly. "Well, how did I handle myself?"

Jed smirked mischievously as he motioned teasingly. "Well, I think two of the men are in love already; one is halfway there."

Hitting Jed in the shoulder playfully, Melissa laughed in delight. "That's not what I meant at all and you know it!"

Rubbing his arm in mock pain, Jed chuckled knowingly... he smiled at Melissa. "You did a good job, I was impressed."

Beaming in delight at the praise, Melissa's expression

sobered as she became serious. "I'm not sure we should have taken Mark and Tomas on until I talked to Victor Gray; I have never known him to just fire someone for no reason."

Melissa thought of her father's friend. He lived directly southeast of here in a log cabin not far from town. Alec tried to talk him into letting them build him a proper home with lumber but he absolutely refused, gripping about getting soft that way. Victor was a gruff fellow; he always treated his men fairly though... as far as Mell was aware.

Frowning in concern, Jed gestured cautiously. "See, that's why I wanted you to meet them in town first; it's not too late, I can get rid of them if you like."

Seriously thinking about it for a moment, Melissa finally shook her head negatively. "No, I'm just being a bit suspicious... I guess; especially with everything that has happened around here lately and now with the threats Brian made I'm a tad jumpy, that's all. We will be seeing him tomorrow so I will ask him about the two men."

Nodding in understanding, Jed sighed in sympathy. "I don't blame you for being wary; I will talk to Wade so he knows to keep an eye on the two men. If they prove untrustworthy, I will let you know immediately."

Sighing in relief, Melissa was glad Jed didn't dismiss her feelings out of hand; they walked the rest of the way in silence. The two went around to the main entrance then went in as dusk was settling in.

Wade met them at the door in a panic. He quickly ushered them into the drawing room. He turned to face Melissa in relief glad she was here. "Mell, I used two excuses to get Mary here. First, I told her about the murders then I told her that Tommy needed her. After I got her here, I told her about my engagement party but I didn't tell her about yours. Right now, she is helping Gloria in the kitchen. I also went out a while ago to see how Giant Bear was doing... it's not good; he said if you weren't back in an hour, he was going to come to the house regardless!"

Melissa turned to Jed in concern. "You better go out and try to keep Giant Bear occupied for as long as you possible can; at least until I have a chance to tell Mary he is here... give me about an hour or so then I will send her to the barn."

Jed nodded and took off in a hurry.

Looking back at Wade, Melissa waved towards the hallway. "Good work, Wade... I will take over in here now. I would like you to go introduce yourself to the new men. They are over at the spot I picked for Brad and Jane's cabin cleaning up. You will need to take them down for a load of lumber; if you ask them, they will show you where your new cabin will be set up."

Looking at Melissa in surprised gratitude, Wade gestured incredulously. "You are going to build a cabin for us?"

Smiling, Melissa nodded affirmative. "Yes, this is our wedding present to the both of you. If you will follow me, I will quickly sketch a plan for Brad's cabin... yours too if you want; or you can do your own design."

Wade hugged Melissa in delight. "Thank you, it's the greatest gift I ever received."

Returning the hug affectionately, Melissa turned away from Wade in pleasure before leading the way to the den; when they entered, Alec was behind the desk writing. Mell walked around it and bent down to kiss her father in greeting. "Oh, just the person I wanted to see."

Alec chuckled in delight as he looked up at Melissa then shook his head in disbelief as he teased her. "No, I'm not; Jed will now fill that space."

Shaking her head emphatically, Melissa joked back. "Never, you will always be my number two man."

Laughing knowingly, Alec looked up at Wade and chortled mischievously; he grabbed at his chest in pretend pain dramatically. "You see, I'm already demoted to second place."

Smiling down fondly at her dad, Melissa changed the subject; she pointed to the desk. "Hand me a paper so I can sketch this while I talk."

Looking up at Melissa inquisitively, Alec moved his chair out from behind the desk before wheeling himself around to the other side curious to see what his daughter was up to. "You can use the desk if you like... paper, pen, and ink are on top."

Nodding in thanks, Melissa grabbed a chair that was in the corner for her use, pulling it to the desk she sat down; Wade found a chair and moved it closer to help if Mell needed it.

Looking across at Alec for a moment before bending down, Melissa began to draw as she talked. "Dad, since you don't know any of this, I will fill you in. As you know we went to town to hire six single men; Jed suggested I hire one family to come out to live, which will give us another man plus an extra woman to help around here. Once I agreed, he hired the Anderson's for this purpose. I highly approve of his choice since I have always liked Brad's wife Jane anyway, so we need a cabin built for them. It was such a good idea that I decided we should also build a cabin for Wade and Gloria as a wedding present. Brad's cabin will have two bedrooms, a sitting room, as well as a large kitchen on the main floor... I want to put a loft above this. The loft should be big enough for his two girls to sleep in. I want the cabin back far enough from the trees so later if they want, we can add on. Wade can decide on how he wants his place set up now or later if he needs some time to think about it."

Finishing the sketch quickly, Melissa stopped talking then handed the paper of Brad's cabin to her father... anxiously she waited for their opinion. The two men studied it in interest; both men nodded at each other before Alec looked at his daughter in approval. "Yes, I like it."

Wade grinned thoughtfully and motioned down at the sketch in admiration. "We can use this sketch for our cabin too; we just won't add the extra bedroom or the loft until it's needed."

Melissa shook her head in disagreement. "Well, I think you should add both; you can always use it for storage, until you have children."

Nodding in agreement, Wade got up to leave. "I'll go out to meet the new men properly; I wasn't sure what you wanted me to do with them so I gave them instructions to stay in the bunkhouse until you got here. I'm going to look over the building sites you picked before taking them down for wood. I can surprise Gloria tonight with the good news... we had wondered where we were going to live."

Alec turned to Melissa once Wade left then waved in praise towards her. "What a good idea; we can buy them some furniture too as a wedding gift."

Shrugging dismissively at Alec, Melissa gestured in explanation. "You will have to thank Jed; it was his idea."

Nodding that he would do that, Alec changed the subject as he motioned curiously. "What about the families you visited?"

Sighing in sad recollection, Melissa thought of their

reaction to the news. Most of them didn't hold her responsible, but she blamed herself. "It was the hardest thing I ever had to do. I gave them all a thousand dollars as you suggested. The bank manager almost passed out when I asked him for eight, one-thousand-dollar bank notes; although, I couldn't find out any information on Chuck... I will keep trying. When I find his relatives I will send them their money, as well."

Alec nodded then reached across the desk for a letter of authority he made earlier; it allowed Melissa to take out two thousand dollars from his account. He handed it to her before smiling stubbornly at her astonished look... he gestured at the letter decisively. "That is half of the money you gave out of your account today."

Sighing knowingly at Alec's inflexible look, Melissa shook her head dumbfounded. Even though she knew the answer, Mell asked him anyway. "What's this for?"

Shrugging dismissively, Alec had known Melissa wouldn't want to take the money. "I wanted to contribute too since I'm part owner now."

Melissa frowned solemnly. "If you insist but there is plenty of money in the ranch account, so it's not necessary."

With an obstinate look, Alec nodded stubbornly. "I know I don't have to, but since I knew you were paying four thousand out of your own account; I wanted to put in my share... they were my friends too."

Nodding in understanding, Melissa not wanting to argue with Alec got to her feet then walked around the desk. After putting her chair back in its corner, she bent down before kissing the top of her father's head in farewell. "I have to go talk to Mary... I will see you later."

Alec went back around his desk to finish what he was doing once his daughter left.

Hurrying across the hall to the kitchen to find Mary; Melissa frowned. Her meeting with Wade took longer than she expected, she was running out of time.

Gloria turned in relief when she heard the kitchen door open and smiled in greeting then winked at Melissa in conspiracy. "There you are we have been waiting for you. I decided to have a late supper; I knew you would need time to bathe before finding something appropriate to wear for the engagement party. Mary will go upstairs with you to help get you ready. We put out some dresses earlier for you to try on. She can have a female talk with you since your mother isn't here to advise you, maybe give you a few tips because she has been married twice. I told her you were getting married with me, but I didn't tell her who you were marrying... I figured you would want to tell her yourself."

Melissa beamed in thanks at her housemaid for giving her an excuse to get Mary upstairs. "Why thank you, Gloria; how thoughtful of you."

Giving Gloria a thumb up sign behind Mary's back, Melissa ushered her out of the kitchen door. She rushed her pale blonde petite friend upstairs; not even allowing her to talk or ask questions... too afraid that Giant Bear would show up before she could explain.

When they entered Melissa's bedroom, she stopped short in surprised delight. The sight before her was unbelievable! Her bed was covered with an assortment of gowns. There were five of them all in a variety of styles and colours... enough to dazzle anyone's eyes! However, even from here Mell could tell that the styles were old; turning to Mary in appreciation, she gestured in awe. "Where in the world did all these dresses come from?"

Mary smirked in delight when she looked at Melissa before pointing up above their heads. "Alec told us there were two trunks in the attic filled with your mother's clothing; some were worn but many of them are still new looking... they should fit you. Your father told me you are about the same size as your mom was, except you are a tad taller than her, we can alter them if necessary."

A knock at the door caused Melissa to stiffen uneasily. "Yes?"

Tommy entered, followed by the new ranch hands; Dusty and Brad. They carried in a tub, with several buckets of hot water.

In relief, Melissa pulled Mary back out of the way.

It took several trips to fill the tub but finally it was full of steaming hot water; before they left Melissa called Dusty over. She motioned in request. "Can you let Tommy eat with you tonight at the bunkhouse?"

Dusty nodded and left the room closing the door behind him.

Leading Melissa to the tub, Mary helped her to undress.

Stepping into the water, Melissa sat down and sighed in bliss as the hot water enveloped her completely... except for Mell's knees sticking up because she was a too long for it.

Walking over to the bed, Mary picked up one gown before turning; she regarded her friend as she held it up to show Melissa. "While you are soaking, I will show you these lovely gowns then you can choose which one you like best."

The two girls spent the next few minutes giggling and laughing over the dresses as Mary showed them off.

Melissa settled on a turquoise gown that was perfect for her.

Setting the gown aside, Mary walked over to the tub and began washing her friend's dark blonde hair.

Groaning in contentment, Melissa enjoyed the novelty of being bathed; it felt good to be pampered. After her bath, she wrapped a towel around herself then sat on the bed to talk.

Mary removed all the dresses except for the one Melissa had chosen to wear. After putting them away, she settled beside Mell. She turned so she could see her younger friend's face better. Mary's curiosity was killing her... she waved chidingly. "You know, I never thought the day would come when I would see you get married. I didn't think there was a man good enough for you and that included my brother, but Gloria assures me the man you are marrying is well brought-up. Of course, I wouldn't know since I never knew you were even seeing anyone let alone contemplating marriage. I'm also quite curious to know who this man is; she wouldn't tell me, so what's all the secrecy about?"

Laughing at her friend's put upon expression, Melissa gestured in apology for not telling Mary about Jed sooner; things just happened so fast... she really didn't have time to tell anyone. "Sorry, it was so quick. I'll explain everything in a moment and I hope you will forgive me. As for me, I didn't think I would ever get married either. This took me completely by surprise; I couldn't find a man strong enough for me! But Jed, that is his name, is definitely man enough to handle me."

Nodding in understanding, Mary remembered that fearful time in her life when she got married to a complete stranger. However, something good did come out of it when she met her second husband... everything was alright for a time at least. "Yeah, I was quite petrified when I left home. Just be thankful you don't have to worry about leaving here. I didn't have a choice in the matter Brian forced me to marry a man I didn't even know. After the war party attacked us, everything changed for the better. I fell in love with my savage. When I found out I was pregnant I got scared then ran away; that was the worst mistake of my life. I should have stayed in the Indian village and waited for my husband to come back. You know I arranged to go back after the baby was born, but my brother killed my Indian guide so I couldn't."

Melissa listened quietly up to this point then decided now was the time to mention Giant Bear. She smiled hopefully before taking a deep breath to calm her nerves; praying this question was not too late for the Cheyenne Indian Chief and her friend's future happiness. "Mary, if your husband was here at this moment... would you still go back with him?"

Mary nodded vigorously, not even hesitating for a moment as she sighed wistfully at the thought of Giant Bear. "Of course I would... I love him more than my life; the only thing that has kept me from trying to find my way back, was our son."

Taking a deep breath for courage, Melissa reached over to take her friends hand in support as she continued. "Mary, the three men your second husband was looking for that killed his first wife all those years ago... were after me. I hired two men a little over two weeks ago, not knowing the outlaws were in North Dakota searching for me. I found out later the two new men I hired were actually after the Shadow Killers, who wanted revenge against me for something that happened when I was fifteen. Luckily, these men stayed to help me catch the murders. One of the men I hired is my husband-to-be, Jed; the other one is a Cheyenne Indian Chief from Montana, his name is Giant Bear!"

Staring at Melissa in shock, Mary remained speechless for a long moment. Finally, she managed to whisper in disbelief; although, her voice was barely above a murmur by the time she finished speaking. Tears filled her eyes then spilled over, but she didn't wipe them away. "Giant Bear is here now... are you sure? Does he know I'm here and about his son?"

Melissa nodded unhappily; she squeezed her friend's hand in compassion. "Yes, he knows Mary, but we didn't tell Tommy about him; we figured you would want to do that. Giant Bear is waiting for you in the barn, very impatiently I might add!"

Sitting still for a few more minutes in uncertainty, Mary continued to allow the tears to stream down her face. She wasn't sure what to do at first... suddenly she sprang up unexpectedly and pulled her hand away from Melissa's grip; reaching down she gave her friend a bear hug in gratitude. "I love you, Mell!"

Standing up quickly; Mary with a cry of joy, raced out of the room not even bothering to wait to hear her friend's reply. "I love you, too."

Smiling ecstatically in relief, Melissa watched Mary disappear; her question to her friend hadn't been too late. She couldn't be happier for her, especially now that Mell found love too. She now understood why her friend had grieved for Giant Bear this long.

CHAPTER ELEVEN

Jed and Giant Bear were in the barn waiting impatiently; for about the third time, the big Cheyenne Chief gestured anxiously over at Grey Wolf. "What is keeping her... do you think my Golden Dove doesn't want me anymore?"

Exhaling noisily in sympathy, Jed grimaced; it was hard to watch the apprehensive Giant Bear. He had never witnessed his friend so agitated or seen his travelling companion show such emotions in all the years they were together. Except the first day when he told Grey Wolf about his wife's brutal murder. He was just about to reassure the chief again when a figure streaked past him then fell into the Cheyenne's arms. He broke into a wide grin of relief... silently he melted away.

Giant Bear stood with his feet braced as the squirming crying bundle he held poured loving kisses all over his face; he grinned as Mary kept repeating in hesitant Cheyenne. "Nemehotatse... I love you!"

Knowing that was the only phrase Mary knew in his language when Giant Bear had left... melted his heart to hear her say it; that she would remember after all these years of them being apart, amazed him. He pulled away and took her hand leading her towards the ladder which led up to the hayloft. The chief helped her up before gently lowering her into a bed of straw. He had placed his bear fur on top, hoping it would keep the straw from digging into his wife's tender flesh then settled himself beside her. Gathering her close, he whispered tenderly. "My Golden Dove, when I found out you're here I was both gladdened and angry. I do not understand why you left the safety of my people. We will discuss that later, right now I want you too much to question you. I will love you first."

Nodding in relief not wanting to talk of unpleasantness, Mary gladly lifted her face for his kiss.

Tenderly, Giant Bear pressed his lips to his wife's tear-streaked face. While she was engrossed in his kiss; he ran his hand up her dress to feel her inner heat. He mumbled irritably to himself as he tried to undo her dress.

Having none of that, Mary too impatient to wait any longer stood up and pulled her bloomers off before kneeling down;

she pushed Giant Bear onto his back and lifted her dress to straddle him.

Giant Bear chuckled knowingly too impatient himself; he flipped aside his loincloth then sheathed himself fully within his wife's body for the first time in nine agonizing years.

Mary groaned in ecstasy; at the same time, she gave a small gasp of pain when Giant Bear's large manhood filled her. It was almost as it had been the first time around... not quite though. Golden Dove held them both still for a long moment so she could adjust to having her savage husband inside her again.

Holding still for several seconds, Giant Bear was relieved at the tight feel of his wife surrounding him. He hadn't missed Mary's small gasp of discomfort either; it made him glad because it meant she had not been with any other man while the two of them were apart. Golden Dove was so tight his manhood wanted to explode immediately... the chief tried to hold back as long as possible.

Feeling the tightness ease somewhat, Mary lifted slightly before sitting back down firmly; Golden Dove groaned in ecstatic pleasure at the feel of Giant Bear's sleek manhood fully sheathed inside her.

They both gasped in unison at the gratification.

Giant Bear grasped Mary by the hips impatiently and flipped her onto her back with them both still joined. Golden Dove could clearly hear the strain in her husband's voice as the chief groaned out in apology. "I'm sorry love... I cannot wait any longer!"

Moaning in satisfaction when her salvage chief slammed into her repeatedly; Mary didn't complain... too impatient herself to wait. Giant Bear fused their mouths together trying to stop some of the noise his wife was making knowing others were still around. Unable to hold back any longer, he started to erupt deep within her.

Mary felt Giant Bear's explosion; instantly, it triggered her own climax. Golden Dove groaned against her husband's lips with an intense mixture of ecstasy and pain.

Giant Bear finally broke their kiss; he dropped his head on the blanket beside Mary's head panting in contentment and relief. He continued to lie on top of her unable to move yet. It took him a few minutes to catch his breath before he was able to roll onto his back beside her in satisfaction. The chief gave a sigh of pleasure when he felt his wife cuddle up against him happily. Once his breathing came back to normal, he turned on his side in order to face her then propped himself up on his elbow... he frowned in demand as he stared down at her intently. "Golden Dove it is now time to tell your story."

Mary sighed apprehensively before motioned pleadingly. "I was hoping for a little more time!"

Mary paused, but Giant Bear made no response just stared down at her intently waiting patiently. She knew she had no choice now. Golden Dove sighed in resignation and looked into the chief's eyes then began reluctantly. "Everything was going well after you left. Little Antelope was helping me to adjust to your way of life. He even taught me a few words of your language. The only problem I was having was adjusting to your medicine man; I was terrified of him. Then when I was sure I was pregnant, he must have suspected too because he started coming to the tepee and chanting when I was inside. Your nephew tried to explain the man was only trying to scare evil spirits away so I would have a healthy baby, but it just scared me even more. So, when I was four months pregnant, I asked your nephew to take me home so my baby could be born there. He refused at first, but I begged... pleaded and cried until he gave in. He said he would only help me if I would promise to return when the baby was born. Of course, I agreed I was already planning to do that. It didn't take us long to reach the ranch. Brian was the first to see us, he came galloping up to us in concern... or so I thought. When he saw Little Antelope, he drew his gun! I tried to get in front of him, but he pushed me off my horse before taking a bullet in his chest. I crawled over to him sobbing it was entirely my fault. I should have known my brother wouldn't stop to ask a question. For several days I was extremely hysterical, I had to calm myself when I realized I would lose the baby if I didn't. Brian didn't know I was pregnant at first, but I could only hide it for a while. I began to show at about six months. When he questioned me whether it was my husband's I answered yes. I couldn't tell him that I married you, I was too afraid of what he might do so I let him believe what he wanted. I think he was planning on taking the ranch my child would have inherited if it was my first husband's baby as he thought. When the baby was born, it was easy to see he was part Indian. His hair was coal black, his skin dusky. He had my blue eyes though. Brian was so furious with me he threatened to kill Tommy, which is what I named the baby. I would not let him get even one-step near the little one. I kept a loaded gun under my pillow Melissa gave me for protection after he tried to sneak into my bedroom one night. After that, he more or less ignored Tommy as long as I kept the baby out of his way. I think the only reason he stopped trying to hurt our son was he thought Little Antelope was the boy's father. It wasn't until he reached the age of five that more problems started; every time Brian came near Tommy, he would yell at him calling him names like dirty half-breed. After many months of this abuse, I decided it would be best for our son if I got him away from my brother. I befriended Melissa just before I had Tommy so I asked her to take him. I figured if he lived at the sheriff's, it would effectively stop him from abusing our son further. Tommy has been here ever since; I come to visit him every chance I get, but now Brian has decided I should marry again. He is looking for another husband for me who lives far away from here so he would not know about our son."

It was deathly quiet for a while as Giant Bear digested Mary's story solemnly. He scowled angrily then stared down at Golden Dove intently... his tone was furious. "Little Antelope is dead?"

Nodding in misery, Mary whispered brokenly. "Yes!"

The fury in Giant Bear's voice was evident. He looked down at Mary grimly. "His family will have to be told when we get back to my people; you will have to tell them how well my nephew died so they will know he gave his life bravely protecting their Chief's wife and unborn child!"

Mary inclined her head mutely in agreement.

Face hardening suddenly, Giant Bear's voice became deadly serious. "As for your brother, I think I should pay him a visit."

Shaking her head in horror, Mary put her hand against her husband's chest in supplication as she begged desperately. "No Giant Bear... please! He is my brother I love him despite all he has done."

Sighing in understanding, Giant Bear's his voice softened as he looked down at Mary's pleading look; he could not refuse his beautiful wife anything. "All right, Golden Dove... this time I will listen to you!"

Giant Bear laid down beside Mary quietly, neither spoke for a while both deep in their own thoughts. He decided to lighten the mood a bit. He turned his head then looked inquisitively at his wife. "Well, my Golden Dove; how would you like to marry me in the white man's way, this engagement party tonight is for us too?"

Shrieking in joy before turning; Mary threw herself on her savage husband ecstatically. "Oh yes, Giant Bear that would give me the greatest pleasure!"

Rolling his wife over onto her back once more, Giant Bear propped himself up over top of her before grinned down at Mary mischievously. "We will find our son then give him our good news later; right now, I want to make love to you slowly without any clothes between us this time. I swear you white women wear too many things!"

Mary sighed blissfully and encouraged her savage husband to have his way with her again.

*****

Gloria walked into Melissa's bedroom shortly after Mary left with a big grin of delight on her face.

Smiling in humour, Melissa looked at her maid. "Did you see Mary go, Gloria; she ran out of here like her skirts were on fire!"

Chuckling, Gloria pointed behind her towards the stairs. "I sure did; we met on the middle step then she grabbed me and twirled me around. I thought we were both going to end up at the bottom of the stairs. Finally, she threw her arms around me hugging me ecstatically before rushing down the rest of them. I couldn't say a thing... I was all out of breath by the time Mary let me go. I figured I better come up to help you finish getting dressed since that is the last we will see of her for a while!"

Melissa sighed as she motioned in confusion. "When I told her Giant Bear was here, all she could do at first was cry then she hugged me before she took off running. You know I have been sitting here thinking about all the tragedy that has been happening around here lately; even amidst the calamity, all three of us women find love because of a disaster... it makes me wonder about life!"

Nodding thoughtfully, Gloria shrugged dismissively. "That is true, life is full of strange occurrences good and bad; unfortunately, sometimes it takes a tragedy to make us realize what we are really missing in life. Enough of this though, I'm not going to let you think anymore about it right now. We have some men to dazzle and only about an hour to get everyone ready. Your Father is already waiting in the den. Jed is almost finished getting ready, so I gave him instructions to go out to the barn in an hour to bring Mary and Giant Bear to the house. It is time for everyone to don their finery. The Judge with his wife is due to arrive any minute... I imagine. Let's see what dress you chose then get you all prettied up, I will go see what I can do about myself afterwards."

Standing, Melissa held the turquoise dress out to show Gloria; she frowned inquisitively. "What do you think?"

Grinning, Gloria eyed the dress in approval. "That is the one I hoped you would pick. It will bring out the colour of your eyes. The beads I brought up will match the dress perfectly... I'll entwine them in your hair. I brought my sewing kit along, so while I take these stitches out you can dry your hair some; we can have a talk about what happens between married couples. I'm sure Mary never got around to it before she left."

Blushing furiously, Melissa recalled what happened between her and Jed last night; she smiled in bewilderment as she eyed Gloria in surprise as her maid worked on her dress. "I thought you were never married... so how would you know?"

Gloria shook her head in wonder at how innocent Melissa was; not even once in the last year, did she notice Wade sneaking into the housekeeper's room or them slipping out to the barn together. Alec knew of course, but kept their secret. Considering the fact that Mell grew up among men, owned her own ranch... plus she was a sheriff, it amazed the maid how she managed to stay so innocent. Well, this was her chance to find out.

Melissa could hear the curiosity plain in her maid's voice.

Pausing, Gloria looked away from her work long enough to gaze at Mell for a brief moment; the housekeeper motioned inquisitively then asked her question. "I don't understand how you can still be this innocent?"

Sighing forlornly, Melissa gestured in aggravation before Gloria looked back down at what she was doing. "It's not so hard really, my mother died before she got around to discussing what happened between a man and a woman. She realized early in my life she couldn't prevent me from becoming a tomboy; to protect me, she forewarned the men to keep me away from all the things she didn't want me to see. She warned them with the threat of death. If you would have known my mom you would have listened too... she was a formidable woman. She didn't need to really, because the men who worked at the ranch were just as protective of me as my parents were. My Father always kept me occupied somewhere else when breeding or calving season was upon us. Even now, I'm not to go anywhere near the corrals at breeding or foaling time. It didn't interest me either so I never thought about it much or tried to find out what all the fuss was about. As for being Sheriff, I still have not had a lot of contact with that side of life. Pam always knew I was a woman. Plus, I was too young to be in her place at that time anyway. When my dad moved up here, he talked to the Madam's in all the towns I'm Sheriff in to make sure I was not permitted inside. Every time I go there on a disturbance, the man who keeps the patrons in line meets me in the lobby with the wrongdoer already subdued. I have never been allowed anywhere in the house except the lobby. None of the girls have been allowed to speak to me directly unless they are giving me evidence in my office."

Snorting in irritation, Gloria continued to pull the stitches out of Melissa's dress as she talked. "Alec should have done something about it; you are definitely at a disadvantage as a Sheriff because of it. One thing you could do before you get married is go talk to some of Pam's ladies, they will teach you everything you need to know... plus things you probably don't want to know!"

Laughing in delight, Melissa nodded in agreement. "You're probably right, I wouldn't want to know; as for talking to me about it you really don't need to, Jed is teaching me but I do have a few questions."

Nodding, Gloria grinned in amusement. "Okay, ask away."

Melissa took a large fortifying breath still unsure if she should ask such a question... the curiosity was killing her though; Mell finally asked in a rush before she could change her mind. "I want to know about the sac that lies between men's legs there are two hard things inside, what's it for?"

Looking up startled, Gloria stared at Melissa in utter amazement; she shook her head in disbelief. "I didn't think you were that innocent!"

Shrugging in embarrassment, Melissa waited impatiently for her maids reply.

Gloria finished ripping out the hem on Melissa's dress without speaking; she wasn't sure how to tell her at first so wanted to have a moment to think. The housekeeper shook the garment out before hanging it up. She sat down on the bed and patted the spot beside her invitingly, bidding Mell to sit down with her. When they were sitting comfortably, the maid turned to her trying to explain as best she could. "Well, that is what makes a man... a man; you did notice your stallion has similar balls on him, didn't you?"

Shaking her head negatively, Melissa grimaced. "Well, no; I've never paid attention to that sort of thing. I guess I should look."

Laughing in delight, Gloria shook her head in humour. "You can check if you want; after I explain it, I hope you won't need to. Now those two hard balls inside his sac store a white substance called semen... it's for making babies. When you make love, the semen goes inside you to make you pregnant."

Nodding thoughtfully, Melissa mussed contemplatively. "Well, that makes sense; last night Jed showed me what the white stuff looks like... he called it his seed though."

Gloria's eyebrows rose in surprise. "You made love last night?"

Melissa blushed in embarrassment then shook her head negatively. "Well not really, I hate to admit it but I was too anxious so Jed is going slowly and showing me different ways of making love; he said this way I will have time to become used to him."

Smirking in humour, Gloria laughed knowingly; remembering Melissa's comment from this morning. "Oh, that's what you meant earlier when you said I needed to get used to Wade."

Nodding Melissa sighed in disgust. "Yes, I didn't know most prospective brides know more than I do."

Chuckling in delight at having that mystery solved, Gloria waved consolingly. "Well, the truth is most women don't know much about it... not until their mother's tells them. I'm sure you would have known earlier if your mom was still alive. Most women don't like to talk about it, so you would be quite amazed at how many don't know even the small amount you now do. My Father was a doctor, which is why I know more than most. Okay, I will let Jed teach you what you need to know, so enough of this; we need to get you ready."

Smiling in pleasure, Melissa went to sit at her vanity. She looked at Gloria behind her in the mirror as her maid picked up her hairbrush to work on the knots in her hair. "What fun to be pampered, maybe being a woman once in a while wouldn't hurt me... after all it might be fun."

Grinning back, Gloria got to work on Melissa's tangled damp hair without a word.

*****

Alec was still sitting behind his desk in the den... he had left briefly though to change; a discreet knock sounding had him looking up inquisitively. "Come in!"

Jed opened the door before walking over to the desk then smiled in greeting as he waved towards Alec. "You shouldn't be working tonight."

Smirking at Jed, Alec put down his pen; he motioned inquiringly. "The work never stops around here, but I'm writing letters nothing serious... what can I do for you?"

Sitting in the chair in front of the desk, Jed gestured down at the suit he was wearing in explanation. "First off, I wanted to thank you for lending me this suit; I didn't bring anything fancy with me. I think I might suggest going to Boston for our honeymoon so Melissa can meet my family. At the same time, I can make arrangements to bring my stuff here... I also wanted to give you this."

Taking the package from his pocket, Jed handed it across the desk to Alec.

Taking the box, Alec smiled in gratitude. "Thank you!"

Gesturing towards the box curiously, Jed continued. "Chelsie asked me to deliver it to you."

Grinning mysteriously for a moment, Alec opened it before passing the box back to Jed so he could see what was inside. "Beautiful aren't they... the necklace was Melissa's Mothers passed down to her from her own Mother. The earrings, plus the bracelet, I had Chelsie make. A friend of mine searched for a long time so the stones matched, but it was Chelsie who actually found them; a friend of hers in Ireland helped us."

Nodding in admiration, Jed handed them back to Alec. He pulled out his own box with Melissa's wedding ring inside. He handed it to his future father-in-law to be inspected. Grey Wolf waved in explanation when his hand was free. "Chelsie said she finished this ring the other day; she did mention being inspired by the design on your commission into making it. So, I have to thank you for that too!"

Smiling in pleasure at the beautiful ring, Alec handed it back. "Chelsie is like that she seems to get inspired easily. She's been talking about opening a goldsmith shop for a while now. She wasn't just talking about jewellery either, but mentioned clocks plus other things. We have a lot of discarded lumber, so we could help her with wooden bases; it wouldn't cost much to build her a shop either, since I have all the lumber here... it would be a good investment."

Jed inclined his head thoughtfully. "I was thinking about that too, I would be really interested if you wanted to do it. A goldsmith shop would be a novelty around here; I don't recall seeing one anywhere that I have been to except Boston of course... it has almost everything."

Rubbing his hands in anticipation and delight, Alec's eagerness was quite apparent. "Great, she will be here for the wedding; if you are really that interested, we can talk to her about it then?"

Smirking at Alec's enthusiasm, Jed grinned. "Fine with me."

Alec changed the subject. "I want to thank you for suggesting the cabins to Melissa, it's a great idea."

Beaming in acceptance, Jed smirked teasingly. "You are welcome, but I'm sure one of you would have thought of it eventually if I hadn't."

Smiling unconvinced, Alec shrugged. "Maybe!"

Alec eyed Jed shrewdly, he motioned invitingly. "You have something else on your mind, don't you?"

Chuckling in delight, Jed winked. "Nothing gets by you, now I see where your daughter gets it."

Nodding, Alec waited patiently for Jed to tell him what he wanted; he had an idea, but waited to see if he was right.

Clearing his throat hesitantly, Jed wasn't sure if he should continue; he didn't want to offend his future father-in-law already. Grey Wolf finally asked in a rush, not sure if he was on thin ice or not "Well your daughter tells me you handle the ranch and all business aspects of it."

Alec gestured inquisitively; this is what he figured Jed wanted. "Would you like to take it over?"

Shaking his head negatively, Jed gave Alec a horrified look at that. "No way, I will leave that in your capable hands!"

Laughing at Jed's dismayed look, Alec nodded in relief. "Okay; although, you do have the right when you marry Melissa to take over if you want?"

Jed shook his head vigorously again in denial, with a decisive gesture. "No, thank you; I would rather be out with Melissa as a deputy then become a rancher. I would like to discuss buying more land though... maybe put some cattle on it. I would pay for the additional land and the cattle, since you look after the business aspects of the ranch, I wanted to check with you to see if it's feasible. I also wanted to make sure the extra workload wouldn't be too much for you."

Leaning forward on the desk earnestly, Alec folded his fingers together staring at Jed curiously. "You do realize now that you are marrying Melissa you will no longer receive a wage from the town for being a deputy... do you not?"

Shrugging indifferently, Jed wasn't worried about that in the least. "Melissa mentioned it, but she was a bit vague on the subject; money isn't an issue, she did say the town supplied everything we needed?"

Nodding, Alec he sat back in his chair and put his elbows on the arms before steepling his fingers together thoughtfully under his chin. He eyed Jed in surprise, obviously there was more to Grey Wolf then meets the eye. "Yes, the town will pay all your expenses while you are on duty. I will explain to you why. When Melissa first came here, she passed herself off as a man. She got away with it for so long because of her height mostly, but also because she used our last name Ray as her first name. Since the men at the ranch where she grew up always called her that, she didn't have any problems with a name change. As long as nobody looked too closely at her, she was able to continue her charade for some time. Longer than even, I thought possible and believe me she made sure nobody came close enough. She got careless though, which was bound to happen eventually so she was dismissed. She had fallen in love with the area so she decided to look for a place to live for the both of us. It didn't take her long to find this place, instead of writing me to get the money to buy it which I would have gladly given her. She decided to be stubborn wanting to do it on her own, so she kept trying to find ways to make money. When she rescued the judge, he agreed to give her this place if she would come back to be the Sheriff again. He was only going to give her the yard site, plus a hundred acres. Mell was not happy about that; she wanted it all. After a lot of arguing and dealing, they compromised. It was decided she would get everything on the condition she never accepts wages again, but all her expenses would be paid when she is on duty. The town got a free Sheriff since this land was theirs only by default. Plus, all the surrounding towns now had a sheriff too... I think the town got the better deal."

Jed chuckled in agreement. "You are right I think so too; Melissa told me some of it, but not all, I understand more now. She also told me you only use part of the land now?"

Inclining his head in agreement, Alec shrugged unconcerned. "Yes, at the moment we don't use the land from here to Devil's Rock. West of here we built a small sawmill, so we have been logging the land over there for some time now. We make sure to replant not wanting to use up our resources. It has been profitable because we have no expenses except for extra men when we cut in the fall, plus the shipping. Since we are not a traditional sawmill... not being on the water; we have to ship overland by wagon. It's a little more expensive, but manageable. There are about six hundred acres that still has nice big trees to the northwest. Right now, we are trying to buy more land beyond that, the trees over there are huge. We still have three hundred acres that would hold cattle if you want. I don't think we will need extra land. The grass is lush enough around here to hold four or five hundred head of cattle right now. If you want to get bigger than that, later we could look at more land. As for buying the cattle yourself, I will have to decline the offer. For one thing, this ranch has made nothing but profit since we took it over. I have been trying to talk Melissa into buying cattle for a while, every time she refuses fearing it would put too much of a strain on me. Oh, she didn't put it into those terms. She just keeps telling me we will do it later when she retires. Now that you are here to help, I am sure we can talk her into it though."

Jed sighed plaintively as he motioned in aggravation. "You give a pretty convincing reason about not needing me to buy the cattle. I agree the ranch should support itself in this venture, but I have nothing invested in it. It would make me feel uncomfortable with no say or control in the project... that's why I left Boston; my brother was inheriting the shipping business, which I didn't want anyway so I had nothing there for me."

Nodding in understanding, Alec gestured towards Jed in appeasement. "I know what you mean I felt the same way when I first came here. So, I will make you the same offer Melissa made me. I'm not aware of your financial situation. Later, not tonight, we will get together to discuss it. At that time, I will let you know how much you can invest in this ranch. Your investment will be on everything, not just the cattle; we can call it, Melissa, Jed, & Alec's Ranch... The MJ&A Ranch"

Thinking about it for a moment, Jed chuckled before grinning; he nodded pleased. "You're right I think investing in the ranch would be better than just the cattle. Love the name too... it's quite catchy."

Standing, Jed got up to go out to the barn to get Giant Bear and Mary for the dinner party. In satisfaction at how well the first meeting with Alec had gone; Jed reached out and held his hand over the desk in invitation, this way his future father-in-law wouldn't have as far to reach.

Alec clasped Jed's hand firmly.

Jed smiled in relief glad that Melissa's father understood his feelings. "It's a deal partner!"

CHAPTER TWELVE

Alec was just pouring himself a snifter of brandy when he heard a knock on the front door; he knew Gloria was upstairs helping Melissa so he wheeled himself over to the door before calling out loudly. "Come in!"

A smile of welcome lit up Alec's face when he recognized John and his wife, Betty. "Good evening, folks; come on in."

John followed closely by Betty returned Alec's greeting; the judge hung up his hat then took his wife's shawl and hung it up too; he turned to Melissa's father with a grin. "Nice night for an evening engagement party... isn't it?"

Patting Alec on the shoulder, John walked around the wheelchair then into the lobby after closing the door.

Nodding, Alec turned toward his two guests before he smiled enticingly then gestured towards the drawing room on their right. "I was just pouring myself some brandy, could I pour some for the both of you; we might as well get comfortable while we wait for the others."

Grinning, John immediately accepted; the judge rubbed his hands together in anticipation, Alec always imported the best brandy around. "Sure, I would love some."

Betty shook her head negatively and declined; she waved towards the stairs leading up to the bedrooms hopefully. "No, thanks... do you think Melissa would mind if I went upstairs to see if she needs some help?"

Beaming pleased, Alec motioned towards the stairs in invitation. "By all means go on up. I'm sure Melissa would be more than happy to see you. She would probably welcome your advice as well; just go to the top of the stairs, it's the first door you come to on the left."

Nodding in thanks; Betty hurried up the stairs before knocking on the door Alec had indicated... while her husband and Alec went to the library instead for a drink.

*****

Gloria opened the door at a knock then peeked out to see who it was; she grinned in surprised delighted before she opened the door wider in invitation. "Mrs. Elton, come on in... Mary just got here as well so we can all make a grand entrance when we go downstairs."

Betty went in and smiled at Mary in greeting since she was the first one, she saw. She turned expectantly looking for Melissa wanting to congratulate her; the judge's wife couldn't help her mouth falling open in delighted shock... she sputtered in relish. "Just look at you, you are absolutely beautiful! A lot of men are going to upset they didn't try to win you over. Mell, you do realize nobody has ever seen you in a dress?"

Chuckling, Melissa imagined all the men from the town seeing her in a dress for the first time; she smirked teasingly at Betty. "You're right I will probably give everyone a shock when they see me at the wedding, maybe I should wear pants instead!"

Betty nodded in perfect agreement then giggled at Melissa's wit. "Heart attack might be more like it though; I don't think Alec or my husband would let you get away with pants... they have both waited too long to see you married as it is!"

Beaming at all three women in turn; Melissa impulsively gave each a hug in gratitude. She stood back so all three could see the love she felt for them. "I don't know if I have ever told you three this, but thank you from the bottom of my heart. You have all supported me all these years, even when I was posing as a man so I could remain the Sheriff. Once I was exposed as a woman... you still stood by me."

Smirking smugly, Betty thought of John's reaction to Melissa being a woman. "Well, we knew right from the beginning you were a woman; I even tried to help you keep your secret. After the boy exposed you to everyone else though my husband wouldn't even let me speak your name, never mind talk to him about keeping you on. He refused to listen to me... bull-headed man anyway!"

Melissa chuckled at Betty's reference to John's stubbornness then waved at the three women; thankful to have such good friends. "I know I appreciate everything you all have done for me over the years."

Hugging Melissa again, Betty stepped back; she grinned mischievously in anticipation. "Come on let's go dazzle some men."

*****

John turned to Alec before grinning... he nodded his thanks for the brandy then sat down in a chair; he settled back comfortably before shaking his head in amazement. "I can't believe Melissa is getting married after all these years."

Grimacing playfully, Alec held onto his chest dramatically as if in complete shock before turning serious. "You can't believe it, what about me; I have been harassing Melissa for the last ten years to find a husband so I could become a grandfather! For a while there, I thought she might pick Brian. Thankfully, after she found out he killed that Indian fellow she refused his marriage proposal... thank God. When she found out how bad he treated Tommy, she refused to have anything more to do with him. I have always suspected there is something not quite right about him. For the last several years I have encouraged her to keep clear of him completely!"

John nodded in understanding then waved anxiously as he changed the subject. "I understand how you feel Brian's always been a strange one. To change the subject, do you think Melissa will quit her job now that she's getting married?"

"No; it's not an option!"

Both men were startled at the voice; they jumped in guilt before they turned towards the door to see Jed entering the room with Giant Bear right behind him.

Grinning at the two men in apology, Jed gestured calmly. "Sorry to make you jump, but the answer to your question is definitely no! We have already talked it over; Melissa will remain as Sheriff with me as her Deputy. If or when she gets pregnant, I will take over for however long she thinks necessary. Afterwards, she will resume her job... I will gladly go back to being her Deputy."

Shaking his head in amazement, John eyed Jed in respect before gesturing incredulously. "I'm glad you are the one involved in this, I could never stand for my wife being that strong willed or independent; of course, it would be unthinkable for her to take on a role like Melissa's in the first place."

Jed just smirked good-naturedly; he motioned decisively. "Well gentlemen I wasn't sure I could either, but Melissa's strong character was the attraction that drew me to her in the first place. When you love someone, it doesn't matter what they do, you will support them either way. Plus, she is the exact opposite of my deceased wife... may God rest her soul!"

Turning to Giant Bear inquisitively; Jed pointed at him curiously. "What about you my friend, could you let your wife be that independent?"

Giant Bear frowned in thought for a moment before he nodded that he could. "Yes, Cheyenne men are mostly dominant. Although, there are stories in our history where a woman became a Shaman... two were Medicine Women. According to legend, our very first Chief was actually a woman. We also have a few brave hearted ones like Melissa. They fight beside their men if the battle is going badly; they also perform many brave deeds."

Heads turned in surprise as Wade walked into the room dramatically before whistling outlandishly to get their attention; he pointed behind him teasingly. "Gentleman... you better come out into the hall to see what visions I saw coming down the stairs!"

Giant Bear and Jed left the room first in an excited rush... followed by Wade, while John pushed Alec out a little more sedately bringing up the rear. Grey Wolf stopped at the bottom of the stairs then stood there speechless for a moment; could the vision floating down the stairs really be Melissa, she was gorgeous!

Melissa lifted her skirt higher so she wouldn't trip on her dress to negotiate the stairs.

Jed couldn't help the grin that spread across his face; Melissa wasn't wearing any slippers but was wearing the moccasins she always wore in the house. Well, he couldn't expect his hard-nosed lady sheriff to transform herself completely... now, could he? Grey Wolf looked down when he heard the squeak of wheels beside him.

Alec winked up at Jed in conspiracy. "Just like her mother, she always knew how to make an entrance!"

As each woman reached the bottom of the stairs, their equally dazed partners claimed them; they were escorted into the drawing room for drinks since it was bigger than the library... more formal too.

Gloria put extra candles around the room to brighten it up more. Shadows flickered almost eerily on the walls from the warm wind coming through the window; constantly moving the flames around. For a while, everyone mingled talking about the day's events... sipping their drinks companionably.

Walking over to the window, Melissa turned then stood quietly by herself observing her guests and fiancé critically. Jed was having a lengthy conversation with John, but every once in awhile he would glance around looking for her. Almost as if he couldn't help himself. Their gazes would meet for a moment then satisfied he would return his attention back to Judge Elton, reassured she was still there. She grinned in pleasure; it was nice to see him so formally decked out, Grey Wolf looked just as handsome in formal wear as he did in buckskins or chaps... Mell preferred the buckskins though.

Melissa's gaze scanned the room; she saw Giant Bear and Mary talking, they looked great together. Her friend and neighbour appeared happier than she had ever seen her. The Cheyenne Chief was wearing his formal buckskins. They were beaded with a unique bear design... very impressive. He didn't look too uncomfortable, being in a white man's house. He seemed tame, compared to other Indian Chiefs that Mell knew. She wasn't sure if it was because his white wife had such a calming effect on him or if Jed actually tamed him on their travels. The sheriff was almost positive it was Mary keeping him in check, like a sleeping lion waiting patiently to be set free. Golden Dove was beautiful in a deep blue dress with a white trimmed lace underskirt she borrowed from the clothes in the attic.

Looking to the right, Melissa gazed at Wade and Gloria next... they looked cozy cuddled in a corner. The housekeeper had chosen a grey silk top with a full black skirt, a white petticoat peeked out at the bottom; the foreman was handsome in a brown western style suit, he looked ecstatic.

Melissa's glance fell on Alec next conversing with the judge's wife; the two were standing by the fireplace. Her father had taken the opportunity to dress up for the occasion. He was wearing his best black suit complemented by a white shirt with silver cuff links. She was always proud of him and tonight he seemed happier than he had been in a long time. Mell smiled in loving pride when her dad threw back his head and laughed in delight at some remark Mrs. Elton made. It was good to hear him laugh with such unrestrained humour... it had been a long time since she heard it.

At that moment, Melissa happened to look up at her mother's smiling portrait. A puff of wind caught the candle flame, making it dance for a split second. She saw her mother's mouth move eerily... almost as if her smile widened in approval. Mell blinked then suddenly everything was back to the way it had been; she shivered slightly in reaction before looking away hurriedly.

Staring sightlessly for a minute; Melissa shook off her fancy then looked at Mrs. Beatrice Elton or Betty, which is what she preferred to be called. She looked beautiful as usual with her black hair artfully swept up. Her green eyes sparkled in mirth as she laughed with Alec. Her spectacles kept slipping down her tiny nose every time she looked down at him. She was slim and petite, her husband looked huge compared to her... Mell couldn't help giggling when she saw them together. The judge's wife could walk under her husband's arm without even misplacing a hair on her head.

Truth be told, Melissa was terrified of Betty when they first met... not because she was uneasy about being discovered either. Over the years she met lots of ladies like Mrs. Elton, they always looked down their aristocratic noses at her since she preferred pants over dresses. Beatrice calmly took her aside on their second meeting to inform her that as long as she didn't disgrace the town or her husband; she wouldn't tell John the new sheriff was actually a woman. The two had been friends ever since. The judge's wife was a lady in every sense of the word too, but she didn't put on airs as others did. Mell was quite grateful to have her as her friend.

Melissa's inspection was broken suddenly; she jumped slightly when Gloria touched her arm unexpectedly. She was so deep in her own thoughts, Mell never heard the housekeeper coming.

Motioning in apology towards Melissa, Gloria frowned, it wasn't often anyone could sneak up on the sheriff. "Sorry Mell, I just wanted to let you know Alec asked Widow Donaldson to come serve supper tonight; Wade picked her up earlier... I forgot to tell you upstairs."

Smiling in approval, Melissa sighed in relief. "I'm glad he thought of it because I sure didn't."

Gloria grinned at the apologetic tone of Melissa's voice before shrugging thoughtfully. "You have a lot on your mind,

I think Alec had another motive for inviting her though."

Frowning puzzled by that remark, Melissa gestured curiously in confusion. "What are you talking about?"

Chuckling low mysteriously, Gloria waved toward Alec in explanation. "Well, in all the years I have known your father. He has never come to the kitchen except for meals. Coffee and snacks I usually bring to him, unless you are around then he will sit at the table with you. Since Mrs. Donaldson has been here, he's been in and out of the kitchen all day; usually, with the lamest excuses."

Pondering that bit of information in surprise, Melissa turned to stare at Alec for several minutes; Mell looked back at Gloria before gesturing in disbelief. "Do you think my father has feelings for her?"

Frowning in worried speculation, Gloria gestured hesitantly. "You wouldn't mind if he has found somebody else, would you?"

Instantly, Melissa shook her head negatively in reassurance at Gloria's expression. "No; in fact, it would ease my mind a lot if I knew someone would be here to care for Dad if something ever happened to me; it just came as a bit of a shock, I had no idea he liked anyone."

Gloria enthusiastically nudged Melissa gently before waving towards Alec knowingly. "Well, keep your eye on them tonight... I will bet you there is another romance brewing; oh, there's Tommy supper must be ready."

Everyone instantly paired up for supper.

Melissa called her foster son over to her then motioned towards Alec. "Tommy, will you do the honours of pushing my father into the dining room for me?"

Inclining his head in agreement, Tommy walked over before whispering up at Melissa curiously; he gestured towards his mom in bewilderment. "Aunt Mell what's with my mother and Giant Bear?"

Melissa put her arm around her foster son's shoulders then gave him a hug of reassurance before pushing him towards Alec. "You will have to wait until after supper Tommy... your mother is going to have a talk with you afterwards."

Nodding in puzzlement, Tommy went over then whispered something in Alec's ear... without asking any more questions. Melissa's father nodded in permission up at her foster son;

he proudly wheeled the man he called grandfather into the dining room.

After everyone was sitting, Melissa called Tommy over to her again; she waited until he got close before waving towards the bunkhouse in invitation. "I talked to Dusty earlier... you are invited to join the men tonight for supper."

Tommy's expression brightened then he sobered in seriousness; the perceptive boy asked Melissa one more question before he left. "Okay, Aunt Mell but before I go; I would like to know if Giant Bear is my dad?"

Melissa looked across the table at Mary with one eyebrow lifted in question.

Mary instantly knew what Melissa was asking; she nodded her head vigorously in permission.

Turning back to her fostered son, Melissa inclined her head in agreement. "Yes, Tommy... Giant Bear is your father."

Smiling smugly at figuring that out, Tommy's face lit up. "Good!"

Turning, Tommy raced out of the room without a word to his mother or his long-lost father.

Glancing towards Mary sadly, Melissa watched the tears fill her friend's eyes then grinned in encouragement.

Smiling back bravely at Melissa, Mary turned away when Giant Bear took her hand; he whispered his own support.

Melissa looked at the food already on the table then smiled knowingly; Mrs. Donaldson had made most of Alec's favourite food. There was a beef pot roast with carrots, potatoes, green beans, as well as turnip artfully set up in the middle of the table. Over to the left was French bread... she also made cabbage with a cream sauce. There were two bottles of thirty-year-old red wine out of the cellar to go with the beef roast.

Mrs. Donaldson came in as Melissa finished examining the table; Brad followed her obediently with a pot of soup, French onion if the widow stayed true to Alec's taste.

Looking at Jessica Donaldson, as if for the first time. Of course, Melissa saw the woman in town often but hadn't paid much attention to the widow... she liked what she saw. Jessica's hair was a shocking red with a hint of grey at the temples. She was a tall willowy woman, not skinny. She was in her early forties with a pleasant smile. She wasn't beautiful in the conventional sense, quite striking though. Her eyes were a deep green almost emerald; they held a glint of mischief as well as honesty. Mell could also see determination in the Scottish widow's eyes with a hint of temper, which undoubtedly went with her red hair.

Going all the way around the table to Melissa's father first, Mrs. Donaldson dished Alec up some soup; she bent down in conspiracy to whisper something in his ear, making him laugh in delight. The widow took the opportunity to touch him then went to the next person.

Turning, Melissa smiled at Gloria who had been watching her expression anxiously; not sure whether her boss would approve or not. The housekeeper sighed in relief when Mell nodded her blessings.

The rest of the evening passed quickly; toasts were made to everyone's continued health and happiness. John and his wife departed after expressing their sentiments that the night had been delightful, but declined the offer to stay overnight even though it was late. Judge Elton joked that the horses knew the way home... he could sleep on route if he got too tired.

*****

As Melissa was getting ready for bed, she turned shy again; she frowned anxiously at Jed. "Can you turn your back while I put my nightshirt on?"

Jed shook his head negatively; he waved towards Melissa's nightgown in disapproval. "I will turn around while you take your dress off but as to the nightdress, sorry no clothes allowed in bed."

Blushing furiously, Melissa nodded; hurriedly while Jed's back was turned, she struggled to get out of her dress.

After a few moments of silence, except for the rustle of clothes; Jed could hear Melissa using a few choice cuss words; he winced slightly at a particularly vulgar word he couldn't remember hearing before. Trying not to laugh at the frustrated curses she was using. Grey Wolf asked mildly with his back still turned. "Having trouble Mell?"

Melissa growled in exasperated anger. "Yes; I can't get out of this damn dress could you come help me, please?"

Turning around slowly, Jed couldn't help burst out in uncontrollable mirth at the sight of Melissa. She had managed to tangle herself up in her dress and the petticoat. It now looked like the petticoat was the dress; it was twisted around her... completely backwards. How she accomplished it, he wasn't quite sure. It took him a few moments to stop laughing before he could even move towards her to help her. Grey Wolf courteously turned his back once she was set straight then waited until he heard the blankets rustling before turning around. He blew out the candle and started undressing to spare her any more embarrassment.

However, the moon was full so there was enough light for Melissa to see; she grinned in pleasure as she watched Jed undress, realizing he didn't know she could see him in the near darkness. Her thoughts turned to Alec as she watched Grey Wolf wondering if he saw anything, she couldn't help asking him curiously. "Did you notice something different about my father today?"

Shaking his head negatively, Jed remembered it was dark so answered cautiously; he wasn't sure where Melissa's question was going. "No, not really... he seemed happy."

Deciding to be more direct, Melissa sighed in exasperation. "Did you notice him paying attention to Mrs. Donaldson?"

Jed shrugged thoughtfully trying to remember the evening while he continued to undress. "I wouldn't say a lot, but yes I think Alec was trying to make her feel more comfortable and welcome."

Scowling Melissa shook her head negatively in frustration; men never notice anything unless it was shoved under their noses. "No, that's not it... I think my dad really likes her; do you think since I'm getting married, he feels free to find a friend or a wife since he doesn't have to worry about me?"

Getting into bed, Jed sighed plaintively. He held up the blankets inviting Melissa to move closer before he changed the subject. "I really couldn't say, but forget about your father for a moment. Come on over here and give your husband-to-be a kiss; I have been waiting for this all night."

Turning to Jed obediently, Melissa cuddled up against him so he could have his way with her.

Sitting up, Jed propped himself up on his elbow. He turned on his side and bent his head to kiss Melissa passionately. He flicked his tongue out, moving back he lightly traced her lips with it then pushed his tongue inside her mouth... deepening the kiss. Lifting his head, Grey Wolf kissed her eyes first then her cute button nose. Moving downwards, he nibbled on her stubborn chin. He moved to Mell's side and flicked his tongue around her earlobe travelling down to her neck, lightly nibbling. Scooting down further on the bed still propped on his arm; he nipped or suckled his way towards his goal, which were her luscious breasts. When he found her nipple, he gently scraped it with his teeth then soothed the hard erect morsel by flicking his tongue around it.

Moaning in delight and ecstasy, Melissa arched her body in invitation wanting more; of what she wasn't sure... just more of something.

Jed began sucking harder on the nipple at Melissa's obvious enjoyment.

Melissa cried out in exquisite pleasure at the shivery feelings racing through her body.

Letting his fingers stroll lightly teasingly down Melissa's belly once Jed was sure she was ready for him; he finally reached her thighs.

Trustingly, Melissa opened her legs to accommodate Jed without any hesitation this time.

The trust Melissa showed made Jed grin in relief against her nipple. He rewarded her by lightly stroking her bud of pleasure with his fingertip. While she was preoccupied, he brought his head down then nibbled on her belly... until she was squirming in delight. He prolonged her enjoyment as long as he could. Looking up he watched Mell's reaction intently as she giggled and writhed; taking advantage of her distraction, Grey Wolf lifted himself up then lay completely between her thighs.

Jumping in shock, Melissa didn't realize what Jed was up to at first. His tongue flicked out suddenly and touched her bud of pleasure for the first time intimately. She shivered in hesitant surprise unsure if she liked the feeling at first but as his tongue continued to caress her; the feelings of astonishment slowly disappeared and excitement took over... relaxing her. It wasn't until Grey Wolf removed his tongue then began rubbing her bud firmly with his thumb that Mell was able to let go and enjoy the moment.

Jed removed his hand once he felt Melissa relax, massaging her thighs, he slowly pushed her legs farther apart to give himself more room. He continued to push them until her knees were sticking up in the air, when satisfied he let go;

this gave Grey Wolf better access to her inner heat. Without any warning he parted her petals then plunged his tongue inside Mell to taste her juices.

Gasping in shocked pleasure, Melissa moaned in protest.

Bringing his mouth back up to Melissa's bud again, Jed began lightly suckling then lapping at it before she could objection further. He lifted his hand before carefully pushing two fingers inside her; Grey Wolf didn't want to pierce her maidenhood accidentally in his eagerness.

Melissa couldn't help a slight scream of disbelief from escaping when she climaxed long and hard. She was still seeing stars when she felt Jed lift his head away; he laid it on her belly to give her time to recover. Reaching down absently she ran her hands through Grey Wolf's hair, but didn't speak thunderstruck plus out of breath. Mell could still feel tremors of pleasure racing through her body uncontrollably. She felt dazed never having experienced anything like this before. When she got her breathing under control again... tears filled her eyes unexpectedly.

Lifting himself of Melissa hastily, Jed had been watching her closely not sure what her reaction would be; he scooted up the bed then gathered her in his arms in concern and alarm. "Did I hurt you?"

Mutely, Melissa shook her head in denial.

Frowning in worry, Jed wasn't convinced in the least since Melissa was still crying; he propped himself up on his arm again so he could study her expression intently. "Then why are you crying?"

Taking a deep unsteady breath, Melissa wiped her tears away angrily then shrugged confused. After her mother died, she hardly ever cried but since meeting Jed that is all she seemed to do anymore. Mell reached up tenderly then stroked Grey Wolf's face in reassurance, trying to explain her tears. "You didn't hurt me... on the contrary; I have never felt such intense pleasure before. I'm just so blissfully happy that's why I'm crying!"

Sighing, Jed was relieved when Melissa dropped her hand and cuddled closer... women were strange sometimes; he was still not sure what to do, so laid down then just held her quietly until she got herself under control.

Suddenly without any warning, Melissa sat up... the tears

were completely gone as if they had never existed; she turned before looking down at Jed then exclaimed in amazement and wonder. "You weren't kidding when you said love making gets better, were you!"

Jed chuckled in delight at Melissa's quick mood change; Mell turned around further before bending down then started feathering light kisses on Grey Wolf's chest and neck. He teased her in amusement. "Just wait until we are married the best is yet to come!"

Grimacing against Jed's nipple plaintively, Melissa whispered. "I'm not sure I'm going to live through it then!"

Laughing at Melissa's response, Jed shuddered in pleasure as she played with his nipple... mischievously nipping it playfully; Mell transferred her attention to Grey Wolf's other nipple giving it just as much attention as the other one had.

Groaning deep in his throat, Jed gasped in surprise when Melissa let her lips travel down to his stomach without him having to prompt her in any way.

Grinning devilishly when Melissa realized Jed was ticklish... she spent several minutes digging her fingers into his ribs; he squirmed trying to get away, but she was relentless. Grey Wolf laughed startled by Mell's playfulness. He inhaled in delight when she moved her head lower and laid her head on his belly gazing at his manhood curiously.

Reaching out experimentally, Melissa tentatively lifted Jed's manhood to feel the texture, shape, and size of him; it was too dark to see details... although, light enough with the moon shining through the window to see a little.

Groaning in tortured amusement, Jed watched Melissa inquisitively trying to see his manhood in the enveloping darkness; he moaned louder when she decided it was too dark to see so lifted it up and used her hand to inspect it.

Satisfied at the feel of him Melissa let Jed go then reached down further and picked up his sac; she squeezed gently feeling the hard pebbles inside with her hand, wondering how those small balls inside his sac produce babies.

Jed gasped in torture as he tried patiently to wait for Melissa to finish her inspection.

Melissa let go of his sac then picked up his manhood again. She frowned puzzled when she noticed some fluid on the tip; she hesitated for a second then finally bent her head before touching her tongue to the tip of his manhood to taste it.

Groaning, Jed arched up in encouragement when Melissa took the tip of his manhood into her mouth then suckled gently. He squirmed in ecstasy and sucked in his breath stunned... waiting to see what she was going to do next; he wasn't sure if he could stand more of this agonizing pleasure.

Smiling in satisfaction at Jed's gasp of delight, Melissa lifted her head to look up at him as her hand continued to caress him intimately. Grey Wolf couldn't hold back any longer... he exploded with a groan of disappointment; he hoped to prolong this a little longer but Mell's inquisitive innocence wouldn't allow that.

Looking back down instantly, Melissa watched Jed's manhood empty itself. She bent down once more before tentatively touching the tip of his manhood with her tongue... she wanted to see what it would taste like. It was quite salty tasting; Mell wasn't sure if she liked it.

Jed's manhood bucked once more in Melissa's hand in reaction... trying to rise again, but then it started shrinking slowly unable to rise so soon.

Squinting, Melissa watched fascinated wondering how something so large and hard could shrink so quickly then become small and limp; she looked up at Jed to find him smiling broadly at her interest.

Reaching down, Jed pulled Melissa up beside him for a deep kiss before propping himself on his elbow... he stared down at her. "I can leave the candle on tomorrow if you want?"

Melissa nodded eagerly up at him. "Yes, I would like that."

Chuckling at Melissa's earnest expression, Jed teased. "What do you think of your second lesson in the art of pleasing your husband?"

Smiling up at Jed mischievously, Melissa couldn't help teasing back. "I like it; I never expected lovemaking to be this enjoyable, if I had known sooner, I might have tried it long before now!"

Growling in mock anger, Jed proceeded to tickle Melissa unmercifully for her impertinence.

Wiggling around, Melissa tried to get away from Jed; laughing and gasping her eyes filled with tears of mirth; finally, she couldn't stand the tickling anymore... Mell gasped out in surrender. "I give up, I was only joking!"

Grinning down at Melissa devilishly, Jed teased playfully. "Don't you forget that I'm the man, the only one for you?"

Giggling again in delight, Melissa sighed in contentment; she reached up and gently stroked Jed's face tenderly, she whispered lovingly. "I love you so much!"

Jed gathered Melissa close to him with a hug smile of pleasure. "I love you too!"

Gently, Jed kissed Melissa then got up and went to the water basin to wash. He brought a cloth back with him so she could wash her hands before throwing it in a corner. Grey Wolf laid back on the bed for some much-needed sleep, changing his mind he decided to continue the discussion Mell had started earlier about Alec. "Now we can talk about your dad, are you worried he might like Mrs. Donaldson?"

Shaking her head negatively, Melissa turned her head towards Jed to talk. "No, not worried really; I was watching them at dinner, they look good together."

Smiling in sympathy, Jed too turned his head to watch Melissa's expression; he couldn't help remembering her pain when discussing her mother. "You're not resenting the fact that your father is thinking of another woman... are you?"

Melissa analyzed her feelings closely before shaking her head decisively. "No, I don't think so; my mother has been dead a long time now. It would actually relieve my mind if there were someone else out there who would love Dad, if something was to happen to me."

Sitting up instantly, Jed propped himself up so he could see Melissa's face; he vowed solemnly. "Nothing will happen to you... I promise!"

Frowning up at Jed in earnest warning, Melissa put a finger over his lips in caution. "Don't make pledges you might not be able to keep; the job we do is extremely dangerous, events can sometime get out of hand and beyond our control!"

Sighing in reluctant agreement, Jed changed the subject again when Melissa dropped her hand from his lips. "I talked to your father tonight."

Melissa's eyebrows lifted inquisitively in surprise. "Oh, and what did the two of you talk about?"

Smiling reassuringly, Jed tweaked Melissa's nose playfully. "We talked about the ranch some, I asked him about the feasibility of putting cattle on here; he said I didn't need to buy land right now because what you have is sufficient to hold a few hundred head."

Melissa nodded thoughtfully. "That is true; if you are going to try cattle here, you shouldn't get too big at first at least until you decide whether you want to stick with it or not."

Jed grinned at that good advice. "You are right... I will start slowly before working up to a full herd; your father also said that I don't need to buy any because there is more than enough money in the ranch accounts to pay for the cattle I need. He did suggest though that I do the same thing he did and invest in the ranch, instead of just the cattle."

Frowning curiously, Melissa wondered where this conversation was going. "Yes, that's what my dad did; we had the ranch appraised first then he gave me half the value so we would be equal partners. Because you're going to be my husband, you'll already have a share so you don't need to worry about that."

Scowling irritably, Jed shook his head earnestly in denial. "No, the ranch is yours; unless I invest in it, I don't want anything to do with it!"

Sighing, Melissa was puzzled by Jed's adamant refusal to share the ranch with her. "So, you are asking me if you can invest in the ranch... is that it?"

Jed nodded definitely. "Yes, could I invest in your ranch?"

Melissa shook her head in impatience. "Well, why didn't you just say so; I don't mind at all, but you don't have to... what's mine is yours."

Smiling down at Melissa's impatient tone Jed nodding decisively. "Yes, I must; I wouldn't feel like I'm part of it if I didn't, and we don't want that."

Reaching up, Melissa brought Jed's head down for a deep kiss to cut him off; when she finally let him go... she smiled up at him encouragingly. "Whatever makes you feel comfortable and happy here, is okay with me!"

Lying back, Jed pulled Melissa against him sleepily content now that he had that conversation out of the way. "Okay, but I still needed to make sure you wouldn't mind."

Turning before cuddling closer, Melissa yawned sleepily. "Goodnight, I love you."

Jed chuckled in delight when Melissa's yawn almost drowned out her words. "I love you too."

CHAPTER THIRTEEN

Waking earlier than usual, Tommy scrambled out of bed eagerly... quickly dressing in anticipation; he raced down the stairs to the kitchen, forgetting his Aunt Melissa's rule about running in the house in his excitement.

Mrs. Donaldson jumped in shocked surprise when Tommy came barrelling through the kitchen door. Jessica on her way to the table, barely got the pot of hot coffee she just took out of the fire up out of harm's way; thankfully avoiding a catastrophe at the last possible minute... just when it seemed they were about to collide.

Coming to an abrupt halt, Tommy gestured in apology; he looked up at the redheaded new addition to the household sheepishly. "Oh, I'm really sorry Mrs. Donaldson... I didn't think anyone would be up yet."

Grinning in forgiveness, Jessica reached with her free hand then ruffled his hair playfully. She turned to put the pot down in the center of the table on its stand, which was an ingenious invention by Alec who hated cold coffee so built a platform with a hole in the center to place a candle underneath to keep it hot until breakfast was ready... before turning back to him. "It's all right Tommy, just be a bit more careful; where are you going in such a hurry?"

Tommy's smile turned shy almost instantly; he shrugged in embarrassment. "I wanted to grab some breakfast for me and Gi... I mean my father."

Turning away to hide the tears that suddenly sprang to her eyes at Tommy's hesitation; Jessica walked over to the oven above the fireplace to give herself time. She took a pan of fresh buns out and set them on the counter. Alec told her the young boy's story last night... The widow didn't think Melissa's foster son would appreciate any sympathy, though.

Once the buns were on the counter, Jessica turned back to Tommy her emotions back under control; she waved towards the cupboard above the counter. "I will put some butter on some of these buns for you, if you look up there you will find the last of the apples."

Nodding happily, Tommy turned towards the cupboard indicated; Melissa's foster son put two of them in his pockets.

Finished putting butter on the promised buns, Jessica placed them in a basket she saw sitting on the back of the counter. As a treat she added a few strawberries out of the jar she found in the cellar... it was dated last year; dividing them up she made sure everyone would get a treat, but it was the last of them until the new season produced more. She put a small jar of cream with two spoons inside then started scooping porridge into a bowl next.

Tommy walked over closer to Mrs. Donaldson and looked at her earnestly; he fidgeted for a moment undecided whether he should ask her or not. Finally, he blurted out in a rush before he could change his mind. "Do you think Giant Bear would mind if I called him Father?"

Mrs. Donaldson caught off guard by such a personal question from Tommy, finished putting the porridge into the second bowl... just to have a moment to think. Jessica hoped her answer would not get her into any trouble; carefully she put the two bowls into the basket. She smiled at Mary's son in encouragement when she turned with basket in hand then held it towards the boy. "I'm sure he would love that; your mother is with your father now so when you go wake them up tell your mom to come see me, I could use a helping hand today."

Beaming shyly in thanks, Tommy took the basket before grinning up at her eagerly. "Thank you, Mrs. Donaldson; I will send my mother over right away."

Racing out of the room with his father's breakfast carefully held out not wanting to spill anything inside; Tommy couldn't help feeling grateful to Mrs. Donaldson for providing him with an excuse to visit with his dad alone... now he wouldn't have to hurt his mother's feelings.

Reaching the barn doors quickly, Tommy slipped inside carefully then walked to the bottom of the ladder; he looked up at the loft earnestly and fidgeted for a moment suddenly unsure of himself... mustering up his courage he called up hesitantly. "Mom, can I come up?"

Mary's head popped overtop of the ladder instantly she grinned down at her son in pleasant surprise. "Just wait down there, Tommy; we will be right down."

Turning without protest away from the ladder, Tommy went to a pile of straw then put his basket down beside it before plopping down gleefully waiting patiently in anticipation. He looked towards the ladder expectantly, but the minutes ticked by without either parent showing themselves. To remind his mother he was still waiting... he called out impatiently. "Mom, Mrs. Donaldson needs you in the kitchen today she said!"

Tommy heard his mother mumble something but didn't catch what she said; he sighed resignedly. Waiting, he tried to be patient.

It was not long before Mary came down the ladder... although it seemed like forever to her son; she stood in front of him then grinned down at his displeased expression but didn't feel one bit sorry. Laughing at his look, she squatted down for a good morning hug. It wasn't until she stood back up that she noticed the basket. Golden Dove cocked her head curiously and looked back at her son inquisitively. "What do you have there, Tommy?"

Getting up eagerly, Tommy whispered in conspiracy. "I brought breakfast for me and... Father."

Hugging Tommy, trying to encourage him; Mary gave a sad sigh at his uncertainty. She held him away so she could see his face before frowning in concern. "You're not too upset at me, are you... finding out about your father the way you did?"

Moving back, Tommy thought about it for a moment; he shook his head negatively... reassuring his mother. "No, I'm just glad I have a dad. Do you think he would mind if I hung around him today?"

Giant Bear stepped into the light having stayed in the background listening... not wanting to intrude; he smiled in encouragement down at his son before nodding pleased that Tommy wanted to spend time with him. "I would be glad to have you with me today!"

Mary grinned at her husband in loving praise. "You speak pretty good English now, when we first met you only knew a few words; I can see you will have no trouble talking to Tommy so I will let the two of you get acquainted."

Kissing Mary goodbye, Giant Bear reached up and tweaked her nose playfully. "You can thank Jed for the English lessons; he taught me well!"

Nodding, Mary would definitely thank Jed later for his good teaching abilities; she turned to Tommy for a final goodbye.

"I'll see you two later."

Mary slipped out the door quickly.

Giant Bear and Tommy stood regarding each other assessingly for a moment in silence. Getting uncomfortable, the boy broke the stillness. He smiled hesitantly at his father then waved down at the basket he brought. "I have some breakfast for us; I wasn't sure what you would like... Mrs. Donaldson helped me put it together."

Tommy's voice trailed off in uncertainty, unsure of what to say next; he was getting unnerved by his father's quite surveillance.

Moving closer to his son, Giant Bear put a hand on Tommy's shoulder in reassurance. "Whatever you have there will be fine with me."

Nodding relieved, Tommy squatted down to unpack their breakfast basket blissfully.

*****

Mary went to the back entrance of the house before going into the kitchen. The delicious smells wafting in the air caused her to inhale deeply in appreciation, unexpectedly her belly rumbled loudly in hunger making her grimace in embarrassment. She turned towards Mrs. Donaldson when she heard a chuckle behind her; Golden Dove smiled in delight as she rubbed her belly hungrily. "Something sure smells good, I'm starving!"

Mrs. Donaldson nodded knowingly having heard Mary's belly growl with a big grin... she motioned in reproach before waving away the Mrs. "First off, please call me Jessica all my friends do. Secondly, with all the excitement going on around here someone had to make sure everyone eats properly. Sit down please; I was expecting you so I have your breakfast ready."

Smirking cheekily at Jessica, Mary sat obediently; she gestured in grateful thanks. "I want to thank you for giving me an excuse to leave Tommy and Giant Bear alone today, now they can get to know each other without my interference."

Looking down, Mary inhaled deeply in appreciation when Jessica put a bowl of hot porridge with strawberries and cream in front of her; she grinned gratefully at the widow in anticipation. "Oh, my favourite... thank you!"

Jessica beamed in satisfaction at Mary's obvious pleasure in the breakfast she had painstakingly made before pointing upwards at the ceiling in explanation. "I already took some to Melissa and Jed. I'm just about to take Alec a tray. Once everyone finishes eating, we can meet here in the kitchen to discuss decorations, dresses, and what not! Oh, I almost forgot... would you tell Mell if she comes down before I get back that Mrs. Elton will be here soon; she told me last night that she would pick up the material for the dresses which will be her wedding present to you ladies. On her way here, she will also pick up Jane and a friend of hers to help make them."

Grinning in relief at having more helping hands, especially on such short notice, Mary nodded in agreement. "That's excellent news; I'll be sure to pass along your message to Melissa. When I finish my breakfast, I will start making bread while I wait for everyone else to arrive."

Jessica turned away from Mary... satisfied everything was in control before picking up the breakfast tray she had waiting. She hurried out; turning right, she went down the hall to Alec's room in anticipation. She knocked softly, but couldn't help hesitating for a moment when she heard a muffled call from inside the room.

"Come in!"

Shaking off her nerves, Jessica entered with a flourish; she walked quickly over to the bed before Alec could protest it wasn't proper for her to be there. She set the breakfast tray across his lap then removed the cloth dramatically. Nervously, she began rearranging things on the tray trying to hide her uneasiness as best she could. Mustering her courage, she peeked down at Melissa's father shyly. The widow had a hint of invitation on her face... she made sure though that it was not too obvious.

Alec smiled up at Jessica in thanks, appreciating the widow's efforts. "Thank you, it looks delicious!"

Smiling bashfully at Alec's approval... Jessica turned away. She knew he had gotten her subtle message so went over to open the drapes to let the sunshine in. From there, she went over to the closet to pull out his chair. Melissa told her this morning where to find it when she had asked. The widow pushed it across the room and left it beside the bed; she returned to the closet before calling over her shoulder inquisitively. "What would you like to wear today?"

Finishing his breakfast... Alec sat back with a contented sigh; he sipped his coffee thoughtfully watching Jessica move about his room nervously. He had noticed the invitation plain in her glance, but wasn't sure what she meant by it. Hearing her muffled question, he thought about it for a moment then answered her. "My black pants with a blue shirt will do for today."

Taking her time, Jessica searched the closet until she found the pants then the shirt; going to the tall dresser next, she took out clean socks and underwear. She walked over to the bed before depositing everything within easy reach of his hand. Turning away so Alec couldn't see her sly smirk, the widow asked with a hopeful tone in her voice... she tried hard to hide it but wasn't quite successful. "Do you need any help?"

Alec coughed to clear his throat after catching a quick glimpse of Jessica's crafty smile; not wanting her to hear the laughter in his voice... he shook his head negatively. "No thank you Mrs. Donaldson, I think I can manage now."

Patting the bed beside him in silent invitation... between the enticement in Jessica's eyes and the sly hopeful smirk; Alec figured it was time for a serious talk. "Come sit for a moment."

Sitting on the edge of the bed, Jessica was ready to get up immediately if he made an improper advance; she quivered in hope, the widow had waited a long time for this... with any luck he would ask today.

Smiling at Jessica's shy uncertainty, Alec set his coffee cup down on the tray and removed it to the bedside table out of the way; he turned back to face her before reaching over then took her hand in his tenderly. "Look at me, please!"

Turning until she was facing Alec fully, Jessica looked him straight in the eye boldly; unafraid, but nervous just the same.

Squeezing her hand gently in encouragement; Alec continued, now even more sure with what he saw in Jessica's eyes. "We have known each other for several years and both of us have been widowed for a long time... I have a unique proposition for you!"

Tensing instantly thinking the worst, Jessica's emerald eyes flashed dangerously... giving away her thoughts.

Alec chuckled in delight at the spirit and fire he saw reflected in Jessica's eyes; he held up his free hand in apology before she could say anything. "I am sorry, I'm not doing this very well... just listen to it all before you yell at me."

Jessica's eyes softened instantly in understanding; she nodded slightly in confusion not saying a word waiting for Alec to finish... still hoping to hear what she wanted.

Smiling in relief when he saw Jessica's eyes soften, Alec put his free hand over top of their locked hands and tried to explain again; this time in a different way. "My late wife was the love of my life, when she died, I didn't think I could ever feel again. It didn't matter because Melissa needed me. I sometimes wonder if I would have survived my wife's death if she hadn't. Now my daughter is getting married so I want to try living again. I will always have a place in my heart reserved for my Patricia, but I would like to try love again. I have always wanted to travel around the country. I just didn't want to go alone. I have liked you for a long time so I wanted to ask you this; after my daughter is married, would you like to come with me. We could get married quietly later if you are concerned about your reputation... or not, the choice is yours. Then we could live here after we are done travelling to help Melissa and Jed with the ranch, since I'm part owner."

Grinning ecstatically at Alec, Jessica ignored the... 'or not' in relief. She nodded emphatically in eagerness. "Yes, I will marry you. I must confess that I have thought about you too; I also loved my husband with an intense passion, but like you I feel it is time to put him away. Surely, we can find as much love and passion together, as we had with our dead spouses. It might be different though more comfortable maybe, not as all consuming. I'm not sure if that is the right words or not, hopefully you know what I mean."

Smiling in understanding, Alec chuckled knowingly. "Believe it or not... I think I do; even though I'm in a wheelchair, I can still make love to a woman so the passion part will be no problem!"

Jessica blushed deeply before leaning forward boldly. "I'm so glad to hear that!"

Alec's response halted in surprise as Jessica took the initiative then claimed his lips for a kiss. He broke the kiss reluctantly, sighing regretfully he pulled away. "As much as I would like to stay here to prove to you that I can still make love to a woman, everybody is waiting for us. I hope you don't mind, but I would like to keep this quiet for a while; at least until after the young ones are married, if possible. Jed wants to take Melissa to Boston on a honeymoon so maybe we could meet them there then have a quiet wedding... if that's okay with you?"

Sitting back breathless, Jessica smiled sweetly in satisfaction glad she initiated the kiss. It was more of a test, thankfully she was right as her body tingled then flushed slightly in passion. "I agree, we shouldn't say anything right now... I like the idea of a quiet Boston wedding. There is no one I care to invite except my children who won't come no matter where it is, so that suits me just fine! As for living here, I like that idea as well; I have always admired Melissa, even before I met you."

Pulling a surprised and giggling Jessica down for another passionate kiss, Alec let her help him get dressed after all. There was a lot of laughter and wrestling before he was ready; both were happier than they had been in many years... it showed in their sparkling eyes.

*****

Finishing the promised bread, Mary put it to the side to rise before covering it with a towel. She was just turning away to get herself a cup of coffee when Jed and Melissa came in.

Melissa took the breakfast tray from Jed then put it on the counter; she turned to Mary with a smile as she accepted two cups from her grinning friend.

Mary gave Melissa the good news about the judge's wife coming with extra help; she waited patiently while the two newcomers found themselves a seat at the table before she poured them a coffee. Golden Dove just sat down when Wade followed closely by Gloria arrived then they too chose a chair... making sure they were next to each other.

Jessica pushing Alec's wheelchair arrived last; both were still flushed from their playful bout in the bedroom... they tried hard to hide their inflamed faces. The widow pushed Melissa's father to his spot at the head of the table before she sat in the last chair.

Standing up instantly, Mary got the newcomers cups for coffee then poured them each a cup before sitting in her seat once more.

It took a few minutes for the morning greetings and excited chatter to settle down before they all sat in comfortable silence, sipping coffee in contemplation; each deep in their own thoughts.

Shaking off her thoughts of last night, Melissa looked around at all her friends and family then grinned in contented pleasure. Her gaze rested on the widow; she beamed across the table at the redhead trying to put her at ease when she noticed a flush in her cheeks. Mell mistook the heightened face colour for embarrassment, so tried to make the new addition to the household feel more welcome by leaning forward earnestly. "How is the guest room, Mrs. Donaldson... comfortable, I hope?"

Jessica smiled over at Melissa before glancing around then included everyone in her look; she turned back to answer Alec's daughter as she motioned pleadingly. "Please everyone, call me Jessica no more 'Mrs.', it makes me feel old! To answer your question, I slept very well... thank you."

Inclining her head in agreement at Jessica, Melissa about to comment paused then caulked her head instead... listening; she heard a distant rumble of a carriage and instantly she got up in excitement. Before she hurried out, she turned to the housekeeper. "I will go greet the ladies arriving. Gloria, will you make more coffee than get everyone settled in the dining room since its much bigger we won't be as crowded in there."

Melissa rushed out of the kitchen after Gloria nodded in agreement then down the hallway. She opened the front door... instantly, she was enfolded in a big hug. Laughing in delight, she pushed away from an ecstatic Jane. "Well, hello there; I'm so glad you could come today."

Jane smiled broadly before letting Melissa go reluctantly. "Wouldn't miss it for the world, besides I need to see where I'll be living from now on don't I!"

Laughing in delight at Jane's boldness, Melissa gestured in affection towards her friend before pointing at the wooden sidewalk behind her in explanation. "To the point as usual, well if you will follow me, I'll show you where you and your family will be staying."

Looking beyond her friend, Melissa grinned at Mrs. Elton before gesturing in invitation. "You and Sarah can come too if you want?"

Betty smiled regretfully then shook her head negatively. "No, I think we will go visit with everybody else if you don't mind... the others don't know Sarah so I want to introduce her."

Nodding in agreement, Melissa stepped out of the doorway before waving down the hallway to the right. "They are all in the dining room waiting for you; tell them we will be back in a bit."

Grabbing Jane by the hand in excitement; Melissa not even bothering to change out of her moccasins, ran down the porch to the stairs... pulling her friend along insistently.

Pulling back so Melissa had to let go of her, Jane couldn't help laughing heartily... out of breath. "Will you slow down already; just because you wear pants don't mean the rest of us do!"

Blushing in embarrassment, Melissa let go of Jane's hand reluctantly; she turned to her friend and gestured in apology. "Oh sorry, I forgot myself!"

Grinning good-naturedly, Jane reached over and grabbed Melissa's hand before pulling her into a hearty embrace; she whispered in her ear, affectionately. "It's okay, I forgive you!"

Jane let Melissa go with a playful push and continued walking beside her friend slowly... chatting excitedly as they strolled along; they both quieted when they heard the banging of hammers before quickening their steps slightly.

Smiling over at Jane, Melissa motioned proudly at the frame of the building already started. "This will be your cabin when it is ready."

Beaming radiantly over at Melissa, Jane turned away then gazed around in approval. "Wow, this is a gorgeous spot... I like it."

Melissa turned away from Jane at a loud shout coming from the new building.

Brad raced over and swept Jane up before twirling her around playfully; he gave his wife a passionate kiss before he set her back on her feet... stepping back, he grinned suggestively. "I missed you last night."

Gazing up adoringly at Brad, Jane reached up... stroking his cheek tenderly. "I missed you too."

Clearing her throat to get their attention; Melissa chuckled when both her friends gave a guilty start at forgetting her presence. They turned to her with identical embarrassed expressions... she smirked, but let them off the hook before motioning at Brad in invitation. "You can show Jane the sketch of her new home please."

Nodding quickly, Brad tried to hide his discomfited face. Pulling the paper out of his pocket, he showed it proudly to Jane in excitement. "See there's two bedrooms downstairs, a sitting room, as well as a kitchen; there is also a loft upstairs, it will be large enough for the two girls to sleep in."

Smiling in delight, Jane studied the drawing in approval before looking up. "It's absolutely gorgeous; thank you Melissa, from the bottom of my heart!"

Turning, Jane pulled Mell into another hug to show her gratitude.

Squeezing Jane gently, Melissa grinned to herself reflectively; if her older friends were going to be staying here with them, she would have to get use to all this hugging. Jane was just one of those types of people that loved to show affection. Mell pushed her away tenderly. "Come on, I'll take you back to the house to meet everyone."

Inclining her head in agreement, Jane stepped back then went to her husband for one last kiss before both women turned away from Brad and hurried back to the house; they went straight to the dining room where everyone was impatiently waiting.

Melissa made introductions, since neither Wade nor Gloria knew Jane then they all sat around drinking coffee while chatting. The excitement in the air was evident as everyone waited for her to tell them what she expected from them.

Everyone quieted when Melissa began handing out assignments. She looked at each group as she called out names to see if there were any objections. "Okay... I would like Mrs. Elton, Sarah, Jane, and Jessica to make the dresses because they will take the longest. Gloria with the help of Mary can do all the cooking. Dad can do the invitations with my help then I will deliver them when I go to work; I'll also gather supplies and decorations for the house while I'm in town. Wade I would like you to take Giant Bear, you might as well take Tommy too then gather poles. Take some of the planks the men are using to make me a platform with an archway. I will give you a sketch of what I want. The new hands can keep building the cabins. Wade, you and Giant Bear can help them after you're finished making the platform for me. Jed can also help Wade until I go to town then he can come help me with supplies and decorations. Anybody who finishes their tasks can help wherever they think that they can do the most good! Would anybody like to add anything?"

Betty spoke up instantly, she pointed in request at Melissa. "Before you do anything we need measurements."

Grimacing, not looking forward to standing in one place for that long; Melissa nodded at Mrs. Elton in agreement before getting up. "Okay, I will meet you upstairs after I make a sketch for Wade."

Nodding in satisfaction, Betty got up and followed Melissa to the entryway; everyone else left obediently eager to start their assignments too.

Moving out of the way, Melissa watched in satisfaction as the groups split up and went their separate ways once in the hallway. She waited until Alec came out before walking behind his chair then pushed him across to the den; Jed was behind her with Wade following him.

Once they entered; Melissa pushed her father to the front of the desk and left him there while she went behind it... gathering her chair that was always against the wall, Mell put it under the desk before sitting down. She took out paper, ink, and pen from the drawer.

The three men gathered around the desk, as close to it as they could get in order to watch what Melissa was doing.

Giving verbal instructions, Melissa drew the design as she talked so they wouldn't miss anything. "Okay, I want a raised platform put along the left side of the house going towards the back door. It will be much easier to get the piano outside from the living room patio doors instead of the front porch, which only has one door. If we stay on that side of the house the guests won't be bothered by the wooden walkway since it will be behind them. I want you to put the planks side by side, but only tack them together lightly so they can be pulled apart when we are done with them. The platform is for the minister to stand on only so the guests can see him clearly. You might want to add a lower platform in front. We can stand on it that way everyone can see us too. I also want two poles about the size of your forearm; it must be tall enough so the minister isn't blocked. Get another pole to nail across the top of the other two. This one doesn't have to be as wide. It should be long though. The archway needs to be set about a foot in front of the platform. I want us to go through it first. I want it big enough it won't block the view of our guests because they will be looking through the archway at us. If you can peel the bark off the poles then tack the archway together, don't set it up right away because we need to decorate it first."

Melissa looked at Alec inquisitively. "Dad, would you start making a list of names to send invitations to? Only make ones for people around here and in town; there is not enough time to invite people from too far away. We will hand deliver them since some cannot read, but they would be quite upset if they didn't get one. I can always read it to them, if they wish. I'll take Wade out and show him where I want the platform set up while you do that."

Alec nodded when Melissa looked in his direction; he wheeled himself around the desk to start.

Putting her chair back in its corner, Melissa led Wade and Jed out of the den.

*****

Betty led her three helpers upstairs into the spare room. It was the one Jessica was using, but she didn't mind at all... she even suggested using it. They pushed all the furniture into a corner to give them more space, making sure though the bed was still accessible for the widow to use; once finished they started bringing in the supplies they needed from the wagon.

Mary walked inside once they finished unloading; she looked around until she spotted Betty then went to her before gesturing apologetically... knowing the judge's wife already bought the material. "Mrs. Elton you only need to make two wedding dresses because I don't need one, I hope you can return the extra."

Smiling in relief, Betty inclined her head in confirmation; that would give them more time to work on the other two. She wasn't worried about the extra material. She would find a use for it sooner or later... she frowned in puzzlement. "Well, it will definitely make it faster but are you sure you don't need one?"

Nodding her head emphatically, Mary waved towards her brother's ranch. "I have my Indian bridal dress hid at home; I think Giant Bear would like me to wear it, if nobody objects."

Shrugging dismissively, Betty didn't see any harm in it; Mary was a grown woman and could make her own decisions... she would make sure nobody else objected either. The judge's wife motioned in anxiety remembering the discussion she had with Melissa last night about her neighbour. "That makes sense, but I heard about the threats your brother made, will you be able to get it before the wedding?"

Shaking her head vigorously in confirmation, Mary pointed towards the town. "Yes, Brian will be going into town today at three o'clock. I also wanted to ask you if I could borrow your wagon for a bit; to gather some stuff while he's gone."

Betty frowned apprehensively at the thought of Mary going to her brother's place; she put her hand over the younger woman's arm before squeezing it in worry. "Sure, you can use my wagon... I don't think you should go alone, though!"

Jane stepped forward immediately, not wanting Mary to go by herself either. "I will get my husband; we will take her."

Smiling in thanks, Mary hid a grimace not wanting anyone else to get hurt if her brother showed up unexpectedly. She turned to Jane when Mrs. Elton's hand dropped from her arm. "That's really kind of you... are you sure; it could cause you and your husband trouble?"

Beaming soothingly, Jane reached out before patting Mary's arm. "Nonsense, we will be happy to help you."

The two women turned to leave; they stopped short suddenly almost in guilty surprise when they noticed Melissa standing by the door.

Melissa scowled at the two conspirators chidingly. "I will go with you as well, just in case Brian comes home unexpectedly; that way there is nothing he can do to stop you since the Sheriff is with you."

Mary's smile was a little edgy... she nodded reluctantly. "Okay, I give up. You do have time to have your measurements taken before we leave; I will meet both of you downstairs when you are done here."

Leaving, Mary closed the door softly on her way out.

Watching Mary leave in surprise; Melissa frowned at the closed door in suspicion. "That was easier than I thought it would be. I was sure she would insist on going alone."

Laughing knowingly when Melissa turned to look at her, Jane gestured in reassurance. "I better go down and keep my eye on her. I think you're right; it was much too easy!"

Turning back into the room when Jane left, Melissa was relieved now that she didn't have to worry about Mary slipping away by herself.

*****

Twenty minutes later, Melissa was striding purposely towards the den to let Alec know where she was going... in case there was any trouble. Knocking softly, she walked in at her father's muffled response to enter. Mell walked to the desk before smiling down at him in apology when he looked up at her inquisitively. "Sorry Dad, I'm going to have to run out on you!"

Alec grinned up at Melissa knowingly before laughing as he motioned teasingly. "That's okay... I'm sure I can manage on my own; I just had this feeling you would find a way to get out of such a boring job as writing invitations."

Chuckling at Alec's put upon expression; Melissa walked around the desk before bending down to give her father a kiss on the forehead. "Good, I am not disappointing you! Unfortunately, I'm not looking forward to this either. I have to take Mary to Brian's to collect her belongings. Writing invitations might be boring, but it's probably safer."

Frowning slightly in apprehension, Alec knew protesting would do him no good Melissa would go regardless of his feelings; he accepted her goodbye kiss before motioning in forewarning when she stood back up. "Okay, but if you're not back by dark, I will send out the cavalry."

Melissa laughed in delight as she walked towards the door, but she turned back before opening it; her expression now serious. Mell didn't argue with Alec's statement that she might need cavalry. "Okay, I will see you later."

Leaving the den, Melissa was almost at the front door when Jane came in from outside.

Smiling in greeting, Jane gestured chidingly. "There you are... we are all waiting for you. Brad saddled Lightning; it was Mary's suggestion, she didn't think you would want to ride in the wagon with us."

Nodding curtly, Melissa thought of Brian and his threats. "Mary is right; one of us should have a horse for a quick getaway... just in case."

Snorting in delighted disbelief, Jane was all too aware of Melissa's aversions to wagons; she couldn't help teasing her new boss... while she waited patiently for Mell to strap on her gun belt, hook her sheriff's badge on her shirt then change out of her moccasins. "That's the lamest excuse I ever heard of for getting out of riding in a bouncing wagon."

Chuckling at being caught red handed by Jane; Melissa didn't comment as they headed out the door together. She sobered in seriousness as she looked at her friend. "It might be a lame excuse, but a true one just the same!"

Before they got within hearing distance of Mary; Jane leaned closer to Melissa... she whispered cautiously in warning. "It's a good thing I went to keep an eye on her; your friend was walking towards the door when I went down the stairs. I pretended I didn't know what she was up to, but I stayed close to her after that."

Mary scowled down angrily at Melissa from the seat of the wagon when they reached her; she snapped irritably. "You sent Jane to watch me... didn't you?"

Melissa frowned up in warning at her angry friend and nodded decisively... not sorry in the least that Mary was upset with her. "Yes, I did! I know you don't want anyone else involved, but think of it this way. If Brian came home unexpectedly, he would lock you up then throw away the key. That would mean Giant Bear, Jed, and I would have to come to your rescue; do you really want your husband fighting with your brother over you, one or both could end up dead!"

Sighing forlornly, Mary nodded pacified; she didn't really want to go alone anyway, but had not wanted to ask anyone. She was just glad Melissa found out in time. "You're right as usual... I'm sorry for snapping at you!"

Reaching up, Melissa took Mary's hand before squeezing it gently. "It's okay, I forgive you!"

Letting go of Mary, Melissa turned away to mount Lightning; she looked over at Brad and nodded. "Okay, let's go before I change my mind!"

Brad nodded then clucked to the horses.

*****

It took them several hours to reach Brian's ranch because of the wagon... Melissa frowned in concern; it had taken longer than any of them expected.

Jumping down instantly without any assistance, Mary was too impatient and afraid that too much time had passed. She hurrying to the barn, making sure Brian's horse was still gone. She came back in a rush a few minutes later then grinned in relief at Melissa. "His horse isn't here; we only have a couple of hours if we are lucky before he gets back... so let's hurry!"

Nodding, Melissa dismounted and handed the reins to Brad after he helped his wife down. "You stay here and keep watch; I will call you when we need you."

Brad took Melissa's reins then tied Lightning with a slipknot to the back of the wagon.

Leading the way, Mary ushered them into the house quickly; she called out questioningly as she looked around. "Mrs. Jenkins, where are you?"

An older woman around sixty came out of the kitchen then hurried over to Mary in obvious relief.

Mary was surprised when the older woman rushed up to her and gave her a warm hug in greeting, usually she never showed affection.

Stepping back, the housekeeper held Mary out at arm's length and eyed her anxiously. "I have been so worried about you, Brian has been storming around the house ever since the Sheriff came here to tell him you were not coming back; he has been muttering nasty things under his breath ever since... figuring nobody could hear."

Smiling reassuringly, Mary gently pushed away from the housekeeper. "I'm okay, Mrs. Jenkins, I come for my things."

Letting Mary go reluctantly, Mrs. Jenkins frowned then wrung her hands in agitation as she eyed her boss's sister pleadingly. "I'm sorry, but I have strict orders not to let you have anything!"

Melissa stepped away from the door with her badge pinned firmly on her shirtfront so the older woman could see it plainly. "It's okay Mrs. Jenkins; I'm here to see that she gets her belongings without any problems."

The housekeeper smiled in relief before nodding. "Oh, that's different... with you here Sheriff, I can let her have them; unfortunately, I can't help or I will get fired."

Sighing in relief Mary reached out to pat the housekeeper's hand in sympathy. "That's okay Mrs. Jenkins, Melissa and her friend Jane will help me."

Relieved, Mrs. Jenkins nodded before hurrying back to the kitchen without another word.

Beckoning silently, Mary directed her two companions to follow her upstairs to her room. She pulled two large trunks out of her closet then started throwing things inside. "Just throw everything in that you find; I'll sort it later."

Melissa and Jane nodded before quickly following her example, none of them bothered to fold anything or look at what they were packing; they just threw it all into the trunk... everything they could lift that is. When they finished, Mary took a last look around then crawled under her bed to retrieve the two large parcels she had hidden there so long ago. Not even once in all these years, did she dare move them. She stuffed them in one of the trunks and lashed the lids down securely.

The three girls pushed with all their strength... groaning they dragged one then the other trunk to the top of the stairs; it had taken them nearly an hour to clean out Mary's room.

Mary sighed painfully when they got the trunks close to the stairs and she stood up in relief. "That is everything except for one trunk downstairs in the storage room; it's my hope chest... thankfully, it's already packed."

Jane nodded then started downstairs quickly, she called over her shoulder. "I'll get Brad to help with the trunks."

With that, Jane hurried as fast as her chubby legs could go down the stairs and out the front door; she returned a few minutes later with Brad.

Grinning teasingly, Brad looked at Mary questioningly. "Only two trunks?"

Shaking her head negatively, Mary shrugged before pointing downstairs. "No, but we can get that one last, it's not as important as these two."

Nodding, Brad heaved one trunk up onto his broad shoulder then carried it downstairs by himself.

The three women managed to carry the second one down by joining forces; by the time they reached the bottom of the stairs, Brad was back.

Hefting the trunk up onto his shoulder, Brad gave a grunt of effort since this one was a tad heavier. Thankfully, he still managed to carry it outside to the wagon on his own. Jane's husband returned quickly and joined the others at the storage room where they were trying to push the bigger hope chest out into the hallway. He tried to lift it by himself, but it was too heavy; they joined forces and got it outside before loading it into the bed of the wagon.

Just as they finished, the unmistakable sounds of horses approaching the ranch echoed in the stillness... deadly silence fell as everyone froze instantly.

Melissa turned towards Brad then spoke urgently. "Untie Lightning and drop the reins; afterwards, get the ladies into the wagon as fast as you can!"

Brad did what he was instructed to do gladly; he was climbing into the wagon when two men entered the yard.

Spinning around, Melissa unhooked the straps on both guns then faced Brian and waited for him to ride up.

Brian stopped in front of Melissa and smiled triumphantly. He gestured rudely first at Mary then towards Mell. "Well, if it isn't my wayward sister and the lady sheriff; what are you doing here sneaking around my house stealing things?"

Relaxing her stance, Melissa dropped her arms in readiness. Just in case Brian got any foolish ideas, now her hands were in easy reach of her guns. "We didn't take anything that was yours... I made sure of that; since I'm the Sheriff everything was done legally."

Dismounting, Brian handed the reins of his horse to his hired man... he turned to face Melissa before copying her stance. "My sister is to marry someone from South Dakota; the rest of you can leave, but she stays!"

Smirking confidently, Melissa shook her head negatively. "Let me bring you up-to-date Brian! Mary is over twenty-five, as well as a widow so she can go where she wants or marry whoever she chooses; your sister doesn't have to marry if she does not want to!"

Calling back over her shoulder, Melissa asked her friend without turning away from Brian keeping her gaze steady. "Mary, do you want to stay here then marry the man your brother has chosen?"

Standing up to face Brian, Mary made sure he could see her gesture as she shook her head negatively before answering verbally; not wanting to distract Melissa by making her friend turn to see her answer. "No! I don't want to stay here. I also refuse to marry anyone my brother has chosen for me!"

Nodding decisively, Melissa kept her gaze locked on Brian's not giving an inch. "You have your answer; I suggest that you go into your house and let us leave now before it's too late."

Brian weighed Melissa's stance, and her willingness to use her guns; he lifted his hands away from his reluctantly then backed away... knowing he was no match for Mell. "Have it your way Sheriff, but you haven't heard the last of me!"

With that parting, Brian turned; he stormed to the house before slamming the door behind him.

Let out the breath she had been holding, Melissa quickly mounted her horse. "Let's get out of here before he tries something stupid!"

Brad didn't need to be told twice; he clucked to the horses glad to be heading back to the ranch.

*****

Jed and Giant Bear were just walking towards the barn when the sound of horses pulling a wagon reached them. They looked at each other in relief; turning they waited for Melissa's party to come into view. Grey Wolf studied Mell intently for any signs of injury. Giant Bear did the same with Mary, when they were satisfied that neither was hurt... both men visibly relaxed.

Melissa reached them first then dismounted; she turned to eye both men warily when they stood there saying nothing.

Dusty rushed up from the barn and took the sheriff's horse.

Scowling at the two men angrily, Melissa asked suspiciously. "Going somewhere you two?"

Shaking his head negatively, Jed gestured dismissively. "Not anymore, why didn't you tell us you were going to Brian's; we were both very worried when we found out!"

Shrugging her shoulders stiffly, Melissa scowled irritably. "I told my father where we were going... I didn't know I needed to report to either of you when I go somewhere?"

Holding up his hands in surrender, Jed dropped them as he motioned placatingly. "I'm sorry; I didn't say that right; I just meant that as your Deputy, I should have been with you."

Sighing in apology, Melissa waved as her anger drained away instantly. "No, I am sorry; I'm just not used to having a Deputy with me all the time."

Pulling Melissa into his arms in relief now that her annoyance had dissipated, Jed tried to soothe her ruffled feathers. "Well, please try to remember in the future; I will try not to question you when you do go without me."

Kissing Jed in apology, Melissa finally stepped back with a nod of agreement.

Giant Bear left the two of them alone then walked over to the wagon and scolded Mary for not telling him her plans.

Eyeing Melissa inquisitively, Jed motioned curiously. "Did you have any problems?"

Frowning grimly, Melissa shook her head negatively. "Not really, Brian wasn't there when we arrived; unfortunately, he did show up just as we were leaving."

Melissa went on to tell them everything that happened before turning to Giant Bear first. When she finished with him, she gave instructions to Jed as well. "Would you take the big trunk to the barn. Mary doesn't need that one. Hun, can you and Brad haul the other two trunks up to the spare room please; she will have to share it with Jessica. We can wait until tomorrow to go to town for supplies since it is already too late... it's almost dark."

Jed nodded then started to lift one end of the trunk obediently, but stopped at his friend's remark.

Giant Bear stepped forward insistently... he pointed towards the barn. "All of Golden Dove's trunks can go to the barn; she will be staying there with me from now on."

Mary smiled widely up at Giant Bear in pleasure and nodded eagerly. "As you wish!"

CHAPTER FOURTEEN

Melissa woke then groaned in dismay at the sound of rain drumming on her window. Drat, just what she needed a wet soggy ride first thing in the morning! She turned to cuddle back up to Jed, but found him gone... she frowned in annoyance. It was the first time since they started sleeping together that he wasn't there when she woke up, and she was disappointed. She turned onto her back before stretching; yawning sleepily, she wondered where Grey Wolf had gotten to so early in the morning.

A soft, hesitant knock caught Melissa's attention... she cocked her head inquisitively; it couldn't be Jed knocking, of course. She called out sleepily after checking to make sure she was decently covered. "Come in."

Smiling, Melissa grinned in pleasure when Jessica entered with a breakfast tray; she sat up now wide-awake. "Good morning... you don't need to bring me breakfast every morning."

Jessica beamed amicably and whispered in conspiracy even though no one else was around to hear. "I know that, but I enjoy doing it... just don't tell anyone!"

Chuckling at Jessica's dramatics, Melissa nodded in gratification; not really having any objections. "Okay, if you insist... I won't complain too much. Do you know where Jed is by any chance?"

Cheerfully, Jessica nodded that she did and put the tray across Melissa's lap before looking at her. "Yes, he told me to let you sleep; I'm to tell you when you got up that he went hunting with Giant Bear this morning."

Nodding in thanks for the information, Melissa dug into her porridge hungrily while Jessica cleaned her bedroom; she finished her meal and sipped contentedly on her coffee... watching the redhead fussily tidy up the clutter in her room.

Melissa smirked at Jessica when she looked over to see if Mell was finished yet... she motioned teasingly. "You're going to spoil me bringing me breakfast then cleaning up after me all the time!"

Sighing wistfully, Jessica thought of her silent house that had once been filled with laughter. "I enjoy doing things for people; it's been a little lonely at home since my husband died... my youngest left the house a year ago, after she got married."

Melissa inclined her head in sympathetic understanding... she gestured curiously. "How many kids do you have, if you don't mind me asking?"

Beaming proudly, Jessica she shook her head negatively. "No, I don't mind. I have two boys who left before my husband died and one girl; my Johnny has been dead three years now."

Frowning wishfully hoping someday to have her own kids, Melissa changed the subject when Jessica walked over to the bed. "Is everyone else up yet?"

Jessica nodded then gestured across the hall towards the spare room. "Mrs. Elton, Jane, and Sarah arrived ten minutes ago... I'm on my way to help them now that you are done. Mary is already in the kitchen cooking up a storm; Gloria will be helping her after she finishes breakfast. Alec is in the den already, finishing up the invitations."

Sighing in satisfaction, Melissa grinned in approval. "Okay, can you find out from the ladies if they need anything from town; if they do, make a list for me. I will pick everything up after work, unless Charlie's boys can bring it here sooner."

Taking the tray from Melissa's lap, Jessica left without another word.

Getting up, Melissa rummaged in her closet for clean pants, shirt, underwear, and socks... quickly she got dressed. She left her room and went across the hall into the sewing room; she grinned at everyone gathered cheerfully. "Good morning, ladies."

Everyone returned the greeting almost simultaneously; they looked up quickly before looking back down... continuing their sewing as if they hadn't stopped even for a second.

Chuckling at the busy women, Melissa turned to Mrs. Elton inquisitively. "Was there any trouble in town yesterday without me there?"

Betty shook her head negatively before smiling up in reassurance. "Nope, John told me to tell you that everything was quiet; he figured you would be asking."

Nodding in relief, Melissa had been worried about no sheriff or deputy around for the last two weeks anything could have happened. She had been in town the day before of course, but not long enough... Mell gestured enquiringly. "I'll be going into work today so is there anything you need me to do?"

Shrugging, Betty shook her head negatively. "No, not today; tomorrow we need to do a proper fitting before the hem can be adjusted, so you are free to go."

Hiding a grimace of relief, Melissa was not looking forward to all those layers of silk she was required to wear. She left the women without another word then went downstairs to see her father next; giving a quick knock on the door of the den before entering... she walked over to the desk.

Alec smiled up playfully at Melissa, he motioned teasingly. "Well sleepyhead, how are you this morning?"

Walking around the desk, Melissa bent to give Alec a good morning kiss. "I'm great, how are you feeling this fine morning?"

Smirking smugly in triumph when Melissa stood back up, Alec waved down at his desk proudly. "I am good; I have two more invitations to make out. Afterwards, I'm done for the day."

Laughing in delight at Alec's self-righteous attitude, Melissa patted her father's shoulder in congratulations. "Well, I guess I'll just have to find something else for you to do!"

Holding up his hands in surrender, Alec shook his head before grimacing as if horrified by that threat. "No, that's quite alright; I already have a lot of things I need to do without you adding more!"

Chuckling at her father's appalled look, Melissa gave in with a nod of finality. "Okay, I'll let you finish them then pick the invitations up before I leave. I will also need a list of provisions for the week; plus, any special items you think we might need for the wedding that might have to be shipped in."

Nodded, Alec motioned down at his desk. "Okay, I'll have everything ready for you in about an hour; is Jed going with you?"

Melissa shrugged grimly in irritation. "I don't know Jed went hunting with Giant Bear this morning... he didn't wake me up; if he isn't back before I leave, he will have to meet me at the office!"

Smirking knowingly up at the miffed Melissa, Alec gestured

consolingly. "I'll give Jed the message when he gets back."

Shaking off her exasperation, Melissa motioned enticingly. "I'm going to the kitchen to have a coffee. Why don't you finish up here and come have a cup with me before I go; hopefully, the rain will let up by the time we are finished!"

Grinning in pleasure, Alec nodded decisively. "Okay, sounds like a good idea to me; see you shortly."

Waving goodbye, Melissa turned before leaving the den; she went across the hallway to the kitchen. Entering, she sniffed in appreciation. "Something sure smells good in here!"

Mary turned in surprise not having heard the door; she smiled at Melissa before waving towards the kitchen table in invitation. "Sit down; I'll bring you a cup for coffee and a bun right out of the oven with lots of butter on it... I already put a fresh pot of coffee on the table warmer."

Sitting instantly without needing a second invitation, Melissa rubbed her hands in anticipation; she beamed over at Mary in delight. "It sounds too tempting to resist!"

Chuckling softly, Mary hummed in contentment to herself as she finished the promised treat. She brought the hot bun, coffee cup... as well as a jar of raspberry jam to the table. Setting everything in front of Melissa dramatically; she stepped back and returning to her cooking.

Just finished putting a generous heap of raspberry jam on her bun, Melissa grimaced in frustration when the redhead entered; she had a list of things the women wanted.

Jessica smiled down at Mell in apology for interrupting her meal.

Groaning in disappointment, Melissa put the bun down to take the paper Jessica handed her.

Pointing down at the items on the page, Jessica reassured Melissa. "Here is the list you requested; there's not much, just a few odds and ends Mrs. Elton forgot to bring with her when she came."

Scanning it before nodding, Melissa looked up at the redhead. "Okay, I'll pick these up later today there isn't enough here to send the boys."

Nodding, Jessica saluted in farewell before turning without comment then left to go back upstairs to help the women with their tasks.

Picking up her bun, Melissa quickly took a bite out of the

tantalizing morsel in pleasure as it continued emitting heavenly smells. She moaned in pleasure before her eyes closed in delight... savouring the exquisite sensation of the hot buttered bun in ecstasy. She sighed in gratification when the raspberries hit her taste buds, causing her to groan in bliss. It was almost better than lovemaking; Mell chuckled to herself thinking of the last few days of lessons. Well, maybe not!

Giggling knowingly when Mary heard the groan of contentment... she turned around expectantly before watching Melissa take her second bite in exactly the same manner; turning away she was satisfied that her friend was enjoying her treat.

Melissa was halfway through her bun when Jed walked in dripping water everywhere; she looked up at his bedraggled appearance then smirked in amusement... it served him right for leaving without her.

Bending down quickly, Jed gave Melissa a thorough wet kiss; making sure to drip on her just because she had such a smug look on her face.

Pushing Jed away in exasperation, Melissa couldn't help chuckling in delight. "Ugh, you are soaking wet... get away from me!"

Smiling down at Melissa, Jed opened his arms invitingly. He made sure to use his English accent with a heavy roll to the r's... a mischievous light entered his eyes. "Come, give me a hug; darrrling!"

Laughing at Jed's dramatics, Melissa shook her head emphatically; she wiggled a scolding finger up at him. "Not on your life buster... go change into dry clothing before you catch a cold!"

Jed saluted smartly in false servitude. "Aye, aye, Sheriff..."

Melissa snorted in amusement, not giving an inch as she watched Jed leave with his head hanging low as if his feelings were hurt. She finished her bun quickly before any more interruptions could wreck her enjoyment; sitting back once done she drank her coffee waiting for her father and Jed to come.

Mary walked over to pour Melissa more coffee from a fresh pot then took the old one off the warmer and replaced it with the new pot.

Smiling her thanks, Mell finished her second cup of coffee.

Hearing the door open behind her, Melissa turned expectantly. She grinned up in approval when Jed walked in with dry clothes and his hair all slicked back. "Well, you certainly look better... not like something the cat dragged in!"

Winking down at her teasingly, Jed agreed. "I feel better too."

Walking around the table, Jed sat beside Melissa; he looked up before grinning in pleasure when Mary placed a cup for coffee in front of him, plus a steaming fresh from the oven buttered bun. "Thank you, the bun looks and smells delicious... the coffee will be appreciated."

Gratified by Jed's appreciation, Mary picked up the coffee pot then poured him a cup before replacing it... it still had plenty in it, so she would wait to make another pot. Turning she went back to cooking.

Looking at Melissa inquisitively, Jed waved towards town. "Are we going to the office?"

Nodded decisively, Melissa watched in satisfaction as Jed enjoyed his bun almost exactly the way she had. "Yep, my father is finishing the invitations right now so I want to deliver them today; I also need to order supplies at the store. Dad's coming to have a coffee as soon as he's finished then we can go."

Jed mumbled his mouth full. "Sounds good to me, the rains letting up some... I saw clearing to the north; hopefully, the rain will stop before we leave."

Sighing in relief, Melissa was glad to hear that the rain was letting up already. "Excellent, I definitely wasn't looking forward to riding in it; speaking of riding, where did you go hunting this morning?"

Pointing to the north vaguely, Jed put jam on his last piece of bun before looking back at Melissa. "Giant Bear wanted to teach Tommy how to track, so we took him to the open field between here and Devil's Rock... deer love high grass; they like to hide in it just as much as they like eating it. We will be having deer steaks tonight for supper. Right now, Tommy is learning how to skin and dress a deer."

Melissa rubbed her hands together then grinned in anticipation. "Good, I haven't had a deer steak in a long time; I'm always too busy to hunt."

Hearing the door being pushed opened behind her; Melissa turned and smiled when her father entered.

Alec beamed back in greeting then turned to Jed. "Did I hear something about deer steaks?"

Laughing in delight, Jed shook his head in amazement. "Nothing gets past you; yes, we got a two-year-old buck this morning... thanks to Giant Bear."

Pushing himself up to the table, Alec rubbed his hands together in delight... almost exactly the way Melissa had. "Oh good, I love deer meat."

Mary brought Alec a coffee cup and a bun; she smirked saucily then set them down in front of him. "Finally decided to join us... did you?"

Grinning devilishly up at Mell's friend, Alec smacked her backside when she turned around to go back to her cooking. "That's for being impertinent to your elders!"

Chuckled benevolently over her shoulder at Alec, Mary looked directly at Mell then winked good-naturedly. "Some men have no respect!"

Smiling indulgently at their antics, Melissa reached over before lightly slapping her father's arm in rebuke... playing along. "Behave yourself!"

Putting on a hurt expression, Alec sighed forlornly before turning to his future son-in-law; he gestured hopefully, looking for sympathy. "See what I've had to put up with Jed over the years; all these women in my household taking advantage of a poor old man in a wheelchair!"

Laughing incredulously in disbelief, Jed shook his head not in the least sorry for his father-in-law. "You love every minute of it too!"

Grinning in delight towards Jed at having his bluff called, Alec nodding decisively. "You already have me figured... do you?"

Smiling affectionately at her father, Melissa changed the subject. "Did you bring everything I need, Dad?"

Nodding, Alec pulled out a pile of papers that he had tucked under his leg and set them before Melissa. "The list of kitchen supplies is on top then the ranch supplies... all the invitations are there too; plus, a list the new hands made of some things they would like."

Looking up at her father for just a second, Melissa dropped

her gaze to the papers as she eyed the lists while she was speaking. "Have you met all the new hands yet, Dad?

Alec inclined his head when Melissa looked back over at him inquisitively. "Yes, I met them yesterday; I added their names to the payroll."

Melissa gave Alec a few minutes to express his concern with any of the new hands, while she finished her coffee. With no further comments coming from her father after a short silence... Mell stood up with the papers in her hand. "Good; I will see you tonight then."

Bending, Melissa gave her father a goodbye kiss then left the kitchen and went to the front door. Taking her gun belt down, she buckled it on before grabbing her badge then pinned it on. Pulling her ponytail over her shoulder, Mell coiled her long blonde hair into a bun on top of her head then put her hat on top firmly, to keep her hair in place... after exchanging her moccasins for riding boots, she was ready to go.

Jed followed Melissa silently after patting Alec's shoulder in farewell. He also buckled on his gun belt before pinning on his deputy's badge; grabbing his hat on the way out, the two of them left and walked to the barn to saddle their horses.

Entering the barn first, Melissa walked over to where Tommy and Giant Bear were hunched over the deer carcass in deep discussion on the best way to skin it. Mell's foster son looked up at her in surprise, not having heard anyone come in... he smiled in childish delight. "I'm learning how to hunt and skin a deer Aunty!"

Smiling down in approval, Melissa patted Tommy on his shoulder in congratulations. "That's great news; with you two big hunters around we will have lots of meat this year."

Tommy nodded eagerly and gestured at Giant Bear ecstatically. "My father is taking me hunting again tomorrow; he's going to teach me how to shoot a rifle afterwards. Dad said he's going to teach me how to fight with a knife too."

Melissa's smile turned noticeably strained before she motioned at Tommy. "Go wash your hands then help Jed saddle the horses for me please, Tommy."

Instantly, Tommy got up then rushed outside to wash at the pump.

Scowling down anxiously at Giant Bear, Melissa pointed

behind her at the retreating Tommy. "Is this really necessary? I know he's going to be living in an Indian village, but maybe you're going a bit too fast; I'm not sure he needs to learn knife fighting yet, he is a little young after all!"

Tommy came rushing back in, anxious to get back to his lessons.

Jed took the boy to the far stall, leaving the two of them to talk privately; he distracted the boy as best he could so he wouldn't hear what the two adults were discussing.

Sighing in aggravation, Giant Bear tried to be as patient as possible knowing Melissa was only protecting his son... as he was. "Mell, I know that you helped raise Tommy but you have to remember Indian children his age already know how to do the things I'm teaching him. If he's going to fit in with the other boys his age, he needs to know everything before we get to the village. If I don't, he will find it extremely hard to fit in. The other boys will make it even more difficult on him to adjust, especially since he's the chief's son they will expect him to lead them. I already had this fight with Golden Dove. I'm trying not to go to fast for him; thankfully, he seems to learn everything quickly then wants more!"

Frowning in thought, Melissa remembered back before the Cheyenne moved out of Northern Dakota into South Dakota and Montana... she had visited one of the villages. She was shown some of the tests of bravery the boys endured to reach manhood at that time. Mell nodded her head grimly, now worried realizing that Giant Bear was right; her foster son would be no match for those boys. "All right, I'll do what I can to help him along."

Giant Bear smiled in relief at having Melissa's support then motioned imploringly. "I was hoping you would teach Tommy your technique of fighting... it will give him an advantage that he will need."

Inclining her head in agreement, Melissa had already decided that she would show Tommy what he needed to know. "I will, but you know Mary won't like it!"

Gesturing resignedly, Giant Bear had already clashed with Mary over this issue, he shrugged dismissively. "I know, but Tommy has to learn!"

Changing the subject, Melissa pointed curiously at the deer hide. "What are you going to do with the skin?"

Giant Bear's smile softened as he thought of Mary and their son. "I'm going to cure it; Golden Dove is going to make Tommy buckskins."

Nodding in disappointment, Melissa had hoped to have it; she turned to smile at Tommy when he handed the reins to her. "Would you like something from town?"

Beaming shyly, Tommy shook his head negatively. "No, Aunt Mell; I don't need anything... thank you though."

Waving goodbye to father and son, Melissa along with Jed left the barn to mount their horses.

Once mounted... Jed motioned inquisitively behind them at the barn when Melissa turned to him before they rode off. "Did Giant Bear ease your mind a bit?"

Jed pulled the lead rope for the packhorse tighter; this way the horse wasn't so far behind then tied him to the back of his saddle... waiting for Mell's answer.

Sighing irritably, Melissa nodded affirmative before turning her horse towards town. "Giant Bear explained why it was necessary to rush Tommy a little... I agree with him but I still don't have to like it!"

Leaning over, Jed reached out and took Melissa's hand as they rode along. "Tommy will be all right; Giant Bear would never do anything to hurt him."

Melissa intended all along to teach Tommy how to look after himself; her original plan was to wait until this winter when they were all stuck inside, now that he was ten it was time for him to learn... but slowly. She didn't want him to grow up too soon like she had. Although, if she was completely honest with herself, that wasn't really why! It was the thought of losing him, wanting to keep him with her as long as possible which stopped her from beginning his training sooner. Mell frowned forlornly, knowing her fear would now be realized. "I know he wouldn't! It's just that he's been my son as well as Mary's for so long I can't help resenting Giant Bear for taking him away from me."

Sitting back, Jed let go of Melissa's hand after giving it a comforting squeeze then nodded knowingly. "I realize that, but Giant Bear is right; if Tommy is going to survive in an Indian village, we have to prepare him before he gets there... otherwise, the other kids will make it impossible for him."

Scowling apprehensively, Melissa gave in as she gestured

in surrender. "Then I guess I'll have to help him as much as I possibly can before he goes. Giant Bear asked me to teach Tommy some of my fighting techniques; I even have a few tricks you haven't seen yet!"

Jed grinned in relief, but deep down he had known Melissa would; he chuckled... thinking about her last statement. "Well, I'm definitely going to have to watch so I don't learn the hard way what tricks I haven't seen!"

Melissa just smiled secretly at Jed without comment and nudged her horse into a faster pace. They reached the edge of town before the rain finally quit completely; a few minutes later the sun came out, she sighed in aggravation... it just figured. She turned to Jed then waved towards town. "I need to hire another deputy today."

Raising his eyebrows in surprise, Jed frowned in feigned hurt. "Oh, are you firing me already?"

Laughing at Jed's expression, Melissa shook her head negatively. "No, but since neither of us lives in town I will need another deputy; I'm sure you don't want to stay here to do night duty, which means we need someone to patrol in the evenings. We also want another deputy here for when we are away checking on the other towns, there's no way we can be in two places at once."

Grinning in relief, Jed nodded emphatically that he definitely wouldn't be staying in town at night by himself. "In that case I'll help you find one... you're right, I wouldn't like night duty; I plan on spending all my nights with you!"

Blushing at Jed's suggestive tone, Melissa smiled back shyly as they rode up main street. She turned away to hide her blush and waved towards their right. "I want to go to the store first to drop these lists off; one of Charlie's boys will deliver the supplies, since Dad added his we now have enough for a delivery... if I can catch him before he goes."

Nodding without comment, Jed followed Melissa obediently; they dismounted at the store before going in together.

Hurrying up the aisle, Melissa spoke to the man behind the counter while Jed stayed behind to browse through some of the clothes on display. She grinned in greeting at the rotund storeowner. "Hi, Charlie; how are you and that pretty wife of yours?"

Charlie shook Melissa's hand firmly in friendly greeting.

"Morning Sheriff, we are both doing just fine; what can I do for you this fine morning?"

Melissa gestured hopefully when Charlie let go of her hand. "Has Graham left to do deliveries yet?"

Charlie shook his head negatively. "Not yet, why?"

Sighing in relief, Melissa held out the lists. "Good, I have some supplies I need; I figured he could deliver them for me."

Nodding agreeably, Charlie took the lists from Melissa. "Sure, thing Sheriff, let me have a look at what you need."

Waiting patiently while Charlie looked them over, Melissa took the opportunity to study him. He was here way before she moved to this area. The store keeper was almost bald with just a bit of silver-grey hair on each side of his head. Huge and chubby, he weighed close to three hundred pounds with a double chin as well as green blue piercing eyes. He was six foot one with a laugh that was heartfelt and deep. The former sheriff that hired her had shown her a wanted poster for him; it wasn't a big reward... a mere hundred dollars. After buying Charlie's Mercantile, he hung up his guns so the old sheriff left him alone as long as his guns stayed hidden.

Besides, how could Melissa arrest someone who smelt like cinnamon all the time; every time she got near him, she couldn't help taking a big sniff... he smells absolutely delicious! After she took over as sheriff, she had written deceased on his poster then sent it to the agency so the bounty hunters would quit looking. Mell had never told him though.

Ticking off the items in his head that he knew for sure he had, Charlie went down the list before looking up at Melissa with a smile of satisfaction. "Yep, I have almost everything you need... what I don't have, I'll order right away; that's a mighty lot of supplies you are getting this time around Sheriff, you having a party or something?"

Grinning mischievously, Melissa dug into her inside pocket where she put all the invitation; she had made sure to put Charlie's on top since she knew this would be her first stop. "I suppose you could say that... this is for you and the Mrs."

Melissa handed him the invitation dramatically.

Taking the envelope in surprise, Charlie opened it; he looked up from the wedding invitation with a smile of pleasure plain on his face. "Well, I heard you were getting married... congratulations!"

Shaking Melissa's hand warmly, Charlie looked over at Jed knowingly. "You must be the new deputy who is marrying our lady sheriff... congratulations to you too!"

Jed walked over quickly then shook Charlie's large beefy hand warmly in gratitude. "Thanks."

Waving down at the invitation hopefully, Melissa grinned pleadingly. "Can you come and bring that beautiful wife with you?"

Nodding emphatically, Charlie put his hand over his heart then vowed gravely. "Sure, thing Sheriff, I'll even close the store down that day; I wouldn't miss seeing you married for all the tea in China."

Smirking in delight at the solemn vow Charlie made because he was always lamenting the fact he couldn't get any tea on a regular basis; Melissa turned to leave then looked back inquisitively... Mell motioned hopefully. "Oh, have you seen Gary around today?"

Charlie shook his head negatively. "No; not since Millie let him get away from her last week."

Melissa sighed in disappointment. "If Gary happens to come in today, tell him to come see me at the office please."

Nodding in agreement, Charlie waved. "Sure, thing Sheriff."

Waving goodbye, Melissa turned then left with Jed following close behind; mounting their horses they rode over to the office to dry out. They were not soaked, but unpleasantly damp; still it was uncomfortable, she needed to show Grey Wolf a few things, anyway. Mell walked into the office then went over to a wood cook stove and lit a fire first to make a pot of coffee. She sat at her desk then pulled out some old reports her other deputies had made and handed them to him so he could study them. "Every night before I leave, I write a report similar to these. My deputies also have to write one, even if they are along with me. That way our judge who is also our mayor... plus, the town council knows what we are doing. I won't look at yours except the first couple to make sure you're doing it right. You will not be able to see mine, that way it's all legitimately told without either of us being able to lie about anything."

Nodding in surprised curiosity, Jed began reading the reports; most were brief less than half a page, some were lengthy filling a sheet of paper... with a few bigger ones.

Getting up, Melissa poured them both a coffee when it was ready then sat at her desk again after she gave Jed his; they both sipped the hot coffee appreciatively while Grey Wolf continued his study of the reports... she smiled over her coffee cup at his intense expression. "These reports have to be handed in to the judge's office at night. Lucy, his secretary makes us a copy of the originals. Once the mayor and town leaders go over the reports, I get the copy not the originals."

Finished reading, Jed handed the reports back to Melissa.

Rummaged through her desk again, Melissa pulled out some more papers. She looked over sympathetically then smiled at Jed's groan of protest at the thought of more papers he would have to fill out. Still, she handed them to him regardless of his protest. "This is an arrest sheet... every time you arrest someone even if it's just a drunk you have to fill out one of these. I made up these forms because my deputies kept arresting people for no good reason. After they had to fill in these, they quit doing it so often. The report we give to the judge is for the town's benefit because I did have a few cases thrown out for lack of evidence, with a lot of your word against mine. So, that is why we both have to fill in one every day without seeing what the other has written; that way the town has more of a case against the outlaws."

Taking the papers, Jed scanned them; they were pretty straightforward. He handed them back to Melissa with a nod, but without comment.

Melissa took the papers then put them back in her drawer so Jed could use them as a reference later when he did his first one. She looked up in warning... her voice became deadly serious at the end of her statement. "You can follow me around for the next few days until you become familiar with my routine. I also want you to read my law book at the house it won't tell you everything, but it gives some good pointers and things to watch for. If you are not sure about something, ask me don't bull ahead trying to solve it yourself. I have lost a few deputies because they didn't check with me so got fired for doing wrong or ended up dead. You will also have to go through my 'wanted' papers you will have to memorize the faces; I don't kill anyone unless I absolutely have to even if the poster says kill on sight. Of course, there are always exceptions to the rule where it is inevitable, but only when I have no other choice or someone's life is in jeopardy! Any deputy that does will be dismissed immediately before being charged as a criminal. Any questions so far?"

Jed shook his head negatively just as serious. "Not at the moment, but I might have some later."

Nodding pleased, Mell stood up. "Okay, let's go."

Walking outside with Jed following, Melissa immediately went to her horse and loosened the saddle girth; she wouldn't need him for a while. She grabbed the whip she always attached to the back of her saddle.

Following Melissa's example, Jed untied the packhorse and tied him to the hitching post before loosening his girth strap.

Waiting for Jed patiently, Melissa finally turned towards the stagecoach office after he joined her; he walked beside Mell listening attentively as she talked explaining why she did what she does. "Every morning, I make this round when I get to town and again every evening before I leave, I always do it on foot. I spend enough time in the saddle during the week I don't want to ride around town too... unless I have to. I always check the stagecoach first since all the other deputies from the surrounding towns send in their reports by stage. Unless it is an emergency then they either come themselves to report or send a pony express rider."

Walking into the building once they reached the entrance, Melissa paused to let her eyes adjust before going to the counter. She nodded cordially to the bald man behind it. Inside Mell was grinning in humour to herself, but she managed to keep her face outwardly expressionless knowing he wouldn't appreciate her amusement; every time she saw him, she wanted to laugh. He reminded her of a weasel with his sharp beak-like nose, thin almost nonexistent lips... his thick glasses made his brown eyes look huge, ferret like. He was scrawny, awkward looking as well as short. "Morning James, do you have anything for me today?"

James nodded that he did; he smiled across the counter in pleasure at the beautiful Melissa... with a fiery blush he knuckled his forehead in greeting before ducking his head to hide his reaction. He reached under the counter to pull out the papers then laid them on the counter. "Morning Sheriff, yes your reports are in and there are new wanted posters."

Melissa inclined her head in thanks... she reached in her vest then pulled out an invitation before placing it on the counter beside her papers. "I have a letter for you too."

Grinning, James picked up his pen to write all the information so he could send it on the next stagecoach. "Where would you like me to send it to?"

Chuckling at the misunderstanding, Melissa shook her head. "Not where; it's for you and your mom."

Beaming in pleasure at getting a letter, James nodded in delight. "Oh, why thank you!"

Taking the letter off the counter, James opened it; he looked up sadly after reading it before shaking his head. "I would love to come, but I can't. I have to look after the stagecoach."

Sighing in disappointment, Melissa gestured hopefully. "What about your mother can she come?"

Shaking his head negatively, James shrugged in apology. "Sorry, she has no way to get to your place without me."

Frowning thoughtfully, Melissa motioned imploringly. "What if I could get her a ride there and back?"

James grinned with a nod. "That's different, if you can get her a ride, I'm sure she would love to go."

Smiling in delight, Melissa waved teasingly. "Good, I will even make sure she gets an extra piece of wedding cake to bring home for you."

Chuckling in anticipation, James nodded in pleasure. "Thank you, I will look forward to the cake."

Melissa turned to Jed and introduced the two men. "James this is my fiancé, Jed Brown; he's also my deputy."

Inclining his head in greeting, Jed reached across the counter to shake hands. "It's nice to meet you."

Nodding, James took the hand offered; he winced at Jed's firm handshake, but didn't pull away until he did.

Jed, realizing he gripped a little too firmly let go immediately so he wouldn't hurt the man further.

Picking up her papers, Melissa turned after waving goodbye; she looked down at the wanted posters as she walked then passed them to Jed one at a time.

Looking them over carefully, Jed passed them back.

Folding them, Melissa tucked them in her gun belt.

They went across the street, turning right Melissa continued to walk until they came to a house at the edge of town; Jed had noticed it on their first trip. It was quiet and dark almost spooky looking being that it was so early in the morning. This must be the place Dan had referred to as, 'Pam's Place'... sure enough just above the door was her name, but not what kind of place it was. They entered, a huge burly man at the entrance nodded pleasantly at them then left without comment to let Pam know the sheriff was here.

Raising his eyebrows in surprise, Jed grinned devilishly at Melissa... he didn't say anything; Grey Wolf looked around at the plush overly lush furniture, with paintings on the wall of naked women lying suggestively on couches, in amusement.

Smiling innocently over at Jed when he looked at her, Melissa sat on a chair without speaking... waiting for Pam.

CHAPTER FIFTEEN

It wasn't long before a plump middle-aged woman with black hair, ample hips, and huge breasts that were almost totally out of her bodice... sauntered into the entryway. Pam had crystal green eyes with huge black irises that almost took over the green. The hair was obviously coloured; it was probably mostly grey since she looked to be in her late fifties or early sixties.

Melissa liked Pam despite her profession, mostly because she was direct and always honest without a conceited bone in her body. She loved to laugh; it was always hearty as well as sincere... especially, at herself.

Pam smiled in delight when she walked in then saw Melissa. "Well, hello Sheriff; I was wondering when you would be back to see us... running a little late aren't you?"

Grinning, Melissa stood up respectfully. "Good morning, Pam; how are you and the other ladies this fine day?"

Laughing boisterously in humour, Pam shook her head in disbelief; she planted both her hands over her ample hips in incredibility. "You know sheriff, you are a gem... you're the only woman who dares to walk in here, never mind calling us ladies!"

Smiling in skepticism... Melissa highly doubted it was only her calling them ladies, but didn't comment; instead, she took out an invitation then handed it to Pam.

Taking the envelope tentatively, Pam fearing the worst opened it. She raised her pencil thin eyebrows in shock then looked at Melissa in uncertainty. "You want me, plus all my girls to come to your wedding; are you serious?"

Nodding innocently, Melissa frowned mystified by the look of mistrust on Pam's face... she gestured anxiously. "Yes, but only if you want to come that is?"

Suddenly reached out, Pam hugged Melissa spontaneously to hide the tears in her eyes; the madam pushed her away so she could look at her. "Darling, I wouldn't miss it for the world, but I can't speak for everyone else... I'll ask them for you though."

Stepping away from Melissa, Pam wiped the tears away; she turned to Jed... the madam eyed him appreciatively before turning to the sheriff then smirked mischievously. "I suppose this gorgeous hunk of a man is the one marrying you?"

Grinning at Pam's direct teasing question, Melissa motioned in introduction. "Pam this is Jed, my fiancé; he's also my new deputy."

Smiling in bemusement, Jed had watched Melissa in disbelief at first then in humour when she innocently asked a woman of ill repute to attend her wedding; as if other women did it every day. Nothing would surprise him about his fiancée now. Taking Pam's hand in his own, Grey Wolf bowed over it making sure to allow his English accent to thicken before kissing the back lightly in greeting. "Charmed..."

Pam giggled in delight; she turned her head back towards Melissa then winked outlandishly. "Well, I have to give you credit you can sure pick them!"

Grinning indulgently, Melissa watched without a shred of jealousy as the two of them flirted back and forth for a few minutes... her faith in Jed's love was unshakable; she broke in finally with business on her mind. "Pam did you have any problems since I've been gone?"

Moving away from Jed instantly, Pam's demeanor turned all business too. "No, it's been really quiet lately."

Nodding in relief, Melissa waved farewell. "Good, we will see you tonight on my final rounds."

Escorting the pair to the door, Pam opened it for them... she gestured in pleasure at Melissa. "Thanks for inviting us, Mell; I'll always love you for that!"

Smiling goodbye, Melissa was still somewhat mystified by the fuss as Pam closed the door behind them.

Jed looked at Melissa sideways thoughtfully. "You really amaze me!"

Turning slightly towards Jed, Melissa smirked nonchalantly... she motioned calmly. "Maybe, I'm just more liberal than most women."

Chuckling in agreement, Jed turned back towards the wooden sidewalk ahead of him. "I guess you are at that!"

They passed several houses, the town office, and the hotel without stopping since Chelsie's Saloon was always third on the list to visit. Melissa pushed the bat-wing doors open then stepped inside... she stepped to the side so Jed could enter also and stopped to wait for her eyes to adjust; she looked around before walking over to the bar and smiled at her friend in greeting. "Good morning, how's business?"

Chelsie grinned in delight at Melissa then turned to pour them the coffee she had waiting; she moved back to the bar and set the cups on the counter before looking at Mell with a sly smirk. "Just fine... how's the bride-to-be?"

Melissa beamed warmly in reply. "I'm doing great, thank you!"

Rummaging inside her pocket, Melissa found Chelsie's invitation and handed it over dramatically.

Opening it in excitement, Chelsie already knew what was inside before she looked up at Melissa then grinned in delight... she nodded in acceptance. "Well, thank you; I will definitely come, but I'll have to ask the girls I can't speak for them."

Sighing in relief, Melissa was glad her friend was coming at least... she became all business as she changed the subject. "Okay, how did things go lately any problems?"

Chelsie shook her head negatively. "No all was quiet, Sheriff."

Nodding glad to hear that, Melissa turned around to see who all was there while she sipped her coffee. She put her cup down then took out her invitations; Mell rummaged through them before pulling out the ones she wanted... putting the others away, she turned to Jed. "Wait here, I'll be right back."

Inclining his head in agreement; Jed's eyes followed Melissa curiously, as she walked away. He turned to Chelsie and accepted more coffee. He smiled his thanks then pointed over his shoulder towards his fiancée in humour. "I think Mell is inviting the whole town to our wedding."

Nodding decisively, Chelsie motioned in emphases. "Of course, if she didn't invite everyone, they would think she was mad at them for some reason; we all love Melissa and appreciate the things she has done for us. This town was quite wild before she came here as a deputy... the sheriff at the time was old so couldn't do much about it. Then this tall skinny boy with a pretty face came out of nowhere and helped clean up the town. Some of us suspected she was a woman, but after she proved herself, we pretended we didn't. As soon as she was fired, the town turned completely lawless again.

We had two sheriff's die one after another then lucky for us she got the opportunity to save the judge and his wife. In gratitude, he asked Mell to take her job back. We have all lived a better life ever since, more women came out here and settled as soon as word spread the town was again safe. Now we have a town growing, as well as prospering, all because she makes sure the law is enforced. Not just for this town mind you, but for several other towns as well."

Jed sighed in understanding. "I can see everyone loves her, I must admit it doesn't take long to fall under her spell either. Melissa emits such an air of integrity and honour; most will be drawn unwillingly to her pure innocence, while some will be repulsed by it. It's extremely intense, allowing those around her to see their own short comings... many will be uncomfortable with it. I fell in love with her from the first day I met her, although I didn't want to at the time."

Chelsie smiled knowingly, but didn't comment; she refilled Jed's coffee cup then Melissa's also when she saw her turn towards them.

Melissa grinned in thanks at Chelsie and looked at the two of them speculatively wondering what they were talking about that seemed so serious. Sipping her coffee... she finally shrugged; knowing if it was important, Jed would share it sooner or later. She turned around curiously when she heard someone enter the saloon, thankfully it was Gary Sanders. Mell smiled in greeting as he sauntered towards her. She studied him speculatively when he got closer. He was six feet, gangling, almost awkward looking, with sandy brown hair, and dark brown eyes. A thick handlebar moustache graced his upper lip which he kept neatly trimmed... he was always playing with it proudly. He was not a fast gun, but he didn't panic in bad situations. She knew that because she kept tabs on him ever since he approached her wanting to be a deputy.

Gary smiled back hesitantly unsure why Melissa would be looking for him. "Charlie told me you wanted to see me, Sheriff."

Nodding, Melissa was relieved she wouldn't have to go looking for him. "Yes, I was, Gary; do you remember asking me for a job last year?"

Frowning in puzzlement, Gary motioned curiously. "Yes, you told me you didn't need anyone."

Shrugging nonchalantly, Melissa tilted her head in agreement. "That's right at the time I didn't, now I'm in need of another deputy; if you're still interested, you will be working from four o'clock until the saloon and Pam's place closes for the night. Once everything is quiet, you can go home but you will still be on call until I arrive in the morning."

Gesturing ecstatically, Gary nodded in excitement. "Yes, I'm still interested; I'll gladly take the job!"

Inclining her head in relief, Melissa waved up the street. "Go see the judge right away, he will swear you in; meet us at the hotel for lunch afterwards and I'll explain your duties then."

Turning quickly before the sheriff could change her mind, Gary headed for the door with a noticeable spring in his step.

Waving goodbye to Chelsie, Melissa and Jed left the saloon; she turned down the street before crossing over to the store then entered... Jed followed curiously.

Walking up to the counter, Melissa yelled into the back so the owner would hear her. "Charlie!"

Charlie came hustling out in surprise then went behind the counter with a troubled frown. "Did you forget something, Sheriff?"

Shaking her head negatively, Melissa motioned pleadingly. "No, but I have a favour to ask; when you come out to the ranch for my wedding, would you mind picking up James' mom. I figured since you live next door to her that you can bring her with you. James can't leave the stagecoach office and his mother has no other way to get out to my place?"

Charlie smiled in relief. "Sure, I will; just tell James I'll pick her up that morning."

Nodding gratefully, Melissa waved goodbye. "Thanks, Charlie; I'll see you later on my evening rounds."

Melissa and Jed walked out of the store then down the street before crossing to the hotel for lunch; as soon as they entered the lobby, she walked up to the desk.

The reed thin clerk looked up and smiled in greeting. "Hello, Sheriff; how's your day going so far?"

Beaming back, Melissa rummaged in her shirt. "Fine, Roger; how's business doing these days?"

Roger shrugged his bony shoulders nonchalantly. "The same as usual... nothing exciting ever happens around here!"

Grinning sympathetically, Melissa handed him an invitation. "Maybe this will help."

Opening the envelope, Roger read it before looking at Melissa with a wide smile. "Wouldn't miss it for the world, your new deputy the lucky man?"

Inclining her head, Melissa made introductions since the two of them didn't know each other. "Yes, this is Jed Brown... Jed this is Roger Boumont."

The two men shook hands cordially.

Chuckling, Roger winked at Jed in conspiracy. "So, you're the lucky man who managed to steal our sheriff's heart. Well, there will be many disappointed men on your wedding day. I think half the men in town are in love with Melissa, even the married ones."

Jed smirked confidently with a dismissive wave. "I'm sure I can handle the competition."

Grinning in exasperation, Melissa shook her head in disbelief at the two of them then beckoned Jed to follow her into the eating room without comment. She picked a table in the back corner; it was positioned so that both their backs were to the wall and the whole room was open to their view.

A serving lady came over immediately then poured coffee for the two of them. "Mornin Sheriff; how's yah doin?"

Smiling up at her in greeting, Melissa studied Gary's wife. She had strawberry blonde hair with steel grey eyes as well as a heavy accent; slim almost scrawny, she was as awkward looking as her husband, but it didn't stop her from controlling him with an iron fist. "Fine, Millie; how are you this beautiful day?"

Millie shrugged nonchalantly. "Doin jus fine, tank yah."

Nodding pleased, Melissa was glad to hear that then rummaged through her invitations before looking up inquisitively. "I hired your husband today as my new deputy, I hope you don't mind."

Shaking her head negatively, Millie grinned. "Nah, he wants ta be deputy for da longest time; I jus hope he does no mess it up likes he does all da udder jobs."

Finding the invitation at last, Melissa handed it to Millie.

Turning it over anxiously, Millie not being able to read finally asked in embarrassment. "Wat dis for?"

Smiling sheepishly, Melissa explained having forgotten that

Millie couldn't read. "It's an invitation to my wedding next week... I hope you can come."

Grateful that she didn't have to pretend to read it, Millie nodded hesitantly but was unsure if she could go. "Well, I can no promise, I try!"

Nodding in understanding, Melissa waved optimistically. "Okay, I hope you can come though. Can we have a couple of your specials Millie; order one for your husband too, he'll be joining us shortly."

Inclining her head in agreement, Millie tucked the invitation in her apron then turned towards the kitchen. "Sure Sheriff."

Looking at Jed, Melissa waved around the room in explanation before getting up. "I'm going to hand out invitations."

Jed watched Melissa as she walked around the room talking and laughing with everybody while handing out her envelopes; she was just returning to their table when Gary came strutting in, proud as a peacock with his new deputy's badge pinned on for everybody to see.

They both sat down together; Melissa smiled over at Gary inquisitively. "The first thing I need to know is can you write?"

Gary shrugged slightly in embarrassment. "I can some, not very well though."

Sighing, Melissa wasn't surprised before motioning placatingly. "That's all right Gary; we will just have to improvise."

Melissa then proceeded to tell him the rules; they were almost exactly the same ones she gave to Jed except for the last part. "Now, you remember if you have any problems, you can't handle come to me or Deputy Brown; we will handle them, absolutely no heroics... do you understand me?"

Nodding anxiously, Gary frowned thoughtfully. "Sure, Sheriff; if a gang comes to town and it looks like trouble I must send someone to get you... I'm not to handle it myself, right?"

Smiling in relief that he understood, Melissa waved pleased. "Correct; plus, every day you need to go over to the judge's office and give Lucy a verbal report, she will write it up for you."

Gesturing eagerly, Gary nodded. "Okay, I can handle that. What about when you are gone on the trail; who do I report to then?"

Inclining her head in approval at the question, Melissa pointed towards the mayors. "When I'm not here, you will report any problems directly to Judge Elton... the same as you would to me."

Gary grinned proudly up at his wife when she set a bowl of soup in front of him. "Millie, look; I'm finally a deputy!"

Millie glanced at his badge briefly before beaming proudly; she gave him a quick pat on the shoulder in appreciation and left, too busy to stay any longer.

The rest of their meal was finished in silence.

*****

Melissa sighed in relief when they headed out of town... it was six o'clock later then she usually stayed. However, she had accomplished everything she set out to do today. Gary had settled into his new job quite well. All the invitations but two were hand delivered and everyone accepted tentatively if not outright except James. She introduced Jed to quite a few people; he seemed to have no problems with anybody or with the rules of being her deputy, so far!

Gazing around curiously, Jed was surprised they were headed northeast. This was the first time she took him in a different direction; they couldn't be headed to Brian's it was farther east of here. He turned to Melissa then motioned inquisitively. "Where are we going, this will take us longer... will it not?"

Turning to Jed, Melissa grimaced in discomfort not really looking forward to the next few hours. She explained to him why they needed to take a different route home. "I have to drop my last two invitations off; we will go to Mr. Grey's ranch first. He's a friend of my father's then swing around to Brian's place."

Jed sighed in aggravation before motioning in annoyance. "I'm definitely not looking forward to seeing Brian again!"

Frowning in agreement, Melissa shrugged consolingly. "Neither am I, but I have to give him one more chance before I give up on him... I really don't know what has come over him lately; he's never been this bad?"

Making a face in reluctant agreement, Jed supposed they should give the man one more chance; as for what had gotten into him, Grey Wolf really couldn't say since he didn't know anything about Brian at all. "I guess so."

They rode in silence for a few minutes then Jed looked towards Melissa inquisitively with a questioning look before gesturing towards the back of her saddle; he just had to ask... the curious question was on his mind all day. "Why do you carry a whip around town?"

Grinning crookedly at Jed's curious question, Melissa shrugged self-consciously. "Well, you know my rules on killing. I don't like to take anyone's life unless I'm unable to come up with another solution; so, I use the whip to control situations that might get out of hand. I've always been better with it then a gun, anyway! I modified my snake whip a bit; the handle is not as long as it was. The thong, which is the center, is also a tiny bit shorter. Instead of the fall and popper, I added three longer extensions on the end so it is in between the snake whip and a bola, but with sturdy hooks... they almost look like fishhooks, they are barbed on both sides."

Melissa shook her head irritably at herself as she tried to explain, it was not really the right description. She snapped her fingers when she got an idea. "Not fish hook exactly, but more like an anchor for a boat. I used antlers from a deer since they are tougher than wood, I carved them myself. It was difficult getting them thin enough so the ends would not be too heavy when released. Now it will snag on someone's clothes or flesh and hold tight, no need for a perfect aim either. It can do a lot of damage if you are not careful, even kill! For instance... if a drunkard starts smashing things or shooting his gun off, I will wrap the whips prongs around him to hold him tight while I disarm him. It's quite effective most of the time, not always mind you. Thankfully, it has helped me to keep my vow not to kill more times than I can count. If, for some reason I figure the whip is no good in a situation or will not help me and I have to use my gun; I always try to aim for the gun hand or arm."

Jed nodded in understanding; they rode in silence for a few more minutes. Grey Wolf turned to Melissa again questioningly. He was thinking of the papers she received this morning... this was the first opportunity he had to ask her about it. "What do you think about the report your deputy from the other town sent you?"

Shrugging undecided, it puzzled her too but Melissa wasn't sure what to do about it yet. "I don't know what to think; Deputy Walters has no idea why a hired gun showed up yesterday... according to him, he hasn't caused any trouble so far. I'm not sure if I should wait until the gunman does or whether I should go check into it myself before the wedding."

Jed nodded thoughtfully before asking curiously. "How far is the town from here?"

Sighing in aggravation, Melissa gestured in the general direction of the town. "Two days from the ranch if we ride hard, three and a half to four days if you take your time; with our wedding only seven days away I'm not eager to go then possibly have to postpone the wedding."

Scowling, Jed didn't like the thought of having to move the date further away either. Unfortunately, another scenario kept running through his head... he motioned towards Melissa in worry. "I see your point, but if we don't go now to stop whatever he has planned he could make a move the day before our wedding; we would have to stop the ceremony at the last moment if that happens. If we go now, we should be back in plenty of time I would think."

Melissa shrugged grimly. "I know that's what I'm wrestling with right now... should we go or not; I'll make a decision tonight then let you know what we are going to do as soon as I decide."

Sighing relieved that Melissa was giving this serious thought, Jed left it at up to her; they rode into a ranch yard a few minutes later.

Riding over to a man who was walking towards the house, Melissa stopped beside him. She tipped her hat cordially in greeting... she studied Victor Grey before grinning in humour. The short, bow-legged old cowboy always wore a huge floppy hat that covered his receding steel grey shoulder length hair. You could just barely see his watery blue eyes or craggy ageing face under the hat. He was close to seventy, unfortunately showing his age more deeply every year. His beard and thick handlebar moustache had finally turned the same colour as the hair on his head. "Evening, Mr. Grey; do you have a few minutes to talk?"

Victor eyed Melissa sourly, but nodded curtly. "What do you want, Sheriff?"

Raising an eyebrow in surprise, Melissa was hurt at his biting tone of voice, as well as the curt nod; the use of her professional name instead of her real name startled her also. Mell ignored his tone of voice then reached into her pocket before pulling out his invitation... she handed it down to him expectantly.

Reaching up, Victor took it reluctantly then opened it tentatively; he squinted at it in the fading light, but was still able to read it clearly. He tried to hand it back to Melissa angrily with a decisive shake of his head in finality. "I'm not coming, neither are my men or I will fire the lot of them!"

Sitting back in her saddle in shocked astonishment, Melissa had not expected that at all... she refused to take the invitation back. Mr. Grey had been her father's friend since they moved to the ranch; not once in all these years, did he ever turn down an invitation to come visit Alec! Mell shook her head in confusion, gesturing anxiously, still ignoring the envelope he was holding up to her. "Why not, even if you don't care to see me married, I figured you would want to come visit my dad at least!"

Growling in rage, Victor motioned in fury towards Melissa. "Me, and your father were once friends... until you killed Greg!"

Melissa's mouth fell open in stunned amazement not expecting that statement to account for his unusual actions at all; she snapped her mouth shut angrily before growling back just as irate now herself in explanation... even though Mell didn't think he deserved one at this moment. "I would not have killed Greg if he hadn't taken my father hostage then tried to kill us both. Plus, he helped murder all my men at the ranch, except Wade!"

Victor scowled up suspiciously; he finally dropped the invitation Mell refused to take on the ground before turning away without any further argument... he stormed to his house without another word spoken.

Ignoring the invitation still on the ground, Melissa turned to Jed before gesturing in livid confusion. "This is unbelievable; I don't understand any of this, he's been my dad's best friend since he moved to the ranch."

Jed shrugged hesitantly, but not knowing Mr. Grey he couldn't really say anything to help with Mell's feelings of bewilderment. "I guess he figures Greg was a better friend then your father."

They turned their horses and headed out, with Melissa brooding in silence totally perplexed by all that happened. Finally, she turned to Jed with an unconvinced expression before shaking her head in disagreement. "That can't be the reason at all, Mr. Grey hardly ever spoke to Greg; never mind spent time with him... I don't even think they liked each other much."

Frowning, Jed gestured placatingly. "Talk to your dad, see what he thinks maybe he has the answers."

Nodding that she would, Melissa was still quite upset; she had even forgotten to ask Victor about their two new hired men, oh well. They turned and continued to ride towards Brian's in silence now going more east then north. They were about a quarter of the way to the ranch when they spotted a rider coming fast. She squinted in the fading light before turning to Jed... Mell gestured for him to stop. "I think its Brian, but I can't be sure yet in this light; we will wait here just in case."

Frowning in suspicion, Jed was also sure it was Brian; he loosened the flap that held his gun in the holster when riding just in case of trouble, he didn't trust the man at all!

Brian savagely pulled his horse to a stop when he was close enough to Melissa that she could hear him clearly, but not too close. His horse squealed in pain at his master's rough handling... he ignored it though. Snarling angrily at the two he hated; Mary's brother leaned forward in rage. "I hope you weren't on your way to my ranch. You are no longer welcome anywhere on my land Sheriff!"

Sighing in aggravation, Melissa scowled grimly... what did she expect though, she knew he wouldn't be giving her a warm welcome after their last visit; still his attitude lately was absolutely appalling. Mell pulled out his invitation then held it towards him. "I was just coming to give you this."

Melissa continued to hold it towards Brian waiting, but he didn't take it.

Spitting on the ground in front of Melissa's horse in disrespect, Brian sneered; he sat back in his saddle and refused to come any closer. "What is it?"

Frowning angrily when Brian refused to take the envelope,

Melissa snapped impatiently. "It's an invitation to my wedding; as well as your sister's renewal vows."

Glancing at the envelope in disdain, Brian looked at Melissa with the same expression of contempt plain on his face; with a last look of rage at the invitation... he cruelly put spurs to his horse before galloping away without speaking or even touching the envelope.

Frustrated, Melissa shook her head in disappointment but had expected he wouldn't accept it. Shoving the envelope back into her pocket; Mell turned to Jed in impotent anger. "I guess the answer is no!"

Turning their horse's west, away from Brian's... the two headed home silently without any more talking; Melissa was glad Mary's brother had shown up here, now they didn't have such a long ride back to the ranch.

*****

It was late by the time they reached the ranch... Dusty followed closely by Tommy ran out of the barn then took the horses reins immediately; the youngest ranch hand unhooked the packhorse's lead rope and the two boys lead all three horses to the barn to be unsaddled then bedded down.

Jed and Mell entered the house still barely talking, both sighed in relief as they took off gun belts, badges, boots then their hats. They just finished undressing when Alec entered the hallway.

Alec smiled in exasperation; he looked both of them up and down in reproach. "Well, look who dragged themselves home; where have you two been... we've been waiting for hours?"

Smiling apologetically, Melissa bent down to give Alec a fond kiss. She stood up still grinning... this time more in repentance down at her father. "I'm sorry we're so late, but it took longer than I thought to deliver the invitations. I also hired Gary Sanchez as the night deputy; I had to show him what to do."

Nodding placated by the confession, Alec smirked up at Melissa in forgiveness. "Apology accepted; we saved supper for you two so come to the kitchen to eat while you fill me in on the day's events."

Melissa pushed Alec, while Jed followed silently.

Jessica turned then smiled in greeting at Melissa and Jed when they entered. "I heard your voices, so I put your supper on to heat it a bit."

Beaming gratefully, Melissa motioned hopefully. "You wouldn't happen to have fresh coffee on, as well; it's quite cool out tonight... plus it is starting to rain again."

Smirking smugly, Jessica nodded agreeably before gesturing at the table. "Of course I do, it's on the warmer already; sit down I'll get you cups."

Jed and Mell sat at the table then thankfully sipped the hot coffee that Jessica poured them, both finally able to relax.

Alec watched the pair relax; he drank his own coffee in silence not wanting to interrupt their time of respite. He decided to tell them all about the goings on at the ranch instead of asking them about their day, questions could wait until after they ate. Smiling over at the two of them, he cradled his cup in two hands. "Your supplies came in just after lunch. The new hands continued building the cabin after the rain quit and it dried up a little. Wade, Tommy, as well as Giant Bear, helped them after your platform was finished. I went out to look just before dark, the house is coming along nicely... it's amazing how fast one can be built when ten people do it together. At this rate, they should be finished in a few days then they can start on Gloria and Wade's cabin. Mrs. Elton left just after supper; she said to tell you that if you didn't get home too late Jessica could help you try the dress on then pin up the hem for them."

Continuing to listen to Alec while they ate, the two late comers made no comments only nodding at the appropriate times.

Finished his description of the day's happenings at the ranch, Mell's father lapsed into silence.

Melissa and Jed finished eating before pushing their plates away, they sat back contentedly sipping their second cups of coffee. Mell smiled in thanks at her father... grateful that he had rumbled on to give them time to finish their food. "I'm glad they are doing well on the first cabin."

Nodding, Alec waved impatiently. "Never mind that now, let's hear about your day."

Smiling in humour at her father's impatience, Melissa obliged him; she left nothing out... if she forgot something, Jed reminded her.

It took a good half hour to tell him everything, when they

finished Alec sat there with a pensive frown; more worried about the hired gun then his friend's strange behaviour. Victor had always been a moody, unpredictable old bastard. He looked at Melissa in concern. "A hired gun showing up before your wedding worries me... is he going to stay where he is or is he going to show up here on your wedding day?"

Frowning thoughtfully, Melissa gestured resignedly. "That's what I've been wondering too, it could be just a coincidence or maybe not; like Jed said we could slip down there then be back before the wedding."

Motioning in worry, Alec frowned. "Once you're in town, you can better assess the situation and the possibility that you might not make it in time. If so, send a rider with a note; I'll let everyone know the wedding is postponed until you get back."

Melissa smiled at both men in surrender. "Okay, I give up. We will go tomorrow as soon as we are up. One of the men will have to go to town in the morning for me and let John know where we went. Judge Elton can deputize him as a temporary deputy; he can look after the day shift until I get back. I would suggest Dusty... he's a little shy, but not a hothead so he should be okay for a few days."

Alec pointed at himself. "I'll look after that for you."

Nodding in relief, Melissa motioned inquisitively. "What about your friend, Mr. Grey, any thoughts about why he is acting so strange all of a sudden?"

Thinking it over for a few minutes, Alec shook his head negatively with a confused shrug. "I have no idea why he's acting as he is; I'll definitely have to find out."

Sighing in disappointment, Melissa had hoped her father could shed some light on his friend's strange behaviour. "Well, if you think of anything let me know."

Inclining his head in agreement before changing the subject, Alec gestured curiously. "Okay; what time are you leaving?"

Melissa shrugged undecided. "I'm not exactly sure, but as early as I possibly can."

Jessica walked over to get their attention; she had been listening, but remained quiet until now. "Can I make a suggestion?"

Smiling up at the red-head, Melissa nodded in permission.

"Of course you can, I'm willing to listen to any proposal that gets me back here before my wedding day!"

Grinning in sympathy at Mell's pleading tone, Jessica gestured upstairs in explanation. "Well, if you come up now and try on your dress... I'll work on it while you sleep. I can wake you up at three o'clock; if all goes as planned you should be out of here no later than four. Breakfast will be waiting for you that way you can eat before you go, so won't have to stop for awhile. The ladies can finish your dress while I sleep in the morning."

Looking at Jed in question, Melissa waited for his nod of agreement... she turned back to Jessica before smiling at her gratefully. "Okay, as long as you are sure you don't mind."

Shrugging dismissively, Jessica smirked teasingly. "Not at all; especially if it will help you get back in time for the wedding."

Frowning, Melissa imagined all the guests showing up here and their disappointed faces when she didn't. "Yes, I would certainly hate to miss it!"

Turning to Jed, Melissa waved inquisitively. "Are you going to bed now or are you going to talk to Dad until I'm done with my dress fitting?"

Jed waved towards Melissa's father. "I'll chat with Alec until you're finished then I will join you."

Nodding, Mell got up before leaving with Jessica.

Alec and Jed talked about the ranch for half an hour then he went upstairs when Jessica came in.

*****

Entering the bedroom, Jed smiled teasingly over at Mell. "Well, how did the fitting go?"

Melissa grimaced in painful aggravation. "Now I know why I don't wear dresses; they are difficult to get into, but even harder to get out of!"

Laughing in delighted at Mell's expressive face, Jed blew out the candle before getting undressed and climbed into bed. "Go to sleep... we only have a few hours, so no lessons tonight; we have a long way to go tomorrow."

Sighing in disappointed agreement, Melissa gave Jed a goodnight kiss before cuddling closer, both were asleep in moments.

CHAPTER SIXTEEN

Waking up to the sound of someone banging on her door insistently, Melissa checked to make sure the blankets covered them fully before mumbling sleepily. "Yes!"

Jessica popped her head in the door then grinned in apology. "Sorry, but it is three o'clock."

Melissa groaned tiredly. "We'll be right down Jessica, thanks."

Smiling in sympathy, Jessica closed the door; Mell nudged Jed impatiently. "You awake?"

Jed sighed plaintively then yawned before mumbling. "Yes, I'm awake!"

Getting up, Melissa dressed quickly; she put a couple changes of clothes for herself into one side of her saddlebag that she pulled out of her closet. She also grabbed an extra buckskin shirt and pants for Jed plus a new pair of pants with a navy-blue shirt he bought before they left town yesterday. Mell put them in the other side of her saddlebag... she turned as she slung it over her shoulder to make sure Grey Wolf was dressed. She smiled compassionately when she caught him sitting on the bed fully dressed smothering another sleepy yawn. "You can carry the other saddlebag with the food and necessities that we will pick up in the kitchen."

Nodding, Jed got up to hold the door open for Melissa; they went downstairs and entered the kitchen together.

Raising an eyebrow in surprise, Melissa hadn't expected to see Alec sitting in his chair at the table calmly eating breakfast waiting for them. She put her saddlebag on the floor then leaned down and kissed her dad good morning before walking over to the counter, Mell helped herself to porridge without comment.

Following her lead, Jed also dished up breakfast; they sat down to eat in silence then sat back sipping their coffee reflectively.

Walking over, Jessica gave Jed a saddlebag bulging with food on one side; the other had flint, medicines, toilet articles, a coffee pot... plus a hand axe was sticking out a little way.

Smiling up in appreciation at Jessica's thoughtfulness, Jed took the saddlebag then set it on the floor beside his chair.

"Thanks!"

Grinning in acknowledgement, Jessica turned back to the sink; she busied herself washing breakfast dishes.

Waving to the door inquisitively, Alec eyed the two enquiringly. "Are you ready?"

Both giving decisive nods got up immediately before grabbing their saddlebags; they followed Alec out to the entryway.

Alec watched the two put on gun-belts, jackets, badges, as well as their hats before grabbing the rifles propped in the corner for them.

When they were ready, Melissa turned to her father curiously. "My rain slicker isn't here?"

Motioning towards the barn in reassurance, Alec explained. "I sent Jessica up to wake Tommy earlier; he's at the barn helping to saddle your horses. He took your rain slickers to tie on to the back of your saddles, since it quit raining. I also gave him two bedrolls... inside you will find a skillet, a hatchet, extra bullets, as well as another hunting knife each."

Melissa smiled gratefully then bent down... she gave Alec a hug and a kiss goodbye. "I'll see you in a few days, please ask the ladies to finish the dresses; afterwards ask them if they can decorate the house, the platform, and the archway for me since I won't be able to do so myself like I planned."

Nodding in sympathy, Alec gestured consolingly. "I'll ask them for you... don't worry so much between all of us we will have everything done by the time you get back!"

Jed walked over and shook Alec's hand in farewell. "I'll take good care of her, I promise!"

Shaking Jed's hand firmly, Alec smirked up at him teasingly... he chuckled knowingly. "I wouldn't be too sure of that if I were you; Mell just might end up taking care of you!"

Laughing in delight with no jealousy evident at all, Jed winked at Melissa playfully; the Englishman was so confident in his own masculinity, he had no need to feel threatened by Mell's abilities as sheriff. "Yeah, you're probably right!"

Rolling her eyes at the two of them, Melissa waved goodbye to her father; they left the house and walked down to the barn. They entered just as Tommy with the help of Giant Bear was leading the horses out of their stalls fully saddled ready to go. Mell walked over to her foster son then put her saddlebag on Lightning... turning when she finished, she ruffled Tommy's hair affectionately in farewell. "You behave while I'm away. I promise when I get back, I'll teach you the proper way to handle a knife."

Tommy grinned up at Melissa in excitement... he nodded emphatically in delight before changing the subject as he pointed behind him towards the packhorses stall. "I'm going to behave Aunty, I promise. We didn't know if you wanted your packhorse this time, but I did not think you would since you want to get there and back in a hurry?"

Shaking her head negatively, Melissa smiled in approval. "You're right; we won't need him this time."

Hugging Tommy goodbye, Melissa turned then led her horse out of the barn while Jed talked to Giant Bear. She was just mounting her horse when Grey Wolf walked out with his; he mounted beside her. They walked for several minutes before urging their horses into a trot to warm them up. After a good ten minutes, they nudged them into a slow lope giving them a bit more time... finally they kicked them into a full gallop.

Melissa led Jed in a southwest direction that would skirt Smyth's Crossing and take them directly to Miller's Creek. They maintained their speed for an hour before slowing to a trot for a half hour then into a walk for an additional half hour; once the time was right, they started all over again. They did this twice more and camped for a quick lunch... they rested their horses for half an hour then mounted repeating their previous routine.

Camp was established around six o'clock, for supper; this time they unsaddled the horses before rubbing them down to give them both a much-needed rest.

Smiling thankfully over at Jed tiredly, Melissa was pleased with their progress so far. "We will have supper here; it will give the horses an hour and a half or better yet two hours to rest up for the last leg of the journey. It's another four hours of hard riding until we get to where I want to camp for the night. Should be around midnight when we get there... I'm definitely not going to feel like cooking that late."

Jed nodded without comment then walked around collecting dead branches to start a fire with.

Taking out their food, Melissa placed it where she wanted

the fire to be so it would be in easy reach. Since Jed was just starting the fire... Mell went over to her saddlebags then rummaged in the extra one that Giant Bear thoughtfully hooked behind her horse; she took out some oats to give the horses. On the other side was hay, but she decided to leave it for when they stopped for the night. She needed to wait for the fire anyway; feeding the horses kept her occupied, while she waited.

The fire was ready when Melissa came back so she threw potatoes, carrots then deer meat into the skillet her father provided; once the vegetables softened somewhat, she added some water from her canteen... plus a little flour for gravy and within half an hour they were enjoying their stew.

Digging in hungrily, Jed quickly finished his portion; it was absolutely delicious... this was the first time he had Mell's cooking. Grey Wolf even had seconds before Melissa could finish her first bowl.

Smiling at Jed teasingly across the fire, Melissa watched his enjoyment in gratification; she was glad he was taking such pleasure in the food she cooked. "I have enough meat and vegetables left over for another stew tomorrow... if you like."

Jed grinned over at Melissa in delight. "Best news I heard all day. I'm surprised you have fresh vegetables; they must be from last year... how did you manage that?"

Laughing in satisfaction when Jed rubbed his belly appreciatively, Melissa finished her stew without answering him right away. She let Grey Wolf have what was remaining in the pot since she was full anyway. She smirked saucily over at him before gesturing at all the dirty dishes. "I cooked so you can do the dishes! Now, to answer your earlier question about how we manage to have fresh vegetables this early in the spring; I got smart after two long hard winters when we barely had any food left. We dug out the cellar so it was larger and added a cook stove. I hauled in several loads of nice dark dirt from the fields until I had a huge mound of dirt down there. Every fall we plant potatoes, carrots, turnip, cabbage, peas as well as beans since they are the hardiest vegetables... they can handle cooler temperatures. Since they are above ground in a mound of dirt, they do not freeze in the winter. We keep a small fire going downstairs so the cellar remains warm, which also helps keep the house warmer too."

Grinning in admiration, Jed would never have thought of that... what a good idea. He shook off his thoughts looking at all the dirty dishes; he groaned in mock dismay before nodding in reluctance then gathered them up and headed for a small creek in the distance.

When Jed got back... he saw Melissa sitting propped against her saddle cleaning, as well as oiling both her guns. Normally this was Tommy's job, but he had been too busy with Giant Bear the last few days; she needed something to do for another half hour, anyway.

Depositing the dishes beside the saddlebag to be repacked later, Jed went over to his saddle... he picked it up then carried it over to Melissa and sat back against it. He rolled two cigarettes. One he handed to Mell after he lit them with a stick out of the fire; the other one Grey Wolf stuck in his mouth. Taking out his own kit, he cleaned his gun too.

Melissa reloaded both guns before putting them back in her holster; she threw her cigarette into the fire and stood up... the two hours were up so Mell started breaking camp, while Jed finished cleaning his gun.

Putting his gun back in his holster, Jed got up to help Melissa; he looked over at her curiously before motioning inquisitively. "What are we doing first when we get to town?"

Sighing plaintively, Melissa hefted her saddle onto Lightning's back. "The first thing we're doing is heading for the hotel; I'm in need of a hot bath."

Jed grinned teasingly over his horse's back at Melissa; afterwards, he went back to doing up the girth on his saddle. "Feeling saddle sore, Sheriff?"

Throwing a quick smile over her shoulder at Jed's bantering tone... Melissa turned back to finish tying the saddlebag in place. "Not really, I just don't usually like to push my horse this hard. Since I need to stable Lightning for a while anyway to let him rest; I might as well relax myself!"

Smirking in disbelief, Jed wasn't convinced by her explanation at all. "Well, I certainly like your way of thinking; I'll even admit to feeling a little saddle sore, even if you won't."

Laughing playfully giving in... Melissa gestured plaintively before mounting her horse. "Okay, I admit to feeling a bit saddle sore; you would think with all the riding I do, I wouldn't have this problem."

Mounting, Jed chuckled at Mell's grimace of pain. "I don't think it really matters how much you ride; the only times I can recall not being saddle sore was when I rode Indian style, with a blanket... no saddle!"

Smiling, Melissa nodded thoughtfully; recalling that at one time it was the only way she would ride. Thinking back, she realized that she never knew what a saddle sore was then. She shrugged dismissively and nudged her horse. "Let's go!"

Melissa and Jed rode hard for the next four hours... lucky for them they had a three-quarter moon so could see quite well. They only slowed once to give the horse's time to rest. Reaching their camp around midnight, the two dismounted. After unsaddling both horses then feeding them hay; they put their sleeping pallets together and dropped into them in exhaustion.

They slept for a few hours then continued their gruelling pace the next day with one exception; they didn't stop at midnight this time, but kept going... hoping to get to the hotel before dawn.

The pair exceeded their expectations, arriving at the hotel just after two in the morning. Melissa was extremely relieved they had made it in two days; not an easy feat by any means, since usually it took three to four days to get here under ordinary riding conditions. They were all totally exhausted, Mell patted her sweat encrusted fatigued horse in sympathy... as well as appreciation.

Immediately, Melissa roused the stableman to look after their horses; she flipped a fifty-cent piece at him for his troubles. "Please take special care of them Tim, we have ridden them pretty hard the last two days... they are both worn out!"

Melissa and Jed gathered their rifles... as well as their saddlebags; except for the one Giant Bear had given them for the horses. They both limped painfully into the hotel once satisfied the stableman was looking after their horses properly.

Deciding not to take her whip, Melissa left it tied to her saddle... she figured it wouldn't do her any good in this situation, anyway; she walked up to the desk while Jed hung back a little waiting for her.

The man at the desk looked up and stared in surprise for a moment not expecting to see Melissa so soon. She only left a few weeks ago. "Sheriff Ray, what a pleasant surprise; we weren't expecting you for three weeks at the earliest."

Smiling at the desk clerk, Melissa's grin widened as she eyed him pensively; he was the complete opposite of the hotel clerk in Smyth's Crossing. He had blonde hair, was short, and chubby... with a friendly twinkle in his hazel brown eyes. The two hotel clerks were so different in looks and mannerisms, it always made Mell chuckle when she thought of the two of them at the same time.

Tiredly, Melissa put a finger to her lips in a silencing motion. "Hello John, I need to speak to Deputy Walters tomorrow but I don't want anyone else to know I'm here; can you keep it a secret please?"

John nodded perplexed then grinned reassuringly. "Sure, I won't tell anybody you're here; I'll make sure the girls keep it quiet too."

Sighing in relief, Melissa nodded her thanks before pointing behind her at Jed. "We will need a room... plus a bath if it's possible at this time of the morning."

Beaming accommodatingly, John waved in agreement. "Both are possible for you, Sheriff; rooms ten and eleven are available if you like."

Leaning over the counter, Melissa whispered in conspiracy to the clerk. "Just one room please, the man over there is Deputy Brown; he's also my fiancé so he can share my room."

Moving over a bit so he could see Jed better, John stared for a moment in amazement. He turned back to Mell with a grin a mile long, he reached over then shook her hand enthusiastically. "Well congratulations, Sheriff; it's about time you decided to get married!"

Nodding, Melissa let go of John's hand and stepped back from the counter with a conspiring grin. "Just don't tell anyone for now, okay."

Frowning in puzzlement, John nodded in agreement without asking why... he motioned knowingly. "You do know there are going to be a few disappointed men around here, especially Deputy Walters. He's been in love with you for years; although, I do know a lady who will be quite happy to hear about this. Claire's been in love with Ted for just about as long as he has been in love with you."

Melissa smiled pleased that her marriage would help Claire with Ted. "I know she is... it should work out for the two of them now that I'm permanently out of the picture though."

Nodding in relief, John hoped Claire would quit moping around here now. "Do you want me to send for Deputy Walters right away?"

Shaking her head negatively, Melissa waved tiredly. "No, send a boy around nine o'clock to bring him here; I would also be much obliged if you sent breakfast up to our room around eight. We have one saddlebag that needs to be put in the cold room please... it still has food in it."

Inclining his head in assent, John took a key from the shelf before handing it to Melissa.

Waving in thanks, Melissa grinned in approval. "Oh, when you make a bill for the town add a half dollar tip for yourself."

John beamed in pleasure. "Thank you, Sheriff!"

Gathering the things she put against the counter while they talked... Melissa handed the one saddlebag over to the clerk; taking the other saddlebag with her, she waved goodbye before heading for the stairs that led up to the rooms.

Jed smiled at the desk clerk and touched the brim of his hat in farewell without saying anything, too tired to talk; he followed Melissa upstairs. He stood back waiting while she unlocked the door then they entered. The first thing he did was walk over to the bed and fall on it in exhaustion. He watched Mell take their clothes out of her saddlebags then hung them up in the closet. Before she too walked over and sprawled on the bed beside Grey Wolf... just close enough, they were touching slightly.

Groaning in reluctance, Jed rolled off the bed to answer a knock on the door; he peered out cautiously then opened it wider to let in the boys carrying a large tub.

Behind them was a brown haired, grey-eyed girl carrying a tray that held a steaming pot of coffee along with ham sandwiches and cake; the girl was willowy slim, but only medium height.

Grinning in delight, Jed's belly rumbled in hunger at the sight of the food. "We didn't order that, but I must say it's more than welcome!"

The woman set the tray down carefully on the nightstand

beside the bed and turned to Jed with a smile... she waved down the hallway. "The clerk told me to tell you there are tubs at the back for men; if you come with me, I will show you where they are. You can return there in half an hour, one of the tubs will be filled for you."

Jed followed her to the bathing area then headed back to the room for a quick bite to eat before his bath; three boys passed him in the hallway. They were already carrying buckets of hot water to fill his tub.

Melissa sat up reluctantly, but the coffee smelt so inviting... finally, she couldn't resist the temptation and poured herself a cup. She was eating one of the sandwiches when Jed came back. Smiling in greeting she pointed at the door. "You can leave it open; the boys will be back with the bathwater."

Leaving the door ajar as bidden, Jed walked over then poured himself a cup of coffee. He began munching on a sandwich hungrily as he waited. He settled on the bed beside Melissa; they sat there companionably sipping their coffee as four boys came in with two buckets of water each and filled the bathtub. He dug into his pocket then pulled out four pennies one for each boy and waited... before they left, he flipped them high in the air.

The boys caught their pennies then grinned in thanks.

Smiling at them sympathetically, Melissa watched them smothered yawns... they were all the clerk's own kids she knew. "You can go back to bed after you fill the tub down the hallway; I'm sure your father won't mind if you wait until later to empty the tub in here."

The boys nodded gratefully before leaving.

The two of them ate everything on the tray; they had another cup of coffee before Jed got up to answer another knock on the door. The same girl that showed him where to bathe earlier was standing there waiting. This time she was carrying a supply of towels and soap... along with a pail of warm water to rinse Mell's hair.

Smiling in greeting, Jed opened the door wider to let the hotel maid in. He grabbed the clean clothes Mell had put on the bed for him then turned and waved goodbye to Melissa before heading to his own bath.

Grinning in welcome at Claire, Melissa removed her shirt. She walked over to the tub so the maid could help her;

bending, she flipped her hair over her head before kneeling. Mell made sure all her hair was floating in the bath water so they wouldn't make too much of a mess.

Claire sighed wistfully. "You have beautiful hair, Sheriff."

Beaming, even though Melissa knew the maid couldn't see it... answered her with a complement of her own. "Thank you, Claire; I think your hair is beautiful too."

Nodding pleased by the praise, Claire tipped the bucket of warm water a little to wet the back of Melissa's hair; she couldn't help asking curiously, never having seen the sheriff with a deputy before. "Who's the handsome man with you... if you don't mind my asking that is?"

Groaning in pleasure when Claire massaged soap into her scalp vigorously, Melissa answered distractedly. "That's my new deputy; he's also my fiancé."

Pausing for a moment in surprise, Claire finally continued washing Melissa's hair.

Not needing to see Claire's ecstatic grin, Melissa could hear it plainly in her voice. "Congratulations, Sheriff; I'm so glad to hear that!"

Melissa chuckled knowingly. "I'm sure you are; it wouldn't happen to be because of another deputy we know, would it?"

Claire giggled in delight. "I think everyone knows I'm in love with him, except the man himself; he just vexes me so at times... he can't see what's staring him in the face!"

Laughing, Melissa stood up a little so Claire could rinse her long hair. "All men can be obtuse when they want to be."

Handing Melissa a towel to wrap her hair in, Claire went over and picked up the tray; she turned then smiled gratefully at the sheriff when she saw the two bits lying on the tray. "Thank you!"

Inclining her head in farewell, Melissa smiled. "I'll see you tomorrow, Claire; oh... can you please keep our engagement a secret for the moment we don't want anyone to know yet?"

Quickly agreeing, Claire closed the door behind her.

Undressing once the maid left, Melissa crawled into the tub with a thankful sigh. She looked at the closed door with a smirk, as she thought of Claire; of course, she would run to see Ted as soon as she could get away which is why she had told her. Mell laid back to enjoy the hot water... she was fast asleep in moments.

*****

Jed finished his bath in record time; he dressing quickly, then hurried back to the room. He looked at the bed when he entered expecting Melissa to be in it already, but she wasn't there. He looked around perplexed and spotted her sound asleep in the tub. Grey Wolf chuckled in delight then threw his dirty clothes into a corner... grabbing a towel beside the tub, he placed it on the bed.

Getting undressed promptly, Jed didn't want to get his clean clothes wet... he went over to the tub. He scooped Mell up into his arms lovingly; leaving a trail of water, he carried her over to the bed and laid her on the towel carefully.

Melissa murmured in her sleep, but didn't wake up.

Drying Melissa off as best he could, Jed rubbed her hair to dry it before he put her under the covers. He grinned down at his fierce sheriff and chuckled in amusement; normally he wouldn't have been able to get away with coming into the room without her being instantly aware of him. The fact that she hardly stirred when he lifted her soaking wet body out of the tub made him glad... she was getting use to having him around. That she trusted him enough to be able to relax and let her guard down meant the world to him.

Snorting softly in disbelief, Jed looked down and found himself in a state of arousal from drying Melissa's body. He ignored his bodies need then snuffed out the light. Grey Wolf crawled into bed beside her and drew her against him; sighing in contentment, he was fast asleep within minutes.

CHAPTER SEVENTEEN

Waking to the feel of Jed stroking her breast tenderly... Melissa stretched before yawning contentedly then turned to him inquisitively. "Good morning, how did I manage to get into bed; the last thing I remember is lying back in the tub?"

Chuckling in delight, Jed remembered finding Melissa fast asleep. "When I came back from my bath, I found you sleeping in the tub; I carried you to the bed then dried you off as best I could before I tucked you in."

Melissa stifled another big yawn still really tired. "What's the time?"

Jed tweaked Melissa's nose playfully. "Our breakfast should be here soon."

Kissing him lightly, Melissa turned before rolling off the bed. "We better get dressed, I really don't want Deputy Walters to see me like this; I just might give him a heart attack or something."

Chuckling in agreement, Jed got up then dressed; they just sat back down on the bed when a discreet knock caused him to grumble good-naturedly. He got up to answer it while Melissa tried to comb the knots out of her hair. He peeked out before opening the door wide to let a girl of about seventeen in. She wasn't the same girl from last night, this one had short black curly hair and she was taller. The young girl set a loaded breakfast tray beside the bed then left with a smile of thanks... after Grey Wolf put a three-cent piece in her hand.

Lifting the cloth away from the tray, Jed smiled hungrily in delight at the bacon and eggs... plus two biscuits with jam spread on top. He sighed loudly in pleasure then looked over at Melissa before grinning sympathetically at the look of pure torment on her face. She was trying to untangle a stubborn knot in her hair; taking pity at Mell's plight, Grey Wolf gestured enticingly. "Come over here and have breakfast then I'll get the knots out of your hair, soon as I'm done eating."

Groaning in relief, Melissa dropped her brush on the bed thankfully; she obediently scooting over to sit beside Jed and started eating hungrily.

Finished first Jed picked up Melissa's brush and knelt behind her on the bed; gently, but methodically he attacked the stubborn knots.

Done her breakfast finally, Melissa leaned her head back in delight. She sighed in pleasure when Jed finally got all the knots out; although, he continued brushing her hair in fascination, loving the feel of her silky tresses.

Jed had never brushed a woman's hair before... nor realized how much he would enjoy doing it, or how aroused he would become from such a little chore. He grinned at himself as he lovingly continued to brush Melissa's long dark golden locks even though there was no need to now. "I love your hair; I hope you never cut it!"

Melissa smiled knowingly at the way Jed phrased his request for her not to cut her hair. He didn't say she could not, only that he hoped she wouldn't... very diplomatic of him she couldn't help thinking. Grey Wolf was not the only one feeling frisky all of a sudden; she grinned savouring the shivery sensation, she would have to get him to brush her hair more often now that she knew how it would make her feel. Mell groaned in disappointment when a knock on the door caused him to lay the brush aside and get up to answer it.

Chuckling knowingly at the moan, Jed looked over and saw the disappointment on Melissa's face; his walk slowed noticeably, now just as reluctant as she was to answer the door.

The man on the opposite of the door looked at Jed in confusion when it opened... he gestured in apology. "I'm sorry; I must have the wrong room!"

Smiling in greeting, when Jed saw the badge pinned to the man's vest; he shook his head negatively in reassurance. "No, you don't... not if you're looking for the Sheriff that is."

Opening the door wider so the deputy could see Melissa, Jed beckoned him to come into the room; he shut the door softly before turning to evaluate Deputy Walters. He was tall at six foot two, but not as tall as Grey Wolf was. He had sandy blonde hair with deep... deep brown eyes almost black, and a handsome rugged face. Slim, almost painfully so it gave him a lanky look, his gun hung low on his hip it looked well cared for and used.

Deputy Ted Walters was studying Jed just as intently.

Getting off the bed, Melissa made formal introductions when both men continued to stare at each other without either looking away; the two men shook hands once introductions were finished, they nodded cordially at each other in greeting.

Ted turned to Mell inquisitively; now that he saw the two of them together, he realized Claire was right... even though he refused to believe her when she told him. "I heard you were getting married, congratulations to both of you. Although I should dislike the man for stealing you away, I have always known you were never interested in me."

Smiling in apology, Melissa knew Deputy Walters thought he was in love with her which is why she told Claire last night... she motioned consolingly before grinning teasingly. "But I do know a lady who works here who is very interested in you."

Blushing in embarrassment, Ted sighed knowingly. "You're talking about Claire of course; I have known for a while how she felt, but I wasn't ready yet."

Nodding in understanding, Melissa waved towards the door. "Let's go down for coffee, it will be more comfortable to talk down there."

Melissa turned towards Jed... she shook her head when he reached towards the table beside the bed; he had put his deputies star on it before going for his bath. "Don't put your badge on right now we don't want anyone to know about you just yet."

Jed frowned in puzzlement, but nodded in agreement before buckling on his gun belt and did up his leg strap. He put his hat on; obediently, he left his badge on the table. He watched Melissa buckle her guns around her waist too then tied the straps around her thighs, which kept her guns from flopping around giving a person more control when drawing. Instead of putting her hat on, she tied her hair back with a ribbon. She also left her badge on the table... Grey Wolf raised his eyebrows in surprise.

Shrugging dismissively, Melissa gestured self-consciously. "I am not on duty; I'm just another woman going down to have coffee in the dining room."

Looking Melissa up and down suggestively, Jed chuckled in

disbelief. "No one would ever take you for just another woman!"

Smiling at the two of them as they bantered back and forth, Ted grinned even wider in delight when Melissa couldn't help but turn a fiery red; not once in all these years had the deputy seen her blush... not even when they went into the whorehouse. He opened the door then led them down to the dining room.

They took a corner table which gave them a view of the whole room.

Ted watched as Jed and Melissa both pushed their chairs against the wall then sat down. He sighed shrewdly before taking a chair across from them, but made sure he wasn't in the way of their view of the room; Deputy Walters smiled over at the sheriff in apology. "Well, I didn't expect you to rush down here until there was actual trouble. I just wanted you to be aware there could be... so far he's keeping to himself though."

The waitress came over then poured them coffee.

Waiting until the woman left Melissa shrugging dismissively. "We are getting married in five days; we figured we better find out what is going on now. I would hate to miss my own wedding!"

Sighing sadly when Melissa referred to her wedding again, Ted shrugging of his feelings; he became deadly serious as he waved in warning. "It is a good thing you did come anyway another hired gun show up last night."

Melissa raised her eyebrows in surprise before she motioned in irritation. "Another one, I wonder what they are up to; do you know who they are?"

Ted inclined his head knowingly. "The one that came to town first, and has been here for a few days goes by Diago... he's Mexican. The one that showed up last night is the same guy you chased out of town a couple of years ago; Samson, I believe his name is."

Jed frowned pensively at the names.

Seeing the look on Jed's face, Ted gestured curiously. "Do you know either of these men?"

Frowning troubled, Jed thought back to that horrible day; he shuddered in revulsion when he remembered what Diago did to that poor girl. "The Mexican, I had a run in with him a few years ago. He was only about twenty at the time, but already a mean son-of-a-gun... I thought I killed him!"

Sighing in aggravation, Melissa turned to Jed. "Well, that sure clinches it; two hired guns both with a grudge against one of us here at the same time. I don't like the sound of this at all!"

Looking from one to the other in concern... Ted directed his question at Melissa in confusion. "You think they are after the two of you, but whatever for?"

Frowning, Melissa explained everything that happened at her ranch since she returned from her rounds of the surrounding towns.

Waiting until Melissa finished, Ted shook his head in disbelief. "That's unbelievable I can see why you would be a bit concerned, but who would hire the two gunmen if all the outlaws are dead; unless they were hired before the others died?"

Shrugging, Melissa was puzzled herself. "I don't know; I suppose it could be just a coincidence."

Nodding thoughtfully, Jed tried to think of every possibility before shaking his head in denial. "It could be, but I wouldn't want to bet on the odds... do you know where they are staying, Deputy Walters?"

Shrugging in apology, Ted shook his head negatively. "No, I don't know where Samson is staying. Diago though is sleeping upstairs at the Saloon. When Samson first arrived last night; they both stayed completely away from each other and totally ignored everyone else."

The waitress came over then refilled their coffee cups; she motioned inquiringly at Melissa. "Would you like some lunch, Sheriff?"

Glancing at the two men questioningly, Melissa waited for their answer... once she had their nod of agreement; Mell looked back up at the waitress before smiling in thanks. "You can bring the men whatever is on special, put it on my tab please but I'm still full from breakfast."

The waitress left and Melissa turned back to Ted; she gestured curiously. "Is there wanted posters on these men?"

Nodding affirmatively, Ted waved decisively. "Yes, for both of them dead or alive... pretty hefty rewards too! Samson's is for five hundred alive or two hundred dead; Diago is one thousand dead or alive, preferably dead it says."

Sighing resignedly, Melissa gestured grimly. "It looks like Diago is one step away from a 'shoot on sight' poster."

Frowning pensively, Ted inclined his head in agreement. "I had the same thought myself, but I figured I better wait for you first; I was sending you another message this morning... good thing Claire came to see me early."

Melissa tipped her head in relief; glad Ted had more sense than to take on a situation he wouldn't be able to handle himself. "You did the right thing those men are far too dangerous for you to handle on your own."

Waving resignedly, Ted nodded emphatically. "Tell me about it, I know my own limitations very well."

The waitress arrived with two bowls of thick beef stew and hot buttered biscuits on the side. The three fell silent as the two men ate. When they were finished the waitress came back with a piece of apple pie each... along with more coffee. She served the dessert first. She even gave one to Melissa before she finished clearing the table; she grinned over at her. "I figured you wouldn't say no to the cook's homemade pie!"

Chuckling in agreement, Melissa smiled in thanks. "You know me too well Linda."

Linda smirked knowingly then left without comment.

Waiting for the serving maid to leave, Ted motioned curiously at Melissa. "Do you have a plan or idea as to what you are going to do now?"

Nodding that she did, Melissa had come up with the idea while the two men were eating... she waved at them in encouragingly. "I do have a plan, but first I would like to hear if either of you have thought of anything; if you have something to add now would be a good time before I tell you what I think we should do."

Ted shrugged in bewilderment. "The only thing I can think of is an ambush, catch them one at a time and throw them in jail then find out what they are up too."

Shaking his head negatively... Jed motioned decisively. "No! Diago is as slippery as a newborn foal. He's been captured and put in jail several times already, but always escapes then ends up killing anyone who has had anything to do with his capture. That's why he's still loose; nobody wants to be his next victim."

Turning to Melissa anxiously, Jed gestured in forewarning. "I know you don't like to kill anyone; unfortunately, I think you are going to have to bend your rules. If these men are after us, they will not stop until we are both dead. If all else fails they will go after our loved ones, which is usually Diago's favourite method of flushing out his prey. He will kill one of them every day, which he has done many times in the past... until we show ourselves."

Melissa frowned pensively drumming her fingers on the table reflectively then they stilled when she finally nodded reluctantly. "I think you are right, but how do you suggest we go about it; should we let it be known we are here and let them come to us or do we go looking for them... forcing their hand?"

Jed shrugged undecided. "A little of both... I think; Deputy Walters can go to the saloon first then let it be known we are coming for a drink to celebrate our upcoming wedding. We will leave fifteen minutes after he does and walk up the street slowly. If they are after us, they will meet us on the street. If not, they will either leave town immediately or hide in their room until we leave the saloon."

Thinking about it for a few moments, Melissa finally nodded... it was almost identical to the idea she had been thinking of. Since everyone in town knew Deputy Walters was in love with her; it would give him a good excuse for broadcasting their coming without the hired guns realizing they were being manipulated. Mell didn't want to go to the saloon and end up in a shoot out there... Jake wouldn't like it if they shot up his place.

Since this wasn't Melissa's hometown... which Samson was aware of. Just the mention of her being in town would hopefully make him leave. If it was just a coincidence that is, but like Jed, she highly doubted it was. She looked at Grey Wolf in approval before gesturing hopefully. "I have mixed feeling about this; in a way I'm hoping they will meet us so we can put a stop to their reign of terror. On the other hand, I hope they will not. It would reassure me that nobody hired them to come after us. Either way I will still have to deal with the pair now or later, as sheriff it is my duty to stop them no matter what!"

Jed nodded calmly... even though inside he was anything but. "I'm also hoping nobody hired them; if there is still someone out there who wants us dead that badly, we need to find out who it is quickly. Without knowing who it is, we can't put a stop to them before anyone else gets hurt."

Ted was looking at Melissa thoughtfully... still not convinced someone hired the gunmen. "I think you might still want to keep in mind that maybe they weren't hired, but will meet you on the street because they hate you. For instance, Samson wants to get back at Mell; having dealt previously with her he knows he cannot handle her by himself, so he gets a hold of Diago. He probably figures he can kill the Mexican after the man helps him get rid of her or they can split up the towns once they take them over. Or, maybe the Mexican finds out Jed is here and wants revenge. Diago wires Samson since he heard the man hates the sheriff out here, they make a deal."

Melissa stared at Ted for a moment in surprise before looking at Jed inquisitively. She could see Grey Wolf had the same thought she did... they both turned to the deputy in admiration, but Mell spoke for the two of them. "Well Deputy Walters, now I know why I hired you; even if you're not a fast gun, you always out think your opponent then manage to get the better of them! I think you are right, all this worrying about who hired them and you give us the reason without even trying."

Blushing in pleasure at the praise, Ted smiled at Melissa in thanks... glad he was able to contribute. "Like you said that is why you hired me; now what time do you want me to go to Jake's Saloon?"

Grinning at Ted's blush of pleasure... Melissa sighed thoughtfully. "Two o'clock is the perfect time; the sun will be down a bit so it should be behind us when we face the gunmen, it will give us one advantage at least."

Linda came back to the table to pick up their dirty plates.

Looking up at the hostess inquisitively, Jed unable to see outside had no idea if it was still morning or afternoon. "Do you have the time?"

Linda nodded. "It's close to twelve-thirty."

Inclining his head in thanks, Jed turned back to Ted. He pointed over his shoulder towards the front entrance.

"Deputy Walters you better go start spreading rumours about Sheriff Ray coming to the saloon, do not mention my name at all; if anyone asks you don't know who I am or whether I will be with her."

Ted got up then left.

Melissa turned to Jed with a troubled frown. "You think they are after me and don't know anything about you!"

Jed shrugged dismissively. "I don't know for sure, but the only way for them to know about me is through someone in your town, if Deputy Walters is right that is. If someone from town told them about me; they would have told them I was at Smyth's Crossing, not here. Everyone knows you travel to all the small communities around your own. It would make sense for them to wait quietly in one of the other towns until you showed up in order to catch you when your guard is down. Then they could not only take over this town, but all the others as well... there would be no one to stop them!"

Sighing thoughtfully, Melissa nodded in agreement. "You're probably right; I just hope they don't figure out what we are up to and hightail it, we need them to stay in town."

They quickly finished their coffee then went upstairs to get ready for the fight of their lives.

*****

Walking out of their room to go to their meeting with the outlaws; Melissa impulsively touched Jed's arm to draw his attention before they even reached the stairs.

Turning immediately, Jed guessing what Melissa wanted and needed... quickly enfolded her in his arms; Grey Wolf kissed her deeply with all the passion he felt for her.

Breaking the kiss reluctantly, Melissa smiled up at him lovingly before whispering passionately. "I love you!"

Kissing the tip of Melissa's nose in reassurance, Jed pushed her away. "I love you too; remember I won't be far behind you!"

Feeling calm now, Melissa was content... Jed had reassured her of his love, which is all she really wanted. They went down to the lobby together; she turned with a final wave before giving Grey Wolf a bolstering smile then left without him.

They decided Melissa would walk out alone to give the outlaws a sense of victory... with Jed following a little way behind her. When the outlaws came out to meet the sheriff, she would go out into the middle of the street; Grey Wolf would catch up to her there and together they would meet the outlaws. They also decided Mell would take on Samson since she had dealt successfully with him before, Jed would take on Diago again.

Turning, Melissa looked up at the sun just behind her then nodded her head in satisfaction; her estimate had been correct... the sun's position would be a definite asset to them today. She turned back towards the east end of town. Mell stayed close to the edge of the sidewalk so she would be as close to the road as possible. Sauntering slowly and confidently the sheriff walked towards Jake's Saloon as if she didn't have a care in the world. Inside though, she was very worried about Jed. Not once since she met Grey Wolf, did she see him use his gun, so had no clue what the outcome of today would be.

Melissa was almost at the saloon when two men walked purposely into the middle of the street arrogantly... both had a confident swagger, they turned staring at her intently. She smiled in relief as the outlaws came out to meet her; Mell stepped off the sidewalk and ambled towards the middle of the street before slowing her pace, so Jed would have time to catch up to her. She was just about to the spot she picked out to stop when he walked up beside her.

Slowing his step to match hers... Jed didn't say a word to Melissa as they walked; neither did either of them take their eyes off the outlaws. He did reach over for a quick moment to squeeze her hand reassuringly before letting go so both their hands would be free.

Observing the two men closely, Melissa saw them look at each other in confusion; she smiled to herself in relief. Well, it looked like Deputy Walters was right, the outlaws hadn't known about Jed. Mell reached the spot she picked out then stopped confidently... she smirked nastily at Samson. "I thought I told you to stay out of my towns or I would kill you next time!"

Relaxing her stance... Melissa fanned her fingers out making sure both her guns were unstrapped before wiggling her fingers to loosen them up slightly. She wanted to be ready to draw at a moment's notice; Mell watched Samson readying himself in a similar manner.

Jed frowned angrily at the Mexican as he too readied himself. "We meet again Diago; do you remember me?"

Diago shook his head negatively in confusion before snapping his fingers when he remembered suddenly. "Yes, it wasn't far from the Montana border if I'm not mistaken. I hardly recognized you without the Indian. I was hired to kill a man squatting on someone's property when you and the biggest native I ever seen shot my employer instead. You also took a shot at me but thankfully, I moved so the bullet missed my heart. It took me six months to recover so I owe you one, where is that big fellow by the way?"

Grimacing grimly, Jed remembered well Giant Bear's rage that day. "Be thankful he's not around at the moment; if I remember correctly, he wanted to talk to you about the Indian woman you cut up after you finished raping her!"

Diago shrugged nonchalantly. "What's it matter; she's just a whore, anyways!"

Samson broke in; he glared in rage at Jed then Melissa before turning to her fully. "Who in tarnation is this man it's none of his business!"

Melissa smirked in delight as she taunted. "This is Deputy Brown... he's also my fiancé; so, you see it is his business!"

Scowling furiously, Samson hissed in warning. "Enough talking, I will give you till sundown to get out of North Dakota or I'll kill you!"

Glaring insolently, Melissa taunted the gunslinger... knowing from other dealings with him that when he was angry, his reflexes slowed considerably. "Sorry to disappoint you Samson, but I am not going anywhere; besides, the minute I turned my back you would shoot me. I'm just surprised you had the guts to face me, usually you lurk around corners then shoot people in the back."

Growling in rage, Samson went for his gun... just as Melissa expected he would. He stared in shock when he saw the sheriff's smoking pistol pointed at him; his gun hardly moved from the holster when Mell's bullet struck his heart. He fell backwards, dead before he hit the ground!

Jed waiting patiently listened to Melissa taunt Samson, but he didn't take his eyes off Diago.

The Mexican drew his six-gun at the same time his accomplice did.

Ready for it, Jed drew his gun too... but, he was a half second slower than Melissa and Diago.

Diago turned his gun on Melissa first... he knew the sheriff was his biggest threat, having perfected his draw since the long-ago day Jed shot him; his confidence dealing with the deputy afterwards was unshakable.

Catching Diago shifting his aim out of the corner of her eye, Melissa was ready; she had already drawn both her revolvers prepared to help her fiancé. Mell's bullet hit first... Jed's entered Diago's body a half second later.

The mistake the Mexican made would be his last; Diago was dead before he even realized a bullet had ripped through his chest... he toppled to the ground lifeless.

Jed and Melissa turned as one to stare at each other anxiously; they both eyed the other from the top of their heads to the bottom of their toes... making sure they were unharmed. The sheriff spun her guns dramatically as she put them away then took a hesitant step towards Grey Wolf.

Taking the final step, Jed swept Mell into his arms for a long passionate kiss of relief at their narrow escape.

It wasn't until a tremendous cheer arose around them that they realized the townspeople surrounded them. Since Melissa took over as sheriff, gunfights were illegal... rarely did the townsfolk get to see one. Everyone gathered were now cheering and clapping their approval; not only because of the demise of the two outlaws, but also for the passionate kiss that they were now witnessing.

Pushing away from Jed in embarrassment, Melissa blushed a fiery red at being caught kissing with such wild abandon. Grey Wolf put an arm around Mell in relief... he bent down and whispered passionately. "I love you!"

Melissa smiled up at Jed adoringly. "I love you, too!"

Ted threaded his way through the crowd then shook Jed's hand first before taking Melissa's hand. "That was the best shooting I have seen in a long time; but I'm sorry Deputy Brown, if I had to put money on one of you it would have to be on Sheriff Ray!"

Jed chuckled... he nodded calmly without a shred of jealousy. "I don't blame you there; if Diago hadn't messed up and turned his gun on Melissa first, I would probably be dead now instead of him. He was definitely much better than he used to be."

Shuddering in Jed's arms, Melissa's mind replayed that scene.

Feeling the shiver, Jed squeezed Mell reassuringly before letting her go. Grey Wolf looked around at the crowd... he shouted loud enough so everybody could hear him. "First drink is on me!"

All the men cheered in approval and rushed for the saloon.

Turning to Deputy Walters, Jed waved down at the bodies. "Will you see to them while I buy my bride-to-be a shot of whiskey to calm her nerves?"

Nodding, Ted flipped a coin at a boy to bring the undertaker here for him; they would need the wagon to get the two men to Luke's funeral home on the other end of town... close to the cemetery.

Putting his arm around Melissa again, Jed steered her over to the saloon; she continued to shiver in reaction at Grey Wolf's narrow escape. When they entered, everyone cheered... a space opened for them so they could reach the bar.

Smiling in greeting at the man behind the counter, Grey Wolf put out his hand for a shake. "You must be Jake; I'm Jed Brown, Melissa's new deputy. Can I get two shots of whiskey, one for me and one for my lady please?"

Jake was tall, although not as tall as Jed was... he was also hefty, nowhere near fat just extremely muscular. He reminded Grey Wolf of a miner turned saloon owner. He had black hair with light brown eyes; when the owner shook his hand it was firm, but not crushingly so. "Sure, thing Deputy Brown!"

Pouring them each a shot, Jed handed them across the counter. The owner watched from the window, but after the shooting the townspeople got in his way so he didn't see the passionate kiss the others did. "Are yeah really getting married to our sheriff or was it a ruse to get the gunmen out?"

Jed grinned in conspiracy... he leaned closer to the bar to be heard above the noise. "That wasn't a lie, Jake; we are really getting married in five days."

Roaring in glee, Jake banged loudly on the bar to get everyone's attention... he hollered above the noise. "Next drink is on me; Sheriff Ray is really getting married!"

Hearing a few groans of disappointment in the crowd, Jed grinned not sorry in the least before lifting his hat in greeting... everyone cheered; they came over one at a time to shake his and their sheriff's hand giving them congratulations.

Melissa smiled in gratitude at everyone in the crowded bar then hollered out. "Next drink is on me!"

The men shout approval again; a toast was raised to their very own one-of-a-kind lady sheriff.

Drinking to the toast, Melissa looked over the counter at Jake. "Make out the bill and send it to the judge, make sure to add a tip for yourself; I think it's time for us to head home!"

Nodding in agreement, Jake handed Melissa a paper to sign before writing all the drinks down and the amounts.

Waiting until Jake finished with Mell; Jed paid for his round in cash and flipped a silver dollar the bartender's way.

Expertly catching it, Jake saluted in thanks.

Touching Jed's arm pleadingly, Melissa gestured emphatically. "Let's go home!"

Nodding in full agreement, Jed steered Melissa through the crowd; it took them a while to get to the doors since everyone kept stopping them along the way for handshakes and more congratulations.

Taking a breath of fresh air, Melissa was thankful when they reached the sidewalk outside the saloon. She looked towards the spot where the two outlaws died; thankfully, the bodies had been taken to the funeral home already... she looked up at Jed then waved down the street. "I need to talk to Deputy Walters and I would like to stop at the store before we go."

Obediently, Jed followed Melissa to the lawman's office before entering the building together.

Deputy Walters was already writing up his report.

Walking up to the desk, Melissa cleared her throat to get his attention.

Ted looked up in surprise before smiling in greeting when he saw who it was. "Well, neither one of you look too bad considering the ordeal you just went through."

Laughing in delight, Melissa motioned agreeably. "It's amazing what a few shots of whiskey can do for a person."

Chuckling knowingly, Ted gestured curiously. "What can I do for you, Sheriff?"

Melissa pointed down at the report Deputy Walters was making out. "We want to leave right away so I would like to know if you would send a note in your report to the Judge for me; tell him we are not going to Smyth's Crossing just yet, but straight to the ranch... we should be home when he gets this."

Sighing in disappointment, Ted waved enticingly. "I can if you like, but why don't you stay over until tomorrow morning... it's getting pretty late?"

Shaking her head negatively, Melissa pointed over her shoulder in the general direction of home. "I made a promise to a boy that I must keep... plus, I need to finish getting ready for my wedding."

Nodding in understanding, Ted got up; he walked around the desk for a congratulatory hug from Melissa before Deputy Walters turned to shake Jed's hand. "I will see you when the sheriff comes back this way."

Jed inclined his head in farewell. "I'll look forward to it."

Saluting in farewell, the two left the building; Melissa walked slowly across the street trying to find a way to get rid of Jed... she looked sideways at him slyly. "Do you need anything from the store?"

Shaking his head, Jed shrugged negatively. "No nothing that can't wait until we get home."

Smiling in relief, Melissa pointed towards the hotel hopefully. "Why don't you go and have our horses saddled while I grab a couple of things then?"

Nodding not suspecting a thing; Jed continued crossing the street, but angled left away from the storefront.

Rushing into the store, Melissa walked up to the counter.

The storeowner stared in surprise at the sight of Melissa. "Well, howdy, Sheriff; what can I do for yah, I wasn't even aware you were back?"

Melissa grinned knowingly at Mike; he was the complete opposite of Charlie. He was short very slim almost mousy appearing with glasses; his blonde hair was thinning and sparse on top, with beautiful dark green eyes. He had an accent he couldn't quite hide. She knew he wouldn't be aware she was in town because he almost never left his beloved store... unless his wife made him go for something. Mell smiled hopefully. "I'm looking for a pocket watch for my fiancé."

Nodding pleased that he had one, Mike reached under the counter. "I have just the one for yah."

Opening an engraved box, Mike pushed it towards the sheriff.

Bending down to inspect the watch, Melissa gasped in surprise; it was beautiful, all gold with a rearing black horse engraved on the front. She picked it up and opened it before smiling in delight when it played a tune... setting it down, she nodded. "I'll take it and some canned peaches too please."

Smiling relieved she liked it; Mike wrapped it while Melissa walked around the store waiting for him to finish.

Noticing a new rifle on the wall in a display case... Mell went over then opened it before taking it down in interest.

Mike walked over after he finished wrapping Melissa's watch. Seeing the sheriff's interest in his new guns, he sensed another sale. "That's the new repeater rifle; it'll shoot fifteen bullets before you must reload, let me show yah."

Handing it to Mike in interest, Melissa watched closely.

Opening a small drawer beneath the display case; Mike took ten bullets out then started shoving them in one at a time.

Watching in amazement when Mike loaded all ten bullets into the chamber, Mell shook her head in disbelief.

Beckoning Melissa to follow him, Mike led her to a door then out the back where he had a target set up ready for anyone who wishes to try the rifles. He explained how the gun worked first. "After yah put the bullets in push this lever over and down, it's now ready to fire the first shot."

Firing the gun, Mike lowered it to show Melissa how to get rid of the empty bullet casing. "To expel the shell, jus pull this lever up and back to where yah had it when it's first loaded."

Watching in incredulity, Mell couldn't help feeling excited when the empty shell was expelled.

Smiling in delight at Melissa's surprised expression, Mike knew for sure now he had a sale. "To fire the next bullet, yah need ta push this lever over... once down its ready."

Lifting the rifle, Mike fired; again, it responded instantly.

Melissa watched closely as Mike expelled the bullet then reset it for another shot.

Mike handed the rifle over to the Mell. "Here, yah try it."

Taking the gun, Melissa hefted it trying to get a feel for it...

it was so light. She put it to her shoulder then fired a shot and waited for the recoil; it was ever so slight in comparison to her nickel-plated one-shot rifle, she hardly even felt it. Smiling in delight, Mell had the rest of the bullets expelled within moments. She looked over at Mike grinning widely in excitement. "How many of these do you have?"

Shrugging in apology, Mike gestured in disappointment. "Not many, only four but they should be at the store in Smyth's Crossing by now. If not, Charlie can get a hold of 'Winchester Repeating Rifles' in Boston; make sure he tells them the model number is one-eight-six-six... they will send him some."

Sighing in disappointment at not being able to get more, Melissa grinned good-naturedly. "Okay, I'll take all four and as much ammunition as you have for them."

Nodding with a grin, Mike led the way back into the store.

Walking to the counter, Melissa waved down at the rifles in explanation. "Just wrap the guns in an oil cloth; the bullets can go in with them."

Smiling enticingly, Mike gestured around his store hopefully. "Is that everything, Sheriff?"

Laughing, Melissa held up her hands in surrender. "It'll have to be, I don't have any room left for anything else. You can put two of the rifles as well as most of the bullets... except for two boxes for the other two guns on the town's tab; everything else, I will sign a bank note for."

Frowning, Mike was disappointed Melissa didn't want more. He loved it when the sheriff came to town because she always bought something out of his store. Within a month, he got his money; whereas most of his clients had tabs... he was lucky if they paid him within a year. Most of his sales were on a bartering system since money was so hard to come by. The storeowner had tabs dating over two years ago. He tallied up the town's bill first, so Mell could sign it. Afterwards; he filled out a bank note on the two rifles, two boxes of shells for each gun, the peaches, and the watch.

Signing it, Melissa tucked the gift away in her shirt pocket under her vest then put the peaches in her pants pocket; gathering the four rifles, which had two shell boxes wrapped in each... she left in a rush and carried her burden to the hotel.

Smiling at her horse when he nickered at her, Melissa passed the hitching post without stopping... in too much of a hurry she didn't stop. She rushed into the lobby then grinned over at the clerk, but didn't stop there either; she ran up the stairs and kicked at the door so Jed would let her in.

Opening the door, Jed jumped back out of the way; he stared at Melissa in surprise when she almost barrelled into him on her way in before setting the bundles on the bed.

Raising an eyebrow in indignation, Jed laughed at Melissa. "Well, what do you have there?"

Smiling up at him in delight, Melissa told him about the rifles.

Walking over speculatively, Jed uncovered one of the guns then examined it... he put it back reluctantly. Grey Wolf grinned at Melissa in approval. "I can't do anything with it here, so let's go; I can try one when we stop for the night."

Melissa nodded in excitement. "The horses are out at the hitching post already; so, all we have to do is pack up, we can stick the rifles in our bedrolls for now."

Motioning around the room with a teasing grin... Jed shook his head. "I've got everything packed too; as you can see there's nothing left in here, it's all on the horses."

Looking around in surprise, Melissa noticed the room was empty... she smiled at Jed in approval. "Okay, let's go I have to stop in the lobby and sign my bill on the way out; oh, did you get our provisions out of the cold room?"

Jed nodded his head in pride. "Both are done, Sheriff; all we need to do is go get on our horse's then ride into the sunset."

Laughing teasingly, Melissa handed Jed two of the rifles to carry. "I just might have to keep you around after all, let's go."

Snickering in humour, Jed followed Mell closely. Racing down the stairs together; they walked across the lobby then waved goodbye to the clerk before leaving the hotel. Putting the guns inside the bedrolls, they mounted... Mell looked over at Grey Wolf. "I want to reach the campsite we used last night, so we will have to ride hard if we're going get there by midnight."

Nudging his horses into a trot immediately; Jed didn't argue, impatient to get there as well.

*****

They arrived before midnight, exceeding Mell's expectation; they unsaddled the horses then rubbed them down good in apology for pushing them so hard. She made beans with hardtack... too tired for anything else.

Jed was stuck doing dishes again. When he got back, Melissa took out one of the rifles. Sitting close to the fire for light, she showed him how to load it and expel the bullets. After practising for a bit; not even sure if they hit anything, but now more proficient in loading and firing rapidly... they sat by the fire then had one last coffee before bed.

Smiling at Melissa hopefully, Jed gestured. "Who are you giving the guns too?"

Melissa grinned at Jed's optimistic tone of voice. "There's one for you and me, of course. I want to give one of them to Tommy... plus one to Giant Bear as parting gifts; I'll go to Charlie's and order more for the men later."

Rubbing his hands together in anticipation, Jed nodded in gratitude. "Thank you, I would love to have one."

Chuckling knowingly at Jed's eager voice, Melissa pulled out his gift and gave it to him dramatically. "I found something in town I think you will like."

Taking the gift in surprise, Jed opened it... he smirked in delight, realizing Melissa got him a watch just because he asked the waitress for the time. He held it closer to the fire so he could see the decoration on the front; opening it, he smiled in pleasure when he heard music coming from it. He leaned over to gather her into his arms before kissing her passionately. Releasing her, Grey Wolf smiled down at Mell gratefully and let her go. "It's beautiful, I will think of you every time I look at it. Come to bed now, we have a long trip ahead of us tomorrow."

Kicking the fire out, Mell followed Jed to the bed he made for them earlier while she was cooking. They kissed goodnight before cuddling together; both were asleep in moments... too exhausted for anything else.

CHAPTER EIGHTEEN

Waking before sunup, Melissa and Jed had a quick coffee then finished off the beans from last night. She got up from the fire and retrieved one of the rifles... plus, two boxes of shells. Mell threw them to Grey Wolf one at a time, so he could catch them. She bent to pick up the rifle they used last night with a box of her shells. Going over to him, they spent twenty minutes practising; afterwards, the two of them went to saddle their horses.

Taking out the old nickel one-shot rifle out of its sheath, Melissa smiled down at it... it had been made in Paris by a man named B. Houllier. She put it in the oilskin to be retired; it had served her well over the years, so she would have it mounted on the wall. Mell put her new lighter repeater rifle in the sheath on her saddle in glee. With a satisfied thump, it settled perfectly inside. Jed did the same; she smiled over at him in delight. "This new rifle is ten pounds lighter; I like it already."

Jed grinned in agreement before mounting. He took out his watch in pleasure and looked at the time speculatively... he turned to Melissa with a hopeful expression. "It's four-thirty, I would like to be back at the ranch in time for supper tomorrow night; do you think the horses would stand such a hard ride?"

Melissa smiled saucily at him. "I'll race you!"

With that, Melissa dug in her heels before racing away. Jed smiled indulgently after Mell; he tucked his new watch into his pocket securely then kicked his own horse into a gallop before giving pursuit... trying to catch her.

*****

Riding into the ranch yard at five the next evening, Mell and Jed grinned at each other... they made it for supper. Knowing they were getting close the two of them only stopped once to give the horses a much-needed rest and for a quick bite to eat just after lunch. Both horses were foam slicked and blowing hard; thankfully, not dangerously so.

Dusty followed closely by Tommy ran out of the barn at the sound of running horses... both stopped short in surprise at the sight of Melissa and Jed. Nobody expected them until at least tomorrow; the two boys looked at each other in concern at the conditions of the horses. They turned back then walked over when the two dismounted.

The two weary travellers grabbed their saddlebags... as well as the new rifles. Melissa smiled in greeting at Dusty and Tommy before her tone became serious. "The horses are exhausted; please, take special care of them for me boys."

Tommy nodded solemnly... already aware of what to do; this wasn't the first time he had seen Lightning like this, but thankfully it didn't happen often. Both boys turned away then trotted the horses slowly towards the barn in concern.

Jed and Mell raced each other to the house... Alec was waiting in the entryway having heard the commotion. Wade had given him a warning twenty minutes ago when the sentry raced in to report that riders were coming fast. He grinned in satisfaction, the two were earlier than he thought they would be; which was a good sign that everything had went well.

Setting her stuff down, Melissa rushed over in relief for a big hug then kiss from her father; not even bothering to remove her outer clothes first.

Alec smiled up at Melissa curiously, as she stood back up. "Well, that certainly didn't take long; I wasn't expecting you guys back until midnight tonight or tomorrow morning."

Smiling grimly, Melissa remembered the ordeal of the last few days. "I'll explain everything when we are all together; are Wade and Giant Bear having supper with us tonight... I want them both here as well."

Nodding that they were, Alec went on to explain the progress at the ranch so far. "Yes, they are; unfortunately, you missed Mrs. Elton, Sara, and Jane they left a little while ago. Betty said to tell you that your dress is ready. She wants a final fitting though to make sure everything is perfect. The archway with the platform is finished except for a few flowers, which we figured you would want to put on yourself. I'm hoping it won't rain until after the wedding, I did see storm clouds to the north this morning. Thankfully, the wind changed sending them in a different direction. The outside of Brad's cabin is almost done... the floor on Wade's cabin has begun already."

Melissa and Jed hadn't been idle while Alec talked; they

both took off their gun belts, boots then their hats. Afterwards they put their badges on the shelf before changing into moccasins; finally, they reached down to gather their new rifles.

Smiling smugly at Alec, Melissa couldn't help teasing him playfully. "I have a surprise for everyone after supper."

Turning to Jed before gesturing down the hallway to their left, Melissa gave him directions. "We can put these in the library until after we have eaten."

Heading there obediently, Jed took the lead with Melissa following him.

Bringing up the rear, Alec tried to pry out more information. "What do you have there, Mell; those are definitely not the rifles I gave you when you left here?"

Depositing her bundle on the divan, Melissa walked over then patted Alec on the shoulder before going behind his chair; she pushed him towards the kitchen. She grinned devilishly at Jed behind her father's back, so he couldn't see. "Sorry Dad, you are just going to have to wait until after supper... like everyone else."

Alec sighed in disappointment.

Pushing Alec's chair inside, Melissa steered him to the table. She smiled in greeting at everyone before sitting down in one of the empty chairs that were left for them... Jed sat beside her.

Tommy came in just as Jessica put a roasted chicken on the table; He smiled over at Melissa hopefully. "Dusty called Brad in to help him so I could eat with you... is that okay Aunt Mell?"

Smiling, Melissa nodded permission; she waved silently in invitation towards the empty chair that was beside his mother... Tommy happily sat beside her. She waited for Jessica to have a seat before giving a quick blessing on the food and everyone dug in; silence prevailed until the meal was finished.

Melissa sat back in her chair to enjoy her coffee... she watched Jessica help Gloria clear the table. Afterwards, they brought more coffee to the table before they sat down again. Once everyone settled, Mell told them everything that happened except for the rifles; she wanted them to be a surprise.

Waiting until Melissa finished, Alec gave a relieved sigh... he gestured thankfully. "So, our fears were groundless; nobody hired them to disrupt the wedding."

Smiling grimly, Melissa nodded in aggravation. "That's right; all they wanted was to get rid of me, so they could take over the towns I look after."

Grimacing angrily in frustration, Alec drummed the fingers of his right hand against the arm of his chair rhythmically... a sure sign of his fear for Melissa. "Well, that's not good either; although, now the story will spread. We can only hope it will make anyone else with the same ideas think twice before attempting it."

Jed shrugged not convinced by that reasoning. "Maybe or maybe not; someone else could still try it, but with a lot more men now that they know two didn't succeed."

Scowling irritably, Melissa nodded agreeing with Jed. "That's the trouble with being a sheriff in such a large area... outlaws, are constantly trying to take over; this isn't the first time it has happened, it won't be the last either!"

Nodding thoughtfully, Alec didn't say anything; very much aware, Melissa was in constant danger.

Looking over at Tommy, Melissa smiled in anticipation before gesturing over her shoulder. "Go out to the bunkhouse then tell all the men to meet us at the target area; the one I use behind the ranch house, we want to show everyone something."

Grinning in excitement at the talk of a surprise, Tommy left out obediently.

Melissa turned to Jed before waving towards the library. "Will you go grab our surprise then meet us outside beside the old oak tree behind the house... you will know it as soon as you see it?"

Jed nodded with a grin of delighted anticipation and left.

Pushing Alec down the hallway, Melissa took him outdoors to the porch. Where he changed into his other wheelchair; the unique design helped her father get around on the dirt and grass in the yard... it had slimmer steel tires from a bicycle for better traction on rough or wet terrain.

Everyone else followed closely behind, chattering excitedly wondering what all the fuss was about.

Gesturing for Wade to come over, Melissa stepped away

from the wheelchair. "Will you push Dad the rest of the way for me; I need to go talk to Jed before everyone arrives!"

Wade nodded with a puzzled frown.

Ignoring the look, Mell sprinted around the house to join Jed.

Waiting patiently for Melissa, Jed handed her the rifle that was hers; plus, the half-empty box of shells that they used the last two days to practise with.

Smiling at Jed in anticipation, Melissa gestured inquisitively. "Should we fire one at a time; or would you rather we shot together... for effect?"

Grinning back eagerly, Jed waved dramatically. "Let's shoot together and give them a real show!"

Smirking mischievously, Melissa gestured ahead of her at the old oak tree. One could tell it had been used for many years as a target... it was riddled with bullet holes. Mell smiled innocently at Jed. "As you can see, I have got two targets against the oak; now that we are more proficient in loading and firing let's make a little wager. We will each fire two full rounds, the one to hit the target the most has complete control tonight in bed. The loser has to do whatever they are told."

Grinning wickedly, Jed nodded eagerly. "You're on!"

Just then, the others from the house arrived.

Handing Jed her rifle, Melissa took four large steps back so everyone would stop in front of her... she didn't want them too close. Mell waited for them to get to her in anticipation. Right behind Alec was Tommy; followed by the men from the bunkhouse.

Melissa waited until everyone was gathered. She listened to all the excited curious questions for a moment before she held up her hand for silence... everyone hushed expectantly. "I'm not going to say anything right now, all I want you to do is watch and listen; when I come back, I will answer all your questions then."

Alec grinned up at Melissa knowingly; he motioned towards the targets. "Going to put on a show for us, are you?"

Smiling teasingly down at her father; Melissa didn't answer him, but winked in conspiracy before turning... she joined Jed.

Handing Melissa her rifle, Jed accepted fifteen bullets from her.

Normally, Melissa didn't allow a loaded rifle in the house... ever; but since she didn't want anyone to see her put the bullets into the rifle, she had reluctantly made an exception this time.

Jed grinned at Melissa cheekily. "Let the best man; or woman win!"

Grinning at Jed in complete confidence, Melissa didn't comment. Both lifted their rifles at the same time and set themselves ready to fire. She waited a few moments dramatically; to extend the silent anticipation behind them before finally shouting loudly so everyone could hear her. "Get set... GO!"

The two rifles fired as one then continued firing for an unbelievable fifteen times; it took them about four minutes to expel all fifteen bullets before both were reloading as quickly as they could. Jed was slightly ahead, but not by much! Three minutes later, both rifles were firing again. When the last of the bullets were discharged, the two of them were dead even. They lowered their rifles and turning to each other in delight... it was a tie!

Wade pushed an excited Alec over to them; her father beamed up at Melissa in amazement then motioned incredulously. "That was unbelievable. I counted every shot... timed you too. Both of you shot thirty bullets in just over ten minutes. I have never heard of such a thing happening before, let me see that rifle."

Smiling cheekily down at Alec, Melissa dutifully handed him her rifle. Jed handed his to Wade, so he could check it out as well. While the rifles were being inspected, the two curiously turned as one in order to go look at the targets in anticipation to see who won the bet.

They scrutinized Melissa's target first. She grinned saucily over at Jed when they counted thirty bullet holes; only two of them were dead center, but she hadn't missed once! They went over and studied Jed's target next. They only counted twenty-nine holes. Mell was just starting to smile in triumph when Grey Wolf noticed that one hole in the center was slightly bigger than the rest. He pointed to it and grinned in triumph at her disappointment. "Looks like neither of us win. We both hit the target thirty times."

Melissa sighed in regret before grinning good-naturedly... she pointed at Jed's target in approval. Twenty-eight out of thirty bullets had hit dead center. The other two encircled the bull's eye. "It's a good thing we never bet on who could hit the middle the most. I would have lost for sure; you're definitely better with a rifle then I am."

Jed smirked devilishly. "I'll have to remember that in the future and bet on it the next time."

Laughing in delight at Jed's gloating look, Melissa turned with Jed following; they went back to join the crowd. The two spent the next hour answering excited questions and showing everyone how to load then reload the rifles. Finally, it was full dark... unable to see anymore someone was sent to find a lantern.

Smiling at everyone, even though Melissa knew none of them would be able to see it now that it was dark. "Tomorrow, when we get back from town, we will do another demonstration then everyone can take a turn... even the women; there isn't much of a kick to these rifles so they should learn how to shoot them as well, but right now I need coffee!"

The men from the bunkhouse left once a lantern was given to them; they could be heard talking excitedly among themselves... all were looking forward to trying the new rifles tomorrow.

Turning to Tommy, Melissa smiled in thanks when he handed her a lantern. "I want you to come to the library with us too."

Tommy frowned perplexed; usually he wasn't allowed in with the adults and was always banished to the bunkhouse or to his room. "I'm not in any trouble... am I, Aunt Mell?"

Grinning tenderly, Melissa ruffled Tommy's hair affectionately then draped her arm around his shoulders; she led her foster son back to the ranch house. "No, you are not... I promise."

Jessica walked up to Melissa and gestured enticingly when they entered the house. "I'll bring a tray with tea and apple pie; if you like."

Nodding gratefully at Jessica, Melissa nodded in agreement; she led the rest to the library, when the widow scurried ahead of them... going to the kitchen. Mell turned to Jed just as they reached the door and handed him her rifle. "Would you please put this in the gun rack in the den for me, grab a couple of extra chairs while you are at it?"

Nodding, Jed left; Wade followed him to the den to help with the chairs. Gloria took the lantern from Mell before going around lighting the candles; she enlisted Giant Bear's help in lighting the big chandelier in the center of the room... wanting more light.

Going to the divan, Melissa transferred both bedrolls to the floor out of her way. She sat down then waited until everyone was present and seated. Finally, she beckoned her foster son to come over so he was standing in front of her. Mell waited until he reached her then she took both of his hands in hers... she looked at him earnestly. "Tommy, since the day you were born and your mother put you in my arms, I have loved you with all my heart. When your mom brought you here for me to look after at the age of six, I have thought of you as a son; always in the back of my mind, I have pictured you staying here with me then taking over my ranch someday. Now though your father is taking you away to live with him, so as your foster Mother I have two gifts to give you. The first one I would have taught you later, but tonight and tomorrow then every day until you leave here, I will teach you my techniques of fighting. This way you can always protect yourself from harm, I'm sorry that I won't be there to guard you myself. The second gift I have for you is also for your protection. I'll give you instructions in its use too, but your dad will have to help you on your journey so you can perfect it."

Letting go of Tommy's hands, Melissa bent down then unwrapped one of the new rifles... with two boxes of bullets; she handed them to Mary's boy. There wasn't a dry eye in the room as everyone felt Mell's pain at the imminent separation from her foster son.

Tommy took the gifts from Melissa reverently. He examined them before setting them on the floor out of his way; freeing his hands. Dropping onto his knees with a heart-wrenching sob... he reached for Mell, crying fretfully on his foster mother's shoulder.

Holding Tommy tenderly, Melissa still crying too stroked his hair soothingly... until he stopped; Mell let him go reluctantly.

Sitting back, Tommy smiled shakily at Melissa before

wiping his face with his sleeve.

Melissa also had to wipe her face clean of tears; she looked around and saw all the others drying their eyes. Everyone in the room couldn't help but feel the pain of Tommy and Mell's parting.

Pausing, Tommy waited for Melissa to look at him again before he motioned down at the rifle in appreciation. "Aunt Mell, thank you for the wonderful gifts. I want you to know that I have always thought of you as my second mother. My dreams over the years were to live here with you forever... until now; I hope you understand why I must go with my father, even though I love you so much. I promise, every single day I'll miss you and be eternally grateful for the unconditional love you have given me throughout the years."

Melissa smiled in understanding before she wiped more tears away. "Yes Tommy, I understand why you must go with him; always remember though if you ever need me, I will come to you no matter what. Now take your new rifle upstairs then come back in an hour. Remember no loaded guns in the house... ever!"

Grinning, Tommy stood up and saluted smartly in humour. "Yes ma'am!"

Tommy scooped up his rifle, as well as the bullets then ran out of the room still crying.

Bending, Melissa unrolled the second rifle. She took it, along with the two boxes of bullets to Giant Bear. The Chief was standing beside his wife's chair, except to eat he refused to sit in a white man's wooden seat; preferring to sit on the ground. Mell sighed sadly when she handed the rifle over to him. "Since you are taking two of the most important people in my life away with you, I give you this gift so you can always protect them."

Giant Bear reached down then squeezed his wife's shoulder in bidding. Mary jumped out of her chair before scurrying from the room aware of what her husband wanted.

Once his wife was gone, Giant Bear turned back to Melissa then accepted the gift graciously. He pointed behind him in the direction Mary had taken. "I thank you for your generous gift; I also have something for you. Golden Dove will bring it. What I have is rare, maybe even the last one in existence and never given to anyone outside the Cheyenne tribes... it's highly prized by all Indians everywhere. I have carried it with me since I started this journey unsure of why I brought it. The Great Spirit told me I would know what it was for when the time came. I'm giving it to you because without your help, my son Tommy wouldn't have survived or grown so strong in spirit."

Mary came back into the room carrying something white; immediately there were gasps of admiration from the others and disbelief at what Golden Dove was holding.

Passing his new rifle to Jed to hold for him; Giant Bear took the white buffalo robe from Mary then placed it around Melissa's shoulders in formal ritual. He took a white medicine bag made from the same buffalo and put it around her neck, so it nestled between her breasts. Finally, he took out his hunting knife before taking Mell's hand in preparation. "From this day forth you shall be known to the Cheyenne as... White Buffalo!"

Giant Bear cut into Melissa's palm then his own before he joined their hands to mix their blood. He continued talking as if they were in an Indian ceremony. "The White Buffalo has strong medicine; it will protect you as long as you are wearing your medicine bag. Her spirit can find you anywhere, but beware... never take it off for too long or your spirit totem will lose you. You are now a blood sister to the Cheyenne Chief of the bear tribe, and friend to all Cheyenne. The drums and signal fires will come to life as soon as I am home to tell the story."

Mary passed Melissa and Giant Bear each a clean cloth to wrap around their hands; she had brought them knowing her husband would want to enfold his blood sister in a welcoming embrace.

After wrapping his hand, Giant Bear hugged Melissa then stepped back... he kissed her on each cheek before releasing her so Mell could see his earnest expression. "If for any reason you need me for anything in the future, find a tribe of the Cheyenne then let them know your need; I will come to you or die trying!"

Melissa smiled flabbergasted... she was so choked up in emotion she had to clear her throat several times before she was able to speak coherently. "This was totally unexpected; I'm not quite sure what to say. I want you to promise me the same thing though Giant Bear. If you have need of me as a Sheriff or as your friend, just get a message to me through any lawman's office. I will come or die trying."

Nodding solemnly, Giant Bear once again embraced Mell; this time in promise to seal their vow.

Stepping forward, Mary embraced Melissa as soon as she moved back from Giant Bear; embracing her friend she could barely contain her glee. "Hello White Buffalo, blood sister to Chief Giant Bear and adopted sister of the Cheyenne! I am Golden Dove, married to the chief of the Montana Cheyenne!"

Jed came over next then hugged Melissa tenderly before speaking in Cheyenne gravely. He stepped back so he could see her face. "White Buffalo, blood sister to Chief Giant Bear; I'm Grey Wolf, blood brother to the Montana Chief... I am also an adopted son of the Cheyenne."

Alec wheeled himself over to Melissa once Jed moved away to let others have their turn with her. Mell bent down then kissed her father's cheek.

Speaking in Cheyenne, Alec was very much aware of what the white buffalo hide represented to the Cheyenne. "White Buffalo, sister to the Cheyenne... blood sister to Chief Giant Bear. I'm 'Stands Tall' friend to all Cheyenne; as well as your loving father."

Melissa smiled down at Alec then tears filled her eyes in joy... she spoke gravely in Cheyenne. "It's been a long time since you spoke your Indian name so openly; not once since mother's death, have I heard you speak it."

Jed and Giant Bear looked at each other in shocked surprise; they had heard many tales of Stands Tall. When the chief was a youngster, he had even been taught a little knife trick by him. Later, he used it to save a young boy's life. Because of the wheelchair though, the Cheyenne Chief hadn't realized who Alec was... plus the Cheyenne heard he died a long time ago.

Stepping forward, Giant Bear nodded eagerly. "Yes! I didn't see you because of the chair, but now that you have spoken your name... I remember who you are! Now I know why I thought you looked familiar even though I couldn't remember where I seen you before. Your daughter's fighting skills were familiar too."

Alec's smile turned nostalgic when he looked up at Giant

Bear recalling that long ago day. "I recognized you; although, it took me some time to remember... it came to me a few days after you arrived; at the time you were only a little older than Tommy and were not yet named Giant Bear."

Giant Bear stroked the hide he was wearing thoughtfully. "It was because of you and the trick you taught me with a knife that I became Giant Bear; without your teaching I probably would have died, instead of the bear!"

Shaking his head negatively in denial, Alec disagreed. "You were fated to become Giant Bear; if the Great Spirit hadn't used me to help you, another way would have been found."

Grinning unconvinced, Giant Bear shrugged unknowingly. "Maybe, you could be right."

Glancing from one to the other speculatively, Melissa smiled in delight; when she was younger, Alec use to tell her bedtime stories of his time with the Cheyenne. "Dad, this is the boy you used to tell me about!"

Smiling in agreement, Alec nodded. "Yes, he is, but his tribe moved to Montana just after you were born; I never did see them again."

Spotting Tommy coming in, Melissa looked down at Alec... she touched his shoulder in farewell. "I'll be in the den if you need me."

Smirking up at Melissa, Alec gestured teasingly in warning before patting her hand that was on his shoulder. "Okay, just don't wreck the place... please!"

Melissa grinned down saucily; she winked mischievously before turning then left without speaking. She took Tommy into the den... they moved the furniture over against the wall to give themselves more room. Mell picked the den because it had the most available space. She put her fur on the divan and placed the two chairs one in front of the other, making sure they were facing each other. Sitting down, she motioned for her foster son to sit in the other one so they could talk. She gestured at him inquisitively. "Did you bring a knife?"

Nodding eagerly, Tommy handed Melissa the hunting knife his father had given him.

Taking it from Tommy, Melissa examined the blade critically then checked it for balance by using her first finger on her right hand. She laid the knife blade down on top of her index finger close to the hilt; it balanced there once she removed her hand... Mell nodded in approval. She noticed movement by the door, but didn't say anything to her foster son when Jed and Giant Bear settled back in the shadows to watch.

Turning her attention back to Mary's son, Melissa ignored everything else as she gave the boy a lesson on knives. "This is a good knife, Tommy. See how it balances when I hold it in the center. It's not too heavy either, which is a good thing. The profile is nicely done, even though it's a little short being only about ten and a quarter inch in length. A Bowie knife seems to be the most popular right now, when used for fighting those blades can run over thirteen inches long or longer. Your knife does have the typical curve and deadly clip point one will need in a fight. I'm glad to see the conclave isn't too deep in the blade though. I like the tang, the guard that protects your hands when two knives come together. It's thin but solid and nicely rounded, so will keep your knuckles from injury. The rawhide handle is unique. It gives it a sure grip and keeps it light so it will thrust better. Overall, I think it will be good for both hunting and fighting!"

Tommy grinned enthusiastically. "Dad gave it to me when we went hunting; he said all hunters need a good knife."

Frowning, Melissa's tone became cautious in forewarning. "Your Father is extremely wise Tommy, so you should always listen to his advice. I have always taught you though that no matter who gives you counsel, all decision in your life is yours to make not somebody else's. Listen to your instincts; gut reaction can save your life just as often as good advice, especially in a knife fight. You have to learn when to use your head and when to use your instinct. Nobody can teach you that it's something you learn as you gain experience. When you are fighting with a knife, never hold it straight out like most people do. Always hold it hilt backwards with the flat of the blade against your arm. The sharp razor edge must be kept pointed down so you don't cut yourself. This gives you better control because your wrist will direct how deep... plus, the angle you are going to drive the knife home at. If your arm is ridged your knife will be pointed straight ahead, so chances are your wrist is locked. At this point, all you can do is lunge forward hoping that your opponent doesn't have a longer reach then you do. Because I was smaller and weaker than the boys my age were, I had to adapt to a different fighting style. Wrestling was difficult for me, one of the hands at the ranch I grew up at seeing the trouble I was having taught me to box. It gave me the footwork I needed to keep away from my bigger opponents!"

Melissa started moving the knife around to get a feel for it, while she talked to Tommy. "To get away from the stiff-armed jabs I'm going to give you some exercises to do, watch me closely and I will explain as I demonstrate. Hold the knife lightly not in a death grip, when you are going to stab someone that's when you need to grasp it tighter. Only the first two fingers... plus your thumb should be holding the handle. The rest of your fingers need to be loose so they are only there to keep the knife in place or to move it into different positions. Move your knife towards the left side of your arm, but don't twist your hand. You should be the only one able to see the full knife blade. Your opponent should only see the tip of the blade just sticking up past your arm slightly. Now move the knife to the right side, which will make the knife completely visible to your opponent. All you should see at this point is the tip of the blade against the side of your arm sticking up. Okay, you can now tighten your four fingers, but loosen your thumb so you can move it to the very end of the hilt. Pull the hilt down slightly so it's fully nestled in your fist. The knife should be pointing out to the side in a horizontal position then tighten your grip fully. You should be ready to use the knife now."

Handing Tommy the knife hilt first, Melissa gestured in encouragement. "Now you try it, but don't cut yourself."

Tommy copied Melissa, but slowly and hesitantly; he had a hard time moving the knife without moving his wrist.

Smiling in approval, Melissa took the knife away. "I want you to turn your wrists counter clockwise in a fist without a knife and with your hand open... now reverse direction. Good now lift your hand then bring it down as if you are waving with it, but strain it some. Go as far back as you can before going downwards; do this with a fist then open handed. Do these exercises twice a day with both wrists. I think at first you should find a stick as heavy as your knife. It should also be the same length. Use that to practise with until you think you are ready to do the exercises using your knife safely! Better yet, ask your father to carve you a knife out of wood.

This is how it should look when you finally become proficient with it. Remember, at first, I don't want your wrists to move. When the time is right though, your wrists will be all you should be moving."

Tommy watched closely as Melissa passed the knife from one hand to the other, not once did the knife stop moving or her wrists. He never saw her once move her arms or shoulders. He watched in amazement as his aunt twirled the knife between her fingers without cutting herself... he sighed dejectedly as he watched her. "It is going to take me years to be able to do that!"

Melissa smiled consolingly over at Tommy. When she finished, she flipped the knife in midair before catching it by the blade and handed Tommy back his knife... hilt first; once he took it, she put her hands in her lap. "Actually, you will be surprised at how fast you can learn to do this if you practise twice daily. You can put the knife away now we won't need it anymore tonight."

Watching in satisfaction, Melissa nodded in approval as Tommy immediately put his knife in its sheath; he then laid it on the divan beside him before turning back to her expectantly. Mell waited until he was facing her once more and she had her foster son's full attention, now she continued her lessons.

Making sure to gestures as she talked, Melissa wanted to make sure her point was getting across to Tommy as strongly as possible. "Now most people who fight with a knife circle each other with the blade held straight out in front of them; when the feeling is right for them, they jump forward stabbing straight ahead. If they manage to hit something, they are darn lucky. That's a crude method, but don't get me wrong it can be effective at times to throw your opponent off balance. You should think of it as a dance instead, one movement should flow into the next freely. As in any dance, you must train yourself to move effortlessly. At first balance, speed, plus the knowledge of what you can or cannot do will come only with time. You always need to remember that every part of your body can be a weapon. Knees, elbows, head, hands, as well as feet can all be lethal if used properly. This method of fighting is extremely efficient with knives, tomahawks, a coup stick, but especially hand-to-hand fighting. When I learned to wrestle then box, I had to teach myself how to stay away from a bigger opponent. It was just natural for me to use my flexibility to my advantage. It helped that we had a strange funny looking man show up out of nowhere one day, nobody could understand anything he was saying. He caught me behind the barn practising my kicks. He stepped in front of me then started doing these slow moves and I copied him, every day for a month he would show up. Mysteriously he disappeared one day and never came back, so I continued doing the routine myself... plus I added many more moves over the years. It's a dance I do usually before bed."

Melissa got up; she walked to the center of the room to give herself more space. She turned to her foster son before pointing at herself. "I will show you my dance first, which will be different from yours. I can do some things that you will not be able to do and it has nothing to do with being a man or a woman. It's how flexible you are that counts, how you are put together is the key. I can kick straight up then touch my nose with my leg. About five years ago, I saw a man in a circus that could wrap both legs around the back of his neck. I tried for a long time to do that; I just couldn't do it. Now, watch me closely Tommy... try to feel the dance, as well as see it."

Moving farther back, Melissa knelt down; she stayed there for a moment with eyes closed listening to something inside her that only she could hear. Suddenly she began to move slowly and was no longer on her knees, every move she made turned into a different one effortlessly. Mell's dance was well practised it had taken her years to perfect, but that didn't mean she never tried to add other moves that she could think up. Always she was changing... never wanting to become predictable.

Watching Melissa in fascination... Tommy had never seen his aunt so intense before or so beautiful. She kicked, twisted, and flipped or rolled sometimes all at the same time. Every move she made was slow and methodical flowing into the next move with no breaks or stops between. Finally, Mell finished in the exact spot and position she started in.

Tommy clapped loudly in approval the awe was clear in his voice. He motioned eagerly when Melissa looked over at him expectantly. "Wow! That was amazing; do you really think I can learn to do all that too?"

Smiling indulgently, Melissa nodded emphatically over at Tommy before gesturing in caution. "Some of it you will learn easily, the rest you will have to train yourself to do. Now, one thing I'll tell you that I probably shouldn't because your mother will shoot me is that I taught her this dance; the only reason I'm telling you is because you will need someone to train with... she can help you."

Tommy stared at Melissa in surprise then grinned in delight before clapping his hands in glee. "She can, I never knew that!"

Melissa nodded before she waved for Tommy to come over to her. "Yes, she can, now come here I'll show you exercises that should be done every day. Once you can do these movements without thought or effort, you will know you are ready to put together your own dance. After you have your routine memorized, it will be time to add your hunting knife; from that time forward, you can practise with it... plus with a tomahawk, coup stick, and of course with nothing in your hands."

Grinning eagerly, Tommy got up to begin his lessons.

*****

Giant Bear and Jed listened and watched quietly without a word spoken between them; not wanting to intrude or distract the pair from their intense concentration. Once Tommy started doing his exercises, the two men now sure they wouldn't be overheard turned to each other.

Jed looked at Giant Bear with a grin of satisfaction. "I have seen a similar technique used by the Chinese in Boston, but its way different; maybe the man she mentioned was Japanese... that's why the moves are a bit unusual. Anyway, Melissa only scratches the surface of what they do... hers are mostly basic kicks, turns, or spins that was put into a dance like rhythm."

Shrugging dismissively, Giant Bear had no clue who the Chinese or Japanese were or even what they are. "I don't know them. My Golden Dove must have learned to fight like White Buffalo after she returned, she didn't know it before! I do remember that Stands Tall had a similar way of fighting he held his knife like his daughter, but he didn't kick like Mell does."

Nodding thoughtfully, Jed waved towards Melissa in amazement. "It looks like White Buffalo trained herself to do most of the things she does... she makes it look so easy. Mell has managed to surprise me completely, now I won't be shocked by anything she does anymore. I have never met a woman like her in all my travels; she is definitely unique!"

Sighing knowingly, Giant Bear nodded in agreement. "That's why the white buffalo spirit claimed her as one of its own. In our history, only two others have been named White Buffalo... it has been over a hundred years since anyone was chosen. At that time, they were both men with strong medicine. This is the first time in our history a woman had such a powerful animal spirit call her. The fact that she is white with no Indian blood in her will cause many of my people to question me on my decision to name her as such. But the Great Spirit showed me that White Buffalo would come to me when my people are in the gravest need; unfortunately, my dream didn't tell me when or why this would happen or even who was to be named. There was only a sense of needing to take the hide, and the medicine bag with me on my journey. With a quick glimpse of a female buffalo walking towards me as my people cried out in the distance. The Cheyenne tribes believe a white buffalo represents a female spirit, but it's still a male totem. As far as I know, no woman has been called before this. The Lakota, here in North Dakota tells stories of a White Buffalo Calf Woman early in their history."

The two men lapsed into silence both wondering what was to come, they turned back to watch Melissa train Tommy.

*****

Grinning down at Tommy, Melissa clapped in approval. "Very good, I think that's it for tonight; remember your kicks should get higher until you reach your limit. Practise tomorrow while I'm at work, I will show you more when I get back. If for some reason I am unable to finish teaching you... your mother can do so."

Tommy nodded; he got up and walked over to Melissa for a goodnight hug before grabbing his knife off the divan then turned to leave. He spotted Jed and his father sitting in the corner... he went over to say goodnight to them first.

Melissa smiled lovingly at Jed when he walked towards her

after Tommy left. "Well, did you learn anything tonight?"

Jed laughed in delight before tweaking Melissa's nose playfully. "Yes, never pick a fight with you!"

Chuckling in disbelief, Melissa didn't believe for a moment they wouldn't fight; she turned away without comment then started moving the furniture back. Jed and Giant Bear helped her. Silently, she picked up the buffalo robe she set aside earlier before turning. Mell smiled at the two men enticingly. "Since I missed my coffee and pie in all the excitement, I think I'll go to the kitchen for some... either of you want to join me?"

Giant Bear shook his head negatively. "I think it's time for me to go back to the barn, Golden Dove will be waiting for me."

Nodding in disappointment, Melissa watched Giant Bear leave before she turned to Jed inquisitively. "What about you?"

Smiling eagerly, Jed rubbed his hands together in anticipation. "I would love some!"

They walked to the kitchen together in silence.

Alec was already at the table enjoying another piece of pie and coffee... he grinned up at Melissa inquisitively. "White Buffalo, how are you feeling now that you have received a Cheyenne name and become a blood sister to Giant Bear?"

Sighing tiredly, Melissa sat down in the chair beside Alec. "I'm not sure yet, everything happened so fast; I don't think I really feel any different except maybe more fulfilled... like I was missing something all this time!"

Nodding knowingly, Alec remembered his younger days. "I had the same feelings when I received my Cheyenne name... how did the lessons with Tommy go?"

Smiling in pride... it was full of maternal approval, which Melissa always displayed when thinking of Tommy. "Very well, he will make a fine warrior one day."

Melissa grinned up at Jessica in thanks as she set pie then a coffee cup before her. "Thank you!"

Looking curiously at Melissa when she turned back to him after Jessica turned away; Alec waved vaguely towards Smyth's Crossing. "Are you going to town tomorrow you two?"

Jed and Melissa both inclined their heads decisively... it was Mell who answered for the both of them. "Yes, I need to make a report tomorrow on what happened with the outlaws; I also have to check on Gary to make sure he's doing all right."

Nodding, Alec had known they would be going but asked anyway making sure. "Good, I want to go to town as well; why don't the two of you meet me at the hotel for lunch?"

Motioning curiously, Melissa cocked her right eyebrow inquisitively at her father. "Sure, we can meet you there... do you have a specific reason for going to town or is it just to get out for the day?"

Nodding that there was, Alec smiled secretively. "I have an eleven o'clock appointment with my lawyer then I'll probably visit with John for a bit. Brad is coming with me to pick up Jane and the kids. They need to get furniture for their cabin, so I need to be with them for that; they are hoping to move into the cabin tomorrow. It'll sure be nice to have the young ones running around."

Melissa's face lit up eagerly, she rubbed her hands together in anticipation. "It'll certainly be different; we have only ever had the one kid around. Unfortunately, he was always so serious and quiet. Usually, you didn't even realize Tommy was here... having three children running around will take some getting used to!"

Grinning over at Melissa, Jed winked... he couldn't help teasing her. "You better become used to it pretty fast if we are going to have one or two kids of our own; although having your own kids is way different from looking after someone else's."

Blushing at the reference to her having children, Melissa concurred. "I suppose it is different, but until we have some of our own, I won't know for sure!"

Smiling devilishly, Jed unable to help himself allowed his grin to turn suggestive. "Well, in three days we can try as often as you like."

Melissa's blush deepened; she quickly changed the subject. "I don't know about you two, but I'm exhausted... if you will excuse me, I am going up to bed."

Mell raced out trying to escape Jed's teasing.

Alec's laugh of delight followed Melissa out the door at the deepening blush staining his daughter's cheeks. He hadn't seen her blush in a long time... it delighted his heart to see it; he chuckled once more then turned to Jed. "It's certainly going to be nice having another man around the house even though I love all the women in my life."

Grinning for a moment, Jed's face sobered before he gestured anxiously. "I hope I live up to all of your expectations for a son-in-law."

Smiling in reassurance, Alec winked encouragingly. "All you have to do is make my daughter happy, that's all I ask."

Jed nodded eagerly. "That's an easy request because it's what I want too. Have you come up with some figures for me so I can buy a share of the ranch?"

Shaking his head negatively, Alec waved dismissively. "No! That's one reason I'm going into town tomorrow; there is an assessment we had done last year on this place at the lawyer's office. I will pick it up and we can discuss it tomorrow."

Inclining his head in approval, Jed finished his coffee before getting up to leave. "I will say good night then sir... I'll see you in the morning or for lunch if you are not up when we leave."

Leaving in a hurry, Jed took the stairs two at a time and quietly entered the bedroom. He quickly got undressed then slipped under the blankets beside Melissa. She turned in her sleep and cuddled close, but didn't wake up; Grey Wolf smiled down at her lovingly before laying back... he drifted off to sleep.

*****

Alec smiled up at Jessica hopefully when she walked over; she pulled him away from the table to take him to bed. "Going to tuck me in Jess?"

Jessica grinned down wickedly then bent down close to his ear... whispering suggestively. "If that is all you want, Alec?"

Nodding solemnly, Alec pretended not to hear the teasing note in Jessica's voice... he looked up with an innocent grin. "That's all I can think of at the moment."

Chuckling in disbelief, Jessica continued pushing Alec into his bedroom. Once inside, she took him over to the bed so that he could lift himself out of the chair; once he was on the bed, she wheeled it over to the closet storing it inside.

Sitting on the edge of his bed, Alec waited for Jessica in anticipation not moving a muscle.

Finished, Jessica walked over to stand in front of him.

Thoughtfully, she stared into Alec's eyes unsure at first if she should continue. Jess only hesitated for a moment; once she saw the passion flare up in his eyes, there was no more indecision. She smiled teasingly, reaching up she started undoing the buttons on his shirt... without asking permission.

Sitting very still, Alec waited eagerly not wanting to push Jessica into something she didn't want to do. His breath caught in hope when she began undoing his shirt; quivering in anticipation... he wondered what Jess would do next.

Pulling Alec's shirt out of his pants once Jessica finished undoing it... she unhooked his cuff links next, and put them on the nightstand. Turning back, she removed his shirt completely. He hadn't worn his long underwear today because it was just too hot out for them, so Jess had an unobstructed view of his chest. She ran her hands over his muscles before smiling in admiration. Because Melissa's father had to lift himself in and out of his chair constantly, his chest plus his arm muscles had hardened over the years; even more so then when he had the use of his legs. The widow smiled mischievously as she looked up teasingly. "For an old man you certainly have nice chest muscles."

Laughing devilishly, Alec wrapped his arms around Jessica so that she couldn't get away. "I'm not that old woman, come here and I'll prove it!"

Grinning saucily, Jessica slipped out of Alec's reach impishly... she paused playfully for effect; unexpectedly, she started to undo the buttons on the front of her dress.

Alec watched breathless... he groaned in torture when Jessica finally dropped her dress to the floor and stood in front of him completely naked.

Jessica wasn't wearing any petticoats or a corset... having planned this moment earlier. She had run to her room while everyone else was occupied in the library then stripped out of them in preparation for this moment; now Jess stood there completely naked.

Catching his breath in delighted surprise, Alec looked her over... Jessica's breasts were not large, but they were high and firm just under a hand full. If he hadn't known better, he would never have guessed that she had any children because her stomach was slim as well as firm; you had to look very closely to see any stretch marks. Jess's hips were nicely curved. The hair at the junction of her thighs was just as red as the hair on her head. Her legs were long very firm with slim ankles. She had surprisingly small feet.

Jessica waited for a moment so Alec could get a good view. Finally, she glided towards him slowly... teasingly. Getting close she pushed him backwards onto the bed, but not near enough for him to grab her. He was now lying flat on his back; she removed his slippers and socks before unfastening his pants then pulled them off. Standing over him once he was completely naked Jess admired his physique for a long moment. Slowly, she crawled onto the bed and up his body wanting a passionate kiss.

Alec groaned against Jessica's lips in pleasure when their bodies came into partial contact. He touched both her breasts tenderly. Lightly, he squeezed her nipples before he ran one hand down the side of her body. Reaching her hip, he brought his hand across her stomach... down then gently cupped Jess's secret place. He shuddered in pleasure feeling her heat and the moisture that said she was ready for him; it was a good thing she was it had been so long he didn't think he could wait much longer. Putting his hands around her waist, he lifted her a little. Without breaking their kiss, he began slowly entering her. He didn't rush her letting her control the penetration, not wanting to hurt her.

Gasping in discomfort then pleasure, Jessica slowly lowered herself onto his engorged manhood... it had been such a long time for her. When about halfway, the tightness eased; she shivered in ecstasy pushing down more fully, but it wasn't enough for her. She broke the kiss reluctantly, now Jess could sit up to get a deeper penetration.

Grasping Jessica's hips in demand, Alec pushed her down harder.

Lifting herself, Jessica sat down hard grinding her hips at the same time.

Unable to hold back any longer, Alec pulled Jessica down for a deep demanding kiss. Grasping her hips, he lifted her up and down faster so they could both erupt together... the pair saw stars for several long moments. He held Jess tightly against him enjoying the pulsating sensation of her muscles contracting around him while he ejaculated deep inside her.

Jessica collapsed on Alec in exhaustion; after a few minutes, she chuckled deeply... panting softly she purred. "Well, you certainly proved to me you are not too old!"

Catching his breath, Alec gasped out breathlessly. "I'm not sure about that I certainly feel old now!"

Laughing in delight, Jessica rolled off Alec... he pulled himself up to the headboard. They cuddled for a bit longer than Jess got up and went to the washbowl; she brought it back with her along with a cloth then proceeded to give him a sponge bath.

Alec's manhood quivered a few times as if trying to rise again.

Chuckling in satisfaction... Jessica watching Alec's manhood twitch couldn't help giving it an extra swipe in approval; she sponged herself off next and put the washbowl away before getting dressed.

Smiling at Jessica sleepily; Alec with a small wistful plea plain in his voice... suggested optimistically. "You don't have to go to your room, if you want. I think my daughter is old enough not to mind if you sleep here with me."

Reaching down, Jessica tenderly stroked Alec's cheek before shaking her head in denial. "I know she wouldn't, but until we are married... we should at least keep up appearances."

Nodding in disappointment, Alec had known Jessica wouldn't stay but had hoped he was wrong. "Whatever makes you happy?"

Bending down, Jessica kissed Alec goodnight then slipped out the door silently without comment.

Yawning sleepily, Alec stared at the door for a few moments hoping Jessica would change her mind before falling asleep... still wishing.

CHAPTER NINETEEN

Jed woke instantly at the sound of an insistent knock... he reached down then pulled the blankets up before summoning softly. "Come in."

Gently, Jed nudged Melissa awake. She grumbled in annoyance, but obediently opened her eyes.

Gloria came in with a breakfast tray and smiled at the two of them cheerfully. "Good morning, it is time to get up; I figured you two would want breakfast before you leave!"

Walking over, Gloria deposited the tray in Jed's lap... ignoring Melissa's discontented mumble. The maid stepped back and folded her hands in front of her. "Brad is up already and seeing to your horses, they will be ready to go whenever you are. Everyone else is still sleeping; do you need anything else before I go?"

Waving Gloria out in dismissal, Melissa sat up. She poured a coffee for Jed... another for herself. "No, you may go."

Turning to the door, Gloria closed it softly behind her.

Melissa grinned over at Jed in sleepy delight. "I could get used to this pampering in no time if I'm not careful."

Laughing in humour, Jed took a sip of his coffee before commenting. "Well, I think you better; between Jane, Gloria, and Jessica you will be waited on daily!"

Smiling in contentment, Melissa didn't comment. They ate their breakfast in silence. After coffee was done, they dressed; she finished first so picked up the tray before gesturing at Jed. "I will take this to the kitchen while you grab our rifles from the gun rack. I will meet you at the front door."

Nodding in agreement at Melissa before she left, Jed finished quickly.

Taking the tray into the kitchen, Melissa put it on the counter.

Bustling over, Gloria shook a chiding finger at Melissa in gentle rebuke. "You don't have to bring me the tray... I can pick it up when I go clean your room."

Shrugging casually, Melissa couldn't keep a note of warning from entering her voice though. "That's okay; I don't think it will strain me too much to carry the breakfast tray down."

Nodding, Gloria held up her hands in surrender before

smiling consolingly. "If you wish..."

Grinning good-naturedly at Gloria's diplomatic answer, Melissa waved goodbye. "See you later."

Leaving the kitchen without another word, Mell hurried to the front door to put on her gear.

Jed was already there waiting for Melissa patiently; as soon as she was ready, Grey Wolf handed her one rifle... plus her last box of shells. They went outside together. Simultaneously, they loaded their rifles then flipped on the safety before going to the barn.

Their horses and the packhorse were already at the corral waiting for them as promised.

Brad came out of the barn to talk to Melissa; he touched the tip of his hat in respectful greeting before waving towards the house hopefully. "If you don't mind, after you are done with the archway, I would like to break it down then make a hitching rail for the front of the house. It would save you time to have your horses tied up there... instead of having to walk all the way here to get them."

Melissa inclined her head in approval. "Sure, you can make one if you like."

Nodding his thanks, Brad turned to go to the bunkhouse for breakfast; his job done.

Tying the packhorse to the back of his saddle, Jed mounted; as soon as he was ready, they headed for town. Once out of the yard, Grey Wolf looked over at Melissa inquisitively before pointing behind him at the packhorse. "Why don't you just keep a horse in town instead of taking one from here all the time?"

Shrugging dismissively... Melissa waved at the horse in explanation. "I have always brought my own because sometimes I don't even get to go to town before I have to leave, so this is easier."

Nodding in understanding, Jed rode the rest of the way in silence.

When they entered town, Melissa stopped at the store first; before dismounting, she turned to Jed and motioned towards the office. "You go on ahead, please make us coffee then start your report. I'll see if Charlie has any of these repeating rifles yet or bullets then I will join you."

Nodding, Jed turned his horse away from the hitching post.

Dismounting, Melissa entered the store; she looked around expectantly then spotted the owner. "Morning Charlie, how are you today?"

Charlie smiled in greeting and walked over to Melissa... he grinned curiously. "I'm doing just fine, Sheriff; I heard you had to run to Miller's Creek, nothing serious I hope!"

Shrugging solemnly, Melissa reassured the inquisitive store owner before changing the subject. "Nothing we couldn't handle; but while I was there, I found some new rifles called Winchester Repeating Rifle... model number eighteen-sixty-six, have you got them here yet?"

Charlie pointed towards the back of the store then grinned in humour. "They came in last night; I haven't even had time to put them on display yet."

Melissa smiled in delight. "Good; I'll take nine if you have that many?"

Frowning in thought... Charlie finally nodded. "I think there's a dozen, but I'm not sure; how much ammunition would you like?"

Deliberating for a moment, Melissa held up her fingers in explanation. "If you have a dozen guns, I think you should add an extra rifle to my nine... I'll need one for the office. If you have enough, I would like two boxes of bullets for each rifle; you can put eight rifles on my tab plus the ammunition. Two rifles with two boxes of ammunition each, along with six extra boxes can be put on the town's tab."

Writing Melissa's instructions as she talked, Charlie looked up inquisitively. "Do you want me to have the rifles delivered?"

Shaking her head negatively, Melissa waved towards the ranch. "No, Dad's coming into town later; he will be stopping here, so you can send them with him... except for the two with their boxes of shells, I'll take them with me now!"

Inclining his head amiably, Charlie waved behind his counter in invitation. He continued the conversation when Melissa followed him. "No problem, Sheriff; are you getting excited about your wedding?"

Sighing irritably, Melissa shrugged resignedly. "Unfortunately, I haven't had time to get excited."

Looking back in concern, Charlie motioned towards Melissa curiously before turning away and continued to walk ahead.

"Being the sheriff is a big job; are you going to continue now that you're getting married?"

Harrumphing decisively, Melissa nodded emphatically. "Of course, that was agreed on before I told Jed I would marry him."

Chuckling knowingly, Charlie stopped at the crates then turned with a grin before he gestured in relief. "I figure it was, but a lot of people are asking that question; now I can relieve everyone's mind!"

Watching silently, Melissa didn't continue the conversation as Charlie grabbed a bar and forced the lid off the crate; it only took a few moments before he was handing the two rifles to her... plus all the ammunition she had requested. She smiled her thanks then turned heading back to the front of the store, Mell called back over her shoulder. "Write it up for me Charlie, I'll see you later."

Leaving the store, Melissa mounted her horse awkwardly; not wanting to put the rifles and ammunition away; especially since she only had a short distance to go then rode to her office. Mell dismounted just as precariously and walked inside before propping one rifle beside the coat rack. The other one she put up in a gun cabinet... with two boxes of bullets.

Gary smiled over in greeting.

Melissa went over to her desk to deposit the ammunition. Afterwards, she walked to the stove to pour herself a coffee; she took the pot over and filled the men's cups before sitting down then sipped her coffee in appreciation... she grinned over her cup at Gary inquisitively. "Did you have any problems while I was gone?"

Shaking his head negatively, Gary waved reassuringly. "Only a brawl between James and Jimmy; they took it outside the tavern themselves so I let them fight, but made sure it didn't get out of hand!"

Sighing thankfully, Melissa motioned towards the door. "Good, you can go home when you are finished at the judge's office. I will be here tomorrow briefly to show my replacement a few things; I have lots to do so I won't be around long. Remember on the day of the wedding, when Dusty gets here go to the judge's office right away to give your report. Once you're done, Lucy will be able to leave the office to get ready for the wedding."

Nodding agreeably, Gary grinned as he thought of his wife's nagging the last few days. "We will be at your wedding too; Millie is very excited about it so I couldn't disappoint her. I guess you could say that I didn't get a chance to say yeah or nay!"

Smiling enthusiastically, Melissa waved in relief. "Good! I was hoping the two of you would come."

Finishing his coffee, Gary got up to leave. "Guess I'll mosey on over to the judge's office. Millie is still at work; I will head there afterwards."

Noticing the rifle when Gary got up, Melissa pointed towards it... after propping it against the wall, Mell had almost forgotten about it. "The gun I brought in is for you; take two boxes of shells off my desk too."

Getting up, Melissa went over to pick up the rifle before handing it to Gary to inspect.

Looking it over eagerly, Gary smiled in thanks. "Well, thank you kindly it's beautiful."

Putting her hand out for the rifle, Melissa motioned towards the bullets. "Bring me a box, please; I'll show you how to load it before you go."

Doing as instructed; Gary watched avidly as Melissa showed him how to insert the bullets before she handed it back to him... with the safety on. "When you get home, you can practise loading and firing it."

Gary nodded eagerly... he took the rifle from Melissa then waved in farewell as he turned to leave. "I sure will and thanks; see you tonight!"

After her new deputy left, Melissa walked back to her desk before taking out paper, pen... as well as ink to write her report; there was absolute quiet except for the scratching of two pens as they both wrote furiously. Only once did she look up, that was to smile in thanks when Jed got up to pour them the last of the coffee. She sighed then threw her pen down thankfully when she finished.

Jed still wasn't done, so Melissa rifled through the wanted posters before taking out Samson's and Diago's; she wrote across the front of both posters in big letters... 'Deceased'!

Dropping his pen on the report, Jed sat back with a sigh of resignation... he looked at Melissa plaintively. "I'm definitely not going to like this part of the job."

Melissa laughed knowingly; she gathered her report plus the two wanted posters before getting up to walk over to Jed's desk. She put Grey Wolf's on top of hers to read critically and smiled distractedly; briefly, Mell glanced at him... quickly she looked back down at the report. "You get used to writing them after a while."

Scanning Jed's momentarily, Melissa nodded in approval before looking down at him. "You did a good job for your first real report; there's some information here that's not absolutely needed, which is okay. As you gain more experience, you will learn what is essential or what can be left out. Now that I'm satisfied, it has everything in it a report should have... I won't read any more of them; it will now be up to Lucy to help you if you do something wrong."

Grinning up at Melissa, Jed nodded gratefully. "Thanks!"

Inclining her head in acknowledgement, Melissa gestured towards the door. "Let's do our rounds so we can meet Dad for lunch."

Getting up immediately, Jed followed Mell out then joined her on the porch. She paused, allowing her eyes to adjust to the sunlight before walking to the hitching rail; both stopped to loosen the girths on their horses first. Melissa grabbed her whip and headed for the stagecoach office. She went in first then smiled cheerfully at James in greeting. "Good morning, how are you and your mother doing today?"

Grinning back, James was certainly thankful to see Melissa back already. "Great, my mom is really looking forward to your wedding. I heard you had some problems at Miller's Creek; the deputy who took over your shift wasn't sure you would be back in time."

Smirking teasingly across the counter, Melissa waved outrageously. "You think I would be late for my own wedding?"

James laughed negatively in relief. "We were all hoping you wouldn't be. We have all been waiting too long for you to get married as it is!"

Melissa chuckled in delight. "Well, I don't plan on disappointing anyone at this late date!"

Dramatically, Melissa handed James the two wanted posters.

Looking them over, James whistled in amazement; he looked up in disbelief. "Both of them at the same time, I have never heard of them working together before!"

Exhaling noisily in satisfaction... Melissa face turned grave. "You won't hear of it again either; will you send a message to all the sheriffs for me. You will also have to send one to the governor and another to the Pinkerton Agency."

Grinning in agreement, James nodded pleased she entrusted him with such an important task. "I will be happy too, Sheriff."

Nodding in thanks, Melissa motioned inquisitively. "Do you have anything for me today?"

Shaking his head negatively, James handed Melissa a couple of letters for Alec. "No nothing for you, just for your father."

Sighing relieved at that good news, Melissa stuck the envelopes in her pocket before waving goodbye as they headed out; she turned to Jed and gestured down the street. "I want to go to the judge's office first today."

Jed followed her without comment across the street then turned left; they went in and Melissa smiled cheekily at Lucy. "Is the judge free, Lucy?"

Inclining her head gravely in greeting, the judge's secretary nodded that he was. "Yes, he is, Sheriff. Your night deputy just left, so go right in."

Groaning in mock anger, Melissa bantered with Lucy for a few minutes while Jed looked on in humour; he grinned resignedly at the two women as they repeated their performance of the other day.

Grinning impishly, Melissa just smiled back at Jed without comment; when they left Lucy's desk, they walked down the hallway to the office.

Looking up from a report, John motioned in relief... glad to see them as he held up the paper he was studying. "I'm glad to see you two are here already; I got this report from Deputy Walters late last night, but I want to hear what happened from you."

Melissa and Jed both sat down before they related everything to John. She handed him their reports so the judge could read them later; usually, she gave them to Lucy but she had known he would want them right away.

Sighing in aggravation, John took the reports and laid them

on the desk for later. "I read Deputy Walter's report last night. If it is not one thing it's another! At least they didn't have anything to do with your wedding... your father did mention a possibility. Maybe we should talk about hiring a marshal. South Dakota has one; it might be time for us to get one too. I talked to the governor about it a few times, but you have always done such a good job that we decided to let it be for now."

Glaring, Melissa broke in as she scowled angrily. Leaning towards the judge... Mell gestured sharply in exasperation. "We don't need a marshal; I can still handle things. Now that Jed is here with me all the time I will have back up if I need it."

John frowned in displeasure before putting his hands up in surrender. "Okay, don't get so mad about it. I agree, now that Jed is with you it will take some of the load off. If you think the two of you can handle it, I will let it be; eventually though, we are going to have to talk about it seriously. We have more and more people coming to settle here with towns springing up every year. You aren't going to be able to keep up pretty soon, even with two of you!"

Sighing in aggravation, Melissa sat back before waving resignedly. "I understand that, but we don't need one yet."

Jed cleared his throat to get their attention. "What's the difference between a marshal and a sheriff?"

Shrugging negligently, John tried to explain to the confused Jed. "A sheriff looks after one town, plus the surrounding area. A marshal doesn't look after any town, but tours the whole countryside then helps any sheriff needing backup; in addition, he looks after people in out of way places that don't have a lawman close to them. A marshal goes from town to town picking up people that are in jail and wanted in other areas. He takes them to a courthouse where the criminal will be tried then if needed executed! Or if it's a long prison sentence, they need to be taken to North Dakota's larger prison, which is near the capital."

Nodding thoughtfully, Jed didn't say anything more wanting to think about that for a bit.

Turning back to Melissa inquisitively, John changed the sensitive subject. "Are you ready for the big day; we are all looking forward to it?"

Shrugging, Melissa motioned impotently. "I'm not sure; you will have to ask my father, I haven't had time to do anything... never mind think about it. That reminds me, Dad is coming into town; he said something about visiting you then we are meeting him for lunch afterwards."

John smiled in pleasure and anticipation. "When you leave, let Lucy know your father's coming; tell her to let him in."

Nodding in agreement, Mell got up then headed for the door.

Following, Jed gave a quick wave of goodbye to the judge.

Stopping at the front desk, Melissa gave Lucy the judge's instructions. Once outside, they turned left... heading for Pam's house. They went in then waited in the lobby while the madam's hired man went to tell her to come out to see them. They didn't have long to wait as Pam came bustling in with a wide smile of pleasure. "Well, Sheriff; it's about time you got back. Thought for sure we were going to have a wedding without its star attraction."

Laughing in horror at that thought, Melissa shook a finger at Pam chidingly. "No chance of that happening; I have waited too long to miss it now. Besides, do you know the first thing I will do after I get back from my honeymoon?"

Smiling puzzled, Pam shook her head negatively.

Grinning mischievously, Melissa waved inside Pam's house... being as dramatic as possible. "I'm going to come here then walk through your house!"

Jed and Pam both laughed uproariously at that statement. The madam was the first one to gain control; she sighed in delight before wiping the tears of mirth away. "Sheriff, once you are married you can come in any time you like; if you ask, I'm sure the girls will give you some good advice as well."

Melissa smirked in satisfaction at the choking noises behind her from Jed, but she made no comment; Mell's expression became serious when she turned all business. "How did things go while I was gone?"

Pam's expression sobered as she thought about last night. "One of my girls was beaten again; I would have handed him over to you, but I didn't know until after he left here."

Melissa motioned knowingly before scowling fiercely. "Was it George again?"

Pam nodded grimly; with a worried expression she twirled

a strand of hair with a finger... a nervous habit she had tried for many years to quit. "Yes! He gagged her this time so she couldn't call out for help. We didn't find her until closing time. George did a real number on her this time. He's been a lot better since you had him in jail last time, so I didn't even hesitate to let him in. Besides, all he usually does is slap the girls around a bit. He doesn't usually hurt them too much. This time, he almost killed her! The doctor's been with her all morning and just told me a few minutes ago she will make it."

Frowning grimly, Melissa sighed in aggravation. "I'll go pick him up and talk to Judge Elton about a public flogging this time; plus, a prison term of at least six months. I will also ban him from all my towns so none of our women will ever have to worry about him again."

Inclining her head in relief, Pam watched Mell stalk from the room in a rage. She had never seen the sheriff this angry before; for just a moment, she felt sorry for George. Until she thought about Jasmine that is then her face-hardened instantly in rage, she didn't feel sorry for him anymore... only furious.

*****

Jed rushed to catch up with Melissa; he hadn't seen this side of her before, she didn't even wait for him. Grey Wolf matched his stride to hers, wisely not saying anything knowing she wasn't in the mood for conversation. It didn't take them long to reach Chelsie's Saloon.

Loosening her whip, Melissa barrelled through the doors in fury. Complete silence fell instantly when a man in the corner jumped to his feet then reached for his gun... he wasn't nearly fast enough.

Jumping to the left knowingly, Melissa with a swift flick of her wrist wrapped the coils of her whip around George... holding him fast. She jerked back hard on the handle in anger causing the man to fall forward; it happened so rapidly, he couldn't save himself from the fall.

George landed hard face first on the floor with a loud yelp of surprised pain.

Instead of loosening the whip, Melissa handed it to Jed to hold. She walked over to disarm George before searching him for hidden weapons. When she was satisfied, she had them all. Mell hauled him to his feet bodily then pushed him towards Grey Wolf in anger. "Take him and lock him up! I want you to fill out an arrest sheet right away. Make sure you put my recommendation on the bottom of it. Take it to the judge immediately for his decision; tell him I'll fill out a report later."

Nodding, Jed didn't dare refute Melissa in her present mood; besides, he actually agreed with her. Keeping the whip wrapped tight around the man, Grey Wolf pushed him outdoors then into the street.

Melissa turned to the bar, her mood improving now that George was so easy to find and catch. She knew this was where he would be waiting for her, the man was always predictable. He even waited at the same table after beating up one of Pam's girls. Mell walked over to the cedar bar then motioned casually before leaning against the counter as if a few minutes ago she hadn't been in a furious rage. "Morning how's business?"

Grinning good-naturedly, Chelsie waved teasingly. "Well, Sheriff that's the most excitement we've had in weeks... to answer your question business is just fine. I knew something was up with George, he came here as soon as I opened at ten then started drinking; he sat in his usual corner and just watched the doors for you without moving. Did he beat up one of Pam's girls again?"

Scowling angrily, Melissa rubbed her chin in aggravation. "Worse than usual this time, the doctor wasn't sure if the girl was going to live; Pam said the worst was over now though, so she should make it."

Chelsie whistled grimly. "Wow, now I know why you were spitting mad!"

Nodding, Melissa accepted the coffee Chelsie offered her; she waited patiently for Jed wanting to finish their rounds together.

*****

Jed pushed the helpless man in front of him, down the main street... exactly in the center of the road. People stared after them wondering at the strange sight of George walking dejectedly with head hanging. Grey Wolf was hoping the riders veering out of their way; plus, the townspeople got a good lesson once the word spread of what the man had done.

Not loosening the whip at all, Jed got George inside the

sheriff's office then into a cell first. When the leather strips were released, the three-pronged snakelike coils dropped harmlessly to the floor... now useless without its mistress to wield it. Grey Wolf eyed the man looking for the marks from the prongs Mell carved out of deer antlers; sure enough, he saw three gouges in George's vest. One was bleeding a bit.

Leaving the cell, Jed closed then locked the door before coiling the whip into an inconspicuous circle. He studied one of the three extensions and frowned thoughtfully. It was as long as his arm, Melissa had braided two thin rawhide strips tightly then put antler hooks on the ends; Mell had described them perfectly. They looked more like an anchor then a fishhook.

Jed frowned thoughtfully; it reminded him more of the bolas some of the natives used then a whip. A bola was two or three strips of rawhide with a rock tied on the end. When thrown, they wrapped around the legs of animals and held them fast. This did the same thing, but it was fashioned specifically for a human. Because a man can undo a bola if given time, Melissa made small hooks that tangled in someone's clothes or flesh instead. Making it almost impossible to get away, the more you fought it the deeper the hooks would dig in.

Standing for a moment longer outside the jail cell in contemplation, Jed looked down at the now innocent looking whip. He had seen men use whips on livestock many times, but this was the first time he saw it used on a person in this particular way. It could be a punishment tool; cat-o'-nine-tails it was called, it would do quite a bit of damage to a man's back. Those whips were used mostly on ships or anywhere there was a slave market, being that it's the preferred method of punishment for sailors or slaves.

The power and precision needed to wrap the long snakelike coils around a body, without injuring or killing him took lots of talent... plus years of practising; now Jed could see why Melissa carried it all the time, she was better with a whip then with a gun and that was saying a lot.

Shaking off his thoughts, Jed left the cells then went to his desk. He took out an arrest sheet and filled it in quickly; at the bottom, he wrote Melissa's recommendations then got up heading out the door.

George hadn't said a word since his capture.

Barely glanced at the man, Jed left; he walked over to the judge's office.

Jane and Brad were turning the wagon around after dropping Alec off then were heading for the store. Jed grinned up at them when they stopped the horses; he waved them on wanting to see the judge right away. "I will see you at lunch!"

Brad nodded before clucking to the horses to continue on without speaking.

Turning away, Jed entered the town office; he approached the receptionist's desk and smiled down hopefully at Lucy. "I need to speak with the judge and Alec, is it okay if I go in?"

Lucy nodded permission as she waved in invitation. "Go right ahead Deputy Brown... I am sure they will not mind."

Tipping his hat politely in thanks, Jed turned away. He walked down the hallway before stopping in front of the door and knocked politely; he entered at Judge John Elton's impatient call. "Come in!"

Smiling in apology, Jed closed the door behind him; he nodded in greeting at the two men before walking over to the desk then held up the paper he had in explanation. "Sorry to interrupt gentleman, but I have an arrest warrant the sheriff wanted me to bring over right away."

Jed handed the document to the judge.

Alec grinned up at Grey Wolf questioningly. "Who is Melissa arresting now?"

Shrugging, Jed didn't really know the guy; he motioned angrily before explaining to Melissa's father the circumstances of the man's arrest. "A man called George seems he likes to beat up on Pam's ladies, but this time he got too rough and almost killed the girl; Mell is recommending a public flogging, six months in prison... plus, a ban from all the towns she presides over as sheriff."

John scowled angrily when he looked up after reading the report. "I agree; except he'll get a year in jail not six months."

Scowling, Alec nodded in agreement. He changed the subject before gesturing inquisitively at the judge. "Any thoughts about hiring another lawman; we have talked about this last year. Now that Melissa is getting married, it would be better to have a marshal so she doesn't have to travel all the time."

Shaking his head plaintively, John remembered Melissa's reaction earlier when he had suggested it... he frowned in annoyance. "I tried to broach the subject with her earlier this morning; she almost bit my head off again!"

Interrupting, Jed sat down in the chair beside Alec's wheelchair and smiled eagerly; this is what he wanted to discuss with both men... he was glad they brought it up. "I might have another suggestion for you, if you would like to hear it?"

Turning to Jed, Alec smiled hopefully over at him; he motioned in invitation. "Sure, we would."

Grinning at the two men enticingly, Jed waved casually in explanation. "The judge described the difference between a sheriff and marshal to me earlier. Melissa fears another lawman will wreck everything she has accomplished, so doesn't want to give up any of her towns; whereas you two want to lighten her load. The answer to your problem is to make her the marshal with me as deputy marshal. This way every town has its own sheriff. It will help because she won't need to worry about being in two places at once or needing to run from one town to another to keep the peace. Neither will she have to be as concerned about desperadoes or hired guns trying to take over her towns. She will still have to travel to each town several times a year which is what she loves to do... that way everybody wins!"

John looked at Alec in amazement at how easily Jed solved their problem then they grinned in agreement at each other. The judge turned to Jed with a smile of thanks. "Well, young man; I think you have the perfect solution to our dilemma."

Nodding proudly, Alec smirked smugly. "Yes! He is definitely going to be an asset to the family!"

Chuckling at the boastful Alec, John looked from one man to the other in contemplation. "Okay, now that we have reached a solution; how do we approach the sheriff with it?"

Jed laughed devilishly at the two men before getting up. "I will leave that up to you two to figure out; if I don't get back to the saloon soon, Melissa is going to come looking for me!"

Alec smiled teasingly up at Jed before motioning resignedly. "He also knows when it's time to make an exit; that's fine leave us poor old men to try figuring out how to approach Melissa on this sensitive issue. I will meet you in about an hour for lunch."

Chuckling in delight at Alec's teasing, Jed inclined his head in farewell to the two men without comment. He didn't stop at the desk this time; although, he did make sure to wave at Lucy when he passed her on his way out. Grey Wolf hurried to Chelsie's hoping Melissa wasn't angry for taking so long.

*****

Melissa smiled across the bar at Chelsie; glad she had gotten rid of Jed so easily. "Do you have wedding bands for men?"

Chelsie grinned and nodded that she did... she waved one of her girls over to tend bar for her. Turning back to Melissa; the redhead beckoned for Mell to follow her. "Come this way, I'll show you what I have."

Following Chelsie into her back room obediently, Melissa watched her friend open a safe behind her desk; she pulled out a small box.

Turning, Chelsie smiled at Melissa before bringing the box over to her desk. "I only have a few at the moment; most men don't wear rings."

Shrugging resignedly, Melissa was just thankful to have a few to choose from and opened the box. There was a dozen rings in total... each one had a different design. She examined them carefully then picked up one that featured three stars and each star held a small diamond. Mell ran her fingers over the surface to make sure it was smooth so it wouldn't catch against anything. She looked back over at Chelsie then held out the ring. "I'll take this one; it looks like it should fit him."

Chelsie grinned before motioning in reassurance. "If it doesn't bring it back; I'll make it fit."

Melissa motioned at the ring. "How much do you want?"

Gazing at the ring critically... Chelsie looked up at Melissa. "There are three tiny diamonds in it and it has a unique design, which took me a long time. It's also the last one I made in Ireland; the ring was made for a duchess to be, but she didn't come back before I left so I took it with me. I'll take twenty dollars for it. If it is too much there are cheaper ones in there that are also very nice."

Shaking her head decisively, Melissa waved reassuringly. "No! I like this one. Hand me a paper; a pen as well, so I can make out a bank note for you."

Handing Melissa the items requested... Chelsie opened her desk drawer and pulled out a box for the ring, while her friend wrote out a note. The saloon owner sighed hopefully when she looked up at the sheriff then handed her the wedding ring. "I heard the railway was coming this way, if it does, I might be able to sell my jewellery cheaper. Most people cannot afford any of the speciality ones I showed you; I do have a separate case full of one's fewer than three dollars. They are not as good as the ones in this case, unfortunately."

Gesturing irritably with a disgruntled sigh... Melissa had heard the same rumours. "You are probably right going to Boston will be quicker and cheaper by train. Speaking as a sheriff I'm not looking forward to it. If it passes too close to any of my towns, it's likely to cause me nothing but grief; I would definitely have to give in to the judge then and let him hire a marshal."

Smiling placatingly; Chelsie was well aware of Melissa's opinion of marshals... she motioned teasingly. "You wouldn't want that now, would you?"

Sighing wryly in aggravation, Melissa ignored Chelsie's teasing tone before shaking her head in denial. "No! I love all my towns; I would hate to have to stay in one, while someone takes over the others then wrecks all the work I did so far."

Nodding, Chelsie's expression became serious knowing Melissa wouldn't appreciate her teasing. She took the box of rings, plus the bank note and put them away in her safe. Both women left the office to go back into the saloon; the owner shooed her girl away before going back behind the bar... she poured Mell another coffee.

Taking a sip, Melissa looked at the clock sitting on the mantel that Chelsie made years ago in aggravation. "I wonder what's taking Jed so long; if he's not back by the time I finish my coffee, I might have to go look for him."

Chelsie laughed. "Now that you are getting married you will have to get used to waiting. You know what men are like when they start gossiping; usually though, they wait until after the wedding before they start making a woman wait."

Melissa was still snickering in delight when Jed came in then gestured in apology. "Sorry, it took me so long; your father was at the judge's office."

Looking at both women perplexed, Jed sighed resignedly when they looked at each other and laughed in conspiracy. He shrugged off their amusement unsure what it was all about. Grey Wolf was positive he didn't want to know either. He continued... ignoring the giggling. "Your father said he would meet us in half an hour for lunch."

Nodding, Melissa took back her whip when Jed gave it to her. Without further comment to Chelsie... she waved goodbye to her on their way out. Mell sighed in anger as her thoughts turned to George; she looked over at Grey Wolf before motioning curiously. "What did the judge have to say?"

Jed grinned reassuringly over at Melissa. "I wrote down your recommendations; he agreed with everything except the jail term. Judge Elton extended the six months to one year."

Sighing relieved, Melissa nodded peeved. "Good!"

They walked down the sidewalk slowly looking into buildings, but not entering any until they reached the hotel; the two turned before going inside.

Walking up to the counter, Melissa smiled over at the clerk in greeting. "Any problems the last few days or is there any strangers in town I should know about?"

The clerk shook his head negatively before waving in reassurance. "No, everything has been way too quiet."

Nodding in relief, Mell turned away.

They went into the dining room to wait for Alec; again, the two walked to a corner table and put their chairs against the wall... in order to see the entire room.

Millie walked over bringing a coffee pot then smiled at both of them cheerfully. "Coffee, Sheriff?"

Melissa nodded before grinning up at the serving maid inquisitively. "Please Millie, my father and the Anderson's will be joining us so we will wait for them before we order; how's home life since Gary started working for me?"

Smiling in pleasure, Millie poured them each a coffee. "Jus great; he loves it so causes me no more grief."

Winking up in approval, Melissa waved reassuringly. "That's good news; I promise to keep him so busy he will hardly have any time to cause you grief!"

Millie laughed in delight. "Suits me jus fine Sheriff."

Sipping her coffee reflectively once Millie left... Melissa looked over her cup at Jed then sighed contemplatively.

"Well, the big day is almost here; are you ready, my love?"

Smirking teasingly, Jed chuckled knowingly. "I have been married before so I do know some of the things to expect... then again, marriage to you will be quite a bit different. You are always so full of unexpected surprises; you're also unpredictable, unlike my first wife!"

Jed was saved from explaining his remarks when Melissa frowned inquisitively... by the arrival of first Jane; followed by Brad pushing Alec's chair.

Jane arrived first and sat down in excitement; she gestured in delight then grabbed Melissa's hand eagerly. "You should see all the furniture your father bought us he said it came with the house and he wouldn't let us pay for anything he even bought us new dishes with lots of pots for the huge wood cook stove that will keep the whole cabin heated with lots of room for cooking we will go pick the kids up from my mother's house on the way out of town we are going to move into the cabin as soon as we get back."

Smiling in pleasure at Jane's excitement, Melissa squeezed her friend's hand but knew better then to try to say anything until she was finished. Her friend could go on for quite some time without taking even one breath. When she finally paused... Mell interrupted hurriedly. "Well, he's right we promised you a place to live and it should come with everything. I'm glad you're happy with the arrangements. It will definitely be nice to have kids around. As for the wood stove, you need a big one because you will be cooking for the men in the bunkhouse; and helping out at the ranch house."

Millie came back then everyone ordered the special.

Alec waited until the serving maid left before looked over at Melissa sadly. "I heard what happened at Pam's last night; any problems capturing George?"

Shaking her head negatively, Melissa scowled angrily. "No! He knew I was coming for him and waited at Chelsie's; she said he was there as soon as she opened. He just sat in his usual corner drinking watching the doors for me."

Alec shook his head pensively. "Something set him off; he hasn't caused any trouble since you had a talk with him."

Shrugging dismissively, Melissa scowled furiously before waving in aggravation. "Doesn't matter sooner or later it was bound to happen again; once someone becomes an abuser it won't ever change, only get worse over time!"

Nodding regretfully, Alec changed the sensitive subject quickly seeing Melissa getting angrier as they talked about it. "I suppose so! John was telling me the railroad is making some progress finally; if they keep on the way they are, they should be here in a few years. It also looks like it will be going straight through our town. He also heard the telegraph is coming too... it might be here sometime next year."

Melissa sighed before pinching the bridge of her nose in frustration. "The telegraph will definitely be welcome, since it takes too long by coach or pony express to get messages; I had hoped the train wouldn't come this way though!"

Jed looked at Melissa in surprise before motioning curiously. "Why would it upset you; with the railroad going through here the towns will grow and prosper."

Trying to explain her fears, Melissa dropped her hand then turned to the confused Jed. "I know it can be a good thing if the town prospers, but think of it this way. The more people in town the more crime; which means I will have to give in to the Judge and let him hire a marshal

The two conspirators looked at each other then smiled secretly before turning their attention back to Melissa; Jed couldn't help asking even though he was sure he knew what the trouble was already. "So, what is the problem with that, what's wrong with being a sheriff in just one town?"

Sighing miserably, Melissa waved plaintively. "They are all... **MY** towns; some strange man will come in here then wreck everything I have accomplished."

The food arrived just then, allowing the conversation to die off as they all ate quietly each deep in their own thoughts. When they were finished eating, Brad got up to leave... Jane stood up also; she smiled down at Alec. "We will grab the kids and the rest of our things before coming back to pick you up."

Alec inclined his head in acknowledgement. "Okay!"

Jane waved goodbye then they left.

Millie came over and refilled their coffee cups before cleaning the table off.

Alec waited until she finished then turned to Jed. He pulled out a paper from inside his pocket and handed it over for Grey Wolf's inspection. "Here is a copy of the estimation done on the ranch; this figure is what you would have to pay to each of us to become a partner. If you don't have enough money; I do have another suggestion. Since it's technically my daughter's ranch, you could just pay me my half then we could each own one quarter with Melissa having controlling interest."

Jed shook his head negatively. "No! I have plenty of money to pay both of you, but Melissa has the final say; if she wants controlling interest, I will just pay you. If she doesn't mind a three-way partnership, I would prefer that."

Melissa looked from one to the other before nodding at the two men agreeably. "Equal partnership is fine by me, it's totally up to you two; I just want both of you to be equally content and happy here."

Sighing in relief, Jed stood up. "I will head over to the bank right away; do you want the money put in your own accounts or in the ranch account?"

Glancing at Melissa inquisitively; Alec looked up at Jed, when she shrugged not caring one way or the other. "Since we are selling a piece to you, it should go in our private accounts."

Nodding, Jed turned to go. "Okay, I'll be back in a minute."

Watching as Jed walked away in surprise, Alec gestured gravely before turning to Melissa thoughtfully. "I'm not sure if that man has more money than brains; or if he's just worried people will think he is using you for your ranch. He didn't even blink an eye at the amount!"

Motioning over at Alec teasingly, Melissa couldn't help a snicker as she reminded him of why there was an estimate. "If I remember rightly; I did have a problem once before with another man who refused to have anything to do with the ranch... unless he paid his own way."

Sighing reproachfully at Melissa, Alec pretended he hadn't heard his daughter's last comment. "Since I was in his place once; I guess I can understand his feelings."

Melissa chuckled in delight when Alec ignored her teasing before changing the subject; she gestured hopefully. "Is everything ready for the wedding?"

Alec grinned in reassurance. "Yes, except you need to try your dress on one more time when you get home tonight. You also had two wedding gifts show up early this morning. A two-year-old steer and a one-year-old sow; they have been butchered already. The pig is probably in the underground oven that we dug this morning... cooking slowly. The steer will be roasted tomorrow evening in the big open fire pit."

Melissa's eyebrows lifted in surprise before waving inquisitively. "Oh, who would send them as a wedding gift?"

Alec chuckled at Melissa's stunned expression. "Victor Grey, you must have made him feel guilty; he still isn't coming to your wedding though, I'm told."

Sighing irritably, Melissa shook her head before tapping her fingers angrily on the table. "I didn't think he would; once that old coot makes up his mind about something you have to hit him on the head with proof before he will budge."

Laughing at Melissa's accurate assessment of his friend, Alec didn't say anything though as Millie refilled their coffee cups.

Jed walked in a few minutes later before smiling in satisfaction. "Okay, all done. The bank manager said the money should be in your accounts within a week or two; once the funds have been transported from my bank in Boston"

Grinning in relief, Alec was glad to have that all settled with. He took another paper from his pocket and handed it to Jed when he sat down. "We all need to sign this; you can read it first then give it to me later. All it says is that you have bought into the ranch on a three-way partnership, your share of the profits will be deposited into your account each year. It also says that if anything should happen to either one of us, their share automatically goes to Melissa since it is her ranch. If something happens to my daughter, her share is divided between us or goes to her children if she has any by then."

Inclining his head, Jed took the paper before putting the contract in his pocket so he could read it later. They had another cup of coffee; plus, a piece of pie, while they waited for the Andersons. Finally, the two showed up and Melissa pushed Alec out to the wagon then gave him a kiss.

Brad and Jed helped Alec get in then put his chair in the bed of the wagon for the trip to the ranch.

Mell and Jed waved goodbye before returning to their duties.

CHAPTER TWENTY

The day of the wedding turned out to be a beautiful one; the sun was shining gloriously with the temperature being mild, not too hot. There was just enough wind to keep the bugs away, but not enough to cause any problems with the outside decorations.

Melissa woke in surprise at the sound of the birds cheerily singing and the sun shining brightly in her bedroom window; she had never slept so late... it was definitely nice for a change. She rolled over to cuddle up to Jed, but he was already gone. Stretching contentedly, she laid her head back on the pillow in excitement. Remembering that today, she wasn't going into work but getting married instead.

The last week had gone well Melissa supposed; while she had been showing Jed the ropes and taking care of the outlaws at Miller's Creek. Gloria, Jessica, Mrs. Elton along with Mary, Jane plus Sarah had spent the week sewing two wedding gowns before preparing food for the wedding feast.

Everyone in town and the surrounding area had been invited; the only ones to refuse their invitations were Brian, Mr. Grey, as well as all their men. Unfortunately, James couldn't come either.

Pastor Dan was going to perform the ceremony. He had balked some when told he would be joining a white woman with an Indian in marriage. However, he came around when told they were already married; a sizable donation to his church helped as well... making him more than happy to renew their vows.

Melissa heard a knock on the door... before she could answer, Gloria walked in carrying a tray laden with food; Mell had just enough time to grab her blankets and cover herself decently.

Gloria grinned teasingly when she saw Melissa comfortably sprawled on the bed. "Well good morning, lazy bones. I brought you some breakfast. You are not to do anything except enjoy the day; you must eat all of your breakfast then in about an hour the boys will bring up your bath water. When they do, Mrs. Elton will come up to help you get ready. Your dress is finished and everything is going smoothly so far. The guests should be arriving around two o'clock or so. You're not even allowed to leave your room... not until your father comes to escort you."

Nodding, Melissa scowled chidingly before shaking her finger reproachfully at Gloria. "What about you; it's your wedding day too. Here you are running around waiting on me."

Laughing good-naturedly, Gloria deposited the tray in Melissa's lap unceremoniously. "I gave Wade instructions last night to disappear until we are finished the morning chores. Afterwards, I will also be banished to my room; Mary will take over for me since they are already married it doesn't matter if Giant Bear sees her. She will have plenty of time to get ready later."

Grinning satisfied with that explanation; Melissa took a sip of her coffee before gesturing to the wardrobe. "Can you hand me my dressing robe, please?"

Nodding, Gloria turned away to look for the robe. "Sure."

Feeling a shiver of forewarning course down her spine, Melissa scowled apprehensively... it was quite unexpected. "Has anyone heard from Brian yet?"

Shaking her head negatively, Gloria put the dressing gown on the bed where Melissa could reach it easily then looked down at her fretfully. "No! It's making Jed quite nervous; he has posted extra men on guard duty just in case there are any signs of trouble. Mary was quite upset about her brother turning down her invitation, but she knew he would. Tommy has adjusted well to Giant Bear, ever since the engagement party he has had a grin on his face a mile wide. He follows the chief around everywhere and tells anyone who will listen to him that he is Cheyenne. The boy never stops asking about his Indian heritage or about the village where he will be living. He practises with the rifle every chance he gets and every time we look for him... he is doing kicks, rolls, or is twirling a wooden knife that his father made for him around."

Grinning in delight for a moment, Melissa's thoughts turned to Tommy. It wasn't long though before her expression sobered restlessly as her mind veered towards Mary's brother again. "I'm glad Jed posted some guards; I have this feeling we haven't seen the last of Brian!"

Frowning irritably at the thought of their neighbour; Gloria turned to leave not wanting to discuss Brian... especially on her wedding day. The maid had never approved of that man and like Alec, she had feared Mell would marry him.

Waiting until Gloria reached the door, Melissa called out curiously. "By the way, how's the romance going between my dad and Jessica?"

Gloria turned the doorknob, but didn't leave right away; she looked back at Melissa then grinned in delight. "Fine, I think Mrs. Donaldson is beginning to enjoy being chased."

With that comment Gloria left the room, softly she closed the door behind her.

Melissa slowly ate her breakfast, but her mind wasn't on what she was doing; her thoughts were on Brian and all his threats. The more she worried about it the more nervous she became. Surely, he wouldn't be crazy enough to attack Mary or Giant Bear here with all these people around... would he! She shook her head negatively when she decided he wouldn't be that stupid.

Melissa shook off her nervous feelings decisively before turning her thoughts to Jed instead. She couldn't help remembering the perfect week they spent together making love... without consummating their relationship. When they were not too exhausted to do so, that is; however, tonight they would go all the way and make love fully. She definitely wasn't afraid of the experience any longer. Truth be told, Mell had lost her fear of him... plus her shyness when it came to Grey Wolf's body after the first night. She hadn't let on though, enjoying their nights together as they were.

Jed explained to Melissa last night that there would be some pain at the beginning when he entered her body for the first time. He promised it would be brief; afterwards, she would never feel discomfort again.

Grinning in humour, Melissa knew it wasn't pain she feared; she had known a lot of it in the years she had been a deputy and sheriff. Especially once everyone found out she was a woman, the men just had to test her abilities out. On more than one occasion, she had been stabbed and shot. She even supported a few black eyes... with a fat lip or two. That was before Mell earned her reputation of never backing down from a fight. It turned to respect once word got around that she always got her man or woman no matter where or how.

Therefore, pain had never entered Melissa's mind when she first looked at Jed. The panic of losing herself was more terrifying than any pain. If she wanted to be absolutely truthful with herself, it was the fear of her own femininity which scared her the most. Grey Wolf made her feel vulnerable, tiny, and for the first time in her life like a woman. That's what really scared her so bad, no other man ever came close to making Mell feel this way; it terrified her and left her feeling defenceless... it almost seemed like she was losing control of herself.

Hearing another knock on the door, Melissa shook off thoughts of Jed; she set aside the tray before hastily getting up then put her robe on. Sitting back on the bed she called out expectantly... knowing it was Mrs. Elton with her bath water. "Come in!"

A beaming Betty entered with Melissa's dress. Immediately, she took it and draped it over the closet door. It was much too long to hang inside with the undergarments. It would be easier for Mell to put it on this way also. Mrs. Elton was followed by the boys carrying a large tub with pails of hot water. After arranging the dress so no wrinkles would spoil it, she walked towards the bed... demandingly; the judge's wife put her hands against her hips in mock sternness. "Come my friend, it's time to get ready."

Melissa grinned up at Betty, but waited for the boys to leave before stepping out of her robe obediently. She crawled into the deep warm water in pleasure. She sighed in delight when Mrs. Elton scrubbed her scalp vigorously... washing her long hair; afterwards, Mell immersed her head for a quick rinse. She then knelt in the tub so the judge's wife could pour a pail of warm water on her head to rinse her hair of any excess soap left behind.

Betty wrapped a towel around Melissa's head then gently pulled on the towel in demand. "Lie back now so your hair is draped over the tub. I'll dry it while you finish bathing."

Once done, Melissa got out of the tub and dried her body off. Betty held her hair out so it wouldn't get wet again. When Mell was dry enough to satisfy her; Mrs. Elton let go of her hair then went to the wardrobe and took out the camisole, undergarments... plus her corset.

Obediently, Melissa put on the camisole. The bloomers

followed before Betty helped her with the corset. She laced it up as tight as she could. Mrs. Elton even went so far as to put her foot against the bride's backside for more leverage... pulling the laces tighter. She was groaning in painful torture by the time the judge's wife felt it was tight enough to suit her; finally, Mell managed to take enough of a breath to wheeze out plaintively. "Why do women want to torture themselves with these contraptions?"

Grinning, Betty smiled sympathetically over Melissa's shoulder. She loosened the laces slightly, not wanting the bride to pass out in the middle of the ceremony. Satisfied, Mrs. Elton peeked at Mell in the full-length mirror... as she explained she went back to fussing with the corset. "They originated in Italy of all places, but it wasn't long before France took up the practice. Originally, the corset was meant to decrease the bust size; they were called bodies or stays at that time. Gradually, they evolved to cover the waist after a woman who went to Europe, saw a large female friend fit into a gown much too small for her. You can imagine that it wasn't long before all women were wearing corsets, now we are stuck with them! Most women only wear them tight when dressing fancy now though, otherwise they are worn loosely for comfort or not at all. Most doctors advise against wearing them, according to them they restrict breathing and can cause many health problems. I have never had any trouble health wise and it actually supports my back when worn loosely. If I don't wear one, I tend to get a pain between my shoulders."

Melissa sighed forlornly at that explanation then waved at the door pleadingly with a smile of innocence. "Betty, could you ask Gloria for the turquoise combs that hold up my veil; I forgot them."

Nodding, Betty didn't suspect a thing and went over to the bed then picked up the breakfast tray. "Would you like more coffee also?"

Grinning eagerly, Melissa nodded; it would keep Betty busy hopefully long enough to do what she needed to do. "Sounds good to me... I will be stuck here for a while so more coffee sounds great."

Betty inclined her head in sympathy before leaving.

As soon as Mrs. Elton left, Melissa rushed over to the bed

and quickly pulled on her stockings. She groaned in pain as she bent in the tight corset... although, she didn't let that stop her. Once her stockings were on, she strapped onto her right leg what looked like a garter; it was actually a small pouch with a derringer. She always carried it, even when she wore pants. Hardly anyone ever noticed that on the right pant leg there was a thin thread which held together her seam just above the knee. It would only take Mell a second to pull the string to get at the pistol, if she needed it.

Hurrying to the closet door, Melissa pulled out her petticoat then quickly put it on. She was gasping for breath now as the tight corset tried to cut off her air supply... not use to wearing one. She hurried as fast as she could, hoping Betty wouldn't catch her in the act of arming herself even on her wedding day. Next, she grabbed a small knife and her white buffalo medicine pouch. Mell had hidden both under her pillow last night; she stuck them into a deep pocket in her underskirt.

Gloria of course, had guessed what the pocket was for when Mell had requested it but she had kept her secret.

Finished with all the required undergarments, Melissa opened the bottom of her wedding gown then pulled it over her head. She was definitely glad Betty had put it where it would be easy for her to get at. She tugged at it carefully trying to pull it off the door desperately without ripping it; she couldn't help a grunt of amusement. Glad no one could see her comical struggles... she was sure she looked hilarious. Mell finally managed to get it off and pulled down over her hips; it was twisted to the left and only one boob was in the bodice, she just managed to get it in place when Betty came back into the room.

Stopping short in surprise, Mrs. Elton stared in disbelief at Mell already dressed in her gown.

Smiling guilelessly over at Betty, Melissa smoothed her dress down. "Oh, just in time to help me do up these buttons. I also need help to put the blue garter on... please."

Sitting the tray down on the vanity, Betty turned before smirking at Melissa impishly. "It took you a long time to decide to get married; now you are in such a hurry you can't wait for me to help you get dressed!"

Betty laughed in delight at Melissa's fiery blush then motioned playfully. "Just teasing you, my dear; how about sitting down at your vanity instead. While you enjoy your coffee, I will fix your hair. You managed to make quite a mess of it before we do up the buttons on your dress?"

Melissa grinned in relief; glad Betty didn't suspect anything. She did as she was told and sat obediently.

*****

Jed then Giant Bear walked out of the house followed by a faithful Tommy; once on the veranda they paused a moment to look around.

Giant Bear turned to Jed inquisitively before waving in demand; he had spent too many years with his blood brother to be fooled by his friend's calm expression. He switched to Cheyenne so Tommy wouldn't understand. "What's wrong, Grey Wolf... you have been extremely uptight all morning!"

Sighing forbiddingly in confusion, Jed turned to look at Giant Bear in trepidation. He shrugged uneasily before he too switched languages. "I don't know my friend; I have had this weird feeling all morning something's not right. I keep thinking about the threats Brian made when told about your re-marriage to Mary. It makes me wonder what he could be up to... it's been too quiet since he made them. Your brother-in-law did not strike me as a man who makes empty promises!"

Nodding, Giant Bear took Jed's unease seriously; unexpectedly, a shiver of foreboding rippled down his spine... he frowned in surprise. "I have to admit I have the same feelings of danger, but the guests will be here in about an hour. We can't call off the wedding on just a hunch, so what do you suggest we do to protect everyone?"

Frowned thoughtfully, Giant Bear turned to Tommy suddenly more worried than he cared to admit; he gestured demandingly before switching to English so his son would understand. "Do you have the knife I gave you handy?"

Nodding solemnly in confusion; Tommy hadn't understood what they were saying, but he could feel the tension in the air between the two men. It was so thick... he could probably cut it with his knife. "It's in my room!"

Giant Bear smiled reassuringly trying not to scare Tommy. Jed had told him about the threats Brian made concerning his wife and son. "Do you remember where I showed you to stab someone if they attack you from behind?"

Tommy pointed down at himself; he remembered his father telling him that stabbing someone in the groin area if he was being held against his will would make them let go of him instantly.

Grinning in pride at Tommy, Giant Bear nodded at the house in command. "Good, I want you to go get it and stick it under your shirt where you can reach it easily; then I need you to stay close to your mother and guard her for me... okay!"

Frowning in surprise at his father's request; Tommy turned towards the house without questioning why. He couldn't help puffing up his chest in pride at having such a serious job as protecting his mother... he ran into the house.

Jed chuckled in approval after the ten-year-old... he turned towards Giant Bear. His expression sobered in anxiety as Grey Wolf waved after the young boy. "Tommy seems quite mature for his age, but do you think he is ready yet? I know you and Mell have been teaching him as fast as the two of you can; thankfully, I did notice yesterday that he has learned quite a few tricks already. Unfortunately, I don't believe he is cunning enough to survive a knife fight any time soon."

Smiling proudly at the progress Tommy was making, Giant Bear grimaced troubled... before shaking his head fretfully. "My son is learning the art of knife fighting well; you are right though he isn't ready yet! I sent him up to Golden Dove for two reasons, one to keep him away from me if Brian attempts to kill me. Two, so I will know where he is at all times. This way I can keep track of him and his mother at the same time."

Nodding in approval, Jed sighed in resignation then pointed up towards his room. "Good thinking, Giant Bear; as for Melissa I already know if it comes to a fight, she will be right in the middle of it. I think we will have to warn our guests to be on the watch at all times and to keep their guns handy. I'm going to check the men I have stationed around the ranch to make sure everyone is on extra alert... just in case of trouble."

Solemnly, Giant Bear gestured towards the barn. "I'll go check on Mark right now; afterwards, I will get dressed in my ceremonial clothes."

Jed walked beside Giant Bear... neither speaking; both, were extremely apprehensive wondering if they had thought of everything. The chief turned to go inside the barn and Grey Wolf walked over to the corral to get his horse. He had left him there earlier, still saddled after positioning all his sentries strategically around the ranch.

Riding towards the North first, Jed wasn't even halfway to his first lookout when he saw a rider approach. He brought his horse to a halt to see who it was... the guests shouldn't be arriving yet. As the man got closer Grey Wolf recognized Mark; he frowned suspiciously in surprise.

Mark stopped in front of Jed then smiled reassuringly; he pointed behind him. "I took a look around and there isn't a soul in sight."

Nodding without comment, Jed waved the man on his way before turning his horse guardedly watching him go. The new hand was riding to the ranch slowly... in no apparent hurry. The bridegroom's eyes narrowed dangerously. He hadn't asked Mark to do any scouting; his job had been to remain at the barn. Changing his mind about checking the lookouts, he rode over to the bunkhouse instead. Grey Wolf would get Tomas to keep an eye on his colleague just in case. He had noticed the two didn't seem to care for each other even though they worked together.

After talking to Tomas, Jed went in search of Giant Bear. He walked around the side of the barn and saw his friend already in his ceremonial outfit... walking toward the veranda; he changed directions quickly. Catching up to the Cheyenne Chief, Grey Wolf motioned inquisitively behind him at the barn. "Did you talk to Mark yet?"

Giant Bear nodded that he had in unconcern. "He was just coming in as I was leaving; he didn't say much, except he was out scouting on your orders."

Shaking his head angrily in suspicion... Jed gestured emphatically. "He implied the same thing to me, but I gave him no such orders. I talked to Tomas; he promised to keep an eye on Mark for me."

Inclining his head in approval... Giant Bear waved at the cloud of dust coming up the road. "I think it's time for you to get ready anyway; I can hear carriages coming. I'll greet the guests and warn the men for you so you can go change."

Smiling in thanks with a hasty grin, Jed totally forgot about Mark in his excitement. He turned then hurried up the steps before slipped in the door.

*****

Melissa stood at the window watching the guests arrive anxiously. She wasn't sure if she could go out there in front of her friends or the town's people. Her gown was exquisitely made; it was all white with turquoise glass beadwork artfully sewn on the bodice. The neckline was low showing off her large breasts to perfection. The waist was snug, but the skirt flared out sweeping the floor. White shoes adorned her surprisingly small feet... they peeked out below her skirts. At first, she had balked at the shoes then gave in when Betty threatened to burn her moccasins if she wore them under her beautiful wedding gown. Mrs. Elton had placed a blue garter above her left knee for Jed to remove and throw to all the bachelors when it was time. The judge's wife had also swept Mell's hair up then held it in place with turquoise combs before attaching the long veil to them.

Unsure, Melissa didn't know if she would be able to manage walking in this dress... without disaster. She grinned at the mental picture of herself getting tangled in the dress and veil; before tumbling down the stairs head first in front of her guests.

Hearing the door opening behind her, Mell turned before smiling in welcome as her father enter the room.

Alec stopped short in shock at the sight of Melissa... in his lap were two cases. Even from across the room, she could see that the long black velvet box was extremely old; with a newer smaller blue one behind it.

Gliding over, Melissa walked behind her father's chair to push a flabbergasted Alec further into the room; unable to move at first, he stared at her in shock. She closed the door before walking back around the wheelchair then turned to face her father.

Smiling mistily up at Mell, Alec wiped a tear away. "Forgive me for staring so, but every time I see you in a dress you remind me so much of your mother... it hurts."

Gathering her dress up, Melissa draped it over her arm so it wouldn't touch the floor before kneeling down... she leaned forward against Alec's legs. She kissed him tenderly, not daring to bend again in the fear of passing out from lack of air. "I know that, Dad! Only once did I wear a dress at the other ranch; I'll always remember the look of sorrow and pain on your face, so until the engagement party the other night

I've never worn another dress. Perhaps it's a good thing, can you imagine me trying to be a sheriff in a dress?"

Alec laughed in humour at the mental picture of Melissa chasing an outlaw with skirts hiked up around her knees, so she wouldn't trip on them. He shook off his thoughts then picked up the long black case before opening it; with a flourish, he turned it around so she could see what was inside. "Mell, I have two things for you. One is very old and once belonged to your grandmother. The necklace was passed down to your mother, so now it rightfully belongs with you. The other one is new and is a gift from me."

Taking the necklace out of the box, Alec held it up so Mell could see it better.

Melissa breath caught in awe; it was gorgeous. The necklace had two perfectly matching small teardrop diamonds one on each side of a large center one... all three were flawless. A delicate chain holding the diamonds was made of pure gold and was so tiny she feared to touch it, not wanting to break it. When the gems caught any kind of light, a bluish green sparkle would flare. She smiled at her father in delight. "It's beautiful!"

Chuckling at Melissa's reverent look, Alec handed her the smaller velvet case.

Opening it, Melissa couldn't help a gasp of surprised delight from escaping at the diamond earrings and bracelet; both were done in a teardrop design to match the necklace. She was so overwhelmed tears sprang to her eyes. It took several minutes before she was able to motion incredulously towards Alec. "Dad, they are absolutely gorgeous; I have never dreamed of owning anything this beautiful."

Smiling indulgently, Alec held up the necklace. "This necklace has always been yours; there has just never been an occasion to present it to you before now. The bracelet and earrings Chelsie made recently for me."

Still kneeling, Melissa turned so Alec could put the necklace on her before twisting back around. She took out the earrings then clipped them on one at a time. Holding out her arm, Mell let her father fasten the bracelet around her wrist. Reaching out, she hugged her dad in loving thanks. When he leaned back, she admired the beautiful gifts and looked at him with a tender smile. "I love you!"

Fondly, Alec grinned before wiping the tears from his eyes so they wouldn't fall on Melissa's beautiful wedding dress; he pulled her back for another fierce hug. "I love you too!"

Pushing Mell away from him, Alec stared at her sorrowfully for a long moment. "You are absolutely exquisite and you look just like your mother did on our wedding day; I still miss her unbearably at times."

Nodding her head, Melissa was too choked up to speak for a few minutes... she wiped tears away. Suddenly, she grinned mischievously then took her father's hand in hers. "I do too; I think Mrs. Donaldson is a very nice lady, though."

Alec eyed Melissa warily for a moment before smiling in relief at her pleased look. "You don't miss much, do you; I'm glad you don't mind. I think it's time I end my mourning for your mother and try living again. Now that you will have a husband to take care of you, I would like to travel some. I think Jessica will be the perfect companion for me."

Melissa was ecstatic that Alec was finally moving on with his life. He had been grieving for her mother far too long as it is. "Dad, I know you will be quite happy with Jessica; this is the best news I have had in a long time. All I have ever wanted is to see you laugh and smile again!"

Hugging Alec again... Melissa stood up then smoothed down her dress; hoping she hadn't wrinkled it. Looking back at him, she couldn't help a naughty look from escaping at her father's reference to Mrs. Donaldson being the perfect travelling companion. Mell couldn't help joshing him just a bit. "Jessica will probably be a good travel partner for you. Although, I think it also doesn't hurt that she is gorgeous too."

Grinning wickedly, Alec changed the subject without comment. "I think it is time, let's go."

Laughing at Alec's refusal to remark; Melissa, catching her father's sinful smirk though decided to let him off the hook. She walked around the chair then opened the door before pushing her dad into the hallway. Brad and Darrel were waiting patiently to carry him downstairs.

*****

Outside in the front yard all the guests were waiting in anticipation in order to witness the marriage of their beloved sheriff; they were sitting in chairs facing an archway decorated with all types of wildflowers. A buzz of excitement prevailed as they talked with friends or neighbours.

Standing in the center of the archway up on the dais was the minister; just below him on a smaller platform on the minister's left-hand side was Jed... on the right side stood Wade. Giant Bear was between the two men on solid ground since they were only renewing vows, this way Jed and Wade would be the focus of everyone's attention.

Suddenly, the guests hushed expectantly as Alec approached from behind; with their backs to the porch and sidewalk that went to the deck they hadn't noticed him. He stopped his wheelchair dramatically at the edge of the guest's seats, his outside chair was decorated with all sorts of wildflowers causing the townspeople to murmur in appreciation... keeping them distracted. This was strategically planned, so that when he appeared and the wedding song began on their left nobody would notice the brides until they began walking between the seats.

Tommy then the judge joined him instantly, both stayed back and to the far right. This way the men waiting on the other side of the archway would have an unobstructed view of their brides-to-be.

The guests all rose to their feet respectfully when Betty stood up to sing the wedding song; she was standing by the drawing room patio doors and accompanied by the piano, which could just be seen inside the room. The men had moved it closer to the doors, and with the window wide open there wasn't even a muffled sound... it was just too large to bring outside.

The three brides... unnoticed as planned; were standing at the bottom of the stairs leading up to the deck waiting for Betty to begin singing. Stepping off the sidewalk, they walked between the seats approached their escorts slowly as Jane and Brad's daughters threw flower petals in front of them. Their son held Melissa's wedding train, with the judge's youngest grandson holding Gloria's long train. Mary didn't have one, since she wore her Indian bridal dress.

Melissa came first; she was a bit ahead of Gloria who was on her left with Mary following behind the two in the center.

There were exclamations of shocked surprise then admiration when the town's people caught their first... undoubtedly it would be their last, glimpse of Mell in a dress.

The three women halted beside their escorts; each woman put a hand lightly on his arm proudly before they slowly proceeded to the front of the archway in anticipation. They halted a little distance from the waiting men so they were directly under the archway... just as the wedding song ended. The minister called out loudly making sure that all the guests could hear him. "Who giveth this woman to this man in holy matrimony?"

Alec looked up at Melissa in pride; he made sure that his voice was loud enough to drown out the excited whispers of the guests before looking away from his daughter then towards Jed with tears in his eyes. "I, Alec Ray... give my daughter, Melissa Ray, to Jed Brown in holy matrimony."

Lifting her dress a bit, Melissa knelt on one knee so Alec could give her a kiss of blessing. She whispered quickly, having rehearsed this speech earlier. "You have stood by me always, even when you didn't understand why I chose the kind of life I did; I will always love you for that, Dad!"

Smiling lovingly at Melissa, Alec whispered back as he lifted her veil for the traditional kiss. "I love you too; may God bless you and keep you happy forever. Remember, I will always be here for you!"

Melissa waited for Alec to lower her veil then she stood up in excitement; she put her hand in her father's and waited for Jed to claim her.

Alec looked up at Jed when he stopped in front of him, with tears in his eyes he reached up to shake Grey Wolf's hand. "I am giving to you the most precious gift a father can give... my daughter; may you both walk with God and have many years of happiness."

Jed shook Alec's free hand; he kept it tightly in his while he made his speech. Grey Wolf proclaimed loudly making sure he was heard by the ones in the back. "I thank you with all my heart for the trust you are showing in giving me your daughter's hand in marriage... I will cherish Melissa always. Remember you are not losing a daughter, but gaining a son!"

Taking both their hands, Alec joined them together. He made sure to keep their hands sandwiched tightly between his. "May you both love each other through good times or bad; always try to remember... love will grow deeper if you nourish it to keep it strong. It will only die if you become complacent then forget to encourage it in the everyday struggles of life!"

Gently pulled their joined hands from Alec's, Jed guided Melissa to the platform; giving Mell's father time to push his chair out of the way... they stood waiting for the others.

Gloria took Melissa's place with her escort... the minister repeated his question; John Elton, the mayor and judge of Smyth's Crossing did the honours for Gloria since her father died many years ago.

Mary was next, and the question was repeated a third time unwillingly; even the now quiet guests could hear the reluctance in the minister's voice.

Tommy forgetting his line in his excitement since he was Mary's escort... yelled in confusion. "I do!"

Kissing his mother on the cheek, Tommy tried to ignore the guest's laughter; she smiled at her son's flustered answer and embarrassed red face... Golden Dove turned away before walking over to stand beside Giant Bear.

The three couples turned to face the minister solemnly holding hands. The guests hushed so they could all hear, not wanting to miss a thing.

*****

Tomas watching from the barn, wiped tears from his eyes before grinning evilly; weddings made him cry. Turning away from the window, he walked over to the dead man lying on the floor. He looked down at Mark then placed his foot on him disdainfully as he nudged him playfully. "Well, Mark... I sure fooled Jed when I sent you to check for intruders on his orders. He thought it was going to be you causing trouble!"

Throwing his head back, Tomas gave a vicious sinister laugh. Going over to the corner, he picked up a can of coal oil. He proceeded to pour it over the straw on the floor at the back of the barn. Turning, he looked at the horses in admiration. "That should give the men plenty of time to get all the horses out of the barn safely. Especially you Lightning; soon you will be mine... he promised me!"

Snorting distrustfully when the man got closer, Lightening backed away from the stall door; he pawed the ground in warning, disliking the stranger instantly. The strong smell of oil had his nose flaring irritably... he nickered apprehensively not liking that smell even a little.

Frowning in anger at the unruly stallion, Tomas went back to the window to watch the rest of the ceremony; satisfied that he was ready ahead of schedule and everything was going according to plan.

*****

Simultaneously six people said. "I do!"

The groom's lifted veils for the traditional kiss.

The preacher waited until the kiss was finished then waved them all over to a small table for their signatures... the judge had put it there earlier for this purpose; once all six signed their names, the papers were given to John Elton and finally taken to Alec to witness the signatures.

A cheer of approval went up from the crowd when the six newlyweds stood on the platform surveying their guests proudly; their lady sheriff was married at last!

Melissa stiffened suddenly in alarm when she saw puffs of black smoke pouring from the windows of the barn... within seconds, she heard her horse scream out in terror; pointing, Mell yelled above the noise of the townspeople's cheers. **"THE BARN IS ON FIRE!"**

Everyone turned as one; instantly, the guests raced forward to help save the horses. Several men reaching the barn doors first tried to get in, but they were barred from the inside.

Jed racing to the barn as quick as he could to save the horses, managed to stay a few steps ahead of Mell... he vaulted over the sidewalk.

A frustrated Melissa, several steps behind Jed was trying desperately to run in her wedding dress. She had gathered the front up and hung it over her arm, which gave her a little more freedom to run.

'BANG, BANG'!

Two gunshots rang out in quick succession.

Coming to a sudden halt in dread, Melissa screamed her new husband's name in panic and horrified disbelief. She watched, as he staggered forward several steps once on the opposite side of the walkway. "JED!"

Jed could feel the bullet tearing through his flesh before bursting out of his back... ripping his shirt as it left a bloody hole. Turning slowly towards Melissa with a look of shocked surprise, he grasped urgently at his upper left chest; he collapsed with blood trickling between his fingers.

A couple second later, Melissa heard Mary scream in grief.

Melissa turned in disbelief; she was in time to see Giant Bear collapse with blood gushing down his face. Everything turned black when something hit her on the head.

*****

Everyone was running around in a panic... screaming; unsure who was doing all the shooting or even where the shots were coming from.

Gloria keeping her head ran over to Betty; she gestured anxiously in fear. "Help me herd all the women and children into the house... hurry please!"

Betty stood there unable to move for a long moment; shocked beyond words... she was as white as a ghost. She stared past Melissa's maid, as if she hadn't heard a word.

About to reach out and shake Betty, Gloria sighed in relief when thankfully she didn't have too. Mrs. Elton visibly stiffened before pulling herself determinedly out of her trance; between the two of them, they managed to get all the children inside safely.

With the help of Chelsie and Pam, they managed to get all the women inside too, Gloria frantically searched among them for Melissa, Mary, and Tommy; she was about to give up, when she spied the boy sitting on the floor in the corner rocking himself. He had his bloody hunting knife clutched in his hand. Racing over, she knelt beside him cautiously. "What happened, are you okay?"

Tommy looked up with a fearful sob. "A man tried to grab me after they killed my father; I did what Dad said I should do and stabbed him in the groin. When I couldn't find my mother anywhere, I ran in here to hide!"

Reaching over tentatively, Mary took the knife from the distraught Tommy then pulled him into an embrace; she kissed the top of his head in reassurance. "You did the right thing, stay here now and I will go find your mother!"

Gloria jumped up, once Tommy nodded in agreement. Taking his hunting knife into the kitchen, she threw it into the sink in disgust. Still unable to find either woman in the house; she ran over to Jessica and Chelsie in panic before waving in urgency. "I can't find either Melissa or Mary in here, so I'm going back outside to take another look... please try to keep everyone calm until I return!"

Jessica watched Gloria leave in concern then turned away before herding all the children into the hallway. With the help of Chelsie and Pam, they got them up the stairs into her room away from any stay bullets. Betty gathered all the towns' women next then led them up the stairs... they followed in relief, unsure what to do or where to go.

*****

Gloria ran out of the ranch house looking for the two missing women; she tried to shout above the noise first as she cupped her hands around her mouth... calling desperately. "Melissa, Mary where are you?"

Giving that up after a frustrating few minutes, Gloria knew nobody could hear her in all this noise anyway... she stumbled over to Alec in fear. "I can't find Melissa or Mary, but I have all the women and children inside safely away from any stray bullets."

Frowning in alarm, Alec pointed to his left towards where the judge was standing surrounded by shouting men. "Good job, Gloria. Now we have to get everyone calmed down; John is over there, please ask him to come here. There are just too many people running around for me to get to him."

Nodding, Gloria did what Mell's dad asked.

Alec looked up at John in relief when the two managed to get to him. He motioned at all the guests still panicking... not sure in which direction they should go. "We need to quieten everyone down; I tried but didn't have much success, do you have any suggestions?"

Sighing in exasperation; John looked around at all the foolish people running around for no apparent reason what-so-ever. Only two bullets had been fired, but by their reaction one would think the townspeople were still dodging stray bullets. "Let's try this first!"

Putting two fingers in his mouth, John gave a loud sharp whistle... nothing happened; when that didn't work, the judge shrugged resignedly and took out his gun before firing a shot into the air expectantly.

Everyone froze then turned to look in surprise; when they saw the judge holding a smoking pistol, a hush descended.

John's voice boomed out in command. "Can I have your attention, please?"

The townspeople gathered around, glad someone was

taking control; even though it seemed to them like hours had passed since the shooting began, in reality it had only been twenty minutes ago.

Alec smiled up in appreciation at John. "Thank you!"

Turning to speak to all his guests, Alec pointed to a group standing off to his right. "I want you men to get the horses out of the barn then put the fire out."

About ten men rushed to the barn instantly.

Looking at the rest grimly, Alec motioned imploringly. "Melissa and Mary are missing, so is Jed and Giant Bear."

Gary stepped forward instantly then waved towards the front deck before indicating the barn next. "Jed and Giant Bear are both dead; one is over by the front porch on the right. The other one is lying on the other side of the walkway not far from the barn."

Gasping in shock, Alec shook his head in denial; he started shaking in reaction... his voice waivered in disbelief. "No, they can't be!"

*****

Melissa blinked several times blearily, trying to clear her head. When she heard the sound of someone groaning, Mell stiffened... instantly alert; at first, she thought it was her that made the sound. Lifting her head to investigate, she saw someone slinging a bound Mary over a horse. She quickly dropped her head towards the saddle when she realized nobody noticed she was awake. Moving experimentally, she concluded in disappointment that she was tied belly down on a horse with a gag which is why her mouth hurt. White Buffalo moved again, this time squirming slightly so she could check for hidden weapons. Feeling the small pistol still strapped to her thigh, plus the small knife hidden under her dress she sighed relieved. No one had thought to search her.

Noticing her necklace hanging over her chin, Melissa peeked over then saw the men still tying her friend down. Lifting her head as high as she could, she brought it down hard so the necklace would catch against the saddle; she was in luck it only took two tried before it caught on a buckle. Pulling back sharply, Mell watched in satisfaction as the delicate chain broke and the necklace fell to the ground in the thick grass. One of her men would find it she hoped.

Hearing footsteps coming closer, Melissa deliberately went

limp; hoping she could fool them into thinking she was still unconscious. Somebody grabbed her by the hair and started to lift her head, but paused halfway to call out to someone instead. "Did she wake up yet?"

Another deep voice answered him; unfortunately, Melissa couldn't tell who the men were by their voices. "I just checked the sheriff... she's still out cold."

The man holding Melissa's head grunted in disgust. Without checking to make sure... he let go without warning; for good measures, he gave a little shove. "Okay, let's go!"

Melissa ground her teeth in pain trying not to make any noise; she let her head hit the saddle with a **thwack**... much harder than she intended as the lights went out once more.

CHAPTER TWENTY-ONE

John pushed Alec over to Giant Bear first; he was the closer of the two men. The mayor looked from the body to the barn and frowned, because the shots had been so close together the shooter must have the new repeater rifle. Which would work in the two downed men's favour since the shooter wouldn't be as proficient with it, being that it was a new type of rifle. With the wind against him, and not being at a forty-five degree angle the bullet wouldn't be as effective over a thousand yards. Although, a bullet can travel four and a half miles in ideal conditions, the shooter had to be a trained marksmen and at the optimum angle... neither would it be as lethal the further away they are. From here it was about three hundred yards; the mayor crossed his fingers that the wind had caused the shooter trouble.

Giant Bear had been chasing the man that had held his son briefly at knife point. Thankfully, his son had stabbed the kidnapper then raced up the stairs and into the house. Ignoring the man now that he was no longer a threat, the chief changed directions immediately... now that his son was safe. Looking for Mary, he was still a long way from the barn searching for his wife when the gunshots sounded. Seeing Jed fall, the Cheyenne Chief's bellow of rage was cut short as a ringing echoed hollowly through his head before he dropped to the ground. The last thing he heard was his wife screaming his name.

Walking around the wheelchair, John bent down to examine the wound on the Cheyenne Chief's head before checking for a pulse. He turned to Melissa's father quickly... motioning in relief. "He's not dead; thank God the shooter used the new rifle. Not having time to become good with it, the bullet just creased him. He should be fine in a bit except for a bad headache once he comes too. Looks like he hit his head on a rock when he fell which caused more damage, it's probably what knocked him out"

Alec sighed in elation before pointing to the men on his left. "You four take him to the house so Gloria can see to him."

Looking up at the housemaid pleadingly, Alec gestured hopefully. "Please, go with them Gloria; I need you to patch him up."

Gloria nodded reluctantly wanting to stay to help find Melissa and Mary, but obediently directed the men to the house.

Walking back around to push Alec's wheelchair, John went over to Jed next. He was laying face down still as death, with blood staining the ground all around him. Being that he was only just over a hundred yards from the barn; the mayor knew that unless a miracle had happened, Mell's new husband would probably be dead. His only hope would be that the shooter wouldn't have had time to line up before having to take the shot.

John left Alec again; he knelt down then gently pushed Jed over in dread fearing the worst by the amount of blood on the ground. The judge examined the wound carefully before checking for a pulse. He turned to his friend with a gratified sigh... waving pleased. "He is alive too, but losing a lot of blood! The bullet went clean through just below his left shoulder, missing his heart by a smidgen. He is pretty lucky, if the bullet had hit a bit farther down and more to the left, he would have died instantly!"

Getting up, John walked back over to Melissa's father.

Alec pointed towards the ranch house before addressing four men standing by waiting. "Please, take him up to the house; Gloria will hopefully stop him from bleeding to death."

Once Alec saw Jed on his way for treatment, he looked up at John pleadingly before gesturing in panic. "What about Melissa and Mary?"

Turning to the remaining men questioningly... John looked at them hopefully, but they all shook their heads at his unspoken inquiry. The judge turned back to Alec then put his hand over his friend's shoulder consolingly. "I'm sorry; no one seems to know what happened to them, they just disappeared."

Giving John a quick anguished look, Alec dropped his head trying hard to hide his expression from the others.

Everyone looked towards the barn at a shout... they saw the men returning carrying someone. Putting the body down gently, Jonathan came over and motioned sadly. "Mark is dead, his throat was slit; the fire is out as well! We put all the horses over in the far corral. Whoever set the fire didn't want to kill the horses, so cleared the area around the fire not wanting it to spread. Earlier, I was one of the first to reach the barn before the shots were fired. It was barred from inside so whoever it was unbarred the door before disappearing out the back."

Exhaling noisily, Alec was pleased none of the horses had been hurt; looking around at all the men gathered... he motioned imploringly. "Pick some men who are good trackers and see if they can find out what happened to Melissa or Mary. Someone must have taken them there's no way they just disappeared without a trace! Gary, I want you to get all the guests together in one group then the new hands in another and see who's missing, Wade will help you."

Turning to two of his hands, Alec waved towards the ranch house. "Paul, will you help me over to the house I need to check on Jed and Giant Bear's progress. Brad, please saddle up their horses plus Lightning... oh, don't forget Mary's horse; I know both men will waste no time in going after the women when they are finally able to ride."

Alec kept his expression under careful control as Paul pushed him towards the house then up the ramp to the front door; he changed chairs before entering the house. Melissa's father looked up at his hired man in gratitude. "Thank you... I can manage now."

Paul inclined his head in farewell and left to help the others.

Waiting until he left, Alec let the emotions he was hiding blaze to the surface for a moment. He shuddered in fear at the loss of his daughter. Dropping his head in his hands in despair Melissa's father stayed like that for several minutes... fighting for control. Taking a deep fortifying breath before finally, he looked back up and his face was expressionless. Once he felt in complete control, again; he went towards the den where he knew he would find their maid working on the two men.

Gloria was just coming out of the den. She put her finger to her lips to indicate that Alec should remain quiet. She had quickly changed out of her wedding dress earlier and put on an apron. It was now full of blood... she wiped her hands to clean them. She went behind his chair so she could push Melissa's father into the kitchen where they could talk without disturbing her patience.

Once inside, Gloria pulled her apron off in distaste... she threw it in the fire so she could burn it later. She pulled a clean apron out then put it on thankfully. The maid washed her hands good and poured them both a coffee still without speaking she brought a plate of sandwiches over to the table before sitting down across from Mell's father.

Sipping his coffee reflectively, Alec put the cup down with a noisy clutter and lowered his head into his hands. He ran his fingers through his hair in frustration. Melissa's father sighed dispiritedly before putting his hands onto the arms of his chair... he looked across the table at the maid pleadingly. "I'm getting too old for this Gloria! I do not know how much more I can stand, if something happens to Mell; I don't think I will survive it."

Taking Alec's hand sympathetically; Gloria held it for a moment already aware he wouldn't survive long if his daughter died.

Squeezing Gloria's hand, Alec was grateful she was there for him before frowning in surprise. He looked around wondering why it was so quiet there should be women and children running around... Melissa's father looked at the maid inquisitively. "Where did you put everyone?"

Gloria smiled mysteriously; she took her hand away from Alec's then picked up a sandwich... she set it before him. "You better eat this or I won't tell you!"

Alec held his two hands up in surrender at Gloria's stubborn look then grinning... he obliged her. "Okay! I will eat if you answer my question."

Waiting patiently without comment, Gloria smiled in satisfaction when Alec picked up the sandwich then bit into it... she smirked before pointing up. "Jessica, with Mrs. Elton's help is upstairs keeping everyone busy."

Waving her hand towards the den, Gloria continued as Alec obediently took another bite of his sandwich. "Jed is lying on the couch in the den; I had a hard time with his wound... it didn't want to quit bleeding. Unfortunately, I ended up heating a blade then pushed the tip inside to cauterize it to stop the blood loss. Afterwards, I put a couple stitches front and back then put some herbs before bandaged it as tight as I could to keep it from opening when he moves. The bullet must have hit a vein which is why there was so much blood on the ground. He came too briefly, but I gave him some willow bark tea and a drop of laudanum for the pain. Hopefully, he should sleep for another half an hour or so. Giant Bear is in the library I had to hold him down physically; he didn't settle until I told him several men were already tracking the women. I promised I would wake him the minute they found out where they were taken."

John walked into the kitchen and sat down heavily in a chair in exhaustion.

Gloria got up then poured the judge some coffee; at the same time, she refilled Alec's cup along with her own, since there was lots left, she put the pot on the warmer.

Looking at Alec, John frowned dejectedly as he held up three fingers in aggravation. "We have three people missing... plus three dead. Missing is your new man, Tomas. The others were guests Gerald and Philip. The three dead are Mark of course; you already know about him. Two sentries, Kenneth as well as Darrel. The men I sent out to track the kidnappers are not back yet, but it shouldn't be too much longer I hope."

Nodding sadly, Alec unexpectedly banged the arm of his chair sharply with a tightly balled up fist in frustration. "I still can't figure out why this is all happening... who would want to kidnap Melissa and Mary; it just doesn't make any sense!"

Shrugging in sympathy, John reached over and patted Alec's hand consolingly. "I'm sorry my friend, but Melissa has a lot of enemies out there. It could be someone she has arrested at one time; or it could be a family member of someone she has had to kill, so they want revenge."

Alec shook his head negatively in disagreement not believing that. "No... I don't think so; if it was for that reason they wouldn't have taken Mary too?"

First Giant Bear then Jed walked into the room. Both were a bit unsteady so they sat quickly; not wanting to fall down and be sent back to the den.

Gloria jumped to her feet instantly in concern... she chided both men for their stubbornness. "You weren't supposed to get up for at least another half an hour!"

John got up then gathered two more cups before pouring the two men coffee and refilled everyone else's; while Gloria checked both men's wounds.

Going to Giant Bear first, Gloria removed the bandage; it

was an ugly red and purple colour, but the bleeding had thankfully stopped. He was getting a black eye from the rock he had hit when he landed. She put a finger in front of his eyes then moved it back and forth. "Let your eyes follow my finger, if you feel dizzy let me know."

Nodding in relief, Gloria was satisfied Giant Bear would have no lasting problems. She decided to leave the bandage off since the gash quit bleeding on its own. Next, she turned her attention to Jed; more concerned about him since his wound was more serious than the chief's. She removed the bandage carefully and was quite happy to see the bleeding hadn't restarted with his movements... the stitches seemed to be holding as well. The housekeeper nodded pleased with her handiwork before bending down then looked into his eyes, but found them clear. "Do you feel at all dizzy or light headed as if you are going to pass out?"

Jed shook his head negatively and answered truthfully. "I felt a little dizzy when I first got up, but right now I feel fine."

Sighing thankfully, Gloria replaced the bandage but tightened it significantly so he wouldn't reopen the wound again. She sat down before pushing the plate of sandwiches towards the newcomers. "I want you both to eat; if the food stays down then I will be satisfied you are recovered enough to leave here!"

Frowning not hungry, Jed looked at Alec for support.

Laughing, Alec waved in sympathy. "Don't look at me I already had this argument with her. She won like usual; you might as well eat Gloria won't let you go otherwise."

Giving in, Jed obediently took a sandwich then bit into it.

Giant Bear followed Jed's example without complaint, knowing that Gloria was right; they would need all their strength to help free their wives.

Turning to Gloria anxiously, Alec waved imploringly. "Can you pack some provisions; plus, anything else you think they will need to go after Melissa and Mary?"

Gloria watched the two men take another bite; satisfied, she left the room without argument.

Turning to Jed, Alec motioned apprehensively. "Do you two have any idea who would want to kidnap Melissa and Mary?"

Giant Bear and Jed quickly; they exchanged a significant glance of perfect understanding. Grey Wolf turned to Alec then answered for the both of them. "Yes! We are both pretty sure it is either Brian or Victor Grey, maybe even both of them!"

Alec stared in shock for a moment before spreading his hands out in stunned disbelief. "But why, I have never really trusted Brian; even so I would never have thought he would stoop to kidnapping. As for Victor, he's been my friend for years."

Sighing sadly at having to accuse Alec's friend... Jed couldn't rule out the possibility though. He was pretty sure Brian had been heading to Victor's place the night they tried to give him an invitation. "We aren't sure about Victor, yet. The other day when we went over to tell Brian about what happened here and about Mary's reunion with Giant Bear, he was furious. It looked to me like he was already mourning before we even told him about his friend, which seemed strange. When we told him Melissa was going to marry me; he got real mean. The man made a lot of nasty threats then he accused me of wanting to marry Mell for her money, which I didn't know anything about. When your daughter asked him how he knew about the money, he said you told him."

Interrupting angrily, Alec shook his head emphatically in denial. "I never told him any such thing; you think he is doing it for the money Melissa will inherit after I die?"

Jed nodded before motioning in explanation. "Yes, but we aren't sure why he took Mary; unless it's to prevent her from remarrying Giant Bear, since he threatened to kill her if she did. As for Victor Grey, he blamed Melissa for killing Greg... he was really hostile about it. The two men we hired Tomas and Mark had both been his before they came to us. Your daughter thought it was strange your friend would just fire two of his men without a reason; then again, we have no idea why he would take Mary so we aren't too sure about him. On the other hand, perhaps the two men are working together. When we left Victor's ranch after he refused the wedding invitation, we bumped into Brian halfway between the two ranches. He could have been headed for Mr. Grey's house, which would make your friend a suspect."

Brad walked in unexpectedly... he was holding a necklace; he gestured in apology for interrupting them then frowned in confusion. "We found the place where they had horses waiting right away; plus, we found this necklace, but we couldn't figure out where they went from there."

Alec held out his hand to take the necklace in fear. "That's Melissa's grandmother's necklace. I gave it to her as a wedding present today; she was wearing it when she disappeared."

Giving it to Alec, Brad had already guessed it was Mell's.

Giant Bear and Jed got up instantly ready to go immediately. "Just show us where we will take it from there!"

Jed turned then looked down at Alec reassuringly; he put his hand over his father-in-law's shoulder comfortingly before vowing solemnly. "We will find them! I swear to you we will bring the women home... this I promise to you on my life!"

Inclining his head in relief, Alec was satisfied by Jed's pledge; he held the necklace close to his heart knowing Grey Wolf meant every word. "Go with God and safe journey to you both!"

The two men left without saying another word... determination written all over their faces. Half an hour later, Jed came back to get the provisions Gloria had put together for him. Alec met Grey Wolf at the front door for news, but there wasn't really anything to report. Mell's dad went back to the kitchen in disappointment.

Entering the room warily, Alec frowned in worry at the mayor and judge of their small town then pushed himself up to the table. "John, I have waited all these years to see my daughter married. I was about to give up on it when Jed showed up out of nowhere! Melissa is such a strong independent woman her ideas scare most men away. Now that she found someone who is willing to accept her the way she is; we might end up losing her before she finds out what she's been missing."

John reached over in sympathy then patted Alec's hand consolingly... he smiled in reassurance. "You will not lose her; Jed will bring her back... he promised!"

Sighing dispiritedly, Alec shrugged in annoyance at himself. After a few minutes, he tried to lighten his tone. "I pray it will turn out all right; I just can't help but feel worried though."

Frowning knowingly, John was just as apprehensive as Alec but tried not to show it... wanting to be strong for his friend. He smiled up at Gloria gratefully as she poured them fresh coffee; the judge turned his attention back to Melissa's father.

Waving off his anxiety, Alec looked at John pensively. "I'm going to send a few men over to Victors to make sure he isn't involved in this. Never mind, I think I will go myself it will keep me busy for a while so I'm not sitting here brooding. Besides, I need to make sure my friend is not tangled up in this mess... it will help put my mind at ease. Can you stay here for me then let the guests know they can go home if they want; or they can stay in the hopes someone will show up tonight. My guess is it will be several days before we see anyone, so maybe just send them all home we can call them back later?"

John got up wanting to help in any way he could then put a hand over Alec's shoulder in support. "Don't worry about the guests... I'll look after them; I will have the men saddle your mare for you, stay here and have a bit to eat before you go."

Alec nodded in thanks then watched John leave.

Jessica came in shortly after the judge left and sat across from Alec then took his hand in encouragement... she was quite concerned about him. "How are you holding up?"

Alec smiled over at Jessica in reassurance before squeezing her hand gratefully. "I was feeling sorry for myself just a few minutes ago... John straightened me out though. I'm taking a few men over to Victor's to make sure he's not involved in Melissa's disappearance. The judge is going to stay here and take care of any of the guests who wish to stay. He didn't think my suggestion would go over well with the townspeople when I told him he should probably send them all home. We can call them back later if they wish to return. Will you help him, please? If any of the guests want to stay, you will have to find places for them to sleep. There's an old bunkhouse we don't use often; ask some of the women to help clean it up then the guests can stay in there if they wish."

Nodding in agreement, Jessica was pleased Alec trusted her to look after his guests. "Of course I will help him; don't fret so much we will look after everyone."

Grinning, Alec gestured gratefully. "Thank you!"

Getting up to leave, Jessica paused... suddenly she leaned over unexpectedly and kissed Alec before turning then left.

Seeing Gloria watching him, Alec smirked at her gloating

expression. He was saved from making any comments when John entered. "Your horse is ready to go; Brad, Deputy Sanders, and Jack... one of the guests, will be going with you just in case you have any problems."

Looking up at John gratefully, Alec smiled in thanks before pointing across the hallway. "Good, can you go into the den and bring me one of the new repeater rifles?"

Turning immediately to leave, John threw over his shoulder before going out. "Sure, I'll meet you at the door."

Alec pushed the wheels of his chair towards the door then left the kitchen and went down the hallway to the entryway. He took his coat off the hook then put it on. Reaching over he took his boots off the rack; it took him a few minutes, but he wrestled them on before he grabbed his hat off the hook. They were put there especially for him and were wheelchair height, this way he didn't have to bother anyone to help him dress.

John came striding down the hallway with the rifle plus thirty bullets; he handed them to Alec then watched him as he put fifteen bullets into the gun and flipped the safety on... Mell's father pocketed the rest of them. The judge motioned at the new rifle in approval. "Those are sure better rifles by far then the single shot rifle, but they are already causing problems... once more people get a hold of them it will be worse."

Aware the new rifles would be more trouble someday; Alec was too preoccupied to worry about it now... he wheeled himself outside. John walked behind his friend's chair then grabbed the handles before helping Melissa's father down the ramp. They didn't bother with his outside chair, not having far to go to get to where Brad and the others were waiting.

Brad grinned down at Alec in pride before waving over to where the new cabins were being completed. "I hope you don't mind, but the men were milling around with nothing to do; I asked them if they wanted to finish Wade's cabin while we are gone. They all agreed, so Wade is directing them. He told me to tell you he wouldn't be able to come with us."

Inclining his head in approval, Alec grinned. "No, I don't mind at all; actually, it's a good idea."

Smiling gratefully at the praise, Brad helped John lift Alec onto his horse once she was sitting; after the horse stood up, they strapped down Melissa's father's legs.

John handed Alec his rifle before shaking his finger up in caution. "You be careful; we don't know what Victor will do if he's involved. I don't want to tell Melissa when she gets back that I let her father get himself killed while she was away."

Reaching down, Alec shook John's hand in reassurance. "Don't worry so much; we will be back before nightfall, I hope!"

Waving goodbye, John watched them ride away in concern.

Brad rode on the left side of Alec; Deputy Sanders rode on the right side... with Jack bringing up the rear. They pushed the horses as hard as Melissa's father dared. Just before they got there, he slowed his horse then turned to the deputy on his right wanting to give him instructions. "Gary, when we arrive can you go to the door and get Victor to come out to see me?"

Gary nodded his head in agreement. "Okay."

Alec spoke up so all the men could hear him. "I'll talk to Victor first then see if it's safe to go in. If it is Brad and Deputy Sanders can carry me in; this way, I can keep both of you with me just in case. Jack you can stay with the horses that way we have someone to watch our backs."

Turning in his saddle, Alec looked at Jack questioningly before smiling in acknowledgement when he inclined his head. He looked at the other two expectantly; Mell's father received their nods too... just as they entered the yard.

Halting a few paces away from the hitching rail in front of the house, Alec nodded at the deputy to go.

Dismounting, Gary handed his reins to Jack before walking up to the door then knocked. He smiled at the man who opened it and pointed behind him in explanation. "Afternoon Mr. Grey; Alec would like to talk to you, if you have a moment?"

Victor looked at the badge pinned to Gary's shirt then frowned puzzled; he wondered why Alec would send a deputy to get him to come out. He looked over the man's shoulder at his friend before looking back at Melissa's deputy... he smiled nervously at him in confusion. "Just give me a moment while I get my boots on."

Inclining his head, Gary turned walking back to Alec.

Smiling down at Gary in praise, Alec nodded in relief. "Thank you; at least we know he's here and doesn't have an armed guard around the place, which would make me nervous."

Shrugging, Gary wasn't worried in the least. "He didn't seem angry to see me or you either, only a little surprised by my deputy's badge."

Sighing relieved, Alec looked towards the front door of the house when it opened; he put the rifle across his saddle and leaned on it... he bent down so he could hear Victor better.

Walking down the veranda, Victor stepped off before walking up to Alec's horse; he smiled hesitantly up at him as he motioned inquisitively. "Afternoon, what can I do for you?"

Inclining his head in greeting down at Victor, Alec tried to be as nonchalant as possible. "I just wanted to thank you for the wedding presents you sent over for Melissa."

Grinning in relief, Victor smiled cordially. "I'm glad you liked them, since I have never been to a wedding I wasn't sure whether it was an acceptable gift or not."

Alec's face sobered suddenly in disappointment; he waved with his free hand curiously. "I also came to ask why you didn't come to Melissa's wedding."

Victor's smile disappeared suddenly... he shifted slightly in embarrassment then he shrugged in apology. "Well, I kind of felt badly at the way I talked to Melissa the other day."

Exhaling noisily, Alec was reassured at the guilty look on Victor's face. "Well, since I'm here now; how about a glass of brandy to toast the newlyweds?"

Grinning thankfully at the forgiveness on Alec's face, Victor pointed behind himself at the house. "Sure, your men can carry you in while I go tell my housekeeper; she will bring us a tray before she leaves for the day."

Turning hurriedly, Victor trotted off quickly before Alec could change his mind.

Brad got off his horse so he could help Gary unstrapped Alec's legs, while the man from town held the reins of the horses... Mell's father handed his rifle to Jack to free up his hands. "Please, keep this handy; hopefully, we won't be long."

Deputy Sanders and Brad held Alec's legs up so the mare wouldn't lay on them by accident... as he whistled. Obediently, she dropped to her knees then her side; she waited patiently for her passenger to be lifted clear.

Gary came around to Brad's side of the horse; the two men locked hands then stepped closer to Alec, they bent a bit.

Waiting until they were in position before reaching up, Alec put his arms around both men's necks holding onto their shirts at the shoulders. The two men moved backwards then slipped their locked hands under Melissa's father's buttocks, now they were able to lift him clear of the saddle; they hefted him carefully so he would settle between them better. Once Brad and Gary had a good hold, he let go of their shirts then relaxed.

Jack tethered the horses to the hitching rail to free up his hands; he casually leaned up against it cradling the rifle as he kept watch.

Carrying Alec between them up to the door which Victor had left opened for them; Gary and Brad took him into the hallway where the older rancher waited impatiently for them. He closed the door before leading them into the sitting room.

The men put Alec on the couch carefully then sat one on either side of him and waited watching expressionlessly.

Victor eyed the three of them in surprise, usually Alec's men left after putting him on the couch but not this time. He didn't say anything; obviously, something wasn't quite right. The rancher didn't recognize any of the men either or the deputy. He sat in a chair across from them before smiling nervously at his friend... unsure of himself now. "The housekeeper will bring a tray in a few minutes."

Alec nodded distractedly not interested in refreshments... he leaned forward before pointing earnestly in demand. "What happened between you and Mell the other day?"

Victor looked embarrassed... he fidgeted. "Well, I had some false information; instead of asking Melissa about Greg's death, I just accused the sheriff of murdering him without giving her a chance to explain."

The housekeeper walked in with a tray of sandwiches, with little squares of chocolate cake... as well as the promised decanter of brandy; she set them all on a small table between them then left.

Pouring the brandy, Victor handed everyone a drink before sitting back with his own.

Continuing the conversation, Alec frowned thoughtfully

then motioned inquiringly at Victor. "It wouldn't happen to be Brian who talked to you would it?"

Looking at Alec in surprise before nodding ashamed, Victor looked down into his glass. He took a generous gulp of the fiery liquid to boost his confidence and looked at his friend with a pleading look for understanding. "Yes, it was; Brian came here then told me Melissa was caught doing something wrong, so she killed Greg to keep him quiet. He said the sheriff did it to keep her ranch... we all know how much she loves that ranch."

Sitting back in relief, Alec was glad Victor wasn't involved in Melissa and Mary's disappearance. "Well, that's not what happened at all!"

Alec spent the next half hour telling Victor the whole story.

When Alec was done, Victor shook his head incredulously. "That's unbelievable! Melissa mentioned Greg was trying to kill you both but I didn't want to believe her, so I just stormed away without letting her explain further. When I thought about it later, I decided Brian lied to me, which is why I sent over the wedding gifts; I was just too embarrassed to come myself."

Frowning troubled, Alec leaned forward anxiously. "Victor you are my friend; all you had to do was come talk to me at any time. I would have explained it to you!"

Shrugging self-consciously... Victor gestured in apology. "I'm sorry Alec, but Brian was just so darned convincing! I suppose in a way; I have always been skeptical about having a woman sheriff. Even though Melissa is your daughter. It didn't take much to persuade me, I'm sorry to say."

Inclining his head acknowledging the confession, Alec was relieved to have this out in the open. "Apology accepted; I do have one more question to ask though regarding Mark and Tomas... why did you fire them?"

Looking at Alec in shocked surprise, Victor waved sharply in denial. "I didn't fire them, Brian asked me if he could use them for a couple of days and I agreed; I haven't seen them since!"

Sighing grimly, Alec explained what happened at the wedding this morning; grateful to have an explanation for two men.

Victor shook his head flabbergasted; he just figured the two men decided to stay with Brian and hadn't checked to see where they disappeared to. The rancher put a fist up to his heart then stared at Alec intently as he vowed vehemently. "I had nothing to do with it... I swear!"

Alec nodded his head consolingly. "I believe you; I think Brian was setting you up if things went wrong for him."

Sighing dejectedly, Victor hung his head in shame. "I cannot believe I fell for it, I should have known better."

Frowning, Alec inclined his head sadly when Victor looked back at him. "Yes, you should have; but I can't blame you completely we were all taken in by Brian."

Finishing his drink before passing the glass back to his friend, Alec motioned towards Gary and Brad to finish up as well. "I must go! Hopefully, Jed is back with Melissa by now; you can come with us if you like, Victor."

Nodding eagerly, Victor quickly got to his feet. "Yes, I would like to come; I want to apologize to Mell personally."

Pleased with Victor's decision to come along, Alec gestured decisively. "Okay; you are always welcome you know."

Smiling, Victor was relieved that he hadn't lost his friend over his stupidity; needing his saddlebag, he went to his room to get ready while Alec's men took him back to his horse.

*****

Alec arrived back at the ranch three hours later then he planned... it was already way after dark; his stomach growled angrily at him, reminding him he hadn't eaten supper yet.

Meeting Alec on the porch with his wheelchair, John smiled in relief... he shook a finger chidingly at his late friend. "I was just about ready to send a posse out to look for you."

Grinning over at John, Alec laughed good-naturedly... he pointed over his shoulder. "No need as you can see, I brought Victor with me; thankfully, he had nothing to do with it."

John inclined his head towards Victor in greeting. "That's definitely good news and you are just in time for supper."

Victor smirked devilishly before dismounting then laughed in delight. "I always time it perfectly!"

Chuckling at Victor's self-satisfied face, Alec waited until Jack and Brad helped him off his horse then carried him up the stairs to his chair. Once the two men stepped back, Melissa's father turned to Victor... he motioned teasingly. "Don't I know it; we are going to have to find you a wife one of these days?"

Laughing playfully, Victor teased his friend... joshing Alec back. "Well, I have been giving the widow Donaldson the eye lately; although, I don't think she is interested in me."

Grinning up at Victor mischievously... Alec gestured smugly. "Normally, I would encourage you and help you if need be but this time I'm going to have to say find your own woman; Jessica is my fiancée!"

Whooping ecstatically, John and Victor took turns shaking Alec's hand in excitement.

Beaming good-naturedly, Victor chuckled in delight. "You old coot; you snatched her right out from under my nose, but I'm really happy for you... congratulations!"

Nodding, John agreed with Victor. "That goes for me too; it's about time you stopped grieving... does Melissa know yet?"

Alec looked over his shoulder at Brad, Jack, and Gary when John walked behind his chair to push him to the house. "Put the horses away then come up to the house to eat; since it's late you three probably missed supper at the bunkhouse."

John pointed in apology over at Gary before he could turn away knowing he would probably want to stay. "Deputy Sanders, I need you to go to town after supper... Paul could use your help to keep an eye on things. I'm sure it will take Melissa several days to get home. I would prefer to have more than one person on duty right now; especially, with the townspeople wanting to stay at least for one night."

Nodding dejectedly, Gary didn't want to go but he concurred.

The three men nodded farewell and left leading the horses to the barn obediently.

Glancing back up at John, Alec continued the conversation. "In a way she does; Melissa knows I have been chasing Jessica for the past few days, but she doesn't know I caught her yet. She likes her though, so she approves fully. If it wouldn't be too much trouble, could you two keep this to yourselves for now... my fiancée doesn't want anyone to know yet?"

Victor looked at John then winked behind Alec's back in perfect understanding before both nodded innocently as they looked down at their unsuspecting friend.

John changed the subject quickly then pushed Alec towards the house. "Oh, by the way almost all the guests stayed tonight. Especially, after I told them there would be a big announcement when Jed returns with Melissa. I sent Paul to town to keep an eye on the businesses. With Gary's help they should be fine. The only one who couldn't stay was Charlie he had to take James' mother home. He said he might return if he could manage it. I told him not to bother coming until I sent someone for him since I'm sure we are going to have a long wait. I told the rest the same thing, but they wanted to stay anyway. If nobody shows up in the morning, they will go back to town. Dusty is here now; he didn't have any problems today luckily. Once he reassured the townspeople everything was okay in town... they decided to stay. They took up a collection while you were gone the townspeople want to divide it between Jed and Giant Bear for saving the sheriff they love so much."

Looking up at John, Alec was totally surprise by that. "That was very nice of them!"

Alec decided he would add to the total too, just as the three arrived at the kitchen for supper. After dinner was eaten, they sat out on the porch waiting as long as possible for the rescue party to show before giving up; Alec's prediction proved correct with no sign of his daughter or the others. He sent Victor out to the bunkhouse with the men to bed down. He put John with his wife upstairs in Melissa's bedroom.

Tommy with all the older kids was ecstatic at being able to sleep in the barn, in the hayloft. The women folk with younger children from town were using every available space; cots were brought in then set up in the den, library, and sitting room.

Sighing dispiritedly, Alec went to bed... even though he knew he wouldn't sleep a wink; however, even he couldn't foresee the length of time it would take before anyone showed up.

CHAPTER TWENTY-TWO

In the four days Melissa hung over a horse, she only came to for short periods but never for long... only to gulp greedily at the water someone poured into her mouth. The concussion she gave herself when her head hit the saddle so hard the first day had been a bad one. It didn't help that the corset she was wearing was keeping her air supply shallow it was contributing to her inability to wake up fully.

It wasn't until the morning of the fourth day when Melissa felt rough hands untying her from the saddle that she was lucid enough to realize what was happening. Someone lifted her off the horse then carried her over their shoulder into a building; she managed to remain limp so they wouldn't guess she was awake. However, she almost gave herself away as she automatically tensed when she felt herself falling... she landed on something soft. Thankfully, nobody noticed she was conscious. Then she felt Mary bounce beside her in relief, her friend was still alive at least. She noticed she didn't have a gag over her mouth anymore and was really grateful at least she could talk now.

A worried voice to Melissa's right that seemed vaguely familiar grumbled anxiously. "Are you sure they won't think to look here?"

Melissa peaked hoping nobody would see her in order to find out who was talking. She wasn't too shocked to find out it was Tomas; one of the new hands she had been highly suspicious of. She sighed to herself mentally in disgust. See she knew she shouldn't have kept him on... White Buffalo stiffened involuntarily when she heard Brian's voice. "Nobody will think to look at Devil's Rock since she killed Greg here."

Mary moaned in discomfort trying to sit up.

Brian grimaced angrily at Tomas before pointing towards Melissa. "Mary's awake again; better check on the Sheriff, see if she is awake yet. She's been out a long time... did your friend hit her too hard? It won't do me any good if she dies from a head wound."

Deciding it was time, Melissa pretend she was waking up too. As footsteps neared the bed... she shifted; unfortunately, her moan of pain was all too real when the corset she was wearing dug into her as soon as she moved.

*****

The two guards Gerald and Philip stationed up on the cliffs died without a sound; a moment later, two shadows drifted towards the miner's shack.

*****

Pushing herself up painfully stiff from lying over a horse for so long, Melissa eyed Brian balefully. "I should have known you would pick my wedding day to ambush us!"

Brian chuckled nastily then motioned in rage. "Well, you strumpet; if you hadn't ruined everything with your stubbornness we would have been married way before now!"

Melissa's voice became deadly when she remembered Alec saying he thought there was another person at his abduction. Things started to make sense to her in a way; although, she was still confused by why. It couldn't be just about the money there must be more to it than that. "It was you, not Greg who planned my father's kidnapping... wasn't it! I don't understand how Tomas is involved though or the three outlaws I had a run in with when I was a kid, how did they get tangled up in all of this?"

Smirking arrogantly, Brian waved towards Tomas in explanation. "My dear, it's quite simple; Tomas here is Greg's brother."

Gazing intently at Tomas, Melissa checked scornfully for similarities. She had never seen the two men together at any time, so never connected the two as siblings. Now that she looked closer, she could see quite a bit of resemblance which is why he always seemed so familiar to her; although, she could never figure out why.

Looking straight at Mary in pleasure, Brian knew it would make him feel good to see every ounce of shock on his sister's unguarded face... as he dropped a bombshell. However, he still directed his speech towards Melissa as he continued without any hint of remorse. "Tomas and Greg are my cousins; the other five you killed were my brothers. After you killed my two older brothers when you were younger, you disappeared so Sam contacted me to find you. Little did I know you were here all the time right in front of me! It wasn't until the kid exposed you that I figured out who you were. When I dug into your background a little, I accidentally found out about your father's money. It took me some time to find my brothers since they were running from the law because of you. I finally found them in Montana. I came up with the idea of kidnapping Alec to get you here then I was going to come on the scene and pretend to kill the bad guys. Regrettably, Alec was going to be shot before I could get to him then I was going to use your grief to get you to marry me. Afterwards, my brothers were going to stage an accident for you and I would end up with everything. Unfortunately, those bootlickers you married came out of nowhere then ruined everything."

Although speaking to Melissa... Brian's gaze never wavered from Mary throughout his confession enjoying her changing expressions. First, one of shock to find out she had other brothers, and they were outlaws wanted by the law. Then disgust before outrage took over when her brother told them his plans for Mell and Alec; finally, she gasped out in total disbelief angry unable to keep quiet any longer. "What are you talking about? I never knew of any other brothers or that Tomas and Greg were our cousins!"

Brian laughed uproariously for a moment enjoying Mary's confusion, his mirth was full of malice... it also had an erratic insane quality to it. When he gained control of himself, he smirked at his sister in obvious pleasure. "My dear, half-sister there is a lot you don't know. You see our father was married to an older widow first with three sons already; after he married her, they had three more children all boys too. I was her last one; unfortunately, she died giving birth to me! I was ten years old when Dad kicked my five older brothers out then married your mother, Irene. When I was twelve years old and you were a year old, my brothers staged a fatal accident for your mother which took her life. Father figured out who was really responsible, so he packed us up immediately then moved us here. I was never allowed to mention my mom or my five brothers again; everybody, including you was told Irene was my mother."

Melissa hadn't been idle while both men kept their attention centered on the confused Mary. Her dress had a tear in the seam between the bodice and the skirt; she was working on making the hole bigger... White Buffalo hoped to retrieve her knife. It was hard trying to rip fabric quietly, but she seemed to be managing it as she worked diligently. She almost had the knife when Tomas happened to look at her; holding herself perfectly still she tried to look innocent, she sighed softly in relief when he turned back to the conversation.

Having a hard time containing her glee, Melissa felt the knife loosened enough for her to pull it out of its sheath... carefully she severed her bound hands. She kept a tight hold on the ropes so they wouldn't fall then give her away. Slipping the knife under her thigh so it was out of sight, she started working on getting the derringer she tried so hard to conceal from Betty. Keeping a close eye on the men to make sure they were not watching her. White Buffalo curled her legs up a bit then started crinkling her skirt to get at the hidden gun secured to her thigh. It seemed to take forever as she lifted the skirt higher to reach it; quickly she pulled the pistol out before placing it under her leg in easy reach. lady luck was with her; she just finished pushing her skirt down then put her hands back in her lap when Brian turned back to her.

Brian grinned nastily at Melissa before looking her up and down insolently with an evil cackle... he rubbed his hands together in satisfaction. "Now that your husbands are dead, I can proceed with my plan. First, since Tomas is not kin to Mary, they can get married it will keep her quiet. As for you my dear Sheriff, we will also be getting married as soon as I get you back to my ranch; I already have an out-of-town preacher waiting."

Mary looked at Tomas in horror; he grinned evilly down at her in anticipation. She shuddered in revulsion, figuring she wouldn't live long under his cruel... barbaric treatment.

*****

The two men listening outside the window heard enough; they nodded to each other then burst into the cabin together.

Brian and Tomas pivoted in shocked surprise then grabbed for their weapons, but they were too late!

'Bang... Bang'!

Two shots exploded almost simultaneously; one shot came from the doorway, the other surprisingly came from inside the room... both men died before they hit the ground.

Jed looked at Giant Bear knowingly, they both turned to see Mell standing awkwardly on bound feet... a little smoking pistol in her hand. He grinned at her devilishly in relief to see her unhurt before putting his free hand on his hip in demand; he waved his gun dramatically. "Don't you think you could let me rescue you just once at least?"

Melissa laughed in delight at seeing her husband still alive as she shook her head negatively. "Never, if I can help it; now get over here and untie my ankles... they are killing me!"

Both men obediently rushed forward to untie their wives.

Mary grabbed Giant Bear's face as best she could with bound hands then began kissing him thankfully as tears streamed down her face; Golden Dove pushed him away as she eyed him in concern. "I thought you were dead, all I remember seeing is blood flowing down your face!"

Mary looked for traces of Giant Bear's head wound; finally, she saw a deep furrow across her husband's right temple... already it, plus his right eye had turned an interesting blue and purple in colour.

Giant Bear sighed thankful Tomas wasn't an accurate marksman with a rifle. "Another two inches to the left I would be dead. Jed got a bullet in his shoulder just above his heart, good thing the man wasn't a great shot! Golden Dove, I think it's time to go home before anything else happens... do you wish to say goodbye to your dead brother?"

Mary shivered in reaction when she thought of her evil half-brother then shook her head negatively. "No; but I must say goodbye to Mell."

Cutting Mary's bound hands and feet, Giant Bear helped her to stand; she wobbled slightly as the circulation rushed into her aching feet... Golden Dove groaned in painful agony. The chief took hold of his wife's arm then helped her over to her friend.

Clearing her throat loudly, Mary tried to get Mell's attention; it took several minutes since the two other newlyweds were in each other's arms engrossed in a deep kiss.

Melissa and Jed broke apart guiltily; White Buffalo couldn't help blushing a fiery red at being caught kissing with such a lack of restraint.

Jed got up instantly so that the two friends could sit beside each other.

Reaching over, Mary took Melissa's hand remorsefully; her voice cracked in strain as she pleaded desperately with tears streaming down her face. "I'm so sorry Mell, please forgive me. It was because of me that my half-brother knew so much about you and the ranch. He was always asking me questions about you after we became friends. I told him you were from South Dakota, plus I gave him the name of the ranch you grew up on. It was me who told him where your father's room was and where to find his chair. I am also the one who told him which horse Wade used and Alec's too. He never asked me more than one question at a time, so I never realized how much I was telling him. Brian always waited a day or two and asked another question, by then I forgot the questions he asked before. Unfortunately, he changed for the worst after I came back from Montana pregnant. When you and I became friends though; he seemed to calm down... turning into his old self again. I figured it was because he was falling in love with you, which is why I never refused to answer his questions."

Taking her hand away from Mary's, Melissa reached up. She wiped the tears from her friends face gently before hugging her fiercely trying to reassure her. "Don't cry... we were both fooled by him for a long time. He manipulated my feelings until I respected, even admired him. That was before you came home again. I might eventually have married him, but a couple of weeks after we met, I saw him beating Lightning. Not too long afterwards, you told me about the Indian fellow he killed. I did try to talk the judge into putting him in jail for murder. Unfortunately, after talking to Brian, John said the charges wouldn't stick because he lied. Your brother swore he thought you were in danger, so he got away with it! The cruel way he treated Tommy was the final straw; it also kept me from saying yes. There's no reason for you to ask for forgiveness it wasn't your fault he was evil!"

Mary sat back wiping more tears away then sighed dispiritedly. "Well, you might not think I need forgiveness; I on the other hand feel I must atone for my actions."

Sitting forward again intently, Mary took Melissa's hand again. "I have a favour to ask. Giant Bear wants to go home so we will be leaving for our Cheyenne village as soon as we pick up Tommy. Will you and Jed look after the ranch for me? I know my son won't want it, but maybe if I have another boy someday; he might want it or a grandchild. Any profit you make from the ranch is yours. You can have control until someone comes to claim it. I will leave a letter of attorney so you can do anything you want with it... except sell it!"

Melissa looked at Jed questioningly... he nodded his assent so she turned back to Mary; she agreed knowing there was no one else her friend could rely on. "Okay, we will be glad do as you ask, but only as a favour to you not because you think you owe me anything!"

Putting her arms around Mary, Melissa hugged her fiercely before whispering sadly in her ear in farewell. "I'll miss you very much my friend, but I know you will be happier with Giant Bear then you were here. I also have a favour to ask of you; will you help Tommy continue to learn my fighting techniques with a knife."

Smiling at Mell when she let her go, Mary shrugged unsure if she would remember much. "I never kept up with it after I took Tommy to you and he was no longer in danger... that's the only reason I wanted you to teach me; hopefully, it will come back to me in time!"

Turning to Giant Bear next, Melissa stood up to give him a big farewell hug... she switched to Cheyenne. "Take good care of Mary and Tommy for me my blood brother; I hope the rest of your life will be a happy one."

Giant Bear returned Mell's hug awkwardly not use to showing affection. "Goodbye, White Buffalo; I will always remember our bond... I will come to you if ever you need me!"

Melissa smiled sadly as she stepped back remembering their pact, hating to say goodbye to her friends wanting to prolong it a little. "I will never forget either, Giant Bear; I promise, I will find you if you ever have need of me."

Jed reached out to Giant Bear next; they clasped forearms in farewell somewhat embarrassed with showing their emotion. "Goodbye my friend, until we meet again."

Giant Bear inclined his head in parting. "Farwell blood-brother it has been a long nine years, but it's finally over. I wouldn't trade knowing you for anything! I thank you for teaching me the white man's language and customs; now I understanding what the Indians will face if we don't find a way to live together. I will never forget you and I'll pass your wisdom down to my children in the hope we can figure out a way to live in peace... even if the other tribes will not listen,

I will find a way myself. I hope when we have a powwow close to the Dakota border you will come with your wife for a visit."

Grinning nostalgically, Jed thought about all the good times he shared with Giant Bear. Grey Wolf agreed... unfortunately, he knew it would be a long time before he was to see his blood brother again. "I wouldn't miss it for the world, thank you for sticking by me through it all; even though I almost gave up, you kept me going. My friend, I'm eternally grateful to you for it. If you ever need anything, don't hesitate to let me know!"

The two quickly embraced then both men turned and helped their wives walk out of the cabin... both still wobbly; they stood quietly for a moment waiting for the two women to find their balance.

Turning to Giant Bear once more, Jed waved towards the ranch. "Will you tell Alec we are going to camp here for tonight, so we will be a day behind you? Take the outlaws horses... give them to Stands Tall, they are branded so he will know what to do with them; we will keep the other two with us."

Nodding in agreement, Giant Bear clasped his friends arm one last time. "I can do that for you Grey Wolf; may the Great Spirit continue to guide you."

Mary turned to Melissa before hugging her once more in parting... tears was still wetting both women's cheeks. Giant Bear and Golden Dove turned away; they mounted the extra horses then were gone.

Turning to Jed, Mell's right eyebrow rose inquisitively. "We are not going home?"

Jed shook his head negatively. "No, we are going down Devil's Rock to your old campsite; I left our horses tethered there because I would like to spend one night before the long ride home."

Nodding in puzzlement, Melissa didn't question him further. Jed helped his frustrated wife mount in her wedding dress; she had to hook her knee over the saddle horn and ride side-saddle. Not wanting to walk down the steep path, they used the horses that the women had been strapped to for four days. Leaving, neither of them looked back. They made it to camp just as the sun was beginning to sink. It was a long silent ride; both were extremely exhausted... physically and mentally. Jed's chest was bothering him quite a bit from the hard ride so soon after the injury. He hid that from Mell, not wanting to worry her.

Lightning saw his mistress coming then nickered in greeting.

Melissa hurried over to him before dismounting. She buried her face in his long mane; quietly, she sobbed out her anger and frustration.

Jed sighed in relief. He dismounted then stood there helplessly watching Mell shake as she cried. This was why he decided to stay the night here; he had hoped his wife would cry now, instead of keeping it hidden to fester until too late. Hate was a powerful emotion... he knew that all too well. Grey Wolf loosened the saddle on the horse he was riding before letting him go. Knowing he wouldn't go far with all the other horses here. Looking around, he was glad to see both Giant Bear and his wife's horses were gone.

Walking over, Jed grabbed the two bedrolls he had removed earlier and made a bed for them; it kept him occupied so Melissa could have a bit more privacy. Picking up the wood leaning against the fire pit, he proceeded to make a fire so he could prepare something for them to eat. Grey Wolf just finished putting the beans and coffee on when his wife came over then dropped down beside him... Mell looked exhausted.

Sighing forlornly, Melissa gestured sorrowfully in regret. "I'm so sorry, Jed; I ripped my wedding dress and our wedding was an absolute disaster!"

Unexpectedly, Melissa's breath caught on a sob. Jed pulled her into his arms tenderly then held her as she wept bitter tears into his shirt. Grey Wolf stroked her back soothingly as he whispered consolingly. "Hush my love, it's all over now; those men can never hurt you again... I promise. It's not your fault the dress got wrecked, I'm sure it can easily be fixed."

The crying ceased as Melissa listened to Jed talking to her softly, but she remained quiet still clutching him closely... afraid to let him go. The fact that Grey Wolf was alive was a miracle; Mell needed a few minutes to hold him while she thanked God silently.

Jed dropped a kiss on the top of Melissa's head before moving so that she could see him smile devilishly down at her then teased. "As for ruining our wedding, I highly doubt that;

you just need to think of it another way. Everyone has been waiting so long for their lady sheriff to get married they would have been disappointed without some kind of action. Now you will not only go down in history as the first woman Sheriff, but you will also be known for having the most talked about wedding of the century. Everyone from here to Boston will remember it... at least for the next twenty years."

Laughing in relief when Jed lightened the mood, Melissa let him go and leaned back in his arms... taunting him back. "I don't think they will be talking about me at all. I think they will put you in the history books as the only man able to tame this, sheriff; plus, you are the only one who has ever had to rescue her not once, but twice."

Hugging Melissa fiercely at her banter, Jed knew the worst was now over. "It was definitely my pleasure. Grab yourself a dish then scoop up some beans before they burn, while I dig out the pants and shirt I brought along for you; oh, I almost forgot I have your boots too!"

Melissa smiled in gratitude at Jed's consideration; especially since having to ride in this corset didn't appeal to her at all... Mell did what she was told. As she filled her dish, she couldn't help commenting in pleasure at his thoughtfulness in bringing her a change of clothing. "It was nice of you to bring them for me."

Leaning against a rock to eat her food, Melissa kept her eyes on Jed as he moved around; afraid he would disappear... that this was all a dream. He had changed back into his buckskins leaving his wedding suit at the ranch before coming to look for her. She was glad, Grey Wolf definitely looked better in them then he did in his finery.

Chuckling in delight, Jed turned around suddenly and caught Mell staring at him. He tried to be as dramatic as possible wanting to make her smile as he gestured flippantly... he fibbed just a little. "I would like to take credit for bringing them to you, but it was Gloria who gave me the saddlebag with the clothes plus the food in it. She thrust it at me as I was going out the door; I was in such a hurry we probably would have starved before I could get you home."

Melissa smiled in pleasure at Jed's first use of the word... home; she filled a dish of beans for him when he came over to sit beside her. Grey Wolf handed her the clothing in exchange for the food; Mell got up and began changing.

Jed chuckled in amused sympathy when Melissa groaned in frustration trying to get out of her dress. He had to leave his food to go help her remove the wedding dress. Now that Grey Wolf had her all untwisted, the petticoat followed soon after. Once he finished helping Mell out of her outer clothes; he stood for a moment eyeing his wife's corset in disapproval. "Whatever possessed you to put that thing on?"

Groaning forlornly, Melissa's voice took on a torturous tone of desperation. "It definitely wasn't my idea, Gloria and Betty insisted. Please, quit staring at it... will yah; I need your help to get out of this dratted thing!"

Moving to provide assistance, Jed couldn't help but grin grimly at the note of misery in Mell's voice; he took out his hunting knife then cut the strings dramatically, but was careful not to cut the camisole under the corset.

Gasping in indignation and relief; Melissa didn't like the contraption, but she hadn't expected Jed to wreck it. "What did you to do that for?"

Laughing, Jed didn't feel one shred of remorse at Melissa's outrage; he watched her strip out of her cotton underwear... it was too hot for them anyway he knew. Grey Wolf frowned slightly in anger as he eyed the deep red marks all over his wife's tender skin, once she removed the camisole. The rigid bone corset had dug really deep into Mell's skin from lying face down for so long over a horse, not even the camisole could protect her. "I did it because I never want to see you in one of these things again!"

Taking a deep breath for the first time in four days; Melissa sighed relieved as she waved in agreement. "Good! Because you definitely won't catch me wearing one of these things again, they are pure torture!"

Sitting back down in satisfaction, Jed finished his supper; he continued to watch Melissa in pleasure as she bent over to put on her socks, pants, and boots. His wife didn't even realize he was staring at her swaying exposed breast. Mell grabbed the white binding she always used to hold her breasts tight against her. She stood up before starting to wrap it around her chest... snug as she could get it.

Frowning angrily, Jed watched Mell for a moment silently... he finally motioned firmly in protest. "I don't think you need to bind your breasts either!"

Looking over at Jed in surprise, Melissa shook her head in irritation as she retorted angrily in disagreement. "That's just too bad, isn't it? I have no choice in the matter; can you see me going at full gallop chasing some man with my breasts flopping all over the place. I'm liable to give myself a black eye or something! This binding controls them. Besides, if I try trotting without the binding it hurts like the dickens!"

Jed thought about it for a moment before bursting out in laughter at the mental image of Melissa's breasts bouncing so hard... they hit her in the face. He held up his hands in surrender still chuckling. "Okay! I concede to that, but at least loosen it a little; I don't like seeing welts all over your beautiful skin."

Melissa inclined her head in agreement; she turned to Jed with one eyebrow cocked in amusement letting him have this victory. "Very well, but I won't loosen it by much. I would rather have welts then sore breasts!"

Loosening the binding slightly as promised, Melissa finished dressing; she picked up her petticoat before extracting her white buffalo medicine bag then put it around her neck... she felt extremely relieved once it was back where it belonged.

Grabbing a cup of coffee from the fire, Melissa also poured one for Jed before walking over she sat down beside him. The two of them sat together sipping their coffee; once finished Mell put her cup down... she pulled on Grey Wolf's shirt demandingly. "I want to see please."

Obediently, Jed pulled his buckskin shirt down so Mell could see the wound. Having used it so much since leaving the ranch it had seeped and a bloody stain marred the white bandage; thankfully it wasn't large... it would wait till they got back.

Shuddering in reaction at how close the wound was to Jed's heart, Melissa thanked God again for sparing her husband. Finally satisfied, she allowed Grey Wolf to pull up his shirt before moving over then snuggled up to her husband contentedly... her expression sobered thinking of all her wedding guests in concern. "Tell me what happened after I was knocked out."

Drawing Melissa closer, Jed kissed the top of her head glad he decided to stay one night before the long ride home; his chest was feeling better. "There was complete chaos... I was told by your father."

*****

It took a good half hour to explain it all.

Tilting her head back inquisitively when Jed finished, Melissa nodded in agreement. "You're right the money was the real reason; did you just barge in when you came to the cabin or did you listen first?"

Smirking down smugly at Melissa, Jed kissed her before lifting away from her so he could answer her. "No; we did not just barge in, but we were tempted at first afraid for the two of you. Brian was just starting to tell Mary about his brothers so we waited, both of us wanted to make sure there were no other people involved. We didn't want to be looking over our shoulders waiting for some other lunatic to come after us."

Sighing relieved, Melissa tucked her head back into Jed's shoulder; she waved pleased that they would be able to live in peace. "I'm just glad it is finished so we can start our life together now with no more worries or threats hanging over our heads!"

Jed nodded then reached out with a stick and banked the fire for the night; reluctantly, he pulled away from Melissa as he yawned. "We will stay here tonight then go home in the morning. I want to wait until we get home to consummate our marriage or go on our honeymoon. Your Father will want to see you first before we go anywhere. I want our first time together to be in our home on our nice soft bed."

Melissa chuckled in agreement then got up after putting her coffee cup down beside the fire pit she would wash the dishes in the morning; Mell walked over to their joined bedrolls before crawling inside clothes and all!

Looking towards the two horses that were still saddled... Jed shrugged; it wouldn't hurt them to stay saddled for one night and crawled in after Melissa then kissed her goodnight tenderly. "Go to sleep, I just want to hold you tonight."

Sighing contentedly, Mell cuddled closer; within moments she was fast asleep completely exhausted from her ordeal.

Jed lay gazing up at the stars for a bit as his chest throbbed painfully... reminding him he over used his left side since the injury happened. Finally Grey Wolf fell asleep content now that Melissa was close.

CHAPTER TWENTY-THREE

John pushed a frustrated Alec in his wheelchair across the veranda. They were on their way back to the house after spending another useless day watching for Melissa and Jed. They had spent eight long days staring out across the ranch yard towards the road leading to Devil's Rock hoping, but in vain. The two were just going through the door for supper; plus, another sleepless night, when they heard the unmistakable sound of several horses racing towards the ranch.

Stopping instantly, John pulled a hopeful Alec back out of the doorway... they turned going back onto the porch. The judge pushed Melissa's father towards the chair he only just vacated a few minutes ago. Both stared intently down the road; they saw Giant Bear and Mary riding into the yard with a string of horses following behind.

Alec kept his eyes glued steadily on the road behind Giant Bear in anticipation, but it remained empty with no sign of Jed or Melissa. He tensed in apprehension before looking back at all the horses, but none of them were Lightning; it relieved his mind only a bit.

Putting his hand over Alec's shoulder, John tried to comfort him... it wasn't hard to guess at his friend's thoughts. He tried to calm him down, but the worry was quite evident in the judge's own voice. "Don't go jumping to conclusions, they may have decided to camp out an extra day or so for some reason; Jed was hurting pretty bad when he left here!"

Nodding, Alec sighed in relief when Mary hurried towards them after dismounting... not even bothering to tie her horse. Golden Dove smiled down reassuringly as soon as she got close to Melissa's father; quickly, she gave him the message not wanting him to worry unnecessarily. "Jed said to let you know they are going to camp out for one night. He also said to give you the extra horses, they are branded but you would know what to do with them. We came back right away because Giant Bear wants to go home immediately, so we came to collect our things and Tommy. I'm also giving Melissa power of attorney with control of the ranch until someone comes to claim it. My half brother is thankfully dead!"

Giant Bear walked over to them then gestured solemnly down at Alec. "Stands Tall, I want to take my family home tonight; will you help me with some provisions?"

Nodding decisively... Alec gestured reassuringly. "Of course, you have wages coming anyway so I'll give you enough provisions to see you home instead of money. We are just going in for supper so come join us. While we are eating, I will have Jessica and Gloria get everything ready for you. You can keep the horses. My men will load them with your supplies; I will write you a bill of sale for them and the John will witness it. Mary, you can tell me the details of what happened as we eat. After we are finished, the judge can help you make out your power of attorney."

Mary looked at Giant Bear then turned back; they nodded in reluctance both wanted to leave immediately, but knew it would be a while yet before they could go. She looked at Giant Bear again and shrugged in silent apology.

Giant Bear grunted in acknowledgement at Mary's look; he knew it wasn't her fault. They both turned and walked into the house with Alec leading the way.

*****

Supper just finished when Jessica came in then walked up to Alec; she put her hand on his shoulder before bending to whisper in his ear. "Everything is ready for Mary and Giant Bear. I also helped Tommy get his things packed to go."

Alec smiled up at her in thanks. He put his hand over Jessica's in silent gratitude. "Good; can you send him to me then ask Paul to put Tommy's saddle on Princess?"

Jessica inclined her head. "Sure, I'll be back in a bit."

Looking around for John after she left, Alec beckoned for him to come over; he grinned up at his friend in anticipation. "You can present Giant Bear with the money now if you want."

Going behind Alec, John pushed him over to Giant Bear and Mary.

Seeing them coming, Giant Bear stood hoping to leave soon.

John walked around Alec's chair then clasped Giant Bear's hand in farewell.

The townspeople that had remained; unfortunately, only a few of them were able to stay. Hushed expectantly, wanting to be witnesses for the others when they came back. Alec already sent a man into town to let the ones who left know Melissa would be arriving sometime tomorrow so they could all come back if they wished. The ones still at the ranch strained to hear what was being said, none of them wanted to miss anything having waited patiently for this moment with silent excitement.

Reaching in his pocket dramatically... John pulled out an envelope then handed it to the Cheyenne Chief expectantly. "Giant Bear, the townspeople wanted to show their appreciation for all your help by taking up a fund for you and Mary; they hope this money will help you on your way home."

Giant Bear looked around at all the expectant faces, he motioned in apology... refusing to take the envelope. "Jed has told me of this custom, but I'm sorry I must refuse; where we are going, we will not need it. Alec has provided us with provisions for our journey, please give the money to him in payment."

Alec frowned in disappointment, but he wasn't surprised. He had known Giant Bear wouldn't accept the money; suddenly an idea came to him, he grinned up at the Cheyenne Chief knowingly. "Would you take horses instead of money?"

Thinking about it for a moment... Giant Bear really didn't want to offend anyone; he finally nodded before looking down at Alec in thanks for suggesting an easy solution. "Yes, if you wish I will take horses instead of money."

Winking up at Giant Bear, Alex was glad to have found an answer so easily. "Good; the Judge will take Mary into the den so she can make out the power of attorney, I will find you some horses."

Reaching up, Alec took the envelope from John. He counted the money then looked around the room expectantly. When he saw Herman Johnson, he pushed himself over to him. He smiled up hopefully as he looked up at the grey-haired old wrinkled rancher that lived on the other side of Victor Grey. It was closer to this ranch if you cut across country. Herman's huge handlebar moustache took up almost his whole lower craggy face; sometimes, it was hard to know whether the man was smiling or scowling. He always joked that it gave him an edge at the poker table. "Do you still have the stud you wanted to sell last year?"

Herman nodded that he did. "Yes, sir I do, why?"

Grinning up in relief, Alec motioned inquisitively. "How much do you want for him?"

Telling Alec the amount; Herman watched Mell's father count out the money then hand it to him before pointing towards one of his hired hands. "Go tell Brad over there which horse it is and where to find him... he will go get him for me."

Counting the rest of the money, Alec frowned; it was short for the mare he wanted to sell, a good saddle horse cost about two hundred these days and there was only a hundred dollars left... he shrugged dismissively, it would do. He beckoned to Giant Bear. "Come out to the corral I will show you which horses are yours."

Obediently, Giant Bear went behind Alec's chair to push him outside. The townspeople followed closely behind them not wanting to miss a thing.

They didn't quite reach the front door when Tommy came running up to Alec; he was really excited to be going home with both of his parents. The ten-year-old had been quite upset after stabbing the man who tried to abduct him, but Melissa's dad spent two hours with the boy... helping him through it. "You wanted to see me Grandpa?"

Alec beamed up at Tommy tenderly in pleasure at the endearment; he crooked his index finger at Melissa's foster son so he would follow them. "Yes, come with us to the corrals... I have something for you."

Tommy was puzzled, but didn't ask any questions; he waited for his dad to pass him pushing the wheelchair. He followed them obediently, while the townspeople followed behind him. They left the house once everyone scrambled into their outer footwear then they kept going.

Once they were in front of the barn... Alec beckoned to Paul. He was standing in front of the doors having a smoke. "Bring the mare that is saddled out first; afterwards, I want you to put a halter and rope on Brandy then bring her out too."

Paul put out his smoke immediately before going into the barn; he came back out a few minutes later leading a dainty mare with a small saddle on her.

Smiling sadly up at Tommy... Alec took the boy's hand before pointing at the mare with his free hand in explanation.

"I wanted to give you a going away present, I figured Princess would be the best one for you, considering where you are going. She was just bred to Melissa's stallion so you will have a foal next spring. Remember, you will always be welcome to return here anytime, we all love you and will miss you dreadfully."

Tommy let go of Alec's hand then bent down and hugged him fiercely in farewell... tears streamed down his face in sorrow. "I love you too, Grandpa. If I ever come back this way, I'll come to see you; I promise! Thank you very much for the horse, I will treasure her always."

Smiling mistily up at Melissa's fostered son when he stood back up, Alec wiped away tears. "May the Great Spirit watch over you and keep you safe?"

Nodding solemnly down at Alec in sorrow, Tommy ran to his horse in sad excitement.

Wiping more tears from his eyes, Alec watched Paul in satisfaction as he went back into the barn. Melissa's father wanted to help Tommy fit in with his new people; Stands Tall was well aware that the more horses you have, the wealthier you were considered in Cheyenne eyes. Hopefully, it would help the boy to be more readily accepted since he had his own wealth already.

Paul led out the mare before walking towards them.

Getting his emotions back under control, Alec looked up at Giant Bear before motioning towards the horse Paul brought out. "This horse is yours from the townspeople... she is bred to Mell's stallion. Brad is on his way to the Johnson's to pick up a stallion for you, it shouldn't take him long. The four horses you brought with you are in the barn they are loaded with provisions. While we wait for Brad the men will help you pack up the mare, I just gave you with your belongings; just show them what you want to take with you."

Giant Bear looked gravely down at Alec then around in surprise at all the grinning townspeople. Never had he been shown such love and respect by the whites before... it gave him hope for the future of the Indian tribes. Maybe someday, they could all live in peace! He smiled at everyone in thanks before gesturing in appreciation. "I want to thank all of you for the gifts, I'll cherish them always; when we have a powwow close to the border you are all welcome to come join us."

The people from town cheered; they came over one at a time to introduce themselves. It took Giant Bear a good twenty minutes before he finally managed to slip away to help pack the mare. Thankfully the stallion arrived ten minutes later, so he too got taken into the barn to be loaded.

The townspeople gathered around Alec expectantly after Giant Bear left for the barn.

Chelsie stepped forward since she was the official spokesperson for the group. She had sent all her girls back to the saloon to look after things for her until she could make sure Melissa was all right. Pam had done the same... both women were very worried about their friend; they knew there would be no rest until they saw her again. "Alec, we would like to know what we should do with Jed's money. Will he accept it do you think or should we find him a gift also?"

Thinking about it for a few moments... Alec grinned up at Chelsie in gratitude. He knew that right now a good breeding bull would go for about ninety to a hundred dollars; cows were around twenty-five and heifers ran about eighteen to nineteen dollars a head. "I think he might take it, but I also know he wants to start a cattle herd. If you would rather go that route there should be enough money for a bull and a few cows here. He would take them for sure."

Tom Carlson stepped forward then fidgeted shyly... he was painfully slim usually too shy to speak out in a group. He was of medium height with mousy brown hair; the only thing that set him apart from his homely appearance was his beautiful crystal green eyes. "I have a Hereford bull for sale."

Herman stepped forward eagerly as well. "I have a black Angus cow and two red heifers for sale."

Alec eyed the two men in appreciation. "Okay, how much?"

They told Alec what they wanted, so he counted out the amount.

Alec looked around at all the expectant townspeople after he handed both men the money they wanted. "There is still twenty dollars left... my suggestion would be to deposit it in the bank for their first child."

Everyone cheered in approval.

It took another two hours to get everything sorted out; finally, Alec sat in his wheelchair on the porch with a few of the townspeople gathered around him waving goodbye to Giant Bear. There wasn't a dry eye to be seen anywhere, Mary and Tommy had always been a favourite among the townspeople... they would surely be missed.

Giant Bear stopped his horses at the end of the ranch yard; the three turned then waved one last time in farewell to their friends before turning away... they never looked back again.

Sighing sadly, Alec looked around in approval at all the familiar faces looking down at him expectantly. These people amazed him sometimes; never in all his travels, had he come across a town so willing to befriend everybody... no matter what race or colour they were. He looked over at Chelsie and Pam standing in the background. Most towns he had been in would have shunned the two women completely, since they were both women of questionable character. Instead, they were standing here among the townspeople talking with the judge's wife. All were friends of Melissa's, which was what brought them together in the first place.

There were two half-breed Indians, a Mexican with his wife, an Asian half-breed plus all his family. There was also an African born black man, who escaped from a slave ship enroute to the slave market; the whole town was quite aware of that... he was talking to the judge at the moment. It amazed Alec that they could all live in one town, not one had a shred of prejudiced feelings towards another that he was aware of.

Frowning in worry, Alec thought of the future. He knew one day it would end, as soon as the railroad went through their town it would all change. More people would come... like Melissa in a way he was dreading it. With that many people in town the crime rate as well as people who are prejudiced will grow; they would end up wreck everything these people had accomplished. He just hoped everyone standing here today would keep their morals and not allowing others to influence them.

Alec looked up at the judge then grinned enticingly... he waved towards the front door of the ranch house. "Okay, I'm sure the ladies have dessert waiting in the kitchen for anyone who wants to have some before bed; there is also brandy in the library for anyone who wishes to have a nightcap?"

John looked around with a grin at all the eager nods of pleasure from the townspeople. He looked back down at Alec;

the judge inclined his head agreeably before walking behind the host's chair... pushing him into the house. "I think we would all like that very much."

The townspeople followed behind Alec and the judge who was also their mayor... they were all talking excitedly about the day; they could hardly wait to see what would happen tomorrow when Melissa arrived back with her new husband Jed.

*****

Jessica sat down beside Alec's chair then sighed in relief when the last guest left for their bed; it had been a long emotional day... she was quite exhausted. She looked over at Melissa's father then opened her mouth to tease him, but paused in surprise when she noticed him staring at her intently.

Alec reached over suddenly without a word and stroked Jessica's cheek tenderly with the back of his hand. He lifted his hand up farther than twined a wayward red curl around his finger teasingly. All the while, he continued to stare at Jess intently. She had done so much for him the last two weeks. He hardly even had to open his mouth and she was there to help him. With so many people around right now it was almost impossible to have a private moment with her; he really needed to tell her how much he appreciated what she was doing for him... now was the perfect opportunity.

Letting go of the curl he was holding, Alec went back to stroking Jessica's cheek tenderly... still staring at her earnestly. "I haven't had much time lately to tell you how much I appreciate everything you have done around here, Jess; I just want you to know, I do appreciate it!"

Smiling over at him lovingly, Jessica closed her eyes... she rubbed her cheek against his hand in pleasure then she looked back at him just as keenly.

Alec caught his breath in surprise at the look of passion suddenly blossoming in Jessica's eyes; he grinned in excitement as his fiancées passion fuelled his own. He leaned over for a kiss, but stopped short of her lips as he whispered lovingly. "I'm such a lucky man, you are absolutely beautiful Jess and you are all mine!"

Without letting Jessica say another word, Alec caught her lips in a demanding kiss refusing to release her. He nibbled then lightly bit her bottom lip playfully before capturing her lips in another searing kiss. While busy, kissing him back passionately... he reached up and pulled out the comb that Jess had holding her hair into a bun on the back of her head. He groaned in pleasure as her hair cascaded down her back in a riot of curly red locks; he buried his hand in the thick mass of hair in pleasure before gathering a fist full.

Reluctantly, Alec pushed himself away from Jessica; he turned his wheelchair, so he was in front of her then pulled her table chair around... now she was facing him completely. He grabbed her by the waist and hauled her into his lap before turning his chair towards the kitchen door.

Jessica giggled in delight... she curled up in Alec's lap not fighting even a little as he wheeled them towards his bedroom. Once inside she waited until he pushed them around the bed then she turned her back so it was facing him as if she was going to get up; she paused suddenly when she felt his erection even through her dress. Instinctively Jess wiggled and heard his surprised intake of breath as he grew harder against her. She grinned devilishly before standing up.

Hearing a disappointed groan behind her... Jessica ignored it. She reached under her dress then removed her bloomers, but left her dress on. She turned suddenly and knelt down on the floor between Alec's legs then undid the buttons on his pants; she looked up at him teasingly as she shook her head chidingly. "Not wearing any underwear, shame on you."

Grinning down saucily at Jessica, Alec winked wickedly... playing along. "Wouldn't want to disappoint anyone now, would we?"

Laughing huskily, Jessica reached inside Alec's open pants and pulled out his engorged manhood; her breath caught in surprise at his obvious pleasure, she lowered her head slowly... her tongue flicked out experimentally.

Gasping in shocked delight that Jessica was willing to do such a thing; Alec groaned in disappointment when she stood up then turned her back to him. He reached out to pull her back, but paused in relief as she lifted her dress up... she was just undressing.

Raising her dress, Jessica looked behind her teasingly; she winked playfully then suddenly sat back in Alec's lap with her dress hiked up around them... she wiggled enticingly.

Frowning, unsure what Jessica was up to for a moment... Alec suddenly grinned wickedly. It didn't take him long to catch onto what she wanted. He couldn't help groaning in pleasure just at the thought of it. He lifted her while she held onto the arms of his chair for support; he guiding her over his manhood then sheathed himself fully inside her wet inner heat.

Jessica cried out in surprise; she wasn't quite sure it would work when she first thought of it, but now that Alec was inside her the pleasure was exquisite... Jess had never felt so full before.

Alec lifted Jessica up... at the same time, she pushed on the arms of the chair then locked her elbows in place to hold herself up; he tried to bring Jess back down once she was up far enough, but her arms were rigid so he couldn't move her.

Just the tip of Alec's manhood was inside Jessica... she groaned as she teased him unmercifully; unfortunately, it was affecting her too as she wiggled around still holding herself up. All of a sudden, Jess relaxed her arms and dropped back into his lap unexpectedly.

Crying out in shocked denial, Alec erupted deep inside Jessica way too soon. He really wanted to prolong this, but the pleasure was just too intense... he couldn't help himself; he wrapped his arms around Jess refusing to let her go before laying his head on her back still shuddering in ecstasy.

Groaning in disappointment, Jessica too had wanted to prolong this, but her pleasure was just as great as Alec's; she cried out in rapture as her body erupted around his pulsating manhood. She slumped against him in exhaustion as her body continued to shudder for a long time afterwards.

Finally, the two calmed down enough that Jessica was able to lift off Alec slowly; immediately, she went over to the washbowl and wet the cloth waiting there for her. Lifting her dress, she cleaned herself first... not wanting to make a mess. Rinsing the cloth good, she walked back over then knelt down between her fiancés legs and gently washed his manhood clean.

Watching Jessica with his eyes half closed... still breathing hard; Alec grinned up at her drowsily as she threw the cloth into a corner and proceeded to undress him for bed. Once he was fully undressed, he reached over then pulled a laughing Jessica into his lap again. He grabbed a fistful of red curls then brought her head down for a deep demanding kiss.

At first, Jessica struggled playfully... she groaned in pleasure and melted against him in surrender. She stayed there for several minutes enjoying his teasing kisses then pushed determinedly away from him; standing back up with her hands on her hips she laughed down at him light-heartedly "Oh no you don't, come on it's time for bed up you go."

Alec groaned in disappointment, but obediently lifted himself onto his bed. He pulled himself up to his pillow so Jessica could put the blankets over him. He waited until she got closer and grabbed her around the waist then hauled Jess on top of him... cloths and all; instantly, his lips found hers in another searing kiss.

Jessica groaned in pleasure, but managed to escape Alec's hold; she rolled off the bed laughing teasingly then turned to face him... she shook a warning finger towards him. "No more tonight, now go to sleep."

Grimacing in frustration, Alec wiggled his eyebrows suggestively. "How about giving, your poor crippled fiancé another goodnight kiss then!"

Laughing, Jessica shook her head emphatically at Alec. "No way that's just an excuse for you to pull me back into bed; I'm not falling for that one mister!"

Smirking in disappointment, Alec stuck out his lower lip in a pout; hoping it would entice Jess to lean closer for a kiss, but it didn't work... she giggled down at him.

Putting her hand up to her lips, Jessica blew Alec a kiss before turning for the door; she opened it then turned back and grinned over at her fiancé tenderly. "Goodnight, love!"

Smiling back sleepily, Alec waved then blew her a kiss. "Goodnight, I love you!"

Nodding knowingly in pleasure, Jess left for her own bed.

Frowning dejectedly, Alec had known Jessica wouldn't stay any longer... he grinned devilishly thinking of his chair; he would never have thought of putting it to such good use, but now he couldn't wait to try it again. Next time there would be no surprises and he would make darn sure he would last a lot longer than he had tonight. He sighed dreamily before drifting off to sleep. The first good night sleep he was to have since Melissa's disappearance eight days ago.

Dreams of Jessica with a future full of love and happiness, filled Alec's evening; it was the first time since the death of his first wife and his inability to walk that his dreams were not full of nightmares.

****

Stopping his horses, Jed waited patiently for Melissa to notice that he wasn't following her any more. He stared up in awe at the bright full moon shining above him. Gray Wolf had always hidden the fact that he was a romantic at heart... even from his first wife; with Mell he felt that he didn't need to conceal it anymore. Never would he hide it again, he swore silently to himself.

It didn't take long for her to notice his absence; Mell rode back to Grey Wolf curiously. "What are you doing, we could be home early in the morning if we ride all night!"

Jed looked at Melissa sitting on her horse; she was totally oblivious to the fact that the moonlight was doing spectacular things to her face and hair. Grey Wolf never thought to bring her hat with him when he left the house to rescue her. For four days now, he had taken immense pleasure in watching it surround Mell in an unruly riot of curly waves... he pointed at the moon playfully. "Isn't it beautiful?"

Melissa looked up in surprise at the moon; she hadn't really paid it any attention to busy concentrating on the ground in front of her horse, not wanting him to step in a hole... possibly injuring his leg. Mell's expression softened as she looked up then gasped in surprise when Jed grabbed her around the waist and pulled her onto his horse demandingly. Grey Wolf captured her lips in a searing kiss. She pulled away laughing huskily as his passion fuelled her own. "What are you up to now?"

Grinning mischievously, Jed getting a wild idea dismounted in a hurry. He pulled a protesting Melissa from his horse then turned and took the saddle off, but left the blanket on his gelding. The mare he was leading would stay here since her halter was still fastened to the saddle; thankfully, he didn't need to worry about her wandering off. Grey Wolf turned suddenly then started pulling his wife's clothes off. First, her shirt dropped to the ground... the binding around Mell's breasts soon followed the shirt. He reached for the buttons on her trousers, but she pulled away teasingly.

Giggling playfully at Jed's haste... Melissa turned suddenly and ran off; she kept her arms across her breasts so they wouldn't bounce quite so much. Mell was laughing so hard it only took her husband a few minutes to catch her.

Grinning lovingly, Jed grabbed a fistful of Melissa's thick blonde hair then pulled gently until she was looking up at him. "I love you so much... my woman, my wife!"

Without giving Melissa a chance to respond, Jed ground his lips against hers in need. His hands were busy undoing her pants while she was distracted by his kiss... suddenly, she was naked. He stepped back and stripped out of his own shirt then his pants and finally his underwear followed; until he too was gloriously naked.

Melissa couldn't look away while Jed stared at her so intently; she jumped in surprise when he whistled for his horse unexpectedly.

Smiling devilishly, Jed vaulted up on his horse naked; he put his hand down enticingly so he could help Melissa mount in front of him.

Frowning in puzzlement as Jed lifted her, Melissa gasped in shocked surprise when he turned her completely around... now she was facing him. Instinctively, Mell opened her legs to straddle his horse; which caused her breasts to flatten against Grey Wolf's naked furry chest.

Jed grinned at Melissa teasingly and grabbed her by the waist; this time, he gently pulled Mell in closer so her womanhood was pressed against his manhood.

Lifting her legs, Melissa draped them over Jed's to accommodate him.

Groaning in pleasure, Jed reached down between Melissa's legs then opened her lower lips so that her bud rubbed against his manhood... he pulled her against him tighter.

Melissa uncertainly wrapped her arms around Jed to keep from falling. Grey Wolf lowered his head to kiss her passionately; however, before his lips touched hers... he whispered tenderly. "Trust me, love!"

Melissa instantly relaxed against Jed as his lips claimed hers; she hadn't realized that she was so tense... her uncertainty was glaringly apparent.

Groaning in approval, Jed nudged his horse into a walk; he couldn't help growling in ecstasy suddenly when every step the horse took rubbed Melissa's bud against his manhood... harder and faster.

Gasping in shock, Melissa's pleasure escalated as Jed kicked his horse into a trot. She couldn't believe they were doing this on a horse. Never in her wildest imagination had she dreamed such a thing would be even possible... never mind pleasurable. Unexpectedly, Grey Wolf nudged his horse into a slow canter causing all thoughts to disappear from her mind as her body took over control. The motion of the horse not only caused a pleasurable friction between their legs. It also made Mell's breasts bounce against the curly hair on her husband's chest. White Buffalo's pleasure was increased two-fold since it was coming from both places.

Crowing in delight, Jed felt Melissa lose control first.

Unable to hold back, Melissa couldn't help screaming out in rapture as she climaxed long and hard.

Jed trying desperately to hold back his climax was incapable of doing so when his horse drove him so hard against Melissa... his control snapped; he too yelled out his intense passionate pleasure. He ground his lips against Mell's in demand before he peaked so hard he almost fell off the horse, but righted himself just in time. Grey Wolf slowed down and turned his gelding back towards the other waiting horses, at a more sedate walk as his wife leaned against him in exhaustion.

Melissa groaned against Jed's shoulder as they rode back; he still had a slight erection and the horse was causing a lot of friction between them... to her astonishment she climaxed again hard.

Jed whooped knowingly, feeling Melissa's uncontrollable shivers in satisfaction... before he even heard her gasp of rapture; he sighed in disappointment when he finally shrank too much for any more pleasurable explosions from his wife.

Sighing disgruntled when her clothes plus the horses came into sight... Melissa squealed in shocked surprise when suddenly without warning, Jed lifted her up. Quickly, she pulled her right leg away from her husband's then holding onto his bulging biceps she slowly let herself drop to the ground. However, Mell's legs were so wobbly they refused to hold her up; with a loud oomph she ended up sitting down hard on the ground right where she was.

Chuckling in delight, Jed dismounted; he had to lean against his horse for a couple of minutes, making sure his own legs would hold him. Finally, he took his saddle blanket off the horse and moving away from animals... laid it on the ground. Walking over he picked Mell up unceremoniously then put her on the blanket not wanting her to catch a chill. Grey Wolf went over to get their bedroll so they could catch a few hours of sleep, they would have to continue on in the morning.

Staring at Jed as he walked around naked making them a bed, Melissa grinned in delight... he had no sense of decency whatsoever! She was definitely glad he didn't; she loved seeing him walking around naked. As Mell watched him, Grey Wolf grabbed his canteen of water and splashed some on his belly to clean himself off. She chuckled before looking down at herself she too was full of her husband's pleasure. White Buffalo hadn't even noticed.

Walking over, Jed washed Melissa off gently without a word. He dried them both off with the saddle blanket before lifting her up again. Mell protested laughingly that she could walk, but her husband shook his head still without a word and brought her over to the bed he made for them. Grey Wolf climbed in with her as soon as he put her down then they cuddled close together. He propped himself up on his elbow for a moment so he could see her expression... he grinned down at his wife enticingly. "Someday we can try that with me inside you, but not yet; goodnight, I love you!"

Melissa smiled up in anticipation sleepily then reached up with her hand and tenderly stroked Jed's face lovingly. "I cannot wait to try it someday soon... I hope; are you sure though it will not hurt you it's an awkward position for you to be in?"

Jed chuckled as he laid back then pulled Melissa closer. "No love it won't hurt me, I promise!"

Snuggling up close to Jed, Melissa yawned tiredly. "Goodnight, I love you."

It didn't take either of them long to fall asleep.

The full moon that caused all the excitement in the first place caressed the lovers as they slept peacefully beneath its loving light.

CHAPTER TWENTY-FOUR

Melissa followed closely by Jed rode into the ranch yard about noon... it was the day after Mary with her husband and son left to go home; they would have been at the ranch sooner if they hadn't stopped to play in the moonlight last night.

When they entered the yard, both were surprised at the sight that greeted them. Alec was the first one they noticed, behind him stood Judge Elton... his wife, plus their daughter. Actually, the people in the background surprised them the most; they had figured after all this time the townspeople would have gone home. Everyone gave a tremendous cheer of greeting at the sight of them.

Feeling overwhelmed by the love... Melissa could hardly believe the acceptance she received from these people. Even though she was a woman, they continued to allow her to be their sheriff and friend. She jumped off her horse in excitement; she wiped the tears from her eyes before rushing over to Alec then gave him a fierce hug of greeting. The tears were more from relief that she was home and everyone important to her was safe.

The two quickly disappeared when the townspeople converged around them in excitement.

Jed sat on his horse watching a little longer amazed by it all... never had he saw the like before; he had visited or lived in many towns from here to Boston. Grey Wolf even lived in Canada for a while, he had never seen a sheriff received or greeted like Melissa. In most towns, a lawman was lucky if they were even tolerated. He smiled when he heard his wife's laughter ringing out joyously as she returned everyone's hugs. At the same time, she tried to answer their questions as fast as she could. He shook his head still baffled by it all before jumping down off his horse then started loosening the saddles.

Brad walked over instantly when he saw what Jed was doing; he warmly clasped Grey Wolf's hand in greeting and pointed over his shoulder at the crowd behind him. "You better go over to join Mell... I'll take care of the horses for you."

Inclining his head in thanks... Jed went to join the throng.

As he made his way through the crowd; he was surprised at how enthusiastically they received him. Everyone clasped his hand firmly in friendship then thanked him for rescuing their sheriff. Grey Wolf nodded cordially, but didn't say anything still awed by it all.

Reaching Alec, Jed shook his hand affectionately in greeting.

The crowd instantly hushed so that they could all hear, not wanting to miss a thing.

Alec tightened his hold on Jed's hand so he couldn't get away from him. Dramatically, he waited for complete silence before starting his speech. Melissa's father gestured around them with his free hand, making sure to speak loud enough for everyone to hear him. "My son, thank you for saving my daughter's life; as you can see, we are all so grateful. To show you our appreciation the judge has a surprise for you. If you will follow us over to the far corral... we will present it to you."

Looking up at John after letting go of Jed's hand, Alec nodded that he was ready; the judge dutifully pushed his friends chair in the direction of the corrals.

The townspeople followed, just as excited to see Jed's reaction as Alec was.

Melissa walked over then took Jed's hand and entwined her fingers with his... they followed Alec obediently; as they drew closer to the far corral, she caught her father's glance then smiled gratefully over at him when she saw what was inside.

Jed could hardly contain his glee when he saw the cattle in the pen waiting for him.

They stopped in front of the corral and John walked around Alec's chair so they would be the focus of everyone's attention... he shook Jed's hand amiably.

An expectant hush fell over the crowd as they waited to hear what their judge and mayor had to say.

John cleared his throat dramatically; making sure everyone was listening before looking at Jed expectantly. "We are all eternally in your debt not only for saving our sheriff, but also for saving our dear friend. The whole town wanted to show their appreciation, so after you left everyone started putting money in a pot then two of your hands went to the Carlson ranch and picked up a Hereford bull that he was selling. On their way back, they stopped at the Johnson's ranch then picked up an Angus cow, and two red heifers... this is our way of saying thank you. We hope that in the coming years as deputy and sometimes sheriff when Melissa is with child!"

Pausing, John chuckled in amazement never having seen Melissa's face turn so red before; everyone laughed at the deepening blush on her face at the reference to her having children. When silence descended again, the judge continued as if he hadn't paused even for a moment. "You will come to know us and serve us as well as Mell does... we also hope to buy cheap beef!"

Everyone hooted again at the rotund judge's hopeful expression at the mention of food then cheered their approval at John's speech.

Jed turned to the crowd waiting for them to settle down; he wasn't sure what he was going to say at first. He took a fortifying breath to calm his nerves as the silence deepened. Finally, waving around in emphasis Grey Wolf gestured at all the people surrounding him in awe. "I'm so overwhelmed by all of this. I don't know what to say exactly. I suppose first off; I would like to thank each one of you for the wonderful gifts. We also appreciate the fact that all of you are still here to finish our wedding celebration with us. I'm sure I speak for Melissa too, when I say thank you. Hopefully, everyone here knows that I would have done the same for any one of you if your woman faced the same situation as mine did. I want to say that I'm grateful for the faith you are putting in me to be your deputy and your sheriff... three or four times I hope."

Melissa blushed furiously again then slapped Jed playfully for the last comment.

The crowd clapped and whistled their approval at Jed's speech; afterwards, the men came over to him one at a time and introduced himself as well as his family... if he had any.

After the last family presented themselves, Alec pushed himself over to Jed's side then raised his hands for quiet dramatically. "Can I please have everyone's attention; Gloria and her helpers are setting out the wedding feast. They have been cooking non-stop since sun up this morning. Better late than never I always say... everyone feel free to go into the house and eat. I would also like to extend my hospitality to all of you who would like to stay over tonight."

As the guests started to leave to go up to the ranch house for the promised food; Melissa leaned closer to Jed then whispered in his ear playfully. "See, I told you they would be talking about you... not me!"

Hugging Melissa before stepping back... Jed shook his head in amazement. "Never, have I had such a warm welcome from people in all my life or such unconditional friendship from folks I don't know; I think I'm going to like it here. What I would like to know is how everyone knew I wanted to raise cattle."

Chuckling when he heard Jed's curious question, John pointed at himself then down at Alec. "We can answer that!"

John explained Giant Bear's refusal of the money, but his acceptance of the horses... as well as Alec's suggestion to the townspeople to give you cattle; he finished with the money put away for their children to come.

Walking around Jed, Melissa moved closer to John with tears in her eyes; she hugged him in gratitude as she whispered brokenly. "Thank you, for all you have done for us."

Hugging Melissa back for a moment, John stepped back... he grinned devilishly. "It is the least we could do after all you have done for this town; you know we do have an ulterior motive in giving these cattle to your husband though."

Moving back instantly when the judge let her go, Melissa's voice became soft and protective before her eyebrows rose in surprise. "Oh, what motive would that be?"

John chuckled at the defensive note in Melissa's voice before he motioned placatingly. "Nothing drastic my dear; we just wanted to make sure you were both so happy here that you would never think of leaving us."

Smiling knowingly, Melissa waved with a giggle in the direction Jed disappeared to... as soon as John had distracted her. "I'm sure you have reached your goal already, look over at the far corral!"

Over by the pen, Alec and Jed were talking excitedly. They were already discussing where they would be keeping the cattle, plus how many new hands they needed; the two men had slipped away while they were talking... the judge hadn't even noticed them leaving.

Laughing knowingly, John nodded in satisfaction towards

the excited Jed before turning back to Melissa then pointed towards the farmhouse. "Come on, we had better get those two to the house or all the food will be gone."

Melissa smirked in humour when John rubbed his round belly in sympathy as it growled at him. They went over and gathered the two reluctant men then headed for the house.

Alec looked up at Melissa curiously, as Jed pushed him. "Have the two of you decided where you're going for your honeymoon?"

Shaking her head negatively, Melissa looked down at her father questioningly. "No; we haven't had time to discuss it yet, why do you ask?"

Smirking up devilishly at Melissa... Alec teased. "Jessica wants to get married in Boston, we thought you two might like to be there; Jed mentioned one time he had family there, so we figured that's where the two of you were heading."

Shrugging in confusion, Melissa opened her mouth to say she didn't know Jed wanted to go to Boston; it snapped shut almost immediately in surprise without a word spoken when the first part of Alec's statement registered. Mell squealed in delight before bending down... hugging and kissed her father in excitement.

Jed quickly stopped the wheelchair before the big wheels could run Melissa over... she exclaimed in excitement. "I'm really happy for you, Dad; it's about time you decided to marry again, when did you ask her?"

Beaming relieved Melissa approved... Alec squeezed her hand as she stood back up, but kept it in his. "Actually, I asked her before you got married; we didn't want to have a wedding with a lot of people so we decided to wait until later."

Walking around the wheelchair... Jed shook Alec's hand. "Congratulations! We haven't really talked about this, but I planned to take Melissa across country so she can show me her routine. I need to know how she makes her rounds; after that, I figured I would take her to Boston to meet my family."

Melissa smiled from one to the other in agreement... she nodded. "It sounds like a good plan to me; usually, it takes me about a week to make my rounds. Since this is our honeymoon, it could take up to three weeks or so Dad; let's say we meet in Boston in four weeks for your wedding."

Alec looked up at John inquisitively. "Do you think you can get by that long without Melissa?"

John's eyes twinkled in delighted mischief... he winked at Alec in conspiracy before looking back at Melissa then nodding that they would be fine. "Yes, Dusty said he would like to remain a deputy; Paul offered to fill in as well until they get back. I told the boys not to expect them for at least a month if not two. The sheriff has never taken a holiday, with all that has happened around here lately I figured she would need to have time to herself for a change."

Grinning, Melissa hugged John in gratitude. "I will take both men to the office tomorrow then show them what to do; I'll make sure to send you a report every so often so you know where we can be reached... in case an emergency arises."

Inclining his head agreeably, John went behind Alec's chair and began pushing him to the house.

Gesturing, Alec smiled at Melissa inquisitively. "Now that your honeymoon is settled, when are you leaving?"

Shrugging, Melissa sighed in disappointment at the thought of having to wait even one more day but they didn't have any choice... there was too much to do yet; she looked down at Alec then shrugged. "Much as I would like to leave tomorrow, I do need a couple of days to get everything organized."

They all stopped waiting patiently as Alec changed chairs.

Jed pushed the front door open once Melissa's father was ready... he held it so everyone could go in; once inside he continued the conversation as he motioned down at his father-in-law curiously. "I think three or four days would be enough time for us. What about you Alec, will you and Jessica be leaving right away?"

Alec shook his head negatively before looking up at Jed. "No, we probably won't leave for a couple of weeks at least; we want to do some travelling, so I need to get everything settled in the office... that way you can take over without any trouble."

Stopping short in shocked surprise... Jed gestured down in panic. "Alec, I don't want to take over the running of the ranch; I was hoping you would continue to stay here with your wife."

Grinning in delight at the note of dread in Jed's voice... Alec waved calmly in reassurance. "I didn't mean for you to look after it permanently, but we want to travel for a year or so; we will be returning here to live afterwards. Wade will be the one who will do most of the work. All you have to do is read the reports with him in the evening and make sure to order enough supplies for the ranch."

Melissa laughed at the look of pure relief on Jed's face.

Sighing in relief, Jed motioned calmly appeased. "Well, I guess I can handle things for a year!"

Chuckling in humour, Melissa grabbed Jed's arm in demand. She pulled him along not wanting to wait any longer... she was starved. "Come on, guys. I'm going to expire from hunger soon; you can discuss business later."

They continued on their way in silence to join their guests for brunch; when they entered the dining room, a cheer came from all the guests waiting patiently.

Immediately, Alec was taken to the head of the table... it was more convenient for the wheelchair. Normally, Melissa would sit at the other end of the table but with this being their wedding the family wanted to sit together. Jed walked past the first chair on his father-in-law's right so Jessica could sit beside Mell's father; he held out the second chair for White Buffalo before taking the chair beside her. Brad plus his wife were next with two of the ranch hands taking up the rest of that side of the table. John took the seat to his friends left with his wife beside him. Gloria then Wade sat next to them. Sara's husband Dan was next with his wife beside him. The preacher's wife was next with the Pastor sitting at the other end of the table.

Once sitting, Melissa looked around in surprise; Jessica had instructed the men to move the dining room table over and bring in the table from the kitchen. Every available space was used to seat people so they could eat. Along the wall was a buffet style table taken from the bunkhouse... it was heaped with enough food to feed an army.

There were a few faces missing of course; not all the townspeople could come back, but almost everyone that could come had. Melissa looked around in wonder, there were about seventy guests still here with all of them in this small room since none of them wanted to miss a thing. She continued to look around gleefully at all her friends then her gaze fell on a face she hadn't expected to see here. She leaned towards Alec curiously. She pointed at the far wall where Victor sat... inquisitively. "Dad, what's Mr. Grey doing here? I thought he wasn't coming to our wedding?"

Alec smiled reassuringly over at Melissa as he explained what had happened when he had gone over to Victor's place.

Melissa nodded thoughtfully when Alec was finished his story. "I'm also pretty sure Brian was going to set him up if things went wrong for him; unfortunately, he never said what his intentions were for involving Victor before he died."

John leaned towards Melissa inquisitively when she sat back in her chair. "Did you notice Gloria and Wade's cabin is finished already?"

Shaking her head negatively, Melissa leaned forward in order to hear better then looked at John in surprise. "No, I hadn't noticed... how did it get finished so fast?"

Smiling in delight, John chuckled at Melissa's shocked look. He waved towards Brad sitting at the end of the table. "It was actually your new hands doing, he asked the guests that stayed the whole time to help. He figured it would keep the men out of trouble while we waited for you two to show up; he was right too and with all these men working together, it took less than a week to complete it. This week, all the finishing touches on both places were done, including painting both cabins."

Grinning in approval, Melissa nodded towards Brad. "Well, I will have to make sure I thank him."

Stomach growling, Melissa thankfully turned when the door to the kitchen opened then the rest of the food was brought out; Mell watched eagerly as the women set everything on the table... she sighed in anticipation. She was so hungry she was sure she could eat a horse all by herself.

Trying to catch Melissa's attention, Alec reached out before tapping her arm then gestured confidently as she turned to him inquiringly. "Princess was given to Tommy as a parting gift... I hope you don't mind; I know you were quite curious to see what colour the foal would be."

Melissa shook her head reassuringly; she was just thankful Alec thought of it... for she hadn't. "No, that was a good idea. I'm glad you did."

Jessica walked to the table with a bottle of champagne.

Alec had hidden three bottles when they first moved in here

hoping for just such an occasion.

Smiling lovingly at Alec, Jessica poured him a glass then continued down the table giving some to everyone.

Sara was at the other end of the room doing the same.

When all the glasses were full and the food ready, John stood up then waited for total quiet. The judge smiled in satisfaction when he looked around at all the silent guests waiting patiently for him to speak. "Ladies and gentlemen... it's very nice to have everyone gathered in one place for a change; I hope we can do this more often in the future. The wedding feast is laid out on the table so everyone can help themselves, but before we do the pastor is going to give a prayer of thanks."

Everyone bowed their heads obediently giving thanks for the food, the beautiful day, everyone's continued health, and blessing all the guests.

John still standing, continued once it was finished. He waved at Melissa, Jed, Wade, and Gloria. "The newlyweds are to go up first then everyone else will proceed in an orderly manner. When everyone is back in their seats again, anyone who wishes to can make a toast. After we eat, everyone is encouraged to go into the drawing room for some dessert and entertainment... where a big announcement will be made."

Finished at last, John sat back down to the excited chatter of the guests; who were all wondering what could be so important that they had to wait until Melissa and Jed returned. That's why they came back since the judge who was their mayor enticed them before they left to go home with the promise of an imperative speech to come. He told them it was essential to the town, as well as the surrounding areas.

Jed grabbed Melissa's hand then led her to the buffet table eagerly... just as starved as she was. His shoulder was killing him, but it could wait until after they ate.

Picking up two plates, so Melissa could fix one for her father; forgetting for a moment it wasn't up to her anymore to look after Alec... it would now be Jessica's job. She turned and smiled in approval at Gloria since she was directly behind her then bent to whisper teasingly. "Everything looks great. I think I'll give everyone a bonus this month."

Gloria grinned in thanks at the compliment; she finally gestured in exasperation. "You have given us plenty as it is just sit back and enjoy yourself for a change!"

Melissa finished filling the plates; she took Gloria's advice and concentrated on enjoying herself in the company of her family and friends. She never noticed the three faces that were missing.

Jed hadn't known of the deaths either having been out cold when the three men were found.

John had cautioned all the guests this morning when they arrived not to mention it to them; Alec would tell them tomorrow... not wanting to spoil their first day home.

*****

Everyone finished eating; the men all went out on the porch for a smoke to give them a chance to clean up. The women kicked Melissa and Gloria out as well... they joined the men.

Taking one last puff, Jed gave his cigarette to Melissa before whispering to Gloria for help. She nodded and went to the den then waited for Grey Wolf, who ran upstairs to take off his buckskin shirt and replaced it with a cotton one. He went back downstairs and into the den so she could check his arm.

Tsking in disapproval at the bloody bandage, Gloria removed it carefully knowing the caked blood would be stuck to the stitches. Once she finally got it off, the housekeeper nodded in approval... her handiwork had held up to his mad dash to Devil's Rock and back. Going to the desk, she grabbed her small satchel that held her doctoring items and brought it over to him. "The skin is healthy and it doesn't look like you did any damage, I'll remove the stitches and put a clean bandage. Tomorrow we can see if there's any more seepage."

Nodding, Jed didn't comment wanting to get back to Mell.

*****

Jessica enlisted the aid of Paul and Brad to take the side table out of the dining room; they set it up in the drawing room against the far wall. The two men brought out a huge wedding cake next and set it in the center of the table. While the men were doing that, a steady stream of women brought in every kind of dessert your heart could desire and set them artfully around the cake.

Paul then Brad each brought out crystal bowls filled with punch. One had brandy in it; the other one had no alcohol. Then whiskey, wine, brandy, champagne, and bourbon decanters, or bottles were brought out then put on the table

at the far end. Three men from town came in to play music...
one with a fiddle, another with a guitar, and one had a mouth
organ. They would play all night if the guests wanted. There
was even someone to play the piano in the corner.

All the younger children had eaten earlier so the older girls
were watching them outside in the front yard.

The couch and the two big chairs were taken away to give
them room for dancing; smaller chairs stacked against the
walls were for sitting if you wished.

Everything was finally ready so Jessica went out to let the
men know; it was not long before everyone was gathered in
the drawing room helping themselves to the much-
anticipated desserts... as well as the drinks.

All the guests stood around laughing telling jokes or stories
with neighbours... the band continued to play softly in the
corner; you could feel the excitement in the air as they waited
in anticipation for the long-awaited announcement.

Melissa smiled down at Alec in amazement as she motioned
around the room. "Wow, I didn't know this room could hold
this many people at once; it's still not full, we could bring in
another fifty people with no problem."

Alec grinned at Melissa then nodded, but didn't comment.
Seeing Jed and Gloria; he turned to John. "Are you ready?"

John rubbed his hands together in anticipation as he looked
down at Alec; he winked in conspiracy before turning to
Melissa and Jed. He crooked his finger demandingly...
wanting them to follow him. "Will you two come with us,
please?"

Looking at Jed in bafflement, Melissa turned back to John
curiously... he was already gone; the judge was pushing
Alec's chair over to where the band was playing already. They
had to scramble quickly in order to follow him obediently.

Unexpectedly, John turned Alec to face the crowd.

Jed and Melissa had to come to an abrupt halt instantly...
one had to sidestep; the other one jumped back in order to
avoid the wheelchair; it was too close for comfort. Grey Wolf
almost got his foot ran over by one of the wheels. The two
newlyweds looked at each other in amusement, chuckling at
their near mishap. They wondered what all the excitement
was about.

The band quit playing immediately aware that the speech

was forthcoming... the guests hushed expectantly as they waited for Alec or John to address them; they had all waited patiently for this moment, none of them wanted to miss the announcement.

Alec waved for Melissa then Jed to stand in front of him. He smiled mischievously up at them, but still didn't say anything; he looked over at Grey Wolf in conspiracy and winked at him in explanation.

Jed smiled in anticipation, aware now of what was about to happen; remembering the discussion they had a couple weeks ago at John's office. After thinking about it for a moment though, he frowned in worry wondering if it was a good idea doing this at what should have been his wedding day. He wished they would have talked to him about it first... this might not go as good as the two men planned. Unfortunately, it was too late now as the judge began his rehearsed speech.

John cleared his throat loudly to make sure he had everyone's undivided attention. He didn't need to bother you could have heard a pin drop at that moment. He gestured solemnly towards Melissa in explanation. "As everyone knows Mell has been with us since 1806, which is when she first became our official deputy. At first, she passed herself off as a man; none of us thought to look twice of course, never would any of us have guessed that a woman could or even would want to be a deputy. Her height plus the shadowy face she managed to keep hidden by her oversized hat was all we ever saw. However, from that day on she has changed all our lives for the better. In 1808, she was sworn in as sheriff after ours got himself killed. She kept our town peaceful as well as lawful for two whole years. Then in 1810, we found out that 'he' was actually a 'she'... some people already knew this secret or had guessed without informing us!"

At this point, John looked directly at his wife in disapproval.

Betty turned with a smug smile to exchange glances with Chelsie and Pam.

The townspeople laughed at John's disgruntled expression as he gazed at the three women, in obvious displeasure.

Harrumphing chidingly at the smug look the three women exchanged, John turned back to the crowd when the chuckles died down. He continued once he was sure Betty had gotten his silent reproachful message and looked around at the guests once more. "Well, most of us were quite shocked of course then because of our bewildered surprise we made the mistake of firing her. Lucky for us Melissa didn't leave completely and in the four months she was gone, our town became lawless again. It wasn't until she saved the life of my wife, who was pregnant with my unborn child, that I came to my senses then rehired her as sheriff. Instead of taking wages though, we agreed she would take over this ranch on condition she would look after all the surrounding towns, as well. So, in 1810 Mell moved onto this ranch and brought her father, Alec, out here to live with her. Now I don't know about the rest of you, but I think we got a better deal."

There was laughter from the townspeople in agreement; most of the heads in the crowd were bobbing in complete accord with the judge... the town had gotten the better deal by far.

John cleared his throat loudly for silence, not finished yet; when silence descended... he continued. "Of course, then there was only one other town besides ours and not too many people lived in it yet. It didn't take long though for the rumours to spread that people could live out here in peace without having to worry about outlaws or desperadoes. It encouraged others to start settling here, so another four towns sprang up overnight. Everyone here has heard rumours of the railroad coming... well it's true, it should pass through our town in two years, I hope! Therefore, our town plus all the surrounding towns will grow more. With the new growth, unfortunately more outlaws will be tempted to come. Now Alec, Jed, and I came up with a solution to keep our towns from becoming lawless again. There's just no way Melissa will be able to keep up to this new growth, even with her husband helping her."

Melissa turned angrily then tried to interrupt with a fierce scowl on her face; John held up his hand calmly to silence her. She turned and threw Jed a murderous look in the process.

Jed just smiled back innocently at Melissa, but inside he was groaning... he knew this was not a good idea today. He turned back to John expectantly, hoping that what was to come would put a smile back on his new bride's face; Grey Wolf, didn't want to end up sleeping in the den all by himself tonight.

Taking a deep fortifying breath, John was still not sure how Melissa was going to take this... he continued hurriedly before he could change his mind. "Now, while Melissa is away on her honeymoon; I want every town to elect a sheriff and they will have one deputy."

The crowd came alive suddenly, shouting angrily in protest... they threw demanding questions at John all at once; they wanted to know immediately what was going to happen to Melissa. The judge's speech was completely overwhelmed, something neither of the two men had expected when they decided to make this announcement tonight.

Alec looked up at John in concern, but all they could do was to wait for the uproar to calm down.

CHAPTER TWENTY-FIVE

John turned away from Alec then scowled angrily; the judge looked around at all the shouting people before raising his fingers to his lips and blew hard... until his whistle drowned out the uproar.

Stunned, a hush descended immediately!

Raising his hands in demand for restraint... John bellowed. "Please, will you let me finish already?"

You could have heard a mouse squeak at that moment, nobody dared make a sound; shocked by the loud whistle, they all waited.

Sighing relieved, John had expected yelling from Melissa but not from the townspeople. The judge quickly continued before they could interrupt him again. "Now, as I was saying. Before Mell leaves on her honeymoon; her and her new husband Jed will come to my office then be sworn in as the new marshal and deputy marshal of North Dakota."

There was a dazed hush for a few seconds as the townspeople absorbed that information. Suddenly, complete pandemonium broke out again; with everyone clapping and cheering their approval.

Melissa stood in dumbfounded astonishment; she was totally speechless... with such a startled look on her face that Jed had to laugh. He leaned closer to Mell then bent down to whisper so only she could hear him. "Congratulations!"

Turning, Melissa looked down at Alec when he took her hand to get her attention.

Alec grinned up at Melissa's amazed look then squeezed her hand encouragingly. "Congratulations sweetheart!"

Raising his hand for silence once more; John sighed in frustration when it took several minutes for quiet to prevail... before he could continue. "Melissa will now be reporting directly to the governor of North Dakota. She will then be travelling from town to town throughout the north keeping the peace. Since she's paid for her ranch, many times over in the seven years she has been with us. Mell will now be paid wages by the governor for her services. We won't be seeing much of her from now on, but I think I speak for everyone when I say we will miss seeing her smiling face every day. I figured it was time to reward her for the many years of service that she has given to our towns."

Walking around Alec's chair dramatically, John went over to the stunned Melissa; taking both her hands in his... he kissed each cheek. He smiled at her before speaking loud enough for everyone to hear. "Congratulations, Mell. I hope you give North Dakota just as many years and as much wisdom as you have given us. We will miss you when you are away, but look forward to the times when it is our turn for your visit."

Melissa smiled hesitantly back at John, still a little dazed by it all; she wasn't sure if she liked being handed over to the Governor without her consent. "Well, you sure managed to surprise me this time! I had no idea you were planning any of this. I'm not exactly sure what to say yet since I have been fighting you for the last two years... whenever you talked about bringing in a marshal. It never even occurred to me that you might have me in mind for the job!"

John grinned as he let go of Melissa's hands then pointed towards Jed in explanation. "You will have to thank your new husband for that; it was his idea to make you the marshal."

Frowning in surprise, Melissa shrugged as she motioned with a laugh of irritation. "I'm not sure if I should thank him or be angry for doing this to me... without at least talking to me first!"

The crowd chuckled in delight at that then a few yelled out suggestions to Jed on how to appease his new wife; trying to be helpful.

Jed smiled confidently when he looked around the room at everyone, but didn't say anything as he grinned with assurance. He appeared not to be worried in the least; inside though, he couldn't help being a little uncertain how all this was going to turn out... Melissa was not looking at all pleased.

Wiping a few tears from her eyes, Melissa thought of all the friends she would miss... she waved in aggravation. "I'm still a bit shocked, I don't know if I should consider this good or bad news. I love this town as well as all my other towns; remaining the sheriff here for as long as I could was always my goal. I'm not sure if you managed to give me more or less work, if I take it, I will be spending most of my time in the saddle. Thank you for the trust you have placed in me to help, North Dakota become lawful. I will miss all of you when I'm away."

Beaming at Melissa once more, but inside John was unsure about her; was she going to accept the position or not? She hadn't really said she would outright. The judge stepped back to let everyone else offer her best wishes; while she was busy with the others, he bent down to Alec troubled... he gestured in confusion. "I'm not sure if she likes the job offer or not, she doesn't look happy about it."

Alec grinned up at him reassuringly before gesturing. "Just give Melissa some time to think about it; she will see that being a marshal is no different from what she is doing now as sheriff. The only difference is she will have a wider area to cover."

Nodding relieved, John stood up straight before turning away from Alec. He stepped forward and called out loudly so everyone could hear him. "I am not quite finished; please bear with me a bit longer?"

When John had their undivided attention again... he continued. "Anyone who wishes to be sheriff of our town must go to Melissa for approval. She will make the decision as to who goes on a list. She also has to agree to the names for sheriff in her other towns; afterwards, a list of suitable candidates will be given out and each town will choose who they want by vote. We already have a deputy as do the other towns, so we don't need to worry about that."

John allowed the crowd to discuss the matter of who would make a good sheriff for a few minutes then cleared his throat for silence. "I have one final statement to make; I would like to congratulate Alec Ray and Jessica Donaldson on their upcoming wedding in Boston."

There was more cheering, as well as clapping from the crowd.

Alec looked up at John chidingly then couldn't help grinning up at his friend good-naturedly. "You just had to do that, didn't you?"

Grinning, John nodded devilishly before waving playfully at Alec. "Of course, I couldn't miss out on such a good opportunity my friend."

The band started playing softly again when John nodded towards them; he had arranged it earlier so once the speeches were finished. They would continue so everyone would start mingling again. Several people came over to give their best wishes to Melissa, Jed, Gloria, Wade, Jessica, and Alec.

The guests helped themselves to more dessert and drinks; several toasts were given to the newlyweds. However, none of these speeches was as exciting as the previous announcements. The townspeople couldn't help discussing the best possible choices for sheriff either... even without a list.

Victor Grey walked up to Melissa hesitantly when he caught her alone... he smiled cautiously then gestured in apology as he hung his head in shame. "I have to apologize for my behaviour the other day, all I can say in my own defence is that Brian was so blasted convincing!"

Melissa smiled sympathetically not really blaming the mortified Victor at all... Brian had taken everyone in. She reached out and patted his arm reassuringly. "It's okay; we were all taken in by him so I really can't blame you for that."

Victor sighed in relief as he looked up then nodded thankfully. "I'm glad to hear that Mell, I was quite worried you wouldn't forgive me; I was pretty nasty about it!"

Melissa grinned teasingly as she dropped her hand from Victor's arm. "I couldn't stay angry with you for long anyway; you have been my father's friend for many years and mine as well!"

Nodding thankfully, Victor turned away and went to find Alec to give him the good news.

A slow waltz started up so Jed walked over to Melissa; he bent down and whispered suggestively. "Will you dance with me, my love."

Beaming in pleasure, Melissa allowed Jed to take her hand then led her over to an empty spot that was cleared for dancing; Gloria and Wade joined them right away. After watching for a few minutes several more couples joined them, as well.

At the end of the waltz; Alec approached Melissa in his wheelchair. He grinned up at her teasingly. "It's my turn for a dance, sweetheart!"

Smiling down at Alec thoughtfully, Melissa tried to figure out how to dance with the wheelchair in the way; she finally bent down so her head was on his shoulder.

Alec grabbed Melissa around the waist unexpectedly then pulled her onto his lap; he laughed at her hesitation.

Chuckling in delight, Melissa settled herself before putting her arms around his neck and her head on his shoulder; Alec manoeuvred the chair around the dance floor. When the music finished... everyone clapped in approval. They had all stopped dancing to watch father and daughter dance.

None of the townspeople had ever seen Melissa's father this happy in all the years he had been here... it was rare to see him even smile; he looked different now, younger without that constant frown on his face. They all definitely approved of the new Alec.

John walked over then claimed the next dance from Melissa.

Wheeling himself over, Alec wanted to talk to Jed since they were both free for the moment... he wanted to talk business. "Are you still interested in building Chelsie a goldsmith shop?"

Jed inclined his head as he looked down at Alec. "Of course, do you want to talk to her now?"

Beckoning, Alec nodded that he did; they threaded their way through the guests until they found Chelsie sipping wine... she was laughing with one of her girls.

Chelsie turned in surprise at a tap on her shoulder; she grinned at the two men before lifting her glass in a toast. "Well, I must say you sure know how to throw a party!"

Alec smiled up at her in thanks before motioning in apology. "Thank you, Miss Chelsie; I'm glad you are enjoying yourself. I hope you don't mind, but we have a business proposition for you?"

Looking at Jed then down at Alec curiously, Chelsie turned then shooed her companion on her way before turning back to the two men. "Sure, I don't mind; what can I do for you?"

Smiling hopefully, Alec pointed at Jed and himself in explanation. "We both admire your expertise designing jewellery. I have also seen your beautiful mantel clock which you have displayed at the saloon. Melissa absolutely adores the one you made her years ago, so we were wondering if you would be interested in going into partnership with us in a goldsmith shop. We would build it then buy all the material you will need. All you would have to do is design the jewellery, the merchandise, and manage the shop; it will be an equal three-way partnership."

Thinking about it for a few moments in surprise, Chelsie shrugged undecided... not sure what to say; it had been her dream when she first came to America from Ireland, but now she wasn't so sure. She loved her tavern, and the girls that worked there. "I don't know. It doesn't seem fair that you two would put in all the capital, but still make me an equal partner."

Waving dismissively, Alec shrugged. "We think it's a fair deal because without you we wouldn't have a goldsmith shop. Besides, I have all the lumber already that we need to build it so it won't cost us much except for labour. We have a lot of beautiful excess wood that would work perfectly for clock bases and such. All you have to do is give us a list of what you will require for the initial start up. When we get to Boston, we can start gathering supplies and look for future suppliers. You will be managing it, which is a lot of work on its own; never mind all the time that goes into your designs. We think a three-way partnership will work best for the three of us."

Grimacing, Chelsie sighed thoughtfully still not sure... she finally shrugged hesitantly. "It's definitely a good deal for me; why don't we get together before you two go away and we can discuss it further I need more time to think about it?"

Looking up questioningly, Alec exchanged a glance of perfect understanding with Jed before he turned back to Chelsie. "We will come to the saloon in a couple of days; I need to buy an engagement ring for Jessica, anyway."

Chelsie nodded enthusiastically. "That sounds good."

The three conversed for a few moments more about the party. Jed excused himself and went to find Melissa; she was standing by the table with a glass of punch in her hand. Grey Wolf smiled teasingly at his wife before bending... whispering throatily in desire. "You definitely look radiant this evening!"

Melissa beamed up at Jed when he bent down for a quick kiss; they turned to survey their guests and both smiled contentedly at how well everything turned out.

John walked over, a grinning Alec following with something shiny in his lap. Once they halted in front of Jed, Melissa's father lifted the knife out of his lap dramatically. All the guests hushed expectantly when he expertly flipped it around to hold it by the blade so it was hilt backwards wanting them to do the honours. "Come on, you two; cut your cake. I think we have all waited long enough."

Smiling in agreement, Melissa nodded before looking around for Wade and Gloria... she waved them over since it was their wedding cake too. The two couples put a hand over their partners and then joined together to cut the first piece. Afterwards, Mell gave the knife to Gloria to finish up. She took the first two pieces; one she gave to her father then the other one to John.

Jed and Wade stepped forward to help then started handing out pieces to all the guests.

Once everyone had one, Jed took his over to Melissa and teasingly held out his for her to have a bite. Just before she could sink her teeth into it; he snatched it back quickly then popped it into his own mouth.

Everyone laughed in amusement at Jed's joke; getting a mischievous look, Melissa held her own piece towards her husband to bite into invitingly.

Chuckling knowingly, Jed pretended to take a bite out of Melissa's cake... expecting her to do the exact same thing that he had done.

Waiting for Jed to get close to the cake, Melissa all of a sudden thrust it into his already closing mouth... it splattered all over her husband's face; Mell laughed uproariously at his stunned look.

Instantly, Jed reached out then grabbed Melissa around the waist before she could make good her escape; he ground his mouth against hers... kissing her with wild abandon; making sure her face got just as full of cake as his was.

Alec and John clapped then whistled their approval.

The guests all joined in as the couple breathlessly pulled apart.

Jed winked at Mell suggestively.

Melissa grinned knowingly and suddenly grabbed Jed's hand; they made a dash for the door leading to the hallway. The newlyweds desperately tried to make their escape.

Instantly, the crowd converged on the laughing pair and their escape was blocked.

Elbowing Jed, Melissa pointed at the door they had been heading for with a laugh.

Snorting, Jed smirked good-naturedly when he saw Wade

with a giggling Gloria make good their escape unhindered... he turned to Melissa plaintively as he chuckled. "Well at least someone got away!"

Smiling, Melissa nodded down at her father in thanks when he handed them towels to wipe their faces on... the two cleaned themselves off; glancing sideways at each other they winked in conspiracy, both dropped their towels at the same time and made another dash for the door.

The crowd cheered before clapping their appreciation when the two made good their escape this time and disappeared.

Sighing in relief at escaping so easily, Melissa turned once inside their room then smiled invitingly over at Jed as he closed the door firmly.

Grinning back, Jed leaned back against it with a thankful sigh at finally getting away from their guests.

The two looked at each other for a moment not sure who should make the first move.

Finally, Jed reached out his hand in hopeful invitation.

Smirking teasingly, Melissa took a step forward then lightly touched her fingertips to Jed's caressingly but only for a second. Suddenly, she withdrew her hand hurriedly before backing away with a sly look on her face. When she was far enough away, she stopped then held her hand out to him and waited in anticipation.

Dropping his hand, Jed laughed in delight at Melissa's implication; that simple caress had tons of meaning. Followed by the quick withdrawal of her hand, gave it even more emphasis as she silently backed away. He pushed himself away from the door and slowly sauntered towards her. When he got close enough, he stopped then put out his hand as if to touch her fingertips as she had done. Grey Wolf watched speculatively as their hands got closer, at the last moment he lunged forward and grabbed her around the waist then threw her on the bed. He jumped after her, hoping to land on top of his wife.

Melissa tried to twist away, but she was laughing so hard she couldn't move away fast enough.

Crowing in triumph, Jed pinned Melissa beneath him then with a growl of impatience he claimed her lips... cutting off her laughter with a searing kiss. Mell felt the kiss right down to her toes; they even curled in pleasure at the sensation. She wriggled around imploringly trying to get her hands loose so she could touch her husband.

Jed would have none of that as he ground his hips against hers, teasing Melissa with his engorged manhood; he firmly held Melissa down refusing to let her hands go... he deepened the kiss insistently.

Groaning in frustration when she couldn't get loose, Melissa waited for Jed to lift his head up. Unexpectedly, she bit his lower lip in retaliation for not releasing her; Grey Wolf lifted his head in astonishment staring at Mell in feigned hurt... his bottom lip came out in a definite pout.

Looking up at Jed, Melissa tried to look innocent but wrecked it by laughing at his injured gaze.

Jumping off the bed suddenly without a word, Jed stood with his hands braced on his hips; still with that appearance of suffering on his face.

Sitting up with a teasing smirk, Melissa wiggled her index finger back and forth invitingly so Jed would come closer. "Awe, poor baby; if you come over here, I'll kiss it better."

Shaking his head in denial, Jed still silent stuck his lip out further as if sulking... he backed away instead; after a few steps, he stopped and watched Melissa closely to see what she might do.

Chuckling in delight, Melissa decided to play Jed's game; she too stood up and advanced a couple of steps. Mell stopped suddenly in indecision when Grey Wolf backed away refusing to let her get closer. Biting the inside of her lower lip, she looked around in confusion trying to decide what to do next. Shrugging resignedly at her husband's refusal to cooperate, White Buffalo pouted for a few moments before getting an idea. She motioned in imaginary hurt before turning her back to him. "Okay, you can stay over there but I'm going to bed!"

While Melissa's back was turned, a sly looked came over her face; she hid the look before checking over her shoulder to make sure Jed was watching her... not sneaking up behind her. She stood straighter then shook her head of beautiful blonde curls behind her so all her hair was covering her back. Arching backwards, Mell ran her fingers through her hair as she spread it enticingly behind her in a waterfall of curls. She turned slightly sideways so Grey Wolf could see some of what she was doing, but not enough for him to see everything wanting to tease him a bit.

Bringing her hands up slowly, Melissa made sure her fingertips lightly brushed against her breasts enticingly on their way up then began undoing the buttons slowly. When it was open, she shrugged her shoulders slightly and let her shirt slide down inch by slow inch until it was at waist height. Mell held it there for a few moments rolling her bare shoulders impishly before letting it drop to the floor in a pool at her feet. Again, she arched her back into a steep curve so her bound breasts were thrust out then lifted her hair up and let it fall back around her playfully. As it fell around her shoulders, she made sure to slump forward so her hair was shielding her... now Jed couldn't see what she was doing. The only thing covering her was her pants, the binding wrapped around her breasts, as well as her long hair.

Melissa had been watching Jed covertly then smiled knowingly when he caught his breath in anticipation. Grey Wolf was fidgeting in expectation; he wanted to see what Mell would do next, but didn't move afraid she would stop.

Smirking slyly, Melissa's hands lifted towards the binding on her breasts before she began unwinding it in slow motion. Just before the last layer of binding fell away completely; she tossed her head so most of her hair would fall forward over her right shoulder... to hide what the binding released.

When the white cloth fell to the floor and Melissa's breasts were still beyond his view... Jed groaned in frustration; he had to put his hands behind his back so he wouldn't be tempted to reach for her.

Lifting her arms up teasingly, Melissa reached behind her to gather the rest of her hair forward; at the same time, she arched her back so Jed would get a better glimpse of her taut nipples through her silky hair. When Mell straightened up... again her hair draped over her breasts hiding them.

Jed closed his eyes for a moment, trying to gain some control of his emotions... he wasn't sure how much more of this he could stand.

Pausing, Melissa had watched Jed covertly the whole time so knew when he closed his eyes. She waited for him to open them again before she unhooked her pants letting them fall to her hips. Holding them there for effect, she tormented

Grey Wolf as long as possible; unexpectedly, she let them drop around her ankles. Mell stepped out of them and halted again before her hands grasped the garter on her right thigh that held her little pistol. Bending she unhooked it, which caused her bare bottom to show through her waterfall of curls... she let the garter fall on the floor beside her clothing.

Unable wait any longer, Jed tugged at the three buttons in front of his shirt; he pulled it out of his trousers quickly then over his head and threw it in a corner.

Giggling, Melissa heard a rip of cloth tearing; she didn't care as she gasped in open admiration when he dropped the shirt to the floor.

Heaving in excitement, Jed's chest rippled with muscles as he clenched and unclenched his hands trying to hold back from reaching for Melissa. He undid his pants then hesitated looking towards the candle; forgetting last night's moonlight streaking episode. He took a step forward to extinguish it, but stopped and turned to his wife in surprise.

Shaking her head emphatically, Melissa gestured reassuringly. "No, Jed; please leave it on tonight I want to see all of you!"

Nodding, Jed slipped his buckskin pants off and walked towards his wife.

Melissa groaned in pleasure at the sight of Jed's completely naked body... he was just so beautiful to look at. The muscles in his arms bulged when he clenched his fists again trying to gain control over his emotions. Turning to face Grey Wolf fully, she took the last step that separated them bringing them so close they were touching. Mell ran a hand over his chest muscles then giggled when he flexed; it caused the muscles to jump in her hands.

Jed's control fled suddenly; he pulled Melissa into his arms completely then backed her up until they were close to the bed. They kissed passionately not able to get enough of each other, until they both collapsed on top of the bed.

Lifting his head, Jed panted in passionate apology and looked down at Melissa uneasily. "I have waited patiently for you to become used to me, but now I find I can't hold back any longer. I don't want to hurt you, but it will the first time; my first wife screamed for hours, afterwards; she refused to let me anywhere near her for quite some time!"

Putting her hands up, Melissa framed Jed's face in reassurance as she stared at him intently. "I must admit I was terrified of you at first... not any longer. I'm aware it will be painful at first, but I'm not some church maid that snivels over a small cut or a wealthy debutante! More than once, I have been shot, stabbed, and even beaten within an inch of my life; the pain I will experience tonight will not be anything compared to that... I'm sure. I love you and trust you. I also need you just as desperately as you need me!"

Opening her legs to accommodate Jed, Melissa wiggled enticingly until she could feel his manhood at the core of her womanhood; she grabbed a fistful of his hair and drew him down until their lips almost met... Mell whispered urgently against them. "Now, love!"

Melissa thrust her hips up hard just as Jed's manhood plunged inside her; she moaned at a small pinch, but it was over in moments. She wrapped her legs around Grey Wolf and squeezed them tightly in demand.

Jed paused to give Melissa a moment to adjust. Thankfully, there wasn't any screaming and crying. When his wife squeezed her legs in command, he took the hint as he drove into her repeatedly. There was no way he could hold back now; Grey Wolf threw his head back desperately trying to control his climax. He wanted... no needed, Mell to join him before he could let go of his own control completely.

Arching up insistently, Melissa tightened her legs even more when she felt her climax beginning to build up. It hurt for a moment... more than having her insides stretched to the limits. She felt her body give in suddenly and she screamed Jed's name in surprise then felt him let his own control go at the same time; his seed poured into her causing her to climax again. She laid there quietly seeing stars for the next few minutes. Mell came back to earth slowly then opened her eyes drowsily as she focused on her husband's concerned expression.

Sighing, Jed grinned in relief when Melissa put her arms around him and purred deep in her throat like a contented cat; she pulled his head down for a kiss of satisfaction then released him... she grinned saucily up. "Can we do it again?"

Throwing his head back, Jed roared with relieved laughter. When he got himself under control, he looked back down to find Melissa scowling in annoyance at him. "I'm sorry; you will have to give me at least half an hour to recuperate before I can give you more!"

Scowling, Melissa frowned in disappointment when Jed rolled away then propped himself up on the headboard. Shrugging, she curled up beside him with a contented sigh; she ran her fingers through his chest hairs teasingly. "Jed, will it always be like this?"

Chuckling, Jed shook his head negatively... he hugged Melissa tightly against him. "No, there will be times when we will fight and shout at each other; at those times, we will turn away not wanting to talk. One thing I will promise you though is that I will tell you every night I love you. It doesn't matter to me why or how mad I get with you at that time. I will still make sure you know how much I adore you. I hope you will also do the same with me!"

Melissa nodded without comment; she yawned sleepily more tired than she wanted to admit.

Jed smiled down at Melissa in gratification; he had worn his wife out. He propped himself up so he could see her face. His tone became serious with a hint of worry. "Are you mad at me for talking the judge into making you a marshal?"

Smiling up at Jed reassuringly, Melissa shook her head negatively. "No not really; after I thought about it some, I realized that I have actually been doing a marshal's job all along. Except that a marshal doesn't concentrate on one or two towns, but every town in the state. Therefore, the only thing that will change is that we will be in the saddle more and I will be dealing with sheriff's rather than deputies. I will also have to report to the governor of North Dakota instead of the judge... I met him only once. I'm not sure if I will like taking orders from him, he was a pompous fool."

Chuckling at Melissa's grimace of distaste... Jed motioned consolingly as he shrugged. "I don't think I have ever met him, but I suppose I will now. At least you won't have to worry about hired guns going out of their way to kill you since you aren't the only one, they will deal with now; although, if they can get past the sheriff and deputy, they might come looking for you."

Sighing grimly at that, Jed paused for a moment; it wasn't something they needed to worry about now and changed the subject as he leaned down then kissed the tip of Melissa's nose tenderly. "I saw you talking with Victor Grey earlier... did you two make up?"

Grimacing, Melissa nodded thoughtfully. Unfortunately, it brought to mind her obligations as sheriff. She shuddered, not really wanting to think about Brian or the others. However, as much as she hated thinking of him; she still couldn't leave him up there for the scavengers. "Yes, he apologized for being taken in by Mary's half-brother. Which reminds me, I should send Brad up to Devil's Rock to bury the dead men up there. Brian must have buried his brothers and cousin because there was no sign of them anywhere."

Jed shrugged grimly with a scowl of anger. "They can rot up there for all I care. I don't want to go up there again, anyway."

Melissa sighed irritably, it was still part of their jobs but nodded in understanding at Jed's feelings; she changed the sensitive subject, she would see to it tomorrow... she asked inquisitively. "I noticed you and Dad talking to Chelsie earlier, anything I should know about?"

Jed grinned mysteriously then shrugged when Melissa slapped him playfully. "It's no secret, your father and I want to build Chelsie a goldsmith shop. We offered to build it then pay for all the materials. All she will need to do, is make jewellery, merchandise, and manage the store; the deal is for a three-way equal partnership."

Grinning teasingly, Melissa tugged playfully on Jed's chest hairs. "Making the town yours already, are you?"

Smirking smugly, Jed nodded emphatically. "Well of course; it's my town now too, so I might as well invest in it."

Smiling in relief, Melissa gestured plaintively as she changed the subject. "Good, I'm glad you feel that way already; now how come you never told me you wanted to go to Boston for our honeymoon?"

Shrugging, Jed tweaked Melissa's nose mischievously. "Well, for one thing I wanted it to be a surprise; I figured we could go across country for a bit so you can show me your routine. Until we reach a train, anyway. I'm not sure how far the railway has come yet but I figured if we have to, we could always ride to Boston. Even though your routes will change now, you still have to visit all your towns and make a list of tentative sheriffs so we can still go. We have to make a stop at the governors now so you can be sworn in properly, anyway. I think we should do that after we visit all your towns though, this way we can have a working honeymoon. So, what do you think is it a good idea or would you prefer to do something different?"

Pleased, Melissa nodded thankful that Jed was willing to have a working honeymoon. "No, your plan is fine."

Melissa paused to yawn sleepily.

Taking the hint, Jed moved down then rolled onto his back and pulled Melissa closer to him in contentment. "Go to sleep sweetheart... I love you!"

Cuddling closer, Melissa curled her fingers in Jed's thick curly chest hairs in pleasure... she murmured sleepily in return. "Good night, love."

They drifted off to sleep listening to the music and laughter of their guests from downstairs; their dreams were similar, they dreamt of having children together then living to a ripe old age, if not in perfect harmony... at least very in love.

EPILOGUE

NORTH DAKOTA

Melissa leaned back with a sigh of contentment as she sipped her tea; she eyed her daughter-in-law sitting across from her pensively thinking back over the years. Pamela or Pam as she liked to be called had married their oldest son, Daniel. Jed was absolutely delighted by her decision to name him after his first dead son. It came as quite a shock to all of them, especially her when her oldest hung up his guns to become a Baptist Pastor. However, Mell was extremely proud of him anyway... after the initial shock had worn off, of course.

Pamela was Giant Bear and Mary's only daughter; she had moved here to live with Melissa so she could go to a white school. Pam had her mother's blonde hair with her father's deep black piercing eyes. A slight dusky look to her skin plus the high cheekbones clearly pointed to her Indian heritage. She was willowy slim so had no need to wear a corset to get a perfect hourglass figure... she already had one.

Mary, plus an ecstatic Melissa were both elated when Pam fell in love with Daniel then got married. The two newlyweds moved over to her friend's ranch house and Pamela made it liveable once again. Both mothers-in-laws and best friends were thrilled to have their families entwined by marriage at last. Now the shadow of Brian, who had plagued their lives... even though they were unaware of it; was laid to rest forever when the kids brought love into the old ranch.

Daniel's twin sister... Patricia or Pat for short was named after Melissa's mother; Pat was following in her mother's footsteps becoming the second woman sheriff in their hometown.

Melissa's third child another boy that they named John after Jed's father and Judge Elton who died last year... since they happened to have the same name. Was becoming a rancher like his grandfather Alec much to John senior's disappointment but her father's satisfaction.

The thought of her father-in-law made Melissa grin in amusement; Jed had been right about his father's reaction to Mell. After the initial shock of her being a sheriff, as well as a soon to be marshal had worn off, of course...

John looked Melissa over carefully in pleasure then he smirked in satisfaction. "Well at least you picked someone as strong as you are this time. I expect to have strapping grandsons and tall ones too from such a good-looking woman!"

Melissa had laughed with Jed over that for many years.

Alec after being married to Jessica for two years made her dream come true then gave her a sister. Unfortunately for the grief-stricken Alec... Jessica died in childbirth; Mell ended up raising her sister as her own, so she always felt little Jessica was more like her daughter because of that.

Giving them all a scare after Jessica passed away, Alec almost died himself. Fortunately, little Jess pulled him away from his grief with her large green blue eyes... fiery red hair that came with her fierce temper. He was starting to show his age now though at seventy-eight years old.

Right now, Alec, Jed, as well as their youngest son was out checking on the new cattle John purchased a month ago. Now they had an even five hundred head, which was always Grey Wolf's dream.

Lightning died a few years ago much to Melissa's sorrow, but not before producing a few dozen healthy offspring.

Judge Elton's prediction proved true; although, he was a few years too early as the railroad went through their town five years after Melissa became the new marshal. The town's population doubled within a year then new towns sprung up everywhere across North Dakota... it had kept them extremely busy; they got so busy she had to hire two more deputy marshals, just so they could keep up.

The gold mine Alec had invested in finally dried up, but he found another one in town when he invested in Chelsie's Goldsmith Shop; Jed along with Melissa's father, tripled their investment since they built the store for her. She ended up selling the saloon shortly after the store opened... she was just too busy with her new shop to keep both.

Shaking off her reflective mood, Melissa turned her attention back to an unhappy looking Pam; it wasn't often her daughter-in-law looked so gloomy. Usually, she was full of smiles and laughter. "Well, you look very grim today... what seems to be the problem?"

Pamela shrugged dismissively, but the worry was evident in her voice. "I don't know; I have been having these dreams lately... I'm not sure what they mean."

Sitting forward quickly in surprise shocked, Melissa had been having strange dreams herself for about a week now; ominously, Mell describing her nightmares to Pam distressfully. "Dreams of Giant Bear calling for help then death and blood all around him?"

Shivering in fear, Pamela waved incredulously in distress. "You are having them too?"

Inclining her head that she was, Melissa's gaze became distant... remembering the last dream two days ago. "Mine always starts out with a white female buffalo running towards Giant Bear; sometimes she goes to him and tells him something then everything is fine. Other times she doesn't, as the white buffalo turns away blood and death appear all around him!"

Melissa touched her white buffalo medicine bag that she was never without; she now knew she was the white buffalo in the dream... she must find a way to help Giant Bear immediately.

Pamela shuddered in panic then dread when she thought of the last dream she had two nights ago before gesturing apprehensively. "All I see is blood and death with an urgent feeling to go to my father immediately; do you hear what the white buffalo is saying in the dream?"

Rubbing her chin reflectively, Melissa scowled perplexed before shrugging pensively. "Yes, but I don't understand it. She just keeps repeating that they must not be forced to marry; an older white man pops into the picture a few minutes later then the white buffalo tells him something important, but I can't hear what she says to him... it's quite confusing."

Looking puzzled, Pamela waved urgently. "That's crazy... who would my father be able to force into marriage?"

Melissa shook her head in frustration totally baffled by it all. "I have no idea that is all she says to Giant Bear."

Sighing uneasily, Pamela opened both her hands in supplication towards Melissa as if she had all the answers. "It doesn't make any sense; how can two people being forced to marry cause so much death. My father would have contacted us by now if he were in danger, right?"

Shrugging thoughtfully, Melissa mussed reflectively. "Maybe Giant Bear doesn't know he is in danger yet."

Frowning grimly, Pamela looked at Melissa knowingly already aware of the answer but asked anyway. "You could be right; are you going and when?"

Melissa nodded emphatically before waving towards town in explanation. "I can't leave right now; I have to telegraph the governor first to let him know I have a family emergency. We will take an extended leave since I don't know how long this will take. I also need to let my deputies know at the same time that they will have to look after things here for me."

Pamela scowled grimly; she got up quickly before motioning towards her ranch. "I will go home to pack my things. I'm not sure if Daniel will come with us or not; do you think Jed will come?"

Melissa inclined her head decisively as she got up to... she waved shrewdly having no doubts at all. "Of course he will; Giant Bear is his blood-brother and friend. I know he will want to do everything he can in order to help us save your father."

Pam nodded relieved. "Okay; I will be back here in a few hours or sooner if I can help it."

Pamela turned with skirts flying, she raced from the room without waiting for Melissa to agree or disagree with her; more scared now than she had been earlier.

Melissa sighed dejectedly; well, so much for her well-deserved vacation... she turned and headed to the kitchen to ask Jane to pack provisions for their trip. Gloria died the year before Judge Elton did, so Jane took over in here. Mell headed upstairs to her room after leaving the kitchen.

At fifty-seven years of age, Melissa was still an imposing figure of a woman. Most people were quite shocked when they learned her age. The only difference now from thirty years ago was that her hair turned almost entirely white, rarely did others see it anyway, so they didn't know that; Mell's face had a few more wrinkles, but her body was still girlishly thin... even after giving birth to twins than to one more boy afterwards.

Jed and Melissa talked seriously about retiring as marshals this year, but they decided to wait three more years. Grey

Wolf would be sixty-five by then and she would be sixty; time enough to retire then spend the rest of their lives together in peaceful contentment.

Melissa grabbed clothes from the closet before throwing them on the bed... she frowned thoughtfully staring in surprise at a pouch hanging in her closet. She had completely forgotten all about it again; inside was her wedding certificate as well as one for Mary and Giant Bear, which she added two months later. A deputy's certificate soon followed. She had one made for Jed then decided to get one for Giant Bear too. Getting an official document was a new thing that only started a few years ago. Judge Elton printed one for their anniversary gift just before his death.

Melissa asked John to make one for Mary and Giant Bear, so next time she saw her friends she could give it to them as a gift. There just never seemed to be an opportunity to give it to them though... until now; she nodded to herself then grabbed the pouch and threw it on the bed to be packed with their things. It would be the perfect gift to bring them. They could laugh about the days when.

Jessica came bounding into the room unexpectedly interrupting Melissa's reflection; her sister waved imploringly in anticipation. "I heard you are going on a trip... would you mind if I came along this time?"

Melissa smiled indulgently at Jessica, but shook her head in denial. "No, I'm going to Giant Bear's village in Montana; it will be too dangerous for you!"

Jessica grinned knowingly then put her two hands together as if in prayer... she tilted her head beseechingly. "I know that I heard you tell Jane, but I still want to come. I need to get away from the bad memories. Please, Aunt Mell. You have taught me how to protect myself so I won't be a hindrance; who knows I might even be able to help out."

Melissa harrumphed in disbelief at the idea of the rambunctious Jessica helping them... it was more likely her sister would bring them additional problems as beautiful as she was. Remembering how depressed Jess had been since her failed engagement to that no-good scoundrel; she finally gave in though with a smile of resignation at the replica of her mother, Jess. Not once in all these years had she been able to say no to her sister when she truly wanted something, this time was no different. Mell nodded reluctantly before pointing a finger at her, she shook it in warning. "Okay, you can come also, but we are leaving in a few hours. If you are not ready, we will leave without you; it's going to be a hard ride with no coddling. You better wear pants and tie your breasts down, they are liable to get us killed!"

Jessica squealed in delight... she grabbed Melissa giving her a fierce hug; Jess picked up her long skirts so she could run then raced out of the room in a rush before her sister could change her mind.

Melissa shook her head grimly; she was already regretting her decision then wondered if she had made a mistake allowing Jessica to come. Mell forgot all about her sister when she heard the door slam shut. It gave a loud resounding crack that she heard even upstairs. "**Bang!**"

Melissa cocked her head listening to the hurried footsteps racing up the stairs. She turned expectantly then waited in anticipation for Jed to burst into their bedroom; he was all out of breath. Mell's gasp of pleasure caught in her throat as she eyed her husband in appreciation. Even after all these years, he still made her heart race in need just by looking at him. His hair was now grey instead of black with a slight hint of baldness on top, but he still kept it long. Grey Wolf's face had gotten craggier over the years from spending so much time outdoors. Nonetheless, it was still a handsome face... only older. He had not lost any of his muscles if anything he had gained more; he still stood at six foot six, with no hint of slouching. Most men her husband's age tended to lose height as they got older, not him. He did have a bit of a potbelly now; it was hardly noticeable unless you knew him for years.

Jed inhaled in relief at the sight of Melissa standing in front of him unhurt. "What is going on around here? Pam raced past us as if her skirt were on fire; so, I came to see what the problem was then seen two pack horses outside being readied for a long trip by the looks of it."

Melissa grinned relieved to see him, at least now she wouldn't have to go running around looking for him; she told him everything she remembered about her dreams of Giant Bear's danger. Followed by the nightmares Pamela was having of her father.

When Melissa finished... Jed nodded not even surprised a

little, he motioned knowingly. "I have been waiting for something like this to happen; I just didn't think it would be this late in the future."

Looking at Jed in shocked amazement, Melissa waved angrily in demand. "You were expecting this to happen... why ever for?"

Jed smiled reassuringly at Melissa's tone of disbelief... trying to explain. "Do you remember the night Giant Bear named you White Buffalo?"

Melissa nodded mutely that she did, but didn't say anything.

Jed frowned pensively when he thought back to that night. "When you were teaching Tommy knife tricks; we were watching you. Giant Bear told me the Great Spirit informed him you would come to him when his people were in desperate need. He didn't know at the time when or why he would have need of you, so I was aware this moment would be coming... sooner or later."

Melissa sighed in confused understanding, not sure if she liked this one bit. Having her future controlled by higher powers would never have been something she thought possible or even about. Irritably, she shook of her disgruntlement because in reality... there was really nothing she could do about it; she couldn't help thinking. She waved at all the clothes laid out on the bed. "Well help me finish packing now that you are here. I want to leave as soon as possible."

Jed nodded without argument then pitched in, helping Mell.

A few hours later, they were all gathered together in the yard. Melissa, Jed, Jessica, Pam, and an emphatic Daniel who refused to be left behind all mounted. They waved goodbye to the people they were leaving behind before racing away to save their friend; not one of them even looked back!

Here ends the story of Jed and Melissa Brown...
Or does it?

Watch for my next book; **'Raven and the Golden Eagle'**

Chief Giant Bear, blood-brother to Jed Brown, had successfully lived all these years by his vow to find away to live in peace with the white man. Now he finds himself in a quandary as a vision gone awry, causes a chain reaction that will not stop snowballing; even Golden Dove his beautiful blonde wife turns against him. In desperation, he tries to save his people by forcing his beloved granddaughter into marriage.

Raven known to the people as their 'Protector', must stop not only her grandfather from forcing her into a loveless marriage, but also the massacre of her people if she refuses to marry the Englishman. In her quest, she unearths a plot to take over the land as greed and hatred for her grandfather's peaceful ways threatens their way of life.

Devon, known as Lord Rochester the second son of the Earl of Rochester in England, had travelled thousands of miles in order to live for one year on a barren piece of land in the middle of the savage Montana wilderness. His grandfather's will stipulates he couldn't sell it otherwise.

Everything changes when his wagon train is wiped out by a Cheyenne war party and he is drawn unwillingly into a struggle between the peaceful bear tribe of the Cheyenne and an unknown source. The only way to save these people is to sacrifice his freedom and marry the granddaughter of the chief, but should he!

Mell and Jed must race from North Dakota to Western Montana to reach Giant Bear with a warning from the Cheyenne's sacred white buffalo before it is too late to save them all.

A BRIEF NOTE TO MY READERS

For all the history buffs out there, that know my dates do not quite coincide with actual events - I am including this little portion for you. I had to manipulate time slightly so my third book to this series 'Dream Dancer & the Celtic Witch' would have a female Queen on the throne in England.

I used the Cheyenne Indians because they were in Dakota first then moved to Montana later and I needed an Indian nation that was in both places. So just to set the record straight here is a summary of actual dates.

— The Cheyenne Indians, lived in North Dakota. According to their history, they farmed corn, squash, and other vegetables. However, in 1776, the Lakota Sioux defeated the Cheyenne and took their land. Some became nomads in Montana like the rest of the Indian tribes. Some moved down into South Dakota and they like the Sioux were involved in the Black Hills War in 1876-1877.

— It became known as Dakota on March 2, 1861. The capital at that time was Yankton until 1883. It was not until November 2, 1889 that North and South became separated. They formed their own identities at that time.

— Gold was discovered in the Black Hills of South Dakota in 1873, which caused a migration boom that led to the Dakota Territories popularity and many settlers flocked to Dakota.

— In 1870, the Northern Pacific Railway pushed westward from Minnesota into North Dakota. By 1872, the company had put down 164 miles of main line across North Dakota. Progress was slow because of Indian raids.

— In 1847, a man in Paris, named B. Houllier, came out with the hammer so that powder was no longer needed for rifles. It was the first single shot rifle.

— In 1857, Winchester made a repeating rifle that had a tube that could hold 15 bullets. Model # 1866 it was to be the most popular rifle used at that time.

— Smith and Wesson also made a repeater rifle in 1854 but it was not as good and had to be perfected in the late 1850's.

— Samuel Colt in Paterson New Jersey made the six-shooter on April 1836 it became the most popular revolver.

BIOGRAPHY

I was born in Dalhousie, NB, but I have lived most of my life in Alberta. Presently, I am living in Falher; it is a town in Northern Alberta, known as the honey capital of Canada plus the home of the largest bee.

I married a wonderful loving man, Michel Pelletier; I have two daughters, a stepdaughter, and two stepsons. So far, I have four grandsons, several step-grandsons, and step-granddaughters. I now have 1 great granddaughter.

I love to fish, dance, and golf... above all is to write. Writing has been a passion for me since I was in my early twenties. It quickly became an addiction; I find hard to stay away from for any length of time.

I was published in 2010 by a company in the US. It did not work out well for me so I recently became self-published. Thankfully, with the help of Page Masters Publications based out of Edmonton.

I have 3 series planned with at least three books in each set. If all goes as planned, I am hoping to have a full trilogy saga in the near future. Possibly, with more on the way, if the writing bug continues to bite me.

The first set of books begins the journey that will tie my three series together; they start from early to the mid 1800's in the USA as a western romance.

The second series is my transition from romance to fantasy, it will become a western fantasy; it's set in the late 1800's and continues into the late 2000's, which starts in England then bring you into Canada, where I will stay until the end!

My third series will be full fantasy. It will be the beginning of a new world and reappearance of magic in its full glory; including forgotten creatures, evil villains, different cultures, and unlikely people. With several surprises that even, I am unaware of yet!

www.ingramcontent.com/pod-product-compliance
Lightning Source LLC
Chambersburg PA
CBHW060137260626
47160CB00001B/13